SHERLOCK HOLMES:
THE DEVIL'S CROWN

SHERLOCK HOLMES:
THE DEVIL'S CROWN

Daniel McGachey

ISBN: 978-1-957121-91-8

Text © 2025 by Daniel McGachey
Cover Art and Interior Illustrations © 2025 by K. L. Turner

Interior and cover design by F. J. Bergmann
Editor and Publisher, Joe Morey

Weird House Press
Central Point, OR 97502
www.weirdhousepress.com

Table of Contents

"What is the meaning of it, Watson?" said Holmes solemnly.... *"What object is served by this circle of misery and violence and fear? It must tend to some end, or else our universe is ruled by chance, which is unthinkable. But what end? There is the great standing perennial problem to which human reason is as far from an answer as ever."*

"The Adventure of the Cardboard Box"

Preface: A Case for Concealment

O ver the course of my long friendship with that
extraordinary individual who has raised the science
of deduction to an art form, I have presented for
publication almost sixty accounts detailing his most
remarkable achievements in criminal investigation and
deductive reasoning. This corpus represents a mere
fraction of the thousands of cases in which we have both
taken active roles during the nigh-on five decades since
first we met, and still, beyond even these, there are those
dating from prior to the commencement of our association,
as well as those in which I played no part. With the tales
of "The Blanched Soldier" and "The Lion's Mane," my old
friend has himself taken up his pen to describe just two
of the latter, while I was once privileged to record his
reminiscences of some of those formative endeavours as
"The *Gloria Scott*" and "The Musgrave Ritual."

*(As an aside—I am suddenly struck by the peculiar quirk
of fate in choosing to list these four particular accounts.
Perhaps they will give credence to what follows for, while
the events I now set out to relate are far removed from any of*

the aforementioned, from each I may draw some element—a stricken face and an apparition in a nocturnal window, a deadly, inhuman terror from beneath the waves, an ill-fated vessel's fatal final voyage and, most tellingly, a treasure whose discovery is marked by tragedy—that you will find woven into the tapestry of this darkly twisting narrative.)

While these published accounts amply demonstrate the range and individuality of the problems my associate has wrestled with, I would not have to delve very far into the vast accumulation of scrapbooks, folders, and files at my disposal to lay my hands on some singular assignment or unique puzzle with which to further reinforce his formidable reputation. However, as discovery of this document—together with any other dossiers and papers with which it has been sealed—must surely indicate, there are certain accounts which may not be brought to the notice of the public during the lifetimes of either the author or the subject of these biographical sketches. I do not treat here of those many endeavours which were never satisfactorily concluded, as with the unfathomable disappearance of the cutter *Alicia* in a bank of mist, or those that were perhaps concluded but in a manner to which I was never made privy, such as the enduring mystery of "The Four Oaks" at Great Tunlow. Nor do I refer to that strand of delicate undertakings typified by the investigation into the peculiar concerns of the self-styled "Amateur Mendicant Society," or the tangled truth behind the Marleigh Towers tragedy. In such instances any ongoing suppression from public scrutiny owes to their particulars being of so sensitive or scandalous a nature that their disclosure's repercussions would be felt at the highest of levels, both here in Britain and across a world still struggling to regain its equilibrium a decade on from the horrors that ensued when squabbling, jostling states flexed their muscles and stamped their feet, and millions fell in the resultant quakes.

Then there are the tales of unease, where rational thought may seem usurped by the uncanny, so that their details read as the improbable entries in an impossible casebook. Against such a global nightmare, what are these other, more personal horrors; the ones that skulk in dark turnings, or lurk in even darker recesses of the mind in all its as-yet-unexplored depths? Is this why I hold back certain tales, the memories of which inspire only disquiet, dread, and sorrow? Has there not been such a surfeit of these emotions that it would be an unwarrantable imposition to unleash more? Or do such sensations perhaps hold less sway in a world that has faced down possible self-destruction? But, no; I think that is not the case. Where there is imagination, there is always room for horror!

I have long since learnt to deal with the fear, dread, and even terror, that have proved frequent ingredients of my adventures—the nagging, insistent fear of discovery while venturing into the criminal's lair; the numbing sense of dread that engulfs a soul while waiting out in the wastes of a lonely moor for a phantom made flesh to strike, or while listening in the confines of a darkened room for the stealthy, gliding movement of a venomous serpent; the stark terror brought on by the administered poison that removes all clarity of thought and puts in its place an unreasoning, unremitting madness. But the fear I experience now stems from the utter conviction that, were certain stories to be told aloud, I would stand accused of being a delusional fool, a fictioneer, or a downright liar. Make no mistake, it is not my own reputation or standing that I strive to protect from any onslaught; such accusations would draw grave doubt upon my other accounts and, in turn, upon the great criminological feats performed by my good friend.

Into this latter category falls the hideous secret of the shadowy inhabitants of "The Paradol Chamber," the grotesque business of the Obsidian Chalice and its dreadful contents, of the repulsive death of the renowned banker, Frederick Crosby, which was in itself merely a preface to "The Crimson Leech Horror," and certain other stories, yet more outrageous-seeming but each utterly true. Some of these I have already recorded—the very action of setting down coherently experiences that had previously maintained the consistency of a nightmare often exorcising the worst lingering traces of anxiety, or imposing order on events once seeming beyond all logical comprehension. That stated, I do not need to put ink to paper to recall the rank breath on the back of my neck, nor to hear again in my dreams the hideous shrieking of the abhorrent creature as it bore down upon us, to recognise that, even were the world to one day to be ready, *I* may never be prepared to relive the story of "The Giant Rat of Sumatra."

It was as part of this small collection of never-to-be-told tales that I had always sworn this current narrative belonged. But while I, so many years on, remain haunted by the cruel horror of the events—a horror which stretches back over several blood-soaked centuries—the emotional strain under which I made my vow to withhold these details has long since passed. What is more, I am now an old man—though not, I should dearly hope, a foolish one—with very few regrets. Therefore, I could not happily live out whatever years I have remaining to me knowing that the full account of this most incredible adventure might one day die with me, thus denying the world the knowledge of how the singular skills of one man brought to a close the bloody tangle of events surrounding the cursed *Corona del Diavolo*—the Devil's Crown!

That man was, of course, Mr. Sherlock Holmes. If this document has not lain undisturbed for too many years, I should hope that name is still a familiar one, even if only to students of crime and its detection, in which field he, more than any other theoretical specialist or practicing investigator, has wrought such advances. Yet at the time to which I invite my unknown reader in their unknowable future to return, the fame that was to make Sherlock Holmes a name whose very utterance brought hope to those in need of justice—and alarm to those villains upon whose trail he had been set—had not yet begun to spread, and his career, which he had honed his every cell and fibre to pursue, showed all signs of having come to a premature and unsensational end before it had even fully begun.

Chapter 1: Mr. Holmes at Home

Even with the passing of so many years, I scarcely need glance at my notes to picture so vividly the commencement of this most alarming episode. It was a chill, dreary morning in 1881, but a scant few months since Sherlock Holmes and I had first been introduced and agreed to share the expense of renting a set of comfortable rooms in Baker Street. My initial mixture of amusement and bemusement at his peculiar lifestyle and, in particular, at his odd habit of extracting precise deductions from seemingly the most trivial of details, had soon turned to respect and admiration, as I found myself closely witnessing the methods by which his unique abilities led to the resolution of the Lauriston Gardens murder mystery. From this rather unexpected series of incidents so early on in our association, I had come to expect that a life of excitement, intrigue, and even danger was to constantly be ours. But in the painfully long weeks that followed we had received not a single visitor of note.

I ought to have been grateful for the respite. I was by no means fully recovered from my ordeal just a year before in Afghanistan, where I had been left with a scarred and nagging leg as a painful reminder of the Jezail bullet that had embedded itself there during the Battle of Maiwand, while fragments of another bullet still lodged in my shoulder. Thus had I found myself pensioned out of the army and not yet capable, either mentally or physically, of facing the task of setting myself up in practice in a capital city already teeming with doctors. Had I walked into a consulting room as my own patient, the advice I should most certainly have received would have involved a long period of recuperation to allow the reserves of strength and stamina to build once more. But, like so many doctors, I make a woeful patient, and I was far from happy to sit idle.

Following that first fateful adventure with my fellow lodger, I had watched in angry amazement as Inspectors Lestrade and Gregson shared between them the glory of a case well solved, while only grudgingly crediting Sherlock Holmes with providing some very minor points of assistance. In truth, with the type of assistance Holmes could really provide, it struck me as a wonder that representatives of Scotland Yard and the various police forces up and down the land were not constantly at our door clamouring for his services.

Holmes himself, in what would in due course become the habitual litany of complaints that marked his spells of inactivity, made no secret of his own feelings on the matter. Following an only too brief burst of elation, gratified that his theories had been proved correct in practice, he had lapsed into a grim dejection which only worsened as each new day passed.

Privately, I was very much concerned for Holmes's well-being. During my convalescence in a North-West Frontier army hospital, I had seen far too many men, most of them fine, courageous soldiers, descend into a form of grief-fuelled madness, brought on by the knowledge that they were henceforth forever denied the chance to use the skills they had spent years of their lives obtaining. I knew that I would be entirely unable to simply stand by while my friend's remarkable talents were so criminally neglected, since I feared that he, in a moment of weakness, would indulge himself in a manner which might, if left unchecked, lead to a serious impairment of his faculties.

Even in those early days, I was already fully aware of the dangerous lengths to which Holmes would go to stave off the crushing boredom of day to day life. No sooner had that air of triumph deserted him than I caught my first glimpse of the gleaming contents of that neat morocco case he kept in the drawer of his chemistry table alongside those small bottles of deceptively plain looking liquids that would, in time, gradually make their way onto the mantelpiece as he either grew bolder or less inclined to care what any might say regarding his vice. Shamefully, after walking in unawares just as Holmes had withdrawn the needle from his forearm, I had said nothing more than a mumbled, "Excuse me, I had no idea you were busy," though I believe my expression of shock before I made my hasty withdrawal had made my view quite clear.

It would be a view that, over time, I would voice, loudly and often. Yet on that first occasion, even as I retreated I was inwardly asking myself was there nothing I could do to help my newfound friend? If only the knowledge of the man's genius was not restricted to the resentful officials of Scotland Yard, he could then bypass their hand-me-downs and have the pick of the most interesting and complex of puzzles.

I cast my mind back over that first incredible adventure we had shared together, and a passing remark that I had made even as the first of those dismissive news reports had boiled my blood came suddenly back to mind. I had observed Holmes intently throughout the entire affair, and my journal was brimming with details of his methods and the steps by which his investigation had proceeded. Reading those pages over once more thrilled me almost as much as had the adventure itself. This was when I realised that I could, perhaps, help Sherlock Holmes

9

after all. I had my plan, or an early notion of one at least, and the first stage was almost complete. Therefore it was with a small smile of satisfaction that I dipped my pen in the inkwell and sat back to ponder for a moment, before drawing a definitive line beneath what I supposed would be my last words on the subject.

Holmes, who had spent the greater portion of the hours after breakfast scraping out a melancholy dirge on his violin, paused in his playing but did not turn toward me before sighing, "It's no good, Watson. No good at all!"

So surprised was I by Holmes's sudden intrusion upon my reverie, I must have become a little furtive as I placed the pages to one side, as if he had somehow read what I was now quietly congratulating myself on achieving and had found it wanting. Whatever response I may have made went unheard, however, as my friend slammed that sorely abused violin down upon the breakfast table with a roughness towards a delicate instrument that made me wince, before throwing himself into his chair, lamenting, "I fear if no interesting crime is perpetrated soon within London, I shall be forced to commit one myself!"

Had I known Holmes better, I would have seen how ill-advised was the chuckle I let out at this unlikely thought. As it was, I could almost have sworn that I felt his eyes bore straight through me, even from behind his closed lids. Attempting another tack, I gathered up the loose bundle of pages from my desk, shuffling them into neat order and preparing to take my chance. "Well, old fellow, if you are that bored ..."

"Bored?" he cried, imperiously. "To label this mire of stagnation into which I sink daily as mere boredom is akin to describing a beheading as rather a nasty cut. I do hope your professional diagnoses are a shade more accurate, Doctor."

I sighed, regrouped my reserves of patience, and remounted my assault. "If you are so deeply enmired, and in need of something to alleviate the stagnation of which you complain, this might interest you." I handed across the pages, which Holmes accepted listlessly, though he barely passed his eyes over them. Instead he took his long, straight-stemmed pipe from the coal-scuttle, lit it, and dropped back languidly into his armchair. "Well? Are you not going to at least skim it? It is my account of the Jefferson Hope case. I have just completed it."

"Completed it?" he once more echoed my words, though less stridently, then handed the pages back without any further perusal. "Ah, I think not."

I rose, my irritation leaving me too restless to be still, and paced upon the hearth-rug. "I have recounted the entire tale! From our first encounter at St. Bart's, through your initial secrecy over your occupation, your association with Lestrade and Gregson and the clues those two officials almost missed of the ring and the message in blood, and on till the aftermath of the investigation, it is all here!"

"Watson, I have seen you read over pages contentedly, only to cross them out and throw them away on the next reading. You have made constant alterations, discarding screeds at a time. An hour passes and there you are, fishing them out of the wastebasket. There are some that have been crumpled then retrieved and unfolded again so often that you might soon require our landlady's clothes iron to press them. You may be happy, for now, that the tale is told, but I guarantee that as soon as you re-read it, there will be scores of changes you will be unable to resist making."

I bridled at the ease with which my efforts had been dismissed, but perhaps even more-so in annoyance that he was, infuriatingly, entirely right. Already I had begun to question certain choices of phrasing or emphasis in the text. Yet I was not inclined to admit as much to Holmes, instead sulkily enquiring, "You think me that much of a fuss?"

"A perfectionist, dear fellow, and I, of all people, can hardly criticise you for that." I was on the verge of thanking him for this unaccustomed compliment when he

11

continued, "After all, I would hardly expect you to be content until you had managed to wring every last lurid drop of sensationalism out of those unfortunate proceedings."

"Lurid? How can you disdain it as lurid if you won't even condescend to read it?"

I felt my anger burn brighter as Holmes took a languorous draw on his pipe before beginning. "That your account is sensational, and not a simple retelling of the facts, I could judge from the long moments you spent staring into space, and the grunts and chuckles of delight you emitted as inspiration struck. I saw you wring your hands, raise your eyebrows, and slacken your jaw more than once. Why, at one point whilst reading it back to yourself you even whistled!"

The flush that came to my cheeks was equal parts embarrassment and anger. "Am I that transparent?"

"Oh, don't look so crestfallen, Watson. I like to believe I have certain advantages in these matters. But as for that title? Dear, dear! My preference, had you sought it, would have been for a brief yet instructive monograph entitled 'An Examination of the Effective Application of Deductive Reasoning Based on Observation in Matters Pertaining to the Efficient Investigation of Criminal Activities'. But from your pen? 'A Study in Scarlet', indeed? It positively reeks of those gaudy yellow-backed novels and high-adventure yarns you so enjoy."

"But these are merely your own words, Holmes! You, yourself, said there was surely a scarlet thread of murder running through those unhappy events. It was our duty to unravel it, isolate it and expose every inch of it."

"Did I really?" said he, an eyebrow arching. "I had no idea I was prone to such melodramatic outbursts; I must watch myself and curb that weakness!"

"Well, I may be paraphrasing, perhaps, just a little. But I trust you can have no objection to my preparing this account?"

"It is really no concern of mine how you choose to pass your time, old fellow."

"My dear Holmes," I declared, "I intend to do far more than pass the time. I intend to have it published."

If I had expected any great reaction to this announcement, I was to be disappointed. Blandly he replied, "Yes, I recall you had threatened such an action at the time of the affair. Though I fail to see how it could be of the slightest interest to anyone."

"In that case, you not only insult my talent as a writer, but also your own talents as a detective! It is my firm belief that the public would be most interested to learn how your methods solved the crime."

Holmes's sigh released a wreath of smoke that hung mournfully above his head. "As far as the public is concerned the crime has been solved and is, therefore, of no further interest. The culprit has been apprehended, the heroes have been honoured, and that is that."

"But that is *not* that! Not at all," I insisted, warmly. "Lestrade and his crony, Gregson, both received testimonials for doing very little of value that I could see. Yet what have you gained? It seems hardly fair. People should be aware of just who the real hero is. And I intend to make them aware. I may take the story to the newspapers; there's enough stimulating and provocative material in these pages to provide a dozen headlines. Or perhaps one of the weekly magazines may be more apt? They might serialise it, or interview some of those caught up in the case."

In fact, I had not yet decided precisely what my ambitions were for the manuscript draft I even then held aloft as if it were some valuable mediaeval document or unearthed Biblical scroll. But even as the possibilities swam through my mind, Holmes waved me to regain both my seat and my composure.

"And how," said he, enquiringly, "would this recognition you promise benefit me?"

"Once your exceptional gifts are known, you would be on constant call to every crime in and around the city, I am sure of it."

"Aha! So that is your real purpose," said he with a smile. "You want to get me out of the house. Am I dreadfully underfoot? You can tell me if it is so."

"Not at all," I replied, stifling my own smile. "But you've evidently been far from happy these past weeks. Perhaps, if your gifts were more widely known, cases would become more readily available to engage your attention."

"There is no shortage of cases, Watson. Crime has not come to a standstill. It is a lack of *interesting* crimes which has led to my current inactivity. Without that rare spark of singularity in a case there is nothing to inspire me, and the criminals we find operating today are a predictably unimaginative bunch." With this declaration, Holmes snatched up a newspaper from the pile that had accumulated next to his chair and tossed it toward me. "You see? Amidst column upon column of unremitting trivia we find only three burglaries of such bungling ineptitude that if the perpetrators are not already known to the police they very soon will be, an arson attack that has all the hallmarks of an insurance swindle, and what the press are terming a double murder and brutal assault."

"Murder?" I cried with an unseemly eagerness as I set about scanning the newsprint.

"Save yourself the trouble. Simply put, the police were called to a suburban house during the night following a report of loud cries and shots being heard. There, a woman was found beaten and unconscious, while two men—the first being her husband recently returned on shore leave, the other a cousin of the husband who lodged with them—were found dead of gunshot wounds; the former to the head, the other to the chest. A man had been seen fleeing the house moments after the disturbance, carrying a bundle in a bag or sack. Described by all as quiet, respectable, charitable people without any enemy to speak of, it appeared that some intruder had entered in the night and shot the husband as he ascended to bed, thus disturbing the wife in her bedroom and the lodger in his own. Both were found in their nightclothes, though only the marital bed was disturbed, hence the conclusion that the wife slept while the lodger prepared to retire, and the shooting of the husband, who had the misfortune to be roaming abroad when the trespasser made his entrance, brought both into the hallway. The wife remains in a comatose state in hospital, while the weapon was found in close proximity to the three victims in the hallway, and the front door of the dwelling lay wide open when the police arrived. They, rather obviously, see this as the culprit's exit point. I, however, believe the perpetrator of these deeds did not leave that house."

The speed with which Holmes reeled off this account had left me too breathless to do more than gesture for him to continue.

"Due to fair weather and good tail winds, the husband's ship returned almost a full day early. While you were busy glowingly writing up your observations of my works, you did not observe as I briefly left to send a telegram to the official conducting the enquiry, instructing him to pay particular attention to the neatness of the lodger's bedding, before directing him to note the dust on his bedposts, and the laundry bills. If, as I suspect, that bed linen has not been in need of laundering since the husband's last return home, it would suggest that the nominal occupier of that room had been sleeping elsewhere in his cousin's absence. The early return of the husband may then have uncovered a betrayal that led to the murder of his rival, the furious brutalization of his wife, and, in a fit of remorse, guilt, or terror over his fate once the crime was uncovered, the taking of his own life."

"But come now," said I with a note of incredulity. "How do you explain the unknown figure sighted retreating with the spoils of his terrible venture?"

"There is no mention of any item stolen, no pillaging or destruction, therefore where you see spoils, I see merely a sack. A burglar would hardly bring baggage to weigh him down, there were no neighbouring properties attacked, yet the bag was described as full. But the premises offered

15

rooms for boarders, and the husband was known for his charity, so might not a fellow sailor in need of a bunk and a place to lay his kitbag for the night have returned with his generous shipmate and witnessed at close quarters the terrible moment of discovery and revenge? In such a situation, staying put to either be included in the husband's wrath, or to find himself caught up in the investigation of a dreadful crime in which he remained the only person unscathed, would present infinitely less appealing prospects than fleeing the scene."

Despite the grim tragedy of this situation I could not help but applaud the methods by which Holmes had seemingly disentangled the case. He dismissed my approval with a deep and heartfelt sigh. "No, no. There is little to tax the brain there. These are commonplace crimes to be tackled by commonplace minds."

"But there must be countless crimes which are not reported in the newspapers."

"Indeed. But if they fail to interest the copy-hungry editors of Fleet Street, then what earthly hope is there of any interest for me? That is why I am a consulting detective and not a private detective. It is why I do not advertise my services, except among the ranks of official policedom. It is only when a case possesses enough points to baffle their occasionally sharp but invariably prosaic minds that I am allowed the opportunity to thrive."

"And so, instead of actively seeking out the type of activity you claim will allow you to flourish, you prefer to allow yourself to sink into the black depression under which you have lived these past few weeks?"

Holmes pushed himself abruptly out of his chair. "I have not been idle. I have made several studies which will prove invaluable to my work—should any work deign to present itself, of course. And I have always the comforts of my violin," said he, and he carefully placed the rudely discarded instrument in its case, before casting a glance toward the locked drawer of his chemical table and quietly adding, "and my needle."

"Now look here, Holmes," I declared, "you must surely know my opinion on that deplorable practise."

Holmes took down a stoppered bottle from the rack above the scarred and discoloured table and emptied some of its contents onto a microscope slide. He kept himself deeply occupied in examining it as I aired my views, only mildly enquiring, "To which do you object, Watson? My playing? Or my very occasional resort to chemical stimulation to make up for the lack of intellectual stimulation?"

"I find your sense of humour strange and ill-timed. Damn it all! 'Very occasional' is still far too often! You are not stupid enough to be ignorant of the dangers."

"You're too kind," he murmured, with the briefest twitch of a smile. I, however, could see little to smile at, and was on the point of stating this fact when the distant sound of the doorbell's chimes reached my ears. At last, thought I, a client to draw Holmes from his mire. But this hope clearly showed on my face for he shook his head, sadly. "No, no. That is the boy from the telegraph office. Though it has been cruelly long since last we heard it, I would recognise that ring—two rapid peels and a more insistent clanging—as his impertinent signature any day. As to what we have been discussing, I have been gravely mistaken, Doctor."

"You finally admit it, then?"

"Yes. I was wrong when I said you weren't a fuss."

"As a medical man," I replied, determined to remain calm despite what I felt sure was deliberate provocation, "it is my duty to stress the great risk you take every time you indulge your ... weakness."

"Then, in turn, it is my duty to do my best to ignore you."

My calm determination flown, the furious exclamation that I was about to let fly was interrupted by a knock at the sitting room door, leaving me to bellow angrily, "Damn and blast it all! Come in, would you?"

Over the years to come our dear Mrs. Hudson would, of course, become a valued friend, an occasional colleague,

17

and a trusted confidant. But back then, during the earliest years of our tenancy, she made quite evident the serious misgivings she nursed over renting her rooms out to such a disreputable pair of madmen as ourselves. As she entered our quarters, I offered immediate and sincere apologies for my raised voice, yet our landlady was too fully engaged in being rendered horrified at the state of the sitting room to take any notice of my contrite niceties.

Irritably, Sherlock Holmes snapped, "Mrs. Hudson, I took the breakfast things down over an hour ago ..."

"Uneaten," she interjected, tartly. "Again!"

"... with the express purpose of preventing you marching in here disturbing me," finished Holmes, as if the interruption had not even occurred.

"Disturbing you at what, may I ask? Torturing that old fiddle, and our eardrums with it?" Having commenced hurriedly picking up fallen newspapers and abandoned teacups, Mrs. Hudson turned her attention on me and insisted, "I do wish you'd talk to him, Dr. Watson. This is the third time this week the tray has come down just as I brought it up. He must eat something!"

"The good doctor has already taken to reminding me how badly I treat myself."

"Holmes believes that hunger helps to sharpen the mind," I added, doubtfully.

"Sharpen it for what? He hasn't been out or done anything for days. Not that he uses any of his spare time to tidy up after himself. No, that's left to me, when I'm not being kept busy cooking meals he doesn't eat and tracking down missing crockery."

"Mrs. Hudson, I'm quite sure you have better things to do than rearrange my sitting room," said Holmes as he rather bravely attempted to take the newspapers from the flustered woman's hands while manoeuvring her toward the open door.

"*My* sitting room," came the sharp response, "and I'll thank you to remember it! Still, if you want your visitor to find you in this ... this pig-sty ..."

"Visitor?" demanded Holmes keenly, swiftly closing the door to bar our landlady's exit. "What visitor? I heard no-one arrive!"

"He turned up at just the same moment as that cheeky imp from the telegraph office did with this message for you." Despite the telegram being addressed to Sherlock Holmes he impatiently gestured for me to accept it, then waved Mrs. Hudson to continue. "A young gentleman who insisted on seeing you. I left him waiting downstairs in the hall. And none too patiently, either! Though impatience seems to be par for the course around here today."

Holmes paced the floor with long, swift strides, suddenly alert. "Describe this young gentleman. Now, if you would."

"Well, you might describe him as a handsome young man, polite, and very smartly dressed. Though he did strike me as being very anxious about something. He was most insistent on seeing you."

Holmes let out a great laugh and seized our surprised landlady by the shoulders. "Mrs. Hudson, I could embrace you and dance you round the room! Unfortunately, I fear Dr. Watson would only write a sensationalised account of such an action, and the resultant scandal and publicity would bring shame upon your good name."

In response, Mrs. Hudson merely dumped the pile of newspapers into Holmes's arms and turned upon her heel to leave.

"Wait! He mustn't see the place like this," exclaimed Holmes, as if only now aware of the chaos with which we had lived these past days. "Mrs. Hudson, would you please go downstairs to our guest and offer him a cup of tea?"

With a countenance that suggested her manners, her dignity, and possibly even her morals had been questioned, she returned, "I don't think either of you gentlemen, or any guests, have ever been given any cause for complaint with the hospitality of this house. But it's usual to wait for a caller to be shown in before offering refreshments, or would you expect me fetch my fine china out onto the doorstep?"

"I don't expect you to do anything of the sort, no, for he will decline the offer. You will insist. He will refuse a second time. Only when you have done all that an admirable hostess can do, short of pouring the infusion straight down his throat, will you then allow him to come up. You understand?"

"No," Mrs. Hudson sniffed. "No, I do not."

"Do it anyway, there's a good woman."

As Mrs. Hudson departed, all the while shaking her head and questioning her own misguided good nature in not simply evicting us on the spot, I quickly scanned the contents of the telegram. "It is from a '*Scotland Yard Police Inspector Peter Athelney Jones*'—hmm, half a bob of the Yard's funds gone on just getting his full name and rank in. '*Wife now conscious. Admits to adulterous affair with lodger. Husband fired both shots. Story vouched for by sailor friend of husband who spent night drinking through shock before coming to senses and telling all. Bad business, but no need after all for theories, laundry lists or dusty bedposts.*' Well, typically lacking in gratitude, but at least your deductions proved sound."

"All it proves is that crime has become as predictable as I feared. However ..." Without another word, Holmes became a blur of activity, and it was difficult to equate the indolent figure who had sprawled in his chair just moments before with this whirlwind of motion that appeared to sweep up every fallen paper and discarded item of apparel in its path. "I hope Mrs. Hudson is as pressing with her offers of tea as she is with her remonstrations. If our caller is as anxious as that good lady claims, he will have no time for such niceties, but her tenacious insistence may buy me some precious time."

Even though Holmes had happily allowed me to share one of his cases, I could not risk assuming this was to be a regular or permanent arrangement. Thus I found myself asking, "Do you wish me to leave?"

"Not at all, Watson. You may be of some assistance!"

"I'm pleased to hear it," I replied, relieved and somewhat flattered by the trust shown.

"Good fellow," said he, then deposited the papers, clothing and crockery into my arms before rushing into his bedroom, so that only the tail of his dressing gown was to be seen, billowing like silken wings as he vanished from view with the cry, "This sitting room is an absolute disgrace!"

"Sorry," said I, with not the subtlest dash of sarcasm, before, with a sigh, collecting yet more debris in a hasty attempt to restore some form of domestic order. "Still, though, a client, at long last? You must be very pleased."

Holmes's voice issued forth, amidst the slam and clatter of wardrobe doors and the muffled thuds of rifled drawers. "We don't yet know that this young man is to be a client. We must hear what he has to tell us before we can decide upon that matter."

"Oh, come now, Holmes! I've not seen you move this quickly since you accidentally set fire to your chemical bench last week. Surely whatever problem he presents you with must be better than nothing? You just admitted to sheer, unmitigated boredom."

"Between the pair of you, you and Mrs. Hudson are determined to force me to seek occupation, if only to escape your nagging," chided Holmes as he emerged once more in his most immaculate morning suit and neatly adjusted his collar. "And that was *not* an accident! Combustion was an integral stage in the experiment."

"The fact that he knew where to find you has to be of some interest."

Holmes rushed to the sofa and, rescuing his jacket from the all-consuming drift of newspapers and journals, threw it on over his slender shoulders. "You think so?"

"I do, indeed," said I, and I marvelled that for one so immersed in mystery and baffling details, he failed entirely to register one when it stared him in the face. "This address was published in none of the accounts of the Hope case which condescended to mention your name."

Holmes seized the stack of papers from my arms but, before he could respond to my point, there was a brisk knock at the door. With a cry of, "Come in, sir! Come in," he threw the entire pile into his bedroom, slamming his door on the blizzard of newsprint that erupted from within just as the sitting room door opened to allow us our first glimpse of the individual whose arrival upon our threshold might, we anticipated, offer us fresh respite from dull and stifling routine, or plunge us into obscure and unknown realms of dread and horror.

Chapter 2:
Introductions and Deductions

The man who entered could not have been more than thirty years of age, though there was care and tiredness etched around his dark, lively eyes, and a mournful quality that lengthened his otherwise handsome face. His dark brown hair was neatly, even severely trimmed, and he was soberly attired, as if suited for the office, with his hat clutched in his hands. Just as Mrs. Hudson had described, he appeared gripped by some anxiety, for he wrung his hat brim quite without mercy, while his smile of greeting failed to mask his state of mind.

"Please excuse my unannounced visit, gentlemen," said he in a voice that was softly well-spoken, "but which of you is Mr. Sherlock Holmes?"

Holmes extended an open palm in greeting and guided our visitor into the room. "I am Sherlock Holmes. This is my friend, Dr. Watson."

The young man grasped my hand, relief already brightening his expression. "And are you also a—what was the term, now? Ah, yes—are you a consulting detective?"

"No, no, my associate is the one man in all the world who can claim that title. I am merely a doctor, and my cases are purely medical. Now you know who we are, sir. And you...?"

"Forgive me, Dr. Watson, Mr. Holmes. My name is Nicholas Wexley, and you have no idea how grateful I am that you have agreed to see me."

Holmes perched himself alertly in his customary chair by the fireplace and indicated that our guest avail himself of the sofa, while I settled into my own armchair. "Now, exactly when did you visit Scotland Yard?"

"Yesterday evening. They were ..." Nicholas Wexley stared at Holmes in amazement, with that slack-jawed, wide-eyed gape that was to become so regular a fixture on so many faces—my own included, I readily admit—over the years to come.

"They were uncooperative?" Holmes supplied, concluding the young man's sentence and eliciting a nod of his head in dumbfounded answer. "But someone there gave you my name and address."

"Exactly so! How did you—no, no—how *could* you know this, sir?"

"Since I have never publicised my work, there was only one way you could have found me, and that is through one of my contacts amongst the official ranks. And, now that you have ..." Holmes gestured for our visitor to swallow his surprise and resume speaking.

"May I tell you my problem, Mr. Holmes?"

"I wish you would. For, apart from the facts that you arrived here in a cab, you are in a good position in a shipping clerks' office, and that, after debating with yourself for some hours, you have only just decided to call upon me within the last thirty minutes, I know absolutely nothing about you."

So startled was our guest, he rose quite unknowingly to his feet and stood staring down at Holmes in wonderment. "But this is utterly astonishing, sir! I mean, it's always possible that you might have observed my cab's arrival from the window, but as for the rest? I am at a loss! An absolute loss!"

"My friend, Watson, will testify that I have been nowhere near the window," said Holmes, airily, and I nodded my affirmation. "As to the remaining facts; that you arrived in a cab is evident from the still wet mud upon your shoes. Had you walked, the mud would have had time to dry and be shaken loose, since it contains traces of a particular blue clay found only in one area, by the docks, quite some distance away. From your build, demeanour and dress, you are patently not a dockyard labourer, while the smudges of ink on your fingers, the creases in your sleeves where your arms rest on the edge of your desk, and the fading but still visible impress of a visor's band across your forehead—quite distinct from the subtler line of your hat—all suggest a career as a clerk. You have obviously been troubled for some time, as your uneven shave and the pouches below your eyes profess, yet you did not call first thing in the morning. And still, you did not wait till standard lunch hours, implying that the decision, having recently been reached, was one that you felt compelled to act immediately upon."

"And," said I, keenly, "your good position is shown by the fact that you could take yourself freely from your office during business hours."

"Well done, Watson! You've been studying my methods."

"Sergeant MacDonald told me that you would amaze me, sir," laughed Nicholas Wexley, "but I certainly did not expect it to happen quite so soon."

"There is nothing amazing about using one's eyes and mind in conjunction, Mr. Wexley," said Sherlock Holmes, taking a fresh fill of tobacco from the old Persian slipper on the hearth. "So, it was Alec Mac, the Scotsman of Scotland Yard, who recommended me? He's one of the few in that establishment who appreciates my methods. I have him marked to make inspector before long, provided he can disguise his native cleverness sufficiently so that they might regard him as one of their own." As those who have followed the somewhat brilliant career of the talented Aberdonian detective will know, Holmes's prediction was to be proved correct, and several well-merited promotions were soon to elevate Alec MacDonald to the forefront of his profession.

"From what he told me of you, and from what I have now seen for myself, I'm surprised you are not at the very least a police inspector, yourself."

"Ha! Thank you," Holmes barked. "I take it you meant it as a compliment?"

"Well, yes. Yes, of course. But I'm afraid that when you hear my story you might think it—it, and myself also, for troubling you with it—all rather absurd and foolish. I know that the police detective I tried to speak to—before your friend MacDonald quietly advised my visit to Baker Street—clearly imagined me deluded."

"That stands as a pretty good recommendation in this household," I smiled. "Perhaps a drink to put you at ease? A wee dram, in honour of the fellow who has sent you our way, or some brandy, if it is not too early? Or I could ask Mrs. Hudson to bring you up some tea?

"My thanks, but no, Dr. Watson. She has already offered a number of times. She seemed quite insistent on the matter." I hid my grin as I fetched a box of cigars from the sideboard. "Thank you," said he, taking and lighting one.

Holmes declined the proffered box and resumed his pipe instead. "Why don't you take some notes, Watson?"

"If you think they will be of use, certainly."

"If they will stop you clucking around like a mother hen and allow our guest to begin his narrative then they will have proved very useful indeed."

Thus it was in rather a sulk that I sat with my journal and a pencil at the ready to jot down any and all salient facts in whatever story this anxious stranger had brought us.

"It is my younger sister who is the cause for my concern." Nicholas Wexley took a small print in its slim, folding frame from his breast pocket and handed it to me. "This is Eleanor. It is a recent photograph."

Even captured in flat, colourless tones on that small oval of card, the face that smiled back from within a frame of darkly flowing curls had such poise and intelligence and, yes, such intense loveliness to it, that I could hardly help but remark, "What a very beautiful young woman. If you don't mind me saying so, Mr. Wexley. She is quite charming. Do you not agree, Holmes?"

"You are probably right," said he, absently, glancing only briefly at the picture before returning it to Wexley. "She looks a somewhat troubled young woman. The smile is very forced."

"Indeed, you are right again, Mr. Holmes." Wexley glanced quickly at the portrait, then returned it to his pocket. "It was taken only a few weeks after the death of our father."

"Oh, my dear chap, you have our sincerest condolences."

"Please, Dr. Watson, you will forgive me if I appear to speak ill of the dead, but Oscar Wexley was not what anyone could possibly have called a good father while alive and, now that he's dead, he is still the cause of our suffering."

"Your sister has yet to recover from the loss? Well, that will come with time."

"It was no loss. Hardly that after all these years!" Our guest's voice rose, startlingly shrill in its vehemence, before, chastened, he resumed in a milder tone, "But you are right. His death struck Eleanor much more deeply than it did me."

"In what way?"

"It has left her open to certain ... certain persons who persist in exerting an unhealthy influence over her." Unable to contain his vexed emotions any longer, Wexley rose suddenly to his feet, and gravely declared "Mr. Holmes, my sister is in the power of witches!"

"Witches?" I glanced at Holmes to gauge his reaction to this extraordinary proclamation. His face, however, remained impassive, though his eyes followed Wexley as he paced in that same spot he himself had gloomily stalked moments before. Very well, thought I, if Holmes will not press the matter, I would have to. "You cannot be serious, Mr. Wexley, surely? Witchcraft in London in this day and age?"

"I am most definitely serious, Doctor. They call their little coven—or society, or gathering, or whatever term they may have for it—'The Most Sacred Spiritualist Church of the Golden Star'."

"I have no expertise in the matter," remarked Holmes, "however, I believe you will find a vast disparity between followers of the current fashion for spiritualism and the practitioners of the more esoteric arts of witchcraft."

"What difference does it make? They are all obsessed with false ideas, crazed beliefs, and plain, old-fashioned mumbo jumbo!"

I am certain that, were these pages to pass before his sharp eye in preparation for publication, my old friend and erstwhile editor, Doyle, would gladly have provided much authentic detail pertaining to the rise of the spiritualist movement, he having become something of an acclaimed authority on the subject. In the mass outbreak of grief that has followed since the Great War, there have been many who have genuinely sought to offer comfort by promoting communion with those whose lives had been so drastically cut short—and, sadly and unforgivably, very many more who would profit from such promises of succour to the bereaved—thus bringing back into vogue those beliefs and practices that had become an international craze during the latter half of the last century. Indeed, before that century was itself laid to rest, Sherlock Holmes and I were to find ourselves in the presence of several self-proclaimed mediums and clairvoyants, and while the majority of them would prove merely fraudulent, or sometimes severely deluded, there are still those I cannot dismiss quite so lightly.

But these adventures were yet to come and, with no

opinion worth voicing on the matter, I could only nod as Holmes observed, "There are many intelligent people, men and women of note included, who believe wholeheartedly that the spiritualist movement can only lead to mankind's progress toward enlightenment."

Sherlock Holmes's calm reply served only to fuel Mr. Wexley's anger. "Are you telling me you believe in this rubbish too? Talking to the dead? Spirit voices? Ghosts?"

"I do not believe, nor do I disbelieve. Beyond certain statements from both advocates and adversaries of the movement in the pages of various journals, I have no data on the subject. So far, my experience has been confined to mortal criminals. If I ever encounter a supernatural one, I'm sure I will find time to research the subject. Now kindly take a moment to compose yourself, then tell me how your sister came to be entangled with this society, and how it involves your late father." And as Wexley took a deep breath or two and offered sincere apologies, Holmes settled back in his chair, his long, pale fingers steepled in front of his face, and allowed his gaze drift to the ceiling.

"As I have told you, my father was far from my affections, and I doubt very much that I was held dearly in his. He was an historian; indeed, he had risen to the post of Professor of Archaeology at one of our smaller universities. Though perhaps 'risen' is a poor choice of word, and I should better have said he scrabbled and clawed and dug himself into his position, and would happily have submerged himself there till the crack of doom.

"We saw little of him at home. That is, when he was even in the country. His first and, I suspect, only care was for things long dead and buried, and he travelled greatly in search of such gloomy articles. What did he care for his own living, breathing flesh and blood when there were old bones for him to coo over? So infrequently did he return to these shores that Mother refused to have us remain cooped up and cloistered in the university's precincts, far away from other families and opportunities that were not so tightly woven in with the stultifying world of academia, and she conveyed us and our home and hearth back to the city.

"Thus my sister and I saw Father rarely as we were growing up, and even then he would more often than not be huddled with his learned friends around some mouldy manuscript they had unearthed, or else be stuck away, solitary and silent in his library, so that Mother must have wished she had left his books and belongings back in his college quarters!"

"What of your mother?" I asked.

"Our poor mother died when Eleanor was only fourteen. We could not even trace our father in time for her funeral. And, when he did at last return, he went straight down to his library and his books. He never so much as visited my mother's grave once, and within the week he was gone."

"He had left the country again?"

"I neither know nor care. Fortunately I was already in full employment with, as you astutely surmised, a respected shipping office, and thus able to support Eleanor until she was of age and found a steady job of her own. This she has since done, as a secretary in a firm of solicitors."

"And you had no word from your father?"

"Not in ten years," replied Wexley, both his face and voice betraying his bitterness. "Then one day, some six months ago, he arrived on our doorstep in a state of considerable excitement. He talked of some great discovery he had made and how, when his work was completed, we would understand why he had deserted us. 'You shall see, at last,' he insisted. 'I have delved into the past to find the future! My crowning achievement, you might well call it! You will both see!' But despite Eleanor's great joy in welcoming him, and the many, many questions we had for him, he simply loaded himself up with more of his damned books and disappeared again, still crying, 'You'll see! Soon enough, you'll see it all so clearly!' But all I clearly saw were the tears in my sister's eyes as he once more left her behind."

"Do you have any ideas as to what his discovery might have been?"

"There was no discovery! Mr. Holmes, my father spent his entire life scrabbling about in the dirt for treasure, but he never once found anything of value. He may have talked like one who had secured some vast fortune, but he knew nothing of wealth. Nor of cost, as whatever money there ever was in our family was squandered on his fool's errands! Finally, it was his work or, more accurately, his overpowering obsession, which killed him.

"Five weeks ago, we received word that our father was still in England, and that he was gravely ill. For Eleanor's sake, we rushed to be with him but, when we arrived, he was already close to death. He was never a strong man and his lungs were collapsing under the strain of pneumonia. He was a babbling half-mad, half-dead wreckage of a man. When he did die, I was almost relieved. I know that must make me sound a very cruel and heartless son."

"I cannot see that you have any cause to feel otherwise, considering the way you were treated."

"Thank you, Dr. Watson. I truly am relieved to find someone else who can understand my anger toward the man."

"Your sister does not share your disdain, then?" asked Holmes. "Is it this that has led her into the troubling company she now keeps?"

"Her heart always was considerably softer than mine, I admit," sighed Wexley. "She never could turn her back on anyone in need, and was forever the supporter of lost causes. And our late father certainly fell into that category. Eleanor had a peculiar sort of faith in him. I would say it was a faith based mainly on the stories our mother had told her of our father when he was a young and brilliant man. I always suspected them to be grossly exaggerated tales, told to stop Eleanor from realising that her father was an eccentric, irresponsible and ultimately purposeless man. So, instead, she grew up thinking of him as some sort of magical and exotic figure, wandering distant isles and gathering their myths and legends, and bringing their treasures to light. It didn't help that, on the few occasions when he did return, his talk would be of the lands he had visited and all the beliefs and superstitions of their peoples. This appealed greatly to Eleanor's romantic nature, and it has now left her open and vulnerable to whatever ridiculous lies this so-called Church has been feeding her."

"Perhaps meeting sympathetic people who have also suffered the same type of loss has been of some comfort," I suggested. It was not a suggestion that found favour with our visitor.

"Comfort, sir? The only comfort Eleanor is likely to find in the company of these villains is that of the feeble-minded, for I believe that it is their intention to drive my poor sister insane! How else do you explain the fact that she claims to not only have seen, but to also have spoken to, the spectre of our dead father?"

Chapter 3: The Sceptical Sibling's Statement

"**Y**our father's ghost?" I repeated, too startled to hide the disbelief in my voice. "Those are your sister's own words?"

"Indeed they are, gentlemen!" Nicholas Wexley accepted the brandy I now proffered with a trembling hand and gulped it down before continuing in somewhat steadier and softer tones. "My sister and I still live in that same house in Battersea that Mother had made into a home for us, and which our father had only occasionally intruded upon. It is a modest household, with no maid or servant, for we live so simply that we have no need of any staff to cater for our whims."

"You have never married?" I enquired in mild surprise, for he was a most presentable fellow.

"There was an engagement. It was a few years ago, now. But the match was not the right one. Perhaps in time, after Eleanor is settled. If this business does not entirely unsettle her, as it has me. Until then, we are the only family each other has.

"The office where Eleanor has worked these past few

years is only a mile or so away, and it is usual for her to be home before me. Not, I must make clear, that her life simply revolves around office and home, and nor does mine. We both have our circles of friends, indeed we share some of those same friends we've both known since our arrival in the city, and if I return home in the evening before her, it's usually because she is visiting with some acquaintance or other. It doesn't often happen, however, as she is generally happier in the company of a good book. So, when I arrived home rather later than usual one evening due to some tedious confusion at work over misplaced dockets, I thought initially that my call of greeting went unanswered because she was engrossed in some romantic tale of intrigue, and her mind was in whichever far-flung location the words on the page had transported her to.

"However, my repeated cries, a stroll around the rooms on the ground floor, and a knock upon her bedroom door all confirmed that she was not to be found in the house. Nor was she in our small, peaceful back garden, where she sometimes likes to sit and look up to the skies. 'Imagine, Nicholas,' she once said, 'all the things those clouds might have seen as they have passed over lands and seas. And all the things that so many eyes that will have looked up at them must have observed.' I leave such imagining to her—to my mind I see only a garden that needs regular maintenance to keep it trim. And on this evening the garden I looked out upon was an empty one, with no sign of Eleanor, not even a forgotten book on the lawn, or her shoes discarded by the door so she might walk through the grass like some unrestrained native of one of those cloud-visited lands.

"It was unusual enough for her to be out at this time, and unheard of for her not to have mentioned any plans she might have made to be away for the evening. It was the unprecedented nature of her absence, coupled with the painful knowledge that her recent bereavement still troubled her, that caused my own thoughts to grow troubled. I paced through every room once more, as if somehow believing that I may simply have overlooked her, sitting quietly in a corner with her nose pressed to the pages of a book.

"Every room, I should say, except for the one that has remained locked these last six months, and had practically always been locked to us ever since we were children—the last door at the end of the hallway, below the stairs, leading down to the cellar that had long since been claimed as Father's study and library. She surely could not be down there? It was logical, I suppose, that if she had found herself striving to feel close to the man once more she might wish to be amongst his belongings. Even so, the thought of her skulking down there amongst those ... those dead things that he had plucked from the ground where they should have still lain was abominable!

"I do not believe in ghosts, let me assure you of that from the outset. But there has long been something about that gloomy, subterranean room that has troubled me. Yet more troubling still was the notion that Eleanor was down there, and so, reluctantly, I put my hand to the handle, knocking gently first in case I should startle her. Then regretting my knock in case—an absurd notion—something else answered, I forced myself to turn the handle. The door was locked. How foolish a source of relief, as I still hadn't found Eleanor, but even so ... Of course, there was the key still hanging in the kitchen, and there, now I had a grip on my needless panic, I saw the note my sister had left for me, stating that she had taken the opportunity to spend the evening with friends, that she would be home before it grew late, and that she had prepared some cold cuts which I might find in the pantry for my supper should I wish to dine before her return.

"There was nothing suspicious or worrying there, indeed I was pleased that she felt up to socialising once more. But still I was uneasy."

"Because of an empty room in your own house?" prompted Holmes.

"I tell you this only because it may give you some idea of the man Oscar Wexley was, and the irrational thoughts that are the lingering effects of his presence. The prospect of investigating the cellar had reawakened old memories. Once, when I was little more than a boy, I found myself wakened in the night by I knew not what. Voices, perhaps? A gruff, loud voice that was both unfamiliar and yet known to me. My mother's calm, reassuring tones issuing from downstairs, and this other voice replying in turn. It was far too late for visitors, and when I at last heard my mother come up and go to her bed, I waited as long as I could and then crept downstairs, only vaguely guessing at who this other person was that even still I heard moving around below."

Nicholas Wexley's voice was barely more than a whisper, as if remembering every stealthy, nerve-wracking step upon that moonlit stairway. "Treading softly, I found that door beneath the stairs open, the first time I had ever seen it unlocked. My curiosity overtook good sense, and I stole down to where I saw the dull, red lamplight flickering below. There the slinking, shuddering shadows caused the primitive masks upon the walls to leer terrifyingly down at me, the old bones to dance under glass, and those many frightful sculptures, and manikins, and hideous dolls with faces like devil-fishes and more limbs than are decent on any creature, to writhe as if living. And there, amidst these grotesque souvenirs of robbed and ransacked graves and burial places, a great red face glowered down into mine.

"Here was my own father, but not the man I had remembered. He had not been so bearded and weathered as now, his hair grown unkempt so that it curled up like horns, and he grimaced down at me with the face of a gargoyle peering down from a church roof as if hunting for trespassing sinners to persecute. I was that trespasser, down there in my father's private sanctum, and as I bolted upstairs I heard his wheezing, cackling laughter following me with every step. That is the kind of father he was, gentlemen. One who looms out of the dark and laughs at the terror of his own child.

"All of these memories now came back as if I were still a whimpering child shivering in his nightshirt and stocking-soles at the thought of some ogre lurking beneath his feet. So much so that I practically leapt from my skin when the front door opened and footsteps pounded down the hallway towards the kitchen, where I sat nursing my dread. A voice rang out. 'Nicholas? Nicholas, are you there?' A voice it took me a moment to recognise, because it was filled with a sound I had not heard in it of late.

"That unfamiliar sound was the sound of joy. It was Eleanor, and she was in raptures. It had been such a long time since I had seen her so elated. She had barely even smiled in the three weeks since our father had passed away. She burst into the kitchen and threw her arms around me, laughing and telling me that she had the most wonderful news. I was truly grateful to see her in such a bright mood, though I was at a loss to divine the cause of it. I had imagined that she may have had some romantic assignation, and was of a mind to offer playfully stern reproaches for such clandestine activity, but my heart sank immediately when she revealed the source of her happiness.

"Smiling, even as my own smile died, she told me, 'They are the most incredible people, Nicholas, dear. Each one of them has lost so much, but still they have such noble courage and strength. And why should they not? After all, they know that those they have lost wait just beyond the veil. They even say that, with the proper knowledge and rituals, the veil can be parted as easily as opening that curtain there to look out through the window upon the world beyond these confining walls and into the thronging streets and peaceful gardens alike.'

"What on earth was she talking about? Ha! Nothing on this earth, she quickly clarified. 'Had I not met poor, sweet Mr. Hammond, I may never have known of these wonderful gatherings. He has lost someone too, and he recognised that loss in me within minutes of our first meeting. How extraordinary a coincidence—if coincidence it truly was, for we must consider that other forces may yet guide our lives—that he and I should find one another in so ordinary a fashion! It was he who told me where they meet, and how they have been allowed those glimpses into the beyond. No, I know that look you wear, Nicholas. I, too, have read of the spiritualists in the newspapers, and the many exceptional claims made for their beliefs and abilities. I daresay I may have pulled that self-same face too when Mr. Hammond first broached the subject. Yet he spoke so clearly and rationally of what he had personally witnessed, and even of the contact he himself had made, that I grew to question my own doubts. If there was but a chance, even the tiniest sliver of a hope that I might reach out and be answered ...'

"I could scarcely credit that my sister, so smart and sensible in her own way, might have been fooled into accepting such a possibility. She accused me of being the proud possessor of a stubbornly closed mind, a rebuke that I had heard more than once over the years. 'You sound just like Father when you say that,' I snapped, immediately regretting my raised voice. Customarily my disapproval when speaking of that man brought her protests, but in this instance she simply laughed. It was not a cruel laugh, neither spiteful nor mocking, but it chilled me all the same.

"'Oh, Nicholas, I know just how Father sounds. Your remark could not be better timed. No, I do not mean from memory. I know because this very night I believe I have— no, I know, as sure as I know that I am speaking to you!—I know that I have been speaking with our dear, lost father. And I know that I heard him answer my call. Yes, Nicholas, I heard him! He called out to me, whispering my name.'"

Nicholas Wexley paused and glanced sharply between Holmes and I, as if expecting to catch us in the act of exchanging knowing looks or rolling our eyes in disbelief. With the smallest of gestures Holmes bade him continue. "It seemed to me that the poor child had lost her mind, and the more I tried to calm her, the more she insisted that it was true. That she had witnessed the apparition of our father's spirit, and that he had spoken her name.

"I was eventually able to persuade her to tell me where this had all taken place, and how a chance meeting with a stranger—this rogue Hammond of whom she had spoken—had led her into the power of this coven. 'He did not believe either,' she told me, 'until he had experienced the wonder of it for himself. It has made him a student of what we might term the occult. Those books of his, which I had so clumsily caused him to spill as I collided with him in the street, were full of genuine, verified accounts of mediumship and clairvoyance.' Verified by whom? That, naturally, she could not answer. 'He had suspected trickery, too, just as you do, dear Brother! Thus he had set about making his own extensive investigations into the matter, and was now convinced that he had not been deceived. As he told me, I would just need to see and to hear for myself what could be achieved and I would be convinced also. And I am! I am more than convinced! For even though I only caught glimmerings of an outline, and heard only a whisper of his voice, I *know* that what I witnessed was real. And next time, next week in fact, when our wonderful, kind, blessed medium is fully rested and her powers have returned to their strongest, I will see more and hear more.'

"Mediums? Powers? She could not possibly intend to go back amongst these people again, I insisted. But Eleanor has inherited much of Mother's determination, and she was adamant! 'Next week, Brother! Next week I shall see him again!'"

"Naturally, you forbade her doing so," said I.

"I did. She tried to suggest I go with her, as if I would willingly accompany her through the gates of Bedlam. I'm afraid it led to quite the most heated argument we have ever had, and for several days afterwards we remained silent and sullen toward one another. It was Eleanor who at last broke the silence; she always was the more forgiving and placatory of us. So I had always thought, at any rate. She told me that she had thought long and hard, and had at last recognised how foolish she had been. She said that, of course, it was impossible for her to have seen what she claimed she had seen, and that her grief must have clouded her mind."

"She was lying, of course."

"Yes. But as I had never known her to be anything but honest and open in all things, Mr. Holmes, I trusted her completely. On the night of the next meeting, she complained of a headache and declared her intention to go to bed early in the evening. It wasn't until I chanced to notice her hat and coat missing from the hallway stand that I realised she must have slipped quietly out. Cursing myself for a gullible fool, I immediately set off after her."

"She had told you the address where these gatherings take place, then?" I asked.

"Only that it was a public hall in the East End, somewhere near the new dock that stands in honour of the late prince. I left my cab in the street, realising it would be quicker to negotiate the alleyways and side-streets of that area on foot, and I might have raced around the whole district before I found the place. A dreary, run-down sort of building, it looked as though it might have been abandoned years ago. The doors were locked, but there was candlelight dimly visible in the windows and, with my ear pressed to the grubby glass, I could hear voices within. One of these was clearly my misguided sister's, and though whatever she said was muffled and unintelligible there was plainly a distressed, pleading tone to her words, just as I'd heard when Father had last left us. And all the while another, more dominant voice coaxed and cajoled and urged her to continue.

"My hammering on the doors received no answer, so I had no option but to force my way in. The old, warped wood of the outer doors gave way under the application of my shoulder while, from beyond the inner doors, I could smell a bitter-sweet smoky aroma that mingled unpleasantly with the air of damp disuse in the place. And still I could hear voices. That stronger voice, which I quickly came to realise was that of a woman with a distinctly foreign accent, rose in its demands for my sister to answer, to speak, to remember, while a lower, vaguer whisper pressed on.

"And then Eleanor spoke again, and her words were horribly clear. 'Father?' she cried. 'Father, is it you?' And without another instant's thought, I threw myself through those inner doors, where I found ..." Nicholas Wexley's voice grew dry and husky, and he regarded his empty glass for a moment. I rose to replenish it, but a sharp shake of the head from Holmes stilled me. Resolving himself, Mr. Wexley pressed on.

"They sat facing a bare stage, as if gripped by some invisible play or show. But the real show was my sister, sitting in the midst of them in some sort of trance, still calling out to our dead father. She was entirely unaware of my presence, although the half dozen or so others in that smoke-shrouded room gaped in horrified shock as I strode in, demanding to know what devilry they were about. Some stood to face me, while others ducked back like rats into the shadows. Yet Eleanor simply gazed ahead of her, as if searching the swirling shadows for something, and when I reached for her and lightly touched her shoulder she called out shrilly and fainted clean away into my arms."

"What was it she cried out?"

"She called out something about a crown. You wish her exact words? As I ran to her, begging her to answer me, there was a sudden flash of something in her eyes. Recognition, I assumed, as if I had roused her from a deep slumber from which she remained groggy before the world resolved itself. But she seemed to look far beyond me, beyond even the furthest corners of that dingy hall, and frantically exclaimed, 'I remember! The crown! Oh, God! The crown! The crown and the circle, Father! I remember the crown and the circle of blood!' Then she fell, as if the life had been drained from her. Whatever those words mean, I honestly could not say, nor could she when I asked her later. In the meantime, my one clear thought was to get her out of that ungodly place."

"No-one attempted to stop you?"

"They wouldn't have dared! Even seven or eight to one, I would have chanced it against them. I was in a fury and, I admit, told them exactly what I thought of them and their squalid society, and made it abundantly clear what action I would take if they came near my sister again. I practically carried her, still swooning in my arms, out into the streets. Then, as the fresh air revived her, I was able to coax her into a cab and get her safely home."

"I take it," ventured Holmes, "your sister did not react as you had hoped to your rescue attempt?"

Wexley shook his head angrily. "Quite the opposite to it, in fact! She was utterly outraged by what she termed my 'ceaseless and overbearing interference' in her affairs. Whatever she had witnessed—had *believed* she'd witnessed—in that room had driven her to the point of collapse, yet even still she scorned my concerns, and indignantly accused me of interrupting the ... the ceremony just as they were reaching a breakthrough! I had believed—had fervently hoped—her experience would drive her away from this unnatural group. Instead, it has only strengthened her determination to return at the next opportunity and go through the ordeal once more."

"Which would be this very evening?"

"At eight o'clock," Wexley confirmed. Then his eyes flew wide and he turned to Holmes to demand, "How could you possibly know it was tonight?"

"You have undoubtedly made every effort to compel your sister to change her mind. When it became clear that your efforts were in vain, you were forced to seek a more desperate solution, namely lodging a complaint with the police, despite your justified belief that they would dismiss your fears. Since you have subsequently taken recourse to attempt engaging the services of a man you had never before heard of and still know very little about, it is clear that the incident you wish to prevent is imminent."

Throughout Holmes's explication, Nicholas Wexley again showed signs of wonderment, and of relief that he had evidently chosen to consult a man possessed of extraordinary gifts. That relief fled upon Holmes's next utterance. "However, I fail to see what you intend me to do. I am a consulting detective. I do not concern myself with family disputes."

"Surely you'd agree that I cannot allow my sister to go through with this?"

"You must admit," said I, "it is a morbid and unhealthy pursuit for a young woman, Holmes."

"Morbidity is no crime, Watson. From what I can see nothing illegal has taken place, as I am sure you were informed at Scotland Yard, Mr. Wexley. You have made no mention of money being abstracted from your sister and, as you have already made plain, there is little wealth in your family at any rate. Furthermore, your sister seems to being acting of her own accord and not under any duress."

"My sister is not acting in her right mind!"

"In which event an alienist would undoubtedly be of more service to you, as I fail to see how I can affect her mental balance."

"Steady on, there, Holmes," I gasped, aware that the brother's anger, already overflowing its banks, was unlikely to be soothed by such talk of his sister's sanity, or lack thereof.

"Something has to be done," insisted Wexley, red-faced and pounding the floorboards with each footstep, so that I imagined Mrs. Hudson in her parlour below offering frantic prayers for the safety of her ceiling plaster. "Something *will* be done, even if I have to lock her in her room to keep her safely out of harm's reach!"

"Then you would be the one committing a crime by holding her against her will. I would strongly suggest you avoid that particular course of action."

"And that is your one and only suggestion?"

"Not at all, Mr. Wexley. I also suggest that you spare yourself some considerable trouble by ceasing your efforts to alter your sister's decision, and allow her to act as she wishes. It should be clear to you by now that you cannot influence her anyway."

"The only thing now clear to me is how badly ill-informed I was about you. You may be good at clever parlour games, Mr. Sherlock Holmes, but I have obviously been wasting my time in hoping that you could assist me!"

As I strove to prevent his storming to the door, Nicholas Wexley brushed past with ease, pausing only as I cried, "I assure you there is more to Sherlock Holmes than parlour tricks. I have personally witnessed his skills in operation during a highly complex criminal investigation, where the only successful results were those provided by the swift actions and keen brain of the man you are currently walking away from."

"Thank you for that spirited defence, Doctor," announced Holmes, and he rose swiftly and moved smoothly round us to the sitting room door. "Mr. Wexley, before you go, please be good enough to supply the address where I may find this 'Church Of The Golden Star'."

"Do you mean to say," asked he, with some suspicion, "that after all that, you intend to help me?"

"At this moment, sir, I believe I may be the only person who can."

I snatched up my pencil and my notebook and handed both to Wexley, indicating that he should write both his own address and that of the gathering place of this mysterious sect. He did so, and all the while he stammered out his gratitude, the red tinge to his cheeks more indicative now of shame than fury. "I apologise for my outburst, Mr. Holmes. If there is anything I may do to repay this ..."

"You might start," Holmes interjected, sharply, "by telling me what it was that you witnessed in that East End hall to alarm you so."

Mr. Wexley's whole attitude grew instantly tense, the hand that held out the notebook gripping rigidly with whitening knuckles before it was surrendered to my grasp. Yet he looked at Holmes as if puzzled. "Witnessed, Mr. Holmes? I have told you all...."

"You told us that we may find you foolish, but I see nothing foolish in wishing to protect your sister. In addition, you paused during your telling of the events of that disrupted gathering, as if undecided on whether or not to reveal a certain detail. Now, what was that, I wonder?"

"This time, I'm afraid you really are mistaken, Mr. Holmes," replied Nicholas Wexley emphatically. "Besides the details which I have just told you, I saw nothing. Nothing at all."

With a slight shrug, Holmes turned his back on us and moved swiftly toward his bedroom door. "In which case, Mr. Wexley, good day to you."

"And is there nothing you want me to do?"

"Go about your normal business and, when you return home tonight, make your peace with your sister." And, so saying, Holmes stepped into his room and closed the door.

I affixed a smile to my face and grasped the young man's hand, shaking it briskly as I led him out toward the stairs. "Good day, Mr. Wexley, and, please, do not allow this matter to worry you further. Once Sherlock Holmes has promised his assistance, he devotes his full energies to the endeavour, and those energies are boundless."

"Thank you, Doctor. I already feel more at ease. Good day."

But the instant the fellow had crossed our front doorstep to be swept along again into the crowds that bustled along Baker Street, I addressed myself to my associate, raising my voice to be heard through the panels of the bedroom door. "I really cannot see how you intend to help in this matter, Holmes!"

"Oh, dear," remarked he as he brushed past carrying a large, well-stuffed carpet bag of dubious design. "You've surely not lost faith in me already, old fellow?"

"Good Lord, no. I simply fail to see how this could be of any interest to you. You said yourself that you could see no crime."

"Which is not to say that no crime is being committed," he retorted, throwing on his overcoat, "only that its nature is unclear. At least for the moment. As yet, we have only heard part of the story. It is now our duty to discover the rest." Donning his top hat, he strode to the door.

"Where are we going?" said I as I reached for my own overcoat. "To the East End, to locate this dismal gathering place?"

"Hardly, at this time of day. Before lunch on a midweek morning is no time for the powers of darkness to be invoked. I am going to the library. The subject of the spirit world is one which should make intriguing reading."

"And what of me, Holmes?"

He paused and regarded me coolly. "You wish to join me in this venture?"

"Most certainly, if I can provide any genuine assistance."

I was relieved to see the faintest glimmer of a smile as he said, "I have not the least moment's doubt of it, Watson."

"Excellent. Then what am I to do?"

"Whatever you please, my dear fellow, as long as you do not leave these rooms." Then, snatching up his cane, Holmes paused only briefly in the doorway to add, "You may wish to clean your old service revolver."

"You believe there is to be danger, then?"

There was no trace of a smile to be found now, as he replied, "I believe Miss Eleanor Wexley to be in the gravest danger. Perhaps not physically, but most definitely emotionally, and very probably psychologically. And now that we have chosen to involve ourselves, we are open to the same dangers."

"But, if she is at risk," I protested, that sweet face in the photograph leaping into my thoughts, "why did you persuade her brother to let her go?"

"Watson, you have no intention of making a habit of being so obtuse, I hope? She is the only link to the perpetrators of this extraordinary scheme. If I am to discover their purpose, it is imperative that Miss Wexley is at tonight's meeting. Now, time is of the essence for, after I have absorbed whatever the library's most exotic shelves have to offer, I must summon an old and trusted friend."

"Which friend is this, Holmes? You think the case so perilous that we need reinforcements?"

But hefting the gaudy baggage, and delivering a high-spirited, "Goodbye, Watson," Holmes marched out, the door slamming shut on any further question I may raise, or protest I might voice.

Indeed there were protests and questions aplenty whirling through my thoughts as I gazed vacantly at that closed door before, on registering the sound of the front door opening and closing, I came to myself and crossed to the chemical table. Yet it was not the tubes and retorts, or vials of malodorous liquids and powders that were my goal, but the drawer beneath, wherein resided the revolver that had been with me on my travels to and from India. It had been put to use there in the heat of battle, and must have seemed a grim souvenir to hold on to. With both its and my own days of army service behind us, how little could I then know to just how much use it was still to be put. Measuring its familiar weight in my grip, before raising it and pointing it at the door, I chuckled to myself, "You won't be much use against ghosts."

It was at this precise instant that Mrs. Hudson chose to enter, carrying a laden tray. "Your tea, gentlemen. I know your guest said he didn't care for any, but I thought I might ..." Unsurprisingly the sight of a revolver pointed directly toward her heart stemmed her flow, though any further words would have been lost in the clash, clatter, and crash of the tray and its contents as they dropped from her hands.

So startled was I that, by the time I had the presence of mind to put the weapon out of sight in the drawer and rush to her full of reassurances, she had already flown from the room. "Mrs. Hudson!" I cried after her, "Oh, my dear woman! I am so very, very sorry!"

Her retreat was short-lived, and her return was far from meek. "Giving decent, hard-working people heart attacks and frightening them out of their wits! And you call yourself a doctor?" she demanded, thrusting a brush and dustpan from the hallway cupboard into my hands and pointing a quivering finger at the shattered crockery on the carpet. "You're just as bad as him!"

And here she did make her exit, slamming the door with such force that I daresay it would have drowned out any actual gunshot. I eased my stiff limbs into a crouch and began gathering the scattered pieces of my landlady's best china, even as, internally, I struggled to slot together the pieces of our recently departed guest's narrative into some semblance of order. Wherever those fragments of a tale would lead, to judge by the startling transformation in Holmes's mood from his earlier lamentation of the lack of mental exercise into his almost improperly sprightly march toward some undefined danger, there was no doubt that—to borrow a phrase which Holmes would regularly borrow in turn from the Bard—the game was afoot!

Chapter 4: A Curious Gathering

The game was indeed afoot, even if I found myself at an absolute loss to declare what, exactly, the nature of this particular game could possibly be. I was left to ponder on this as Holmes, as he would do on so many occasions throughout our subsequent adventures, went stalking off in pursuit of his own researches, leaving me without the slightest idea as to his theories or his plan of action. It rankled then and, while experience has taught me to view it as nothing other than Holmes's way, it would continue to irk me for years to come. At that time, however, I could scarcely help but feel some personal slight in what seemed a hasty desertion.

True, Holmes had assured me that my assistance was keenly sought, but what, then, of this trusty old friend he raced to confide in? While it now seems unthinkable that I might ever have felt such envy to this unknown ally, in that moment I struggled to ignore the notion that I may be just one in an interchangeable array of helpmates, and sought instead to focus on how best I might play my own role when the time came. Whether I was to act as junior partner in his detective consultancy, or march as but one of many foot-soldiers in a battalion against crime and injustice, I would do what was demanded of me, such was my faith in my new friend.

With no indication as to when he might return—and after no little time spent in tidying away the crockery shards and spillage, and also the general mess that tended to accumulate during Holmes's inactivity, all in an attempt to assuage Mrs. Hudson's justifiably sharpened temper—I chose to look upon my afternoon confined, so to speak, to barracks as an ideal opportunity to apply Sherlock Holmes's own methods to what we had been told. As ever, the first step was to eliminate the impossible.

Obviously the apparition of Professor Oscar Wexley had not visited an abandoned public hall in the East End of London. So, why should someone try to persuade his daughter that such a thing could happen? Apparently not for money, as there was none to be had. And if not for financial gain, then to what end? Could it, perhaps, be a cruel and elaborate scheme to drive her insane and, if so, for what possible purpose? It seemed an extreme step for some personal grudge and—though I was aware that Holmes would have favoured me with one of his most withering glares and a sternly worded lecture on the dangers of theorising without possession of all the facts—I could not believe that this lovely, kind-hearted young lady could possibly have made such an enemy.

And, so, once I had removed the readily apparent impossibilities, there seemed little left to consider, not even the vastly improbable. No matter from which direction I chose to approach the problem, my questions uncovered no answers, and yielded only more questions. Who were the organisers behind the self-styled 'Most Sacred Spiritualist Church of the Golden Star'? How could an unhappy young lady have been so fully convinced of seeing her late father's phantom? And what was the meaning of her strange cry? What was 'the crown'?

I had no doubt it was this very lack of any clear answer that had fuelled Holmes's desire to entangle himself in this strange affair. But for me, it led to a very long and anxious afternoon—an afternoon made all the more unbearable by the knowledge that, somewhere in London, a beautiful, defenceless woman was soon to be placing herself into what Holmes had described as 'the gravest danger'. And, the realisation that, should any harm befall her, we were responsible for sending her there.

Yet even as I paced and worried, steps were already being taken. The remainder of this chapter and both chapters that directly follow it comprise as thorough and accurate an account as I can provide, based upon my own notes of the testimonies of several participants in these unfolding events; events into which I would not enter until a later stage.

Thus we now fly from the warmth and safety of the Baker Street rooms in which I restlessly prowled, and out into streets slickened by a steady, dull rain that commenced as the afternoon lengthened yet achieved little in lessening the heavy darkness which had all day overhung the city like a grey and looming ghost. Leaving luckless travellers to splash and wade through the puddles below, let us soar up and above the buildings, their rooftops glistening, their chimneys sending up columns of smoke to mingle and swirl with those swelling clouds, and thenceforth fly eastwards over the vast metropolis. The buildings beneath us grow meaner, more cramped and huddled, the broad thoroughfares narrowing, the thick arteries scattering off into a multitude of scrawnier veins. And as a distant church clock chimes out the hour of eight, we drift gently down once more to find ourselves at the threshold of a squat building whose peeling sign proclaims it the 'Cyrus Road Public Hall and Assembly Room'. There are lights beyond the begrimed windows, and murmured voices from within, but from those who have already gathered and wait unseen, we turn our attentions to one who has just arrived.

This young woman steps lightly down from a cab and nimbly avoids a deep and murky puddle at the pavement's edge. She pays the driver, adding a cheerful smile and a small but not ungenerous tip, and stands alone in the lightening drizzle as the cab clatters off to lose itself in the warren of streets around Cyrus Road. Alone now, the smile which favoured the cabman turns its corners down into a frown of apprehension before, with a determined snap of irritation at her own nervousness, the lady gathers herself and steps briskly inside.

Before she allows the gloom within to swallow her up, however, let us take advantage of the last look she casts over her shoulder, for even so fleeting a glimpse is enough to fix her lovely aspect in the mind's eye. Her heart-shaped face is clear complexioned and pale, though against the sombreness of her dress—still displaying unmistakeable traces of mourning—and the darkness of her lustrous chestnut hair and her large, inquisitive eyes, the pallor is all an illusion. She is evidently healthy and in full possession of herself, as can be seen by the resolve that brings a sparkle to those green eyes and a tight smile to her expressive lips before she walks confidently on out of sight. We might recognise that same smile and same fixed look from the photograph her brother had shown two new acquaintances just that morning. Though we may also note that the sadness captured in that image is almost entirely absent. For, as nervous and uncertain as she may be, at this precise moment Miss Eleanor Wexley is pleased and excited, and keenly anticipating what lies ahead of her.

As we follow her past freshly painted and newly re-panelled outer doors and on through the dank and musty foyer, its notice-board bedecked in a tatty rainbow display of the fluttering scraps of unread and out-of-date signs, bills and announcements, we pass into the hall itself. It is a room one might typically find attached to a church or town hall, with a low stage at one end, the shabby curtains closed, the dust in their folds more disturbed

by moths than by any recent performance, while the
floor before it looks sufficient to accommodate twenty
or more wooden benches. This seating has been pushed
against the furthest wall, next to a table upon which sit
a scattering of glasses and decanters, the larger of which
lies nearly empty of sherry, while the smaller still brims
with brandy. The shifting aside of the benches leaves
the floor almost bare, save for the circle of furnishings
and objects that have been arranged at its centre. Tall,
elaborate wrought-iron candle-holders form a wide ring,
while positioned in a yet wider circle around the room are
large, ornate bowls of glazed enamel depicting far-flung
and exotic scenes. And at the heart of these we find an
inner semi-circle of around a dozen wooden chairs. They
face the stage in a horseshoe formation, though the chair
that should mark the apex of the curve is placed forward,
toward the centre of the grouping, whether by accident or
design rendering the horseshoe a cloven hoof.

There are six people already in the hall. Their
descriptions can be given simply, based upon their
demeanour and their mode of dress. Thus we have a
wealthy old woman with a kindly face and staunch but
tragic mien, a middle-aged dock worker in his flat cap and
unaccustomed Sunday best suit with its collar too tight at
his throat, a seasoned sailor still in his uniform, eyes as
bright as his jerkin's buttons, an off-duty housemaid, her
cap still in place and her uniform visible beneath the hem
of her coat, and a nervy, pale-faced fellow with spectacles
balanced upon the bridge of his nose and a selection of
dusty volumes clasped in the crook of his arm, who one
might take for a librarian or scholar. A sampling of all
walks of life is seemingly represented in this gathering,
and they stand in a close group, whispering animatedly
amongst themselves, occasionally sipping politely at their
glasses of sherry as they chatter.

Amongst this group our attention must fall upon
the young man who goes by the name of Mr. Francis
Hammond. Here is an elegant fellow, fashionably attired

and moustached, and from his voice and the easy command with which he compels the attention of his cohorts, evidently well-educated and possessed of some authority.

This, then, is the scene that sets itself, and we may now only sit back and observe as the foyer doors swing open and Eleanor Wexley, cast in the role of ingénue, makes her entrance into the drama!

And as she entered the hall, gently easing the door closed behind her, only too mindful of how loudly those doors had slammed and crashed on her last visit to this place, Miss Wexley was distinctly aware of the hush that descended on those already gathered. Their lively conversation drifted into low murmurs and glances, before the larger body broke into smaller groups, each resuming their chattering and laughter with what seemed to her a conscious effort at animation. How grateful she was that young Mr. Hammond, his face breaking into a most unforced and welcoming smile, bounded across the room to greet her, his jollity smoothing away the harder edges of her nervousness.

"Miss Wexley, you came," the handsome fellow declared enthusiastically. "Oh, I am so pleased. We all are, I'm sure." This latter was expressed in tones loud enough to encourage smiles, raised glasses, and murmurs of welcome from the others in the hall.

Miss Wexley, aware of her cheeks colouring as her eyes darted to the floor, forced a few words of thanks to the assembly then, in a much quieter tone, added, "I didn't know if I should have come along at all, Mr. Hammond."

"Why on earth not?" gaped Hammond in slightly overdone surprise. "Have we done something to upset you? Oh, dearest girl, I do hope that is not the case."

"You know exactly what I mean, though I thank you for your chivalrous pretence. I rather feared it would be the other way around, and that I would have offended you when ..." She bit her lip, as if she might succeed in biting back the embarrassed jumble of memories from the previous week. "Well, upon my last visit."

"Good Lord, not at all! No, not in the least, my dearest Miss Wexley. You mustn't go blaming yourself. The intensity of the ceremony can be terribly draining, and you are, after all, still stricken in grief. It was a natural thing to occur. I'm only glad that you have managed to withstand the shock so well." Yet even as he spoke so cheeringly, Hammond subtly led the new arrival to one side, whereupon he confided, "I've been worrying all week about you, Miss Wexley."

"Please, call me Eleanor. Miss Wexley is far too stuffy and formal. It makes me sound like some old spinster."

"Oh, you are far from that, Miss—Ha! Forgive me— you're far from that, Eleanor. But I do mean what I said, about being worried. We all were. The Contessa, especially. I would have so liked to call upon you and to check that all was well, but," he shrugged, "I thought it might not be the wisest move."

"Because of Nicholas?" A frown obscured that pleasant face. "I fear I owe you another apology for my headstrong brother's actions. I knew he disapproved of my attending your meetings, but I had no idea that he would react so appallingly and come bursting in like some marauding invader." Her eye strayed to the gleamingly new lock and handle on the inner door. "Perhaps my passing out of consciousness wasn't because of the ceremony, and I merely fainted out of sheer embarrassment instead."

"It *was* a rather dramatic entrance, I will say. A nice little burst of excitement for us. Our Miss Garthorn was thrilled to bits by it all. She was only too disappointed to learn that it was your brother who stole you from us, and not some dashing lover come to carry you off to distant lands." Smiling as he spoke, Mr. Hammond raised his glass to the old woman, who, on hearing her name invoked, waved across benignly.

Eleanor Wexley returned the wave and a smile, though her voice remained low as she remarked, "Miss Garthorn has read rather too many penny-dreadfuls, I fear. There's nothing you might call dashing about Brother Nicholas, unless a boorish, pig-headed, narrow-minded busybody is one's idea of a romantic hero. Why he cannot accept that I'm a grown woman and no longer need to be watched over like a little girl escapes me."

"You shouldn't be too harsh, Eleanor. He's your brother, he cares about you, and it really is only natural that he should wish to protect you."

"Protect me from what?" snapped the young lady. "And if he cares so much, why can't he allow me to do the only thing I feel can give me any lasting comfort?"

"He's simply afraid. So many fear what they cannot understand. And many cannot understand the good and positive effect that our movement will have on the lives of all, once it has been accepted throughout society. We've all faced rejection or mockery for our belief in the spiritual world, but we cannot make room in our hearts to nurture any hostility toward those who do the mocking. We must be patient with them, because we know they're really only afraid that we are right in what we seek to promote. You need only ask the Contessa."

"I don't know if I would dare," admitted Eleanor, and she glanced around shyly, as if expecting some other presence to have silently entered the room. "She must have taken some offence."

Hammond sadly shook his head. "More than any one of us, the Contessa Nascosta has had to face the prejudice of those unable or unwilling to learn. Her powers long ago made her an outcast in her own country. The great Christian nation of Italy could not come to terms with what they believed to be an opposing ideology, a competitor for the hearts, the minds, and even the souls of the people, even though we believe in the same God and the same Heaven and Hell. We differ only in that we of our church do not believe there to be so great a barrier between our world and the next. And, because of that difference in belief, this remarkable woman has been accused of every abomination from sorcery and consorting with the Devil, to being a confidence trickster, seeking only to take money from the grieving and the gullible. I tell you, if money was the goal, there are infinitely easier ways of making it! Ways that wouldn't involve being hounded from your homeland like vermin!"

"I so wish you and Nicholas could talk. I'm certain you could persuade him to let me follow my own path."

"But you surely must have persuaded him yourself?" said Hammond, mildly alarmed. "He doesn't seem to have stopped you from joining us at any rate."

"He didn't put up all of the objections I had expected to hear, but he was by no means gracious about it, either."

"Then perhaps he's beginning to realise that his sister has grown into a woman, and is capable of running her own life as she sees fit."

"Either that, or he's realised he can no longer stand in my way. If he had dared try to stop me tonight ..."

"Why, I do believe you would have bloodied his nose."

Miss Wexley regarded him evenly. "Are you patronising me, Mr. Hammond?"

"Not at all," said he, solemnly. "I rather like my nose the way it is."

Despite her best efforts, a laugh escaped from Eleanor Wexley's lips. "It's so good to see you laugh," said Hammond, whose own smile lingered even as his voice took on a more thoughtful edge. "I'm sure, now, that you are indeed ready for what is to happen this evening."

"And why is that? Is the Contessa going to entertain us with some merry jokes and tricks?" Even through her merriment, Eleanor Wexley grew abruptly aware of the others turning, their spirited conversations tailing off sharply. Under their curious scrutiny, she felt her own laughter die in her throat. "I meant no disrespect. It was simply that you seemed so very serious after appearing so amused, Mr. Hammond, that I thought you must still have been teasing me. Why must I be ready? What is to happen tonight?"

The entire group now slowly drew in around her, and Eleanor Wexley felt that same uneasiness she had thought to have left outside on the pavement overshadow her once more. She looked from one blandly smiling face to another—old Miss Garthorn, sad-eyed but beaming, Mr. Rundall, the sailor, grinning through his bushy moustaches, the scholarly Mr. Scribsham's glimmering eyes magnified behind his spectacle lenses—then gasped out another attempt at a laugh. "Come, now! You must tell me, after all that! Or are you planning to keep a lady in suspense?"

"Of course not." Hammond sipped lightly at his sherry, and this simple motion lead Miss Wexley to realise just how dry her mouth and throat had become. "You have nothing in this world to worry about, Eleanor. Nothing in this whole, wide world."

"The oddest thing is, any time someone says that to me, I begin to worry. Even when I wasn't in the least worried in the first place." She laughed again, the sound brittle to her ears. "Why not tell me what it is that I have no call to worry about?"

"The Contessa is most pleased that we have found you."

"Then I'm pleased that she's pleased."

"You don't quite understand, Eleanor. The Contessa has never before encountered someone with such a strong psychic aura. She was deeply impressed by the results of our prior meetings."

As she stepped forward to place a hand gently on the young lady's arm, old Miss Garthorn's lined face wrinkled further into a smile. "You have been blessed with the gift, my dear."

"That's right, miss," nodded the dockhand, who went by the name Seward, and who removed his cap as if mindful of being in exalted company. "You've got the ghost vibrations, and most powerful strong they are, too."

"The Contessa Nascosta has rarely seen such a natural connection with the spirit forces," explained Hammond. "With her powers acting through you, she easily managed to establish a direct channel to the world beyond. Through you, she was able to talk directly to your dear father and, if the ceremony had not been so drastically halted and the channel so abruptly closed, she believes she might have been able to summon your father into this very room. Not simply as a voice from beyond, Eleanor. You would have seen him, standing before you."

"I have seen him! I truly did. I saw him here. Here in this room!"

"Mere glimpses," sighed Hammond. "Nothing more. But had we been allowed to continue, you might have reached out your hand to touch him. He would have been as real as you and I, and he would have been right here to walk among us."

"Then ... tonight?"

Francis Hammond gripped Eleanor Wexley's unsteady hands and gazed into her wide green eyes. "Yes, tonight, Eleanor. The Contessa wishes to try again. The ceremony was well begun when last you were with us, but left dangerously unresolved, and we have a duty to complete it. Otherwise ..." The young man paused and considered carefully his next words. "You're entirely sure your brother won't try anything to disrupt our proceedings?"

"Quite sure. Nicholas has gone out for the evening. Quite likely to avoid the argument he knew he'd have faced if he'd thought to change my mind. He knows it would be pointless to try."

"Then the only thing that matters is that you feel strong enough to take part."

"Ah, go you on, miss," urged Mr. Rundall. "Say you will." The sailor's hopeful plea was swiftly echoed and amplified by the others in that clustering press of expectant faces.

"Healthy girl like you?" grinned Mrs. Maynard, the sturdy young housemaid, her cheeks gleaming like polished apples, her eyes gleaming yet brighter with eager expectancy. "You'll be all right. Get to see your dad again. What harm can your old dad do you?"

"There's no possible harm, nor any danger," insisted Hammond. "Well, dear, courageous Eleanor, you must decide. We stand on the verge of that moment of which we have so many long years dreamt. On the verge of that which our noble Contessa has searched her entire life. It is the proof that we have not been wrong in our beliefs; the final confirmation that the spiritual world is real, and that it may not only be reached but can also reach out itself and so aid humanity in its suffering. And for you, more importantly, this is the opportunity to say all those things you never had a chance to tell your father while he walked upon this plane, and to take comfort in his words of love."

"Otherwise?" Eleanor stared fixedly at Hammond. "You said we had a duty to complete the ceremony now that it had been started, 'otherwise ...' What more were you going to say?"

The young man grimaced, and a nervous forefinger brushed at his trim moustache. "Our ceremony last week opened the passageway between the land of the living and those who have passed onto the next stage beyond that which we know as life. And, in doing so, your beloved father was summoned by your devotion to navigate that passage and join us in this realm. We know that he heard that summons and responded to it, for we heard his voice as if from the air around us, and thus we see that he had begun his journey to be with us. But before he could fully reach us, we were disturbed! Thus he did not entirely manifest. Yet even so, without completing the full ritual that makes up the ceremony, we were unable to ease him back onto his return voyage into the dominion he now occupies."

All colour fled from Eleanor Wexley's face. "Then he may still be trapped, somewhere between this world and the next? Is this what you're telling me we may have achieved? Have we lured my poor father from his rest into some limbo, trapping him there, neither alive nor truly dead?"

"We can't know that for definite," insisted Hammond, easing the frantic young woman toward one of the chairs within the ring of candles. "There's so much we don't yet understand. But if there's the merest chance, then you surely see that we must resume the ceremony, discover what it was that your father would have wished to communicate with you, and send him peacefully back to his reward."

That dreadful thought, of some endless, formless, lifeless existence as a wraith without actual substance inhabiting some featureless landscape, but possessed, maybe, of the maddening awareness of being confined forever, was more than Miss Wexley thought she could possibly bear without herself running mad. "I must," she said, trembling under the weight of sudden responsibility.

"God bless you, dear," cried Miss Garthorn, though the younger woman only vaguely heard her.

"There's no other possible answer. I must do it!"

"Sit for a moment. You must think clearly before you give your decision."

"I've made my decision, Mr. Hammond. I had made it before I came here tonight. But if what you now tell me has even the slimmest possibility of being my poor father's fate, any other resolution I might otherwise have made would have been entirely overthrown."

"Be sure," Hammond urged. Then he left Eleanor to sit alone with her hectic thoughts, only dimly aware of his moving across to the table bearing the drinks. To the scholar, the maid, and the old woman, he issued quiet instructions. "Go and bolt the outer door, Mr. Scribsham. Double bolt it! The ceremony must not be interrupted. Miss Garthorn, Mrs. Maynard, the candles, please."

Without demur, the two women set about lighting the candles in their tall holders, while the academic gentleman rushed out of the hall.

"I'll see my father again. I can tell him so much. I can ask him so much." Eleanor Wexley's quiet mutterings were disrupted as Hammond returned to solicitously press a glass brimming with a healthy measure of brandy

61

into her hand. "No. I'm perfectly fine. At least, I will be so in just a minute or two."

"Drink it. You've had more than your fair share of shocks. Oh, we have been very unfair. We should never have crowded around you like that, and I should certainly not have put such dreadful fears into your thoughts. I wouldn't wish for you to feel pressurised into making your decision! Yet I still felt it vital you should be aware of what may have been at risk."

Eleanor Wexley sipped her drink and replied, "That's quite all right. I would have made this decision anyway. I know this is the only way I might ever find peace."

And it was then, just as that sentiment had been uttered, that whatever sense of peace there may have been in that room was shattered by a furious commotion from beyond as the doors crashed and shuddered on their hinges.

Chapter 5: The Skipper's Sorry Story

From the outer foyer beyond those rattling doors, Mr. Scribsham's thin and petulant voice struggled to be heard over a gruffer, more insistent voice, as the pale little librarian protested, "Sir, please! You mustn't go in there. I beg of you, sir, step aside!"

"And what would be givin' the likes o' you the rights to be tellin' the likes o' me where the likes o' me can and can't be goin'?" growled the other.

The naval man, Rundall, and Seward, burly and brawny as befits one whose days are spent labouring in the dockyards, took a step apiece closer to the source of the disturbance, while Mrs. Maynard and Miss Garthorn both circled protectively around Eleanor Wexley. Francis Hammond, a fierce scowl in place, strode toward the doorway gesturing irritably for the others to hold back for the moment.

"What in the world is going on?"

Eleanor Wexley's unsteady rise to her feet was met by Miss Garthorn's hand lowering onto her shoulder, where it patted maternally yet with a strength that belied her age, so that the younger woman felt compelled to remain seated. "Oh, no need to look so panicked, dear. The Contessa looks after us all." Then, pressing the glass of brandy on her, the ancient lady urged, "You drink up now. Trust me, child, long before you reach my advanced age you'll come to learn there's nothing better than brandy for lifting the chill in your blood."

"Please, sir. I tell you this is a private meeting," Mr. Scribsham's voice shrilled out once more as the door was knocked ajar.

"Out of me way, sonny-boy," wheezed the diminutive figure that threw the doors wide to stand defiantly, though none too steadily, in the doorway, while Scribsham's helplessly gaping face loomed at his shoulder. Evidently more than a touch the worse for drink, the newcomer slumped back against the wall, forcing a rattling cough from his lungs in the process. He was a bespectacled, plump little fellow, with the strands of white hair that were as sparsely visible beneath his hat's brim as they were profuse in his sideburns tinged yellow with nicotine. Red of face, even while not undergoing a coughing spasm, and more particularly red of nose, he had the clear look of a habitual imbiber, and the prominent teeth that he bared in his efforts to still his coughing looked by far the healthiest part of him, not least because they appeared to be dentures. His trailing brown overcoat, his loose scarf, baggy checkered trousers, and dented bowler hat all spoke of better days long flown. With patched and unravelling fingerless gloves he smeared his spectacles and wiped at watery eyes, then peered suspiciously at the curtained stage and demanded, "When's the concert start, then?"

"I just couldn't stop him, Mr. Hammond," came Scribsham's tremulous apology.

Said Miss Garthorn, with a disdainful sniff, "It seems like someone has already had an encounter with the spirits this evening."

"What, no sing-song?" The newcomer fixed a beady eye upon the old woman and waggled a finger in admonishment. "So what kind of concert would you call it without a sing-song, I asks you? Here, let the old skipper give you a saucy song as'll knock you flat! No, tut-tut, wait up, Skipper, ladies present, so better not! Don't know, though, you looks like you might just know it, Love! Fact, it might even be about ... No, I'm being wicked cruel. Just my joke, missus! No need to look so po-faced. Anyone'd think we was in a bleedin' church.... Oh, now hang about just a tick, somebody, somewhere, said something...."

Hammond, having summoned the necessary control to hold his annoyance in check, crossed spryly to this unexpected arrival, to amiably enquire, "Perhaps I can help you, sir. Are you looking for somewhere or someone in particular?"

His wheezing finally abated, the old fellow in the dilapidated suit drew on some deep well of dignity, straightened up, and focussed an eye on the younger gentleman. "This is some kind o' church, I'm told?"

"Now, who on earth might have told you that?"

A crooked finger was directed at the glowering Scribsham. "Laddie, over there. See, there used to be concerts in 'ere, upon a time. Load o' bloomin' rubbish mostly, but there was one or two good turns. I thought he was the comic havin' a laugh on me when he tol' me it was a church." His face crumpled a little as a thoughtful look drifted vaguely into place. "I could prob'ly do with a church more'n a concert, truth be told. Best place for an old sinner, so my old lady would've tol' me. 'Get you along to the church an' beg forgiveness for bein' such an old rogue, Jasper. You'll only be on your knees for the whole month, but it'll be a start, my lad.' Aye, she knew the ways o' it, true enough."

Lamely, the scholar protested, "He asked what was going on, then just barged in past me. I tried to stop him. You heard me try."

The old man coughed raucously, another fit threatening. Mr. Hammond, close enough to be discomfited by the attack, turned his face away, with a sardonic mutter, "It's obviously not the Temperance Society he was after."

The callous dearth of charity in the young man's remark brought a sharp hiss from Eleanor Wexley. "Mr. Hammond, you surprise me, sir." Allowed no pause to apologise, Hammond could only step reluctantly aside as she rushed to help the spluttering old man toward a chair. "Sir, please. You are plainly tired and a little confused. Would you like a seat and time to regain yourself, Mister...?"

"Montague, young miss. Jasper Montague, at your service. Though what service a wretch such as me could offer I'm at a loss to declare." He lowered himself, groaning, into the chair with Eleanor's support at his arm, and displayed those tombstone teeth in a smile of gratitude. "And it's delighted that I am to meet such a fine, kind young gentlewoman. Kindest and fairest, a queen among womenfolk. Oh, you may blush, an' most fetchingly too, if I may make so bold, but the offer of a seat is more kindness than has been shown to me in many a year. An' I can't rightly remember the last time anyone called me 'sir'. Not since she ..." The old man sighed a mournful sigh. "No, it takes a very kind an' fine person to offer such gentleness to a drunken old fool." He coughed again, weakly, a frayed handkerchief finally reaching his mouth.

"You mustn't call yourself that, Mr. Montague. It's not true."

"Ah, but it is. You see," he beckoned her closer as he whispered with a wink, "I am drunk. Just a wee bit. But not so drunk as I can't spy, even with my weak old eyes, that you're a frightened lady, miss."

"Frightened, Mr. Montague? Not at all! Merely a little— well, maybe more than a little—nervous. This is to be a very important evening for me."

"For all of us, Mr. Montague," Hammond interjected, and he stepped anxiously to Eleanor's side. "A most important and solemn occasion, so if you would, sir ..."

"Again with the 'sir'? Twice in the one day? Ahhh, the

old skipper here's in danger o' startin' to feel rather grand."

"Mr. Montague, we really must proceed with our meeting."

"Oh, your church meetin'? Are you the vicar? No, course you ain't! But I'm not holdin' you back, am I? I do humbly apologise," insisted Montague, rising unsteadily to his feet. "Here am I, babblin' away like an addled old whatchermacallit, when you good people is tryin' to go about your devotions."

"Think nothing of it, sir. It's just that time presses on, and we have much still to achieve." Hammond's relief at the old man's willingness to depart was proving short-lived, however, as his attempts to usher Jasper Montague to the door came to a sudden halt in mid-step as another coughing fit loudly commenced.

With a frown, Eleanor Wexley drew the young man to one side. "You cannot mean to send him out in his condition, Mr. Hammond. This unfortunate gentleman is plainly ill."

"He's not ill, Eleanor, just drunk. He positively reeks of cheap gin!"

"Just somethin' to warm the old blood, sir." Mr. Montague thirstily eyed the contents of Eleanor Wexley's glass. "Not as good for insulation as brandy, per'aps, but nothin' near as hexpensive neither."

"I don't doubt we could offer you a warming glass of brandy before you go on your way," smiled Eleanor. "Mr. Hammond, we could delay the meeting for just a moment or two longer, couldn't we?"

"Well, I don't know, Miss Wexley.... No, but, of course, Eleanor, we must be charitable. Yes, I suppose we might just spare a moment.... Ah, but I see now that we have no more glasses."

"Then Mr. Montague must take mine."

"But you've not finished your own drink, my dear. I'm quite sure Mr. Montague wouldn't object to my glass," declared Hammond, reaching for the decanter.

"You are all too kind. Too, too kind," sighed Mr.

Montague, whose raucous blowing of his nose into his florid handkerchief evidently masked his struggle with some strong inner emotion. "Such uncommon kindness. Ah, sherry, is it? Not as effective as brandy. But it'll serve, at a pinch. Your good 'ealth, sir, and my thanks to you." So saying, Jasper Montague raised the proffered glass and its meagre contents to the assembly. "My thanks to one an' all. God bless you an' yours!"

An array of reluctantly raised sherry glasses returned the toast before the assembled guests fell back into their muttering clusters. Montague, rapidly revived after his first noisy sip of the golden liquor, caught Rundall's arm in a surprisingly firm grasp, and enquired, "Been ashore long, Jack?"

The sailor recoiled from the old man's lurching proximity, but managed to reply, "A couple of weeks, matey. I'll be off out again come first tide Sunday, bound for Cairo."

"Cairo, is it? A fine, fine city," nodded Montague, approvingly. "Though a bit dry an' dusty for them as likes the wet. Still, a flask in your pocket'll keep you wet from the inside out. I wish to God I was sailin' out with you, Jack, lad. This London climate'll be the death of Jasper Montague, mark my words. But Cairo! Aye, that's the place. The heat an' the drink." With a nudge to the sailor's ribs, he chuckled lasciviously, "An' the women. You'll know all about them, Jolly Jack, eh?"

"Well," mumbled Rundall, his swarthy features reddening further as he grinned, "I'd not be complainin' at the chance to find out."

"Never been, eh? Well, where did you last drop your anchor? If you'll pardon a nautical phrase."

"Cyprus. That was a hot one."

"Pah," snorted Montague. "This one 'ere calls Cyprus hot? I remember the time I sailed into the Bay of Bengal. That were a voyage, an' a hot one. Aye, Jack! Skipper Jasper here, an' you just ask about that name round any port you'd care to mention an' some you surely couldn't! Finest captain to sail the China Seas, they'll tell you straight. From east to west an' back again, from the Cape o' Good Hope to the Cape o' No Bloody Hope—beggin' pardon, ladies—an' all in search o' treasure. For were it not the old tales of pirates, an' legends o' golden trinkets an' jewelled fancies what I'd a-heard since I were a nipper as gave me the wanderlust? An' me never dreamin' that the only treasure I'd ever need were the one I left behind? Ah, but it were for her I sailed, for if ever I found the gem whose sparkle were 'alf as bright as one o' her smiles, I'd 'ave had the riches to buy her a palace an' perfumes an' paintin's, an' what-so-ever her blessed heart desired. So I sailed, ever searchin'. Till the old demon rum got me! The scourge o' sailors, an' our only blessed release."

"Nothing wrong with a drop of grog, Skipper," laughed Rundall.

"A drop's one thing, laddie. Half a barrel a day's another! An' that were on a good day, though even they led to many a bad night. Lost me my commission an' the best livin' a man could hope for. But it helps sometimes to forget. 'Cept when it causes you only to remember, damn it all!" A wet glimmer came into the old skipper's eye as he spoke, before that damp eye fell upon Mr. Seward. "What say you, fellow?"

"I wouldn't know, would I?" came the brusque rejoinder. "I only fix the boats. I don't sail 'em."

"Any connection with the sea makes you a fine man in my eyes, be it on the decks or in the docks." Montague's laughter at his attempted jest spluttered on into yet more violent coughs and wheezes, and these were matched by an intense shuddering. Staggering blindly, the old man gripped tightly to Eleanor Wexley's arm for support, the contents of her glass spilling and soaking into the dusty floorboards as she jolted in shocked surprise at this sudden rough handling.

Hammond, with more than necessary force, dragged Montague upright. "For Heaven's sake, man, take care there!"

"It's perfectly all right, Mr. Hammond. It was hardly

deliberate, and, to be entirely honest, I'm not much of one for strong drinks."

"You're too kind-hearted, Eleanor. You mustn't allow people to take advantage of that."

"And you are beginning to sound dangerously like my brother."

Dismay shadowed Mr. Hammond's handsome features. "Then I apologise."

"No, young miss. If anyone deserves to apologise, that man is I," Montague snivelled, his expression a mask of perfect misery. "What have I become? I were once a respected man. Now I'm a wretched soak. This would never've happened if—oh—not never, if only ..."

Eleanor Wexley laid a gentle arm around the pathetic figure's heaving shoulders and urged, "Please tell us what it is that has brought you this unhappiness. You spoke of a woman more dazzling than any treasure."

"Emma Kate, miss. My poor, lovely Emma Kate. Why'd she go? She knew I needed her to keep a watch on me. To keep me from becomin' this miserable creature."

"She was your wife?"

"Aye, but I loved her nonetheless. Thirty years we would have been married, if the consumption 'adn't got her."

"How long have you been missing her?"

"Three years. Three long, wretched, drunken years. I weren't even near when she went. The word was sent that she were goin' rapid but, by the time it caught up to me in the Azores...? Aye, well, it were just too late, weren't it? Too late for her. Too late for me. Losing her was like losing my old brass compass, for I 'ad nothin' no more to point me in the right direction. It was like all the jewelled stars had fizzled an' gone out in the night sky, leavin' me in the dark with nothin' to set a steady course by. An' I never got to tell her how losing her took me. I never got to tell her that she were my world. My whole life an' soul."

"My poor, sad Mr. Montague," said Eleanor Wexley,

decisively. "Would it ease your burden if you could tell your dear wife what you have just told us?"

"It's the one thing that could ease it, aye. If I could speak to her one last time, I know that it would bring some shred o' peace."

"Miss Wexley, just what are you doing?"

Eleanor Wexley looked imploringly into Francis Hammond's handsome, dubious face. "Only what I must do! We can help this man. Is that not exactly why we're all here?"

"How can you help?" Jasper Montague's look of utter confusion shifted suddenly to one of suspicion. "You don't jus' mean with prayers, do you? Jus' what kind o' church is this?"

"You may have read of spiritualists, and of our beliefs," began Miss Wexley, mildly.

"Oh, I've a-heard of you," the little man cried. "I don't want nothin' to do with any o' that! Not the way I hears your lot do things! I don't want none of your ... your dark ways!"

"The only darkness is the loss that overshadows us all. I've suffered that loss, just as you have. I believed I would never see my poor, lost father again. But our dear, kind, gentle Mr. Hammond introduced me to the Church of the Golden Star. Here we have all lost someone. Mr. Seward, too, has lost a wife. Miss Garthorn, her brother. Mr. Scribsham, his beloved fiancée. Mrs. Maynard ..."

"My Petie." The maid dabbed at her eyes and let slip a heartfelt and wistful sigh. "My little boy. Seven years old when he was took from me, and though he'd been sickly all his days it was still so sudden, and with hardly no warning at all."

"And I lost a shipmate and a right good friend to the sea," ventured Rundall, his eyes downcast.

"And Mr. Hammond, more than all of us, has suffered greatly."

Hammond cleared his throat and bit his lip before affirming in a deep, dry voice, "My entire family, sir. Father, mother, two sisters, all gone in a dreadful fire. I

71

wasn't there to save them, or I would happily have walked into those flames if I might have brought even one of them out alive." By his side, Eleanor offered a sympathetic nod to urge him on. "But we've all found comfort here. We have found a friend who can truly help us. A remarkable woman, the Contessa Nascosta ..."

Jasper Montague's sudden wheezing bark stilled Hammond's words. But Miss Wexley picked up his lost thread, undeterred. "Through the Contessa, we have been able to talk to our loved ones. And they to us."

"Then it's true, right enough? What everyone says about you people is on the level genuine? That you talk to ghosties an' spirits o' the dearly departed?" Jasper Montague cringed in his seat and his eyes swept around the occupants of the hall, peering and darting, as if suspicious that any one of them might not be a living, breathing person, but an inhabitant of another, more shadowed domain.

"He's frightened out of his wits," Hammond hissed. "We simply cannot let him go through the ceremony with us. The strain would be too much for the fellow."

"Have you forgotten so soon what you said to me?" urged Miss Wexley. "That when people don't understand, they become frightened? If we can help this one unfortunate soul to understand, if we can bring him some momentary respite from his grief, then that must count as a victory for our cause! It surely must!"

"Miss?" stammered the old man. "You really can bring my Emma Kate back to me? Even if it were only for a minute ... Oh, that might jus' about be the one an' only thing as could brighten this old fool's sorry life."

"Well? Would you be the one to deny him that, Mr. Hammond? Yes, I know your concern is for his own feelings. Yes, I see how alarmed he was. But I too was nervous, you will surely recall. And I would never, not ever, exchange my experiences here. Not for the world."

"No, my dear, and nor would I," Hammond admitted, though not entirely without reluctance. He then moved with swift strides to the short flight of steps that lead up to the low stage. "I had better inform the Contessa of our new guest's presence."

There was in that instant a sudden flurry of rustling cloth, and the young fellow took a sharp step back in his own tracks. A cold, dusty draught swept out as the worn stage curtains parted onto a thick darkness beyond. And from out of this darkness a yet darker figure materialised. Draped from head to toe in black and with not a single human feature visible, this living shadow glided as silently as drifting smoke into the open, its unseen eyes moving across the gathering, before gravely announcing, "The Contessa already knows."

Chapter 6: From Beyond the Veil

Grey dust rose like hazes of fine mist as the dingy curtains dropped back into place, sealing the darkness behind. The slim, tall woman who strode across the front of the stage was clad like a mourner, in a long, rich dress of suitably funereal black whose hem only narrowly missed sweeping up further wafts of dust from the floor with each step. Gloves of fine, dark lace adorned the slender, long-fingered hands which she let drop to her sides. She paused at the stage's edge, quite as still as any statue, the only movement being the very gradual turning of her head as she surveyed the room before her. Whether what she viewed pleased or angered her, or left her entirely unmoved, was impossible to judge, as her face was naught but a pallid smudge behind the thick folds of a black veil.

Finally that unseen face turned fully upon the young man who shared the platform with her. Stepping sharply aside to allow this dark apparition to pass, Francis Hammond croaked, "Contessa! We—that is I—didn't know you were waiting."

Stout little Mr. Montague, cowed by the faceless form that descended from the stage, clutched nervously at Eleanor Wexley's arm, and a whine emerged from his sagging mouth. The veiled woman twisted her head abruptly in his direction, and hostile eyes seemed to blaze as they regarded him, however impossible it was to discern her gaze behind the dark covering.

"You have no need to be afraid. The Contessa is here to help us all," said Miss Wexley, and she patted the old man's quivering hand for reassurance. Yet her own confidence seemed less assured as she nervously bowed before addressing the dark woman. "Contessa Nascosta, the group has found a new member in need of your assistance."

Hammond, who followed hesitantly at her heel, addressed the veiled woman's back. "Miss Wexley believes that ... That is, we all feel that, well ..."

The woman gave no acknowledgement, just glided forward to regard Miss Wexley solely. Indeed, as she faced that inscrutable shrouded figure it appeared to Eleanor that every other occupant of the room faded into an incorporeal haze. With an effort of will she found her voice.

"Mr. Montague has suffered greatly since losing his wife. I believe we may be his only hope of finding peace."

"I do miss my Emma Kate so very badly," sniffed the old man. Then, as if suddenly recognising his place, he removed his hat and presented a balding dome fringed with a snowy halo as he bowed and added a mumbled, "Your most gracious ladyship."

The Contessa, in a deep, refined tone that carried with it traces of all things Italian, spoke softly, and not unkindly. "If the young lady believes that we can help, and if the gentleman has belief in the spirits ..."

"If these good people says as such things are true, then who is a broken soul like me to deny it?"

The Contessa stood a moment and her concealed gaze scrutinised the shabby, ill-favoured little fellow who cringed before her. His own trembling ceased, as though frozen to stone under a Medusa's baleful glare. At long last, the woman silently nodded, as if resolved to some course of action. Hammond saw this signal as the cue to break from his own watchful trance, and moved swiftly to lock the doors against any further intrusion, while his fellows, reacting in turn, solemnly took their places in the half-ring of chairs.

"It grows late," intoned the Contessa, and the rustlings of her gown and veil seemed like whispers of agreement while she settled into the central chair around which the others clustered. "I tire. We must begin!"

Eleanor Wexley tenderly guided Montague's faltering tread toward the seats. But it was she, herself, who stumbled, as her legs suddenly weakened beneath her, and her vision blurred and swam. Thus Jasper Montague instead found himself offering her his support while he plaintively asked, "Are you sure you're all right, young miss?"

Within an instant Francis Hammond had taken Eleanor's other arm. He led her to be seated at the immediate left of the veiled woman, which left Mr. Montague to hobble his own way around to seat himself by the flustered but weakly smiling young woman's own left-hand side. Here he listened with steadily more sober concern to her dismissal of his worries.

From one of the ring of softly fluttering candles, Hammond carefully lit a taper and set aflame the contents of those ornamental bowls that widely circled the room Then he himself took his seat in the inner crescent. An incense-heavy smoke lazily drifted from the bowls to merge and flow with the fluttering shadows, and to dim the light outside the ring of candles until, for those within that inner circle, it appeared that beyond those shivering flames could be seen the fringes of the known world, fading off into an infinite, all-consuming shade-laden darkness.

With the gathering at last seated, and with all looking upon her expectantly, the dark woman spoke, her tone low and placid and musical. "We have gathered once more to lift the veils that separate our short spans of earthly existence from the eternal spiritual life that lies beyond. Only our belief can make this possible. We all believe?"

As he saw all around him silently nod, Jasper Montague bobbed his head in agreement, albeit with markedly less certainty than his fellows.

"We all believe," was affirmed, as one voice.

"We seek those who have gone before to ease the burden of our unhappy lives. We seek their words of joy at what lies beyond, that they may lighten our sorrows. We seek their wisdom to enlighten our minds. We seek their love to gladden our hearts. There is one among us who has the great gift. The powers within her are strong, yet she has only the dimmest awareness of them. She seeks the love of her father, and she believes that he is with us tonight." The Contessa took Eleanor's hand in her own, the younger woman's skin pale within the dark embrace of the lace glove, and urged, "You know what is to happen, child?"

Eleanor Wexley stared dead ahead, and her answer was a slow whisper. "I am to see him tonight."

"She is prepared," Hammond said. "We are all prepared, Contessa."

"The world of spirits is vast, and many voices call out to me," intoned the veiled woman, her voice quiet and distant. "A chorus of happy greetings. They call out in every tongue, yet there is but one universal language here. There are men and women, and now ... now a child laughs. He can see his mother, and feel her love for him. That love is like the candle's flame, a nightlight so that he need not sleep in darkness or fear."

It may only have been a noise from outside, but from somewhere in the shadows, beyond the drifting smoke, a gentle sound like that of far-off laughter reached all within that stilled room. Backs straightened and nervous feet ceased their shuffling, as ears strained to hear if the laughter would chime again. Which it then did, sounding so much nearer, a whisper close by, as if a tiny, giggling figure might dart out of the gloom to present a smiling face to them all.

"My Petie," gasped the maid, and it was only the grip that old Miss Garthorn took on one hand and Mr. Scribsham on the other that prevented her leaping to her feet. "That's my little boy! Peter, my little pet."

"He asks that his mother not cry for him," soothed the Contessa. "He is so very happy now. There are many children in the world of spirits. He has such good friends, and there are beautiful fields for them to play in, and lakes for them to swim. His one single sadness is that his mother cannot be happy. His wish is only that she does not grieve any longer."

"I won't, Petie son. I just miss you, that's all," sobbed Mrs. Maynard, tears flowing freely even while her flushed face beamed rapturously. "But I just needed to know that you was happy where you are now, and that you're not suffering no more."

Another laugh, gentle and merry, chimed through the scented air.

"Oh, my poor boy, you had so much pain in your short, short life. Though I want only to see you, and to hold you close, I would never bring you back to that, even if I could. I know that you'll be happier there than you could ever be here. Take care, Petie, love."

The laughter was joined by a mellow lapping, like that of a shallow stream. Heads turned, seeking the source, and at the sound of furling cloth Eleanor Wexley felt her gaze drawn to the stage. Where the curtains had previously been closed, they now lay slightly parted, and in the gloom between the musty velvet draperies, a small, pale shape seemed slowly to rock back and forth.

"It's his boat," cried Mrs. Maynard, as the trim white sail and pale blue body of the little wooden model, with its string rigging and carved and painted crew, became clearly visible. "We used to take it to the park, when he wasn't too poorly to go out of doors, and he'd play in the stream with it. It was his favourite toy, until it got swept away too fast for us to catch up. He treasured it, and I thought we'd lost it forever."

"Nothing that is loved is lost forever," murmured the Contessa. "All beloved things await us still. And the bond of love, of care and affection, between parent and child is never broken. It is the thread that connects through eternity. Like he who was cast into the great labyrinth with no clear route to freedom, that golden thread will guide one to the other always. But now, the other children are waiting. The little one goes to play their game. He is smiling and, oh, but he sings such a lovely song. Farewell, little one. Farewell ..."

A single sob escaped from behind Mrs. Maynard's beaming smile.

"But even as one departs, another approaches. You see how great is the longing for communion from both sides? Who is it that you seek, beautiful one?"

Mr. Montague's loud wheeze prompted stern glances from those around him. Yet his laboured breaths were soon drowned out as the lapping of the gentle stream grew in intensity, swelling to proclaim itself the roar and rumble of the distant sea.

"You speak of someone called Callum?" called the Contessa, voice lifting to be heard above the roll of the waves. "Your 'old mate', Callum?"

"I'm Callum," announced Rundall. "Bernie? Is that you, you old sea dog?"

Timbers creaked and groaned, and the billowing of mighty sails penetrated the smoke, which roiled and rolled in turn like heavy sea mists. That innocent toy boat beached upon the stage boards cast colossal shadows as it swayed in time with the creaking and with the lapping of the waves, as if some great intangible vessel might sweep through the room, cutting through the sweet-smelling smog like a ship sailing steadily on toward distant climes. The sailor sat rapt while—in the contrition-edged voice of the Contessa—his former crewmate confessed to an eternal, relentless guilt over an infant child fathered in some remote port. With tears in his eyes, the sailor swore on oath to ensure that the offspring was cared for, and promised that she would grow knowing her father had loved her truly and wanted only what was best for her.

"Now, at last, he knows his words are safely delivered to one who understands, he can rest easy," came the voice from behind the veil. "So your friend boards the great ship that has waited these many years to take him to his journey's end. The waters are clear, and a warm breeze carries him across the great shining lake."

"We'll share a tot or two of rum again, Bernie, one of these years soon, an' we'll toast your fine, bonnie lass, and what she's made of herself in this world."

Mr. Montague squirmed in his seat as the shadow of the great hull shrank and contracted. He craned his gaze, as if searching for whatever horizon it had sailed in pursuit of. The Contessa turned her shrouded head toward him, and her voice, when it came, had a harder focus to it. "A woman now approaches. She has heard echoes of the great ship's passage, and she comes to see if it carries the one she has awaited so many times before."

A groan of misery escaped the lips of Jasper Montague.

"The woman's name is Emma, yes? No? Ah, her name is Emma Kate. She seeks her husband. When she was called, he was far from her, and never did they share their last good-bye...."

"It is she," the old man howled. "It is she! I'm here, my lovely wife! Does she see me? Can she hear my voice? I'm here, my treasure! I wish you was here with me!"

"She always sees you when you dream of her, and always hears as you call her name. She has always remained with you. She has watched over you. She does not wish you to mourn her."

"Emma Kate was all I had. Everythin' else, I ruined. I let the damned drink ruin it. Destroyed the lot!"

"It is but grief you are suffering. Grief and guilt. These bring forth a pain that burns so deeply you try, time and

81

again, to drown its agonies. Where your loved one is now, there is no pain. There is no guilt. Only forgiveness. She wants your suffering to end. You cannot allow your life to be ruled by despair. Take succour from her words, and let yourself live."

"I swear, from now on I won't touch a drop. I'll be the good man she knew an' loved." This promise delivered, the old man let his head drop, a quiet snivelling sporadically issuing forth as his shoulders quivered in waves of grief.

With an abrupt shudder, the veiled woman tensed, her entire frame drawing rigid, and her grip on Miss Wexley's hand tightened sharply, causing her to turn to the Contessa, her eyes wide and fearfully expectant. "There is another presence. A strong soul who has pierced the veil once before, and who wishes to pierce it yet again and so to finish what he has once begun." She rose smoothly and drew Eleanor to her feet, then guided her into the centre of the half-circle. There she eased the young woman into the chair she had herself just vacated. "Come, child, he is waiting. Your father calls to you."

Very quietly, very slowly, Eleanor Wexley murmured, "Father? I cannot hear him. Are you there, Father?"

"He hears you, child. You must call him forth, and invite him to be with us. Entreat him to cross the divide between our world and that which lies beyond."

"Are you there, my poor father?"

A voice emanated from the wispy, cloying air, soft, low and distantly echoing. "Eleanor … Please …"

The Contessa stood firm at Miss Wexley's back, and her slim fingers pressed into her shoulders like a perching blackbird's claws. Stooping so that her veil caressed Eleanor's cheek, eliciting a tremor of emotion, as in one who has accidentally brushed through a cobweb in the dark, the Contessa whispered close to her ear, "He waits for you. Assure him you are here."

"Father? Can it really be you?"

In the shift and swirl of smoke it seemed that, in the deepest shadows beyond the parted curtains, a tall shape had begun to take on an indistinct yet vaguely human form.

"I'm here, Eleanor. I am here, and I hear you."

"Speak to him, child," urged the Contessa, while the eager faces of her congregation nodded and smiled their own encouragement. "Answer your father."

"I thought ..." Miss Wexley fought back a sob, "I thought I would never speak with you again."

"Nor I with you, my daughter," whispered the disembodied voice. "Nor that I ever deserved to hear your sweet voice again. I have been so sorely remiss as a father."

"Don't ever say that! Whatever failings you think yourself guilty of, I forgive you. I love you, and always have loved you."

"I love you too, dearest Eleanor, and I feel your warm and kindly thoughts even here. But my heart is so heavy I cannot rest. Must I carry such a cargo of pain and doubt with me throughout all time?"

"Why is it so? What can possibly make you so unhappy?"

"I must be certain! Certain that you have remembered! That you have never forgotten ..."

"Forgotten what? Father, if I am to answer, you must tell me! What must I remember?"

The outline in the smoke grew more defined, until it was clearly seen as the figure of an imposing, well-built man of middle years. He was outfitted finely in a top hat and morning suit, with a heavy black moustache and thick beard framing handsome, intelligent features from which searching eyes shone out. Not a speck of colour was there to be found about the pale form, which stood proud and motionless, any appearance of movement owing to the shifting of the smoke. That floating, distant voice appeared to find its source now that the shadow form had resolved itself. "The words, Eleanor. The last words ever I spoke to you. It's so important that you always remember those words. With my dying breath, I whispered them to you and you alone. They were my only legacy. I may not rest, will have no peace, ever, until you can show that you haven't forgotten."

"No," protested Eleanor Wexley, as she lurched forward in her seat, desperate only to run to the shimmering man who stood just feet away from her, yet compelled to remain still for fear that any movement might disturb the ceremony at its crucial second, and that the revenant should disperse and vanish. Worse yet, that it should remain behind, imprisoned in this incorporeal, unliving, undying form for all time. Her hand rose to clasp the black-gloved fingers that pressed down at her collar. "No, I have not forgotten, Father. I have always remembered your words. Yet I don't know what they mean!"

"This you will learn, Eleanor, when the time is right. But the words are vital. You must be sure that you have remembered them correctly."

"Tell him, child," murmured the Contessa. "It is your father who asks. Look! You know him, Eleanor. His voice may be distant, a mere echo cast out into the void, but you plainly see that it is surely him!" The Contessa released herself from Eleanor's slackening grip to point a lean, long finger at the smoke-wreathed presence. As she did so, the monochrome man in the formal suit seemed to flicker and shift. The strong face remained the same, bearded, stern, and intensely thoughtful, while the clothing now suggested further flung climes, the linen shirt loose, sleeves rolled up, hands thrust into the pockets of dusty shorts.

"There's something else there!" Hammond directed a quivering finger toward the apparition's heart. From seemingly within the very substance of its being, a glimmering circle resolved itself. Wide enough to enclose a man's head, its rippling golden band glittered with reflected light, while jewelled encrustations gleamed and sparkled. "A crown! It's surely a miraculous crown!"

With a further rapid flickering, the shadows swam to replace the form with a differing view of the same man;

more solemnly attired once more, the great beard greyer, the face more deeply lined and careworn. Yet the eyes still flashed with piercing inner light, and still that golden circlet shone within his chest. "You see him, as he was in life, and as he still is," the veiled woman crooned. "Throughout that life he sought something. And still he seeks. That seeking consumes all happiness. If you wish your father's pain to end, you must speak the words. You must let him hear!"

"You must let me hear so that my suffering will end, and I may join your sweet mother in eternity. What will matter those brief years parted in life when we may be as one throughout aeons? She waits, and the waiting pains her as it does me. Ease our pain. Say the words, Daughter. My words!"

"The words?" Eleanor Wexley rose slowly and wriggled loose from the hands that hovered still at her shoulders to stare in a daze toward the blazing coronet that encircled her father's heart. "I remember ... 'The crown'? I remember, the circle, and the crown."

"The crown ..." shivered the voice, eagerly urging her onwards. "Already my burden lightens. The crown, Eleanor. Tell me all that you remember of the crown."

Eleanor Wexley smiled suddenly, remembrance and recognition clear in her relieved expression. But with a whisper of fear, just as suddenly her face fell, and she threw her hands up as if to ward off some hovering threat, and screamed, "There is something in the darkness at my father's back!"

Francis Hammond reached out a steadying hand. "There's nothing there but your father, Eleanor. Your father and the crown."

"The coiling darkness of the deep, he called it. A darkness filled with leeches, and ravening carrion birds, and faceless, nameless horrors."

"You must speak the rest, child," insisted the Contessa, a swift gesture driving Hammond back to his seat. "These nameless abominations are the dread things that lurk in waiting for those who cannot be gathered safely into the light. Do not let their grasp enfold your father. Say the words, that he might be free of their hexes and spells. Cry them aloud so that even those clutching phantasms might hear, and banish all doubt as you free his eternal spirit!"

"Yes," cried Eleanor, fervently, and she stumbled toward the stage and its phantom occupant, held back only by her trailing hand, still enclosed in the loose grip of Mr. Montague's nervously twitching fingers. "Yes, I shall!"

"No!" Jasper Montague's clutch tightened instantly, as he leapt to his full height—a height considerably taller than any of those gathered had been given cause to suspect. His bowed back uncurled, and with his abrupt growth in stature so his manner grew instantly commanding. Yet none of these metamorphoses were quite as startling as the transformation in his voice, as he stridently issued the order, "This sham ends now!"

The veiled woman whirled savagely to face this intrusion. "How dare you interrupt?"

"Sit down and shut up, you old drunkard, or I'll have your scalp," hissed Hammond, and he roughly tried to push Montague back into his seat. His surprise at the ease with which the old man shrugged him off showed plain in his face. Mouth agape, he stepped back as the startlingly transfigured Montague strode defensively into the line of vision of the confused and frightened young woman whose hand he still clasped.

"This is nothing but a hoax, Miss Wexley. These people are liars, and they are trying to trick you!"

"No!" The Contessa reached imploringly out to Eleanor. "It is he who tries to deceive. Will you listen to a man who has heard his own wife's words of love, but even still refuses to believe?"

"I've never had a wife! That was my own deception, to prove you false."

As she turned desperately to the vaporous figure that hovered before her, Eleanor Wexley implored, "Father? What is happening?"

"That is *not* your father, Miss Wexley! You mustn't tell him what he wants to hear."

The Contessa's insistent fingers scrabbled tightly at Eleanor's free hand, yanking her round so that the cobweb-folds of the heavy veil again brushed the young woman's face. "It is he, Eleanor! You know him. Can you stand by and watch him suffer? Speak the words!"

"We must take the crown from 'round Father's heart, for it feasts upon his life's blood," whispered Eleanor, her face drawn into mask of abject certainty. "Even though he no longer live, it still craves the blood. For four hundred years, it has supped on blood. It is a circle of blood."

The man who had introduced himself as Jasper Montague nimbly drew Eleanor away from the Contessa Nascosta. His voice, no longer slurred and hesitant, was smoothly coaxing as he urged, "You must listen to me. Your father is dead. It is not he who speaks to you. You are being used. You must not tell them what they wish to know."

"He's ruining everything," snapped the veiled woman, her unseen but deeply felt glare freezing her scattered cohorts as they edged their cautious way toward the doors. "We cannot lose the girl now, or she is lost to us forever! Bring her, now!"

It was the burly Seward who obeyed the command. He lunged sharply at Montague, his bulk considerably greater, even despite the old man's dramatic increase in stature. His grim look of threatening rage became one of startled dismay, however, as his arm was caught in an iron grip and pinned far up into the crook of his back, and his opponent brought him crashing to his knees with a grunt of pain and eyes that sprung sudden tears.

"Make no foolish moves, any of you. If anyone attempts to touch this young lady, I shall deal just as severely with them." So saying, the shabby figure released the breathless dock worker to scuttle away, red-cheeked and crab-like and still half on his knees, wincing as he gingerly rubbed his abused arm.

"I must congratulate you on your little display. It was an almost-convincing fraud."

"Who the hell are you?" growled Hammond, the veneer of gentility stripped away and entirely forgotten in his panic.

"Another fraud, I'm afraid. I am a consulting detective."

"The police?" yelped Rundall. "A legit job, we was told! We was not told nothin' about the flamin' law!"

Jasper Montague's long fingers flexed and then flew to the back of his head, gripping and peeling away his bald pate and its fringe of hair and sideburns, to reveal the full head of dark hair underneath. In a series of short, swift motions, he removed both eyebrows and eyeglasses, extracted the cotton and putty that had swollen his nostrils to create his bulbous, broken-veined nose, then finally passed a hand across his mouth to detach those prominent dentures from the straight and even teeth that resided below. So expertly and fluidly was it done that, within a very few seconds the shambling, pathetic old drunkard had flown, to be replaced by a far more formidable figure. "My name is Sherlock Holmes, and Miss Wexley is under my protection," he announced, before, as an amused afterthought, he tossed the crumpled wig into Hammond's hands. "I believe you said you would have my scalp, sir."

It was a few seconds more before the gawping, scarlet-faced Hammond threw down the wig and found his voice to yell to his equally slack-mouthed and wide-eyed confederates, "He's not the police! Get him!"

Whatever authority the young man might once have possessed had crumbled, as the others looked between Hammond and Holmes, weighed up the chances against each, and opted to back cautiously away.

"Do you want to get paid or not?"

Still rubbing his aching arm, Seward grumbled ominously, "We're not being paid for this!"

"You told us there could be no possible problems, Vincent," hissed the old woman, provoking a dismayed groan from Hammond, whose attempts to signal for her to be silent were entirely in vain. "And this after last week, and the brother nearly giving us all heart attacks, too!"

"Was it he who sent you?" demanded the veiled woman. "The brother?"

"He was far from convinced that you were all you claimed to be," replied Holmes. "That much was obvious to me from the moment I entered the room, *Contessa*. A sailor who claims to have recently returned from warmer climes, yet has obviously never even had a genuine suntan beneath that swarthy greasepaint that still shows his wrists and a goodly portion of his neck to be as pale as any typical English summertime could produce? A dockyard worker with hands as clean and soft as a dowager's? And, as for the noble Contessa Nascosta? Haha! In my work, I've found it useful to gain and maintain a precise knowledge of Europe's noble houses. There is no such a title among Italy's noble lines. Your deceptions and disguises may appease a seated audience from a safe distance behind an orchestra pit and the footlights' glare. Indeed, they may have been enough to fool a naïve and trusting young woman still blinded by grief. But, to one who has any observational skills at all, it was woefully transparent. Now, let us lift the veils for real this time."

Sherlock Holmes reached out to remove the supposed noblewoman's dark veil and finally reveal the face of his adversary. As his long fingers found the lace, she shrieked her defiance and pulled sharply out of reach, allowing only a portion of the veil to rise in Holmes's hand. My friend is not one who could ever be described as squeamish. Nor is he prone to flights of fantasy and wild imaginings. He has presided over dissecting slabs, exhumed gravesites, murder rooms, and scenes of the most depraved criminal brutality. Yet still he drew back, shocked to that steely core of his by what he believed he had glimpsed. For there, in that dimly lit and smoke-enshrouded chamber, the fleeting impression he gained in those seconds before the Contessa snatched back her veil and concealed herself once more in darkness, was that he was looking upon a madly glaring skull. A skull with living, hate-filled eyes!

A howl of anguished fury reverberated from every corner of the room at once, as if the very building shrieked its dismay. Still reeling from the sight of that ruined visage, Holmes spun just in time to see the jewelled crown drop with a hollow clatter to the stage, where it rolled absurdly before coming to rest with a heavy thump. The curtains billowed, dust clouds adding to the smoke, as somewhere in the darkness a door slammed back against the bricks.

Hammond, taking desperate advantage of this fresh distraction, grabbed hold of the still only semi-aware Miss Wexley, who appeared to drift as listlessly as the smoke in the direction of the insubstantial figure upon the stage. Her wanderings were halted by Hammond's arm, which snaked around her slender neck and, with an application of pressure that caused her to gasp, he started manoeuvring her toward the doors. "Out! Everyone, move," he shrieked, as his cronies fumbled and fought to unlock the doors and flee into the maze of streets outside. "Not a step, mister detective, or it's her pretty neck."

"I don't believe you have the nerve for violence," replied Holmes, coolly.

"But you're not willing to find out, are you?" leered Hammond, and he tightened his grip so that Miss Wexley's startled eyes widened and her fingers plucked ineffectually at his sleeve.

"Contessa! Come quickly!" With that shout, Hammond pushed Eleanor Wexley away from him, and sent her hurtling forward on unsteady legs, choking and gasping for breath. Holmes stepped across swiftly and caught hold of the young lady at the point of collapse.

In that instant Hammond flung himself through the door, but the Contessa remained, hovering in the doorway, where her entire form quivered with scarcely contained fury. "Our work is ruined. *Il Corona del Diavolo* remains lost, and the darkness even still hovers at all our backs!"

A black-gloved finger pecked at the air like a savage beak. "I place the curse upon you! The blood of four hundred years is on your heads! *La maledizione!* You too are now as cursed as ..."

From outside the hall Hammcnd's pleas cut across her words. "Contessa Nascosta! Hurry!"

"*Attenta! Attenta! La maledizione!*" And, with a final anguished snarl of thwarted rage, the veiled woman fled, the doors slamming at her back.

Holmes lowered the weakened Eleanor into a chair and only then raced to the doors, which he reached in long strides just as the snap of drawn bolts rang out. With a snort of frustration he slammed a palm against the door panel, which juddered but did not yield.

Alone and reeling from all that had happened so suddenly around her, Eleanor Wexley gazed fearfully about the shadows as they swarmed and gathered, amassing and multiplying in every corner, as if ready to spill forth and submerge the room in midnight darkness. The smoke pouring up in twisting columns from the ornamental bowls resolved into white grasping fingers of vapour—skeletal fingers that in turn became pillars, just as in those temples and churches her father had told her of so long ago. A smile came at this memory, as she vaguely recalled that she might even now be standing in a church of some description. Was it, perhaps, a church with stark white pillars, she drowsily wondered? But if so, what were those dusky, unsettling forms that darted and hid behind each pale column, peering out with glittering eyes before ducking away teasingly out of sight the instant she turned to look back at them? Might these skulkers within the swarming shadows have been the source of the whispering, crowing voices that mocked her with every harsh word? "Eleanor ... remember ... the crown ... You are cursed ... dearest Eleanor.... Cursed and suffering..." A chorus of those goading voices rose till they attained shrieking pitch, yet others whispered in choked tones, croaking like things that had been buried in the damp earth for a long, long time, or had crawled out from even deeper recesses, from nightmare depths in which they had waited such unbearable ages.

Eleanor Wexley moaned, and her hands covered her ears in a futile attempt to block those hideous whispers out, but her own words merely echoed their grim insistence. "No! The crown is cursed, and all who find it are lost. Yet it must be found or all truly is lost!" Then, as her cries finally gathered into a scream, she begged, "Father? Will you please help me, Father?"

In answer to those shrieks, Sherlock Holmes, oblivious to the prowling creatures and their obscene babble, rushed to her side. I may, in other accounts, have suggested that Holmes thought of women as practically another species, worthy of cold, unfeeling study, but meriting no more thought than that he might expend on an amoeba on a microscope slide. Such a suggestion is careless and facile, for as well as quite freely voicing his admiration of many of the women we encountered, in particular those who demonstrated the same courage, tenacity and level-headedness that he found admirable in men, Sherlock Holmes was entirely capable of displaying great chivalry and understanding with the opposite sex, and was peculiarly adept at dealing with those in a heightened emotional state. This he now strove to do, as he gently took hold of Eleanor Wexley's face in his hands, directed her gaze toward him and attempted to hold it there. "Miss Wexley? There's nothing more to fear. I'm here to help you. You must concentrate and listen."

"Help me? No, you silly fellow, you cannot help me! No-one can. Not all the king's horses, nor all the king's men, for I am cursed! The blood is on me! They will catch the scent of the blood, and then they will come for me, clothed in night! But not even the king's men or the king himself can find the crown!" Eleanor Wexley pulled free of Holmes's arms and resumed her inexorable motion toward the stage and the phantom figure that hovered there even still. Holmes grabbed once more at her hand, but she ignored his efforts entirely. All she said was, "Can you not see him? It is he! Oh, Father, I am cursed. The crown has cursed me!"

"I know you're afraid, but you must listen. You're acting under an unnatural influence."

"No! It is my father. My dear, dead father!" Eleanor slipped from Holmes's grasp and, unmindful of his warnings, staggered toward the phantom, her hands reaching for it. "He won't let the curse take me. Will you, Father?" Her hopeful face darkened suddenly in dread realisation. "But, oh! Oh, why is he here? Contessa? He's still here, and he mustn't be! Contessa Nascosta, we need to finish the ritual! He must be sent back!" Her frantic eyes darted in search of a veiled form. "Contessa, you raven-dark witch, stop hiding in your shroud of shadows! We must send my poor father back, for he cannot be left amongst the ghosts!"

Her questing fingers brushed against something soft and yielding, and as chill tendrils wrapped themselves around her hands and wrists, the face of her lost father rippled and distorted, splitting and reforming, stretching and retreating, before finally tearing itself apart as she struggled to free her arms from whatever it was that entangled them. Something soft and cobwebby pressed against her face, choking her moans, and only relinquished its grip with a sudden tearing sound as she fought her way free. Before her dizzying senses the room appeared bathed suddenly in a hellish red glow. As the walls of the blood-shaded chamber expanded and contracted, she momentarily saw that they stood within an enormous heart, while some unyielding thing squeezed tightly round it. The figure before her, its familiar façade finally collapsing, stretched hideously, and its mouth opened in an impossibly widening yawn of hideous darkness that seemingly emitted the ghastly moan which filled the room—the moan that emerged instead from her own lips. "Eleanor, you are cursed! It is the blood, Eleanor! The blood of four hundred years!"

Sherlock Holmes, recognising that she was nearing the limit of her strength, lightly touched Eleanor's shoulder and drew away the torn and flimsy tatters of whatever had enshrouded her. "Miss Wexley," he insisted, "you are quite safe! There is no blood and no curse!"

Holmes stooped lithely to retrieve something from the edge of the stage, then gripped her lightly but firmly by the shoulders until she looked up to meet his unblinking grey eyes. "You're hallucinating. There is nothing here to harm you beyond the dreadful fear those people deliberately put into your mind. The things that alarm you, the terrible visions you think you see and hear, aren't real, and they cannot touch you." He raised aloft the golden circle he had snatched up. "No, don't shy away from it. You see the crown? Yes, I see it too. But look closer and you'll see only painted wood and coloured beads, and a length of fishing line to make it float."

"It's ... it's not real?" Miss Wexley repeated, and her shuddering slowly subsided as her fingertips cautiously brushed the golden painted circlet.

"None of it. You're perfectly safe."

The grotesque voices that assailed her died down to a whisper, and then into a silence broken only by Holmes's reassurances. The ghastly figures melted swiftly away, leaving only the swirling of the smoke and the tattered remnants of some gauzy material that Holmes discarded in a heap by their feet, before finally putting an arm around the exhausted young lady's shoulders. And as a weary numbness crept over Miss Eleanor Wexley, her slowly receding sobs lacked even the energy to scream as the locked doors abruptly parted with a splintering crash and three figures lunged into the hall.

"Take your hands off her, you damned swine," cried the first of these sudden arrivals, Nicholas Wexley, aghast and infuriated at finding his sister struggling in the embrace of this most peculiar looking stranger.

The second, who Eleanor dimly recognised as Mr. Francis Hammond, said nothing of note, but gave an aggrieved little grunt as he was shunted none-too-gently back into the room from which he had so recently escaped, any argument quelled by the persuasive presence of the revolver that nudged at his lower ribs.

The third newcomer, wielding that same revolver in one hand, and a stout walking stick in the other, surveyed all before him in that smoky room with utter amazement, before crying out, just in time to prevent Mr. Wexley from striking at his sister's apparent assailant, "Holmes? Good Lord, it is you, man!"

"It is, indeed," grinned Sherlock Holmes. "It's good to see you too, my dear Watson, and not a moment too soon."

Chapter 7: The Actor's Account

My arrival upon this extraordinary scene can be very briefly explained. Following a long afternoon awaiting the rallying cry in whatever form it might arrive, where I had practically leapt from my seat every time Mrs. Hudson stepped on a creaking floorboard or opened a door somewhere in the house, I had finally settled myself down for what looked liable to stretch into a long night's vigil when there came an urgent ringing of the doorbell, followed by an even more urgent rumble of footsteps on the stairs, and a brisk rapping at the sitting room door. Outside, stood young Wiggins, the proud lieutenant of Holmes's Irregulars, that motley gang of street urchins and waifs my friend had described as 'the Baker Street division of the detective police force', and had put to work as paid messengers, spies, go-betweens and upholders of a variety of other useful tasks that I have little doubt kept many of them on the right side of the law, and safely away from far less legal and savoury lines of work on the treacherous city streets.

"There's a cab waitin' downstairs for you, Doctor, an' a gentleman in it who Mr. Holmes asked me to fetch."

Rubbing a red ear with a grimy palm, he darkly muttered, "Though I near enough got me ears boxed clean off for knockin' on 'is door before I got to tellin' 'im who'd sent me. It's *'a most vital matter o' 'uge hurgency'*, accordin' to Mr. Holmes, so step lively, 'e says. The cabman's got the address you gents is headin' on to, an' the other gentleman has the message I was to give you both. Now I best be off, an' since I can't very well ask you to slip the gent waitin' below a thick ear if the chance comes, if you could remind Mr. Holmes that it's a sovereign 'e owes me, I'd be obliged to you, sir." And with that, the lad tore off again, leaving my landlady standing by the front door wearing an expression dark enough to match his grubby knees and collar.

Inside the waiting conveyance, I had found Nicholas Wexley, more bemused even than I to find himself summoned in such a manner, and as the cab proceeded eastwards, he produced the envelope, somewhat grubby and finger-marked by its time spent in the tender care of its delivery boy, and its contents, written in Holmes's neat script.

> *Gentlemen,*
> *You will be deposited across the street from the meeting hall our opposite numbers are using for their venture. Imperative you do not attempt to enter or intrude unless you witness obvious signs that assistance is required.*
>
> *S. H.*

Wexley and I had pondered, without any measurable success, on what these obvious signs might be, and were still doing so from the shadows in the doorway of an abandoned shopfront when we first heard voices raise to a commotion, then scant moments later spied a motley scrabble of bodies pouring out from the door opposite and taking to their heels. Declaring this most certainly a sign for action, we had been crossing the street when a smartly attired fellow had burst out with an extraordinary shrouded figure following. The dapper man had pleaded with the veiled woman to hurry, just as a carriage, its driver muffled and darkly cloaked, clattered out of the side street in which it had been concealed in the shadow of the hall. It had swiftly departed, but without one of its potential passengers, charging off the instant the veiled woman was aboard, leaving I, with my service revolver to reinforce my argument, compelling the young man to return to the building he had just fled, as Nicholas Wexley, unencumbered with any bullets in his shoulder, performed the duty of applying his own weight to the locked doors.

"I do owe young Wiggins that sovereign," admitted Holmes. "He wagered his Irregulars were more efficient than any telegraphic system."

Nicholas Wexley lowered his fists as comprehension dawned and stammered, "Mr. Holmes? My God, I didn't recognise you. Is Eleanor all right?

"Nicholas? Is that you?" his sister cried, and she threw her arms around him as he attempted to reassure her that whatever ordeal she had endured was all over.

"The others got away, I'm afraid, Holmes," said I. "I caught this one pushing a woman into a carriage."

"A veiled woman? That is a pity. I would rather have liked you to meet her."

"It had been sitting in wait, I think. The carriage, that is. Bolted as soon as she was inside, and I could hardly hold him and try to catch up with it. Though whoever it was holding the reins didn't seem too bothered to lose one of their own, did they?"

The young man's look of dismay was the only answer I was to receive. Holmes paid his cringing presence no heed, but gently ushered the Wexleys from the stage, then bent to grasp the fallen pile of flimsy material at his feet. "Miss Wexley, please try not to be alarmed," said he, just as he straightened up and to allow the substance to hang between his upraised hands. Where a moment before there had been only thin air, there now hovered the phantasmal face of a bearded man.

It was not Eleanor Wexley but her brother who cried out, "Oh, God! Father?"

"An impressive trick, is it not?" Holmes allowed the thin fabric to fall, drifting to the floor, the face vanishing in an instant. "But a trick nonetheless." His long arm extended, pulling the grubby curtains aside, and a beam of bright, piercing light became visible, shimmering across the stage and off into the wings. On a low table sat a large cabinet device of wood and brass with a thick glass lens, which I recognised instantly as a lantern slide projector and the source of the beam of spectral light. "As you can see, there's nothing supernatural about this apparition. I've seen similar illusions created on more professional stages than this, employing lighting tricks and reflections upon a sheet of clear glass which itself remains invisible to the audience. Dircks devised it for his *Phantasmagoria*, and Pepper helped perfect it. This is merely a variation.

"Mr. Wexley, did your father possess a camera?"

"Not that I could imagine, no. Any invention conceived later than the early mediaeval period would likely have been of little interest to him."

"Ah, well, merely a thought. That cellar you spoke of might have made an admirable photographic dark room. You see? Lantern slides, taken from photographic plates of your late father, projected on a scrim of hanging gauze create a suitably ghostly vision, and with smoke drifting through to add movement and an ethereal shimmer, the illusion is complete. I would imagine the briefest sight of this is what alarmed you when you were last here, Mr. Wexley."

"You were right," admitted Nicholas Wexley. "I thought you would have dismissed me completely if I'd admitted to having seen such a thing as that! I should have trusted your keener wisdom."

A toy boat lay abandoned by the table, a length of fine thread or catgut attached to its prow so that an unseen hand might create its rocking motion, while a number of bizarre objects lay about which produced sounds like thunder when shaken or babbling water when tipped. Holmes rapped a knuckle on a grille set into the wall, and it echoed and reverberated through similar barred apertures around the room. "Flues for heating, but ideal for the projection of voices from other realms." The smoke that had obscured these vents was now dying away as the last of the incense burned down. As it swirled and thinned, the draught revealed a door lying ajar at the back of the stage. Sherlock Holmes darted toward it, calling, "Watson, would you see that Miss Wexley is all right? She has had rather an alarming experience, and I believe she may be suffering the after-effects of being drugged."

Nicholas Wexley flew suddenly at Hammond, eyes ablaze. "You filthy devil! I ought to kill you where you stand!" Wincing with the strain on my old wounds, I still managed to drag Wexley from the quaking, jabbering Hammond before he could deliver anything more serious than a glancing blow. "Let me go, Watson! I'll make this foul villain suffer!"

"Your sister needs you! You'll be of little use to her in prison, and this wretch will be no use to any of us if he's dead or in hospital."

Wexley, the fires of fury dimming yet still smouldering, shrugged me off, and briskly pulled himself together. "You're right, of course."

"What's this, Watson?" cried Holmes on his return across the stage, "Miss Wexley still requires attention."

I looked on that bewildered and fatigued young lady and inwardly cursed her brother's hot temper for distracting me from her care. "Yes, of course. You are going to be quite all right, Miss Wexley. I'm a doctor. Doctor John Watson. If you don't mind, miss?" With tender fingers I tilted her head to the light of the nearest candle so to examine the pupils of her eyes.

"Please," she said softly, "would you call me Eleanor?"

"Of course, Eleanor," said I, smiling I supposed to reassure her, though perhaps I had my own reasons to smile that I could not then admit, even to myself. Even as I rolled up her sleeve, and gently took her wrist in one hand and my old pocket watch in the other, I silently reminded myself that, first and foremost, I was a doctor and could allow myself no further distraction from duty. Nonetheless, I listened intently to the confrontation taking place close by.

"Look," the grovelling specimen I had dragged back indoors protested, "I don't know anything about any drugs. If I'd had any idea ..."

Nicholas Wexley growled in disgust. "Don't try to wriggle your way out of this, you fawning little liar."

"He isn't lying. Are you, Mr. Hammond? At this precise moment, you are far too frightened to even attempt to think of a lie."

"I ... I don't even know what's happening, Mister...?"

"I have already told you my name," said Holmes, who unwound the threadbare scarf from his throat and removed his stained old overcoat to reveal a stomach padded out to swelling with the bulk of that grotesque carpet bag I had earlier seen him hefting. Releasing it from the sagging waistband of his trousers, he opened it and unfolded his customary dark overcoat and morning jacket, from whose wadded depths he retrieved a small bottle of water and a towel before placing them on the table before him. Throughout this shedding of his outer guise he continued in a casual, conversational manner. "If you have forgotten that name, it is Sherlock Holmes. Now, why don't you tell us your real name?"

My examination of Miss Wexley complete, I removed my own overcoat and draped it around her shoulders for, though far calmer now, she still quivered with shock. My gesture must have awoken something within her, as she looked up at me, directly into my eyes, and smiled. It seems ridiculous for an old man, so many decades after the event and with so much more experience since gained, to write of a mere smile as something golden and transforming, but I must be truthful and admit that this was precisely what I then felt, and that giddy feeling is easily summoned again should I choose to do so. I returned the smile, doubtless looking somewhat more foolish and dumbstruck than she, and sat by her side, trying not to shiver myself with nerves as she huddled into my side. That examination had revealed something surprising, with both the roof of her mouth and her tongue being strangely affected. I had mentally noted it, having no intention at that moment of alarming the young lady with this discovery, or of interrupting Sherlock Holmes as he pushed for a response.

"Come now. Silence cannot protect you, only implicate you further in these events."

"Fitzhugh," sighed the man previously known to us as Hammond. "Vincent Fitzhugh. That's my name. Not that you'd have heard of it, there's the injustice! Listen here, I knew that what we were doing probably wasn't totally above board. I'm not going to play that daft. But I don't know anything about any drug! I swear it, on my life!"

"Your life? I ought to ..." began Nicholas Wexley, before putting a stopper in his own anger at a pointed glare from my friend. "I ought to keep quiet, I know. But you surely can't believe him, Holmes?"

"I do. He knows nothing about what was really happening here. How can I be so certain? From the fact that he referred with all sincerity to the woman at the heart of the plot by a name which I know to be false. He has no notion of her real identity. Also from his expression of pure horror upon realising just how deep were the waters into which he had been dropped. He had no idea that the brandy he was instructed to give to Miss Wexley contained an unusual vegetable alkaloid, the purpose of which was to leave her susceptible to hallucinations built around the lies fed to her in this room. Look at him! Even now his slack expression shows the difficulty with which that concept penetrates his skull. Now," he turned his gaze back to Fitzhugh, "how did you first meet the woman you believed to be the Contessa Nascosta?"

"It was at the theatre. The Citadel Theatre."

103

"An actor? I suspected as much."

"An actor, yes, though not a successful one."

"That much I also suspected."

"Not a patch on you, sir. That was an uncanny performance as the old drunkard...."

"Get to the damned point, man," snapped Nicholas Wexley.

"There was an audition for a new show, a musical comedy review. I went up for the lead, and I would have been ideal for the part too, I should add. But the director had other ideas. They always do when it's my turn in the limelight—Sorry, yes, to the point!—Anyway, that was where I met the Contess— well, the woman in the veil.

"I never even noticed her at first. Gave me quite the turn, I confess, sitting there in the dark at the back of the stalls, draped all in black with that veil and all, like one of the Weird Sisters from the 'Scottish Play'. She beckoned to me with one of her black talons. I could have told her I don't give private performances, but you never know where you might find a patron, so I lent her my ears. But even in those first minutes she gave me the creeping shudders. It's one thing addressing yourself to a faceless audience, and with some of the audiences I've played to, that's a positive benefit. But sitting in the shadows talking to a woman with no face—at least not one I suspected I wanted to see—was different. So when she told me she needed actors, I just laughed and said how, if she'd seen my audition, she'd know she'd come to the wrong man."

"The money helped change your mind."

"I'm not too proud to admit it, Mr. Holmes. At first her idea sounded a bit odd to me—as if it was the first oddity here!—but in my few years in the profession I've spent more time out of work than in it, so I wasn't in any position to turn down paid employment, no matter how strange it struck me. And when she said that there was a mint to be made from gullible folks, with this spiritualism lark, how was I to refuse?"

"Gullible folk?" echoed Wexley. "Like my sister?"

"It was the Contessa made the choice, sir! She pointed the young lady out to me, and I did as I was bid. I had my props, as my peculiar employer had given me a pile of books on the spirits. I even memorised some of what was in them by reciting the information aloud, just as I might rehearse a monologue or patter song. I also memorised the young lady's routine, so that I might act when ordered. Thus prepared, on the elected day I followed Elea— that is to say, Miss Wexley, for a time, ducking ahead of her so that I might approach from the opposite direction. Being as careless as I could manage, and with every step choreographed, I allowed myself to be knocked into by her, thereby spilling my heavy cargo of books.

"I was prepared, I swear, to back out of my plan of action when I saw the kindness with which your sister treated this clumsy-seeming oaf. Regrettably, the lure of the Contessa's coin was more than equal to my good intentions, and the young lady had already sprung the trap upon herself by her favourable comments regarding my choice of literature as she helped gather up my bookish burden. 'You are a believer in such things?' I enquired, as ingenuous as any lead soubrette in a romantic melodrama.

"Smiling on me, she told me gently, 'Sir, there are so many different beliefs in all the world that to reject them all would leave us an empty existence indeed.' From where had she developed such a marvellous philosophy, I had asked. Oh, my, how her smile did falter, only briefly but revealing such a depth of tragedy. 'From my father, sir.' This was the very cue I needed! Had the words been put in her mouth by a playwright, they could not have been more leading, and so it was, then, that I used the information I already had about her father to 'sense' that she had recently lost him and still grieved. So impressed was she that she begged to be told how I could possibly have known. To which pleas I replied, 'I know the shadow that loss leaves upon a person, for I have seen that shadow in the mirror, lurking behind my own eyes.' And I told of the fire that had razed my home—rather, Mr. Francis Hammond's home—to the ground, and of the family who had perished in the flames. 'But even so, I have found them again, those I had thought parted from me forever more, or until my last breath has been breathed, at least.' And then, having kindled the hope now flaring in her bosom, I told her of how I had found the Church of the Golden Star, and of the comfort it had brought me, and from that moment on it was simplicity itself to persuade her to join us here."

"How easily the trap was set," mused Holmes. "But, as to its purpose? This is a more complex matter. You realise by now that this was no mere attempt to defraud Miss Wexley?"

"I do, sir," Fitzhugh nodded vehemently. "Leastways, I do now. But the reason behind it all is entirely a mystery to me. The Contessa told me nothing other than what she wanted me to do and say. She needed other actors to aid in the illusion, and I have many associates who are also failing to make a living upon the stage, just as happy to earn a guinea apiece for one hour's work. Poor Herbert Pope, whose arm you nearly dislocated, Mr. Holmes, may not win laurels for his fighting and duelling, but he's the finest unheralded baritone this side of a Seville barber's shop! I rounded them up, and we each took on characters which best fitted our demeanour. I, the sophisticated but good-hearted leading man and potential suitor, should a dash of romance be required. Please, Mr. Wexley, do put down your fists! I merely meant with honeyed words and stolen glances! There would have been no impropriety, I swear! We all had our roles, even if Madame Dulcie Jameson—our elderly Miss Garthorn—had to be cajoled out of donning paste diamonds and playing the grand duchess. Our instruction was to remain strictly in our roles with their agreed upon histories at all times while in this building."

"And your instruction concerning the contents of those decanters? That you were not to touch the brandy?"

"Miss Wexley was to be persuaded to take a drink before each ceremony. I supposed it to be laced with gin, or something a little stronger, just to soften the young lady up for the show. If I'd had any idea, sir ..."

"So you keep saying," Holmes murmured, cutting him off with a dismissive gesture. "Who provided and operated the slide lantern, and no doubt acted as the driver to facilitate your employer's swift escape?"

"I never knew who it was, nor ever asked. There was something about the Contessa that didn't encourage idle questions. The others were answerable to me, and I took my orders directly from her. But him behind the curtains, he never spoke a word to any of us. We never even saw him properly. He was dressed nearly as black as her so as not to be seen in the shadows. He was here whenever we arrived, at work with his machine and his effects. The only words we were to hear from him were during the ceremony. It was he who spoke as your father, Miss Wexley. I am ... I am sorry about that, truly."

"And how did you know when you were next to meet?" asked Holmes, ignoring the man's show of penitence.

"The Contessa would tell us at the end of each meeting. Apart from that first day at the Citadel, and when I'd assembled my cast and had a few rehearsals, I only ever saw her the three times that we were here. I swear to you, that's truly all I know."

Sherlock Holmes studied our craven prisoner in silence for a long moment, before deciding, "Then you should go, Fitzhugh."

"What's that you say?" roared Nicholas Wexley, and I was inclined to agree with his astonishment. "You're letting him go?"

"What else do you expect me to do with him?"

"What about the police?" I asked.

"The police?" Vincent Fitzhugh's fear-filled eyes strayed to the door, and his mind turned to thoughts of flight.

"What of them? They'll discover no more from this witness. He's completely ignorant of what he has allowed himself to get involved in, and his continued presence is not only obstructing my enquiries into just that, but is also making me quite nauseous." Then, with ice beneath the calm, he quietly instructed, "Get out, Fitzhugh."

"Thank you, sir. Your kindness, Mr. Holmes, is a credit to you." And with more and similar tearful platitudes, the actor scurried from the room and out into the night.

"A lamentable lack of backbone," remarked Holmes.

Nicholas Wexley, halfway to the door in pursuit of Fitzhugh's rapid steps, rounded on my friend with a livid face of fury, crying, "Damn it, Holmes, I must protest!"

"Must you? I can't see it serving any purpose," replied Sherlock Holmes, as he soaked water into the towel and proceeded to dab the florid make-up from his face. "However, it may be of some comfort to know that the cringing Fitzhugh is liable to receive some exceptionally rough justice when his compatriots realise that their mysterious employers have flown and they are not to be paid. I can hardly imagine that they will be as lenient as I."

"But can you be sure that he told all that he knows?"

"I can, Watson. While at our mercy the snivelling creature was far more alarmed by us and the idea of becoming entangled with the police than of any action the real instigators of this scheme may take against him. In whatever dark corner he chooses to hide, he may reconsider as he realises he is alone with naught but enemies on all sides, be they us, his brother actors, or his secretive patrons. Patrons who may now consider him a traitor and seek retribution, perhaps even to still his tongue for good."

"Do you know who they were?" demanded Wexley. "Or what reason they had to go to all this trouble?"

"Their identities are still unknown to me. But their purpose?" Holmes paused, deeply thoughtful, then turned to me. "How is Miss Wexley following her troubling experience, Doctor?"

"She's still in a highly nervous condition."

"I am perfectly all right, I'm sure, Dr. Watson." Eleanor rose to her feet and walked with halting but steadily more confident steps forward. "Mr. Holmes. I do not know how to begin thanking you."

"Then save yourself the trouble, Miss Wexley, for our task is far from over. As, I fear, is our opponent's."

"But you've succeeded in your mission," protested Nicholas Wexley. "My sister has been rescued from their snare."

"On the contrary," returned Holmes, a warning finger raised. "A great deal of planning and organisation has gone into their operations. My intervention prevented them achieving their goal on this night, but their failure may only make them more determined. Miss Wexley, I offer my deepest apologies for allowing their deception to carry on so long, but I was unable to discern the motive behind their actions in any other way. Had I halted the ceremony sooner, the veiled woman would never have revealed her true purpose. Hence this deception of my own." A sweep of his hand indicated the discarded remnants of his disguise.

"But why change your appearance so utterly?" said I. "Unless you had expected to encounter someone who might recognise you amongst this sect, I cannot see a reason for it."

"I invariably have a reason, old fellow," said Sherlock Holmes with a rapid smile, "and you will come to realise that I can never resist a touch of the dramatic. The idea itself was formed when you, Mr. Wexley, mentioned that your sister never could turn her back on a lost cause."

Eleanor Wexley smiled at this revelation. "You have always said it would be my undoing, Nicholas. It seems, instead, that it was my salvation."

"It was the one chance I had to observe the crime in progress. Even though I know my concerned friend, Watson, already fears I may be just such a lost cause, I felt that Miss Wexley was more likely to look kindly upon a harmless, pathetic old soul who had lost his way in life. And I'm afraid I borrowed a few leaves from your father's biography, for good measure."

"I thought there was some bond there that drew my heart to the poor man's plight."

"So this was the reason for that hideous carpetbag," said I, as I indicated the luggage into which Holmes had begun to pack away the outlandish costume.

"Yes. I had the disguise already. Mr. Jasper Montague has been of invaluable assistance in the past, though the abominable Signora Ricoletti and her club-footed husband may not have found him quite so helpful in their pretty little schemes. Mind that pocket, it contains my chewing baccy!"

"You don't indulge in chewing tobacco, do you?"

"I thought it might add to the character of the old sailor, whose accoutrements I'd already set aside lest that boarding house incident of such dreary predictability had proven otherwise and I required an incognito to make neighbourhood enquiries in person. But, in truth, such a touch would have been a little too grotesque for this evening."

I regarded the skullcap, thick-lensed spectacles and oddly-proportioned dentures with some wryness, only to be told, "No-one so loud, garish and obtrusive could possibly be acting by stealth or concealing secrets, therefore his motives are never questioned. But there is a fine line and the truly grotesque attracts interest. Besides, teeth such as these aren't cheap, and Mr. Montague must share them with an elderly gentleman cleric, who would most certainly draw unwelcome comment should he benevolently look down upon some sinner with a tobacco-browned smile."

"So, an 'old and trusted friend', I see, this Mr. Montague," said I, relieved to have had this slight mystery, as well as some nagging doubts of my own making, cleared away. "Jasper 'Montague', you say? Aha! Named, no doubt, in honour of your former lodgings in Montague Street."

"Indeed so, for it was there that he first drew breath, even if that breath was accompanied by a wheeze and a cough. And that cough was a saviour tonight, as I may well have laughed aloud more than once at the brazenness of their cheek. But, just as I hope I present a healthier specimen than the dear old skipper, you are also looking much improved following your ordeal, Miss Wexley."

"Now that the panic's over, I feel only shame. Yes, shame. For reacting so to ghosts and monsters conjured out of my own imagination. And more so for allowing myself to be so easily led in the first place."

"Nonsense," I insisted. "By all accounts, they were extraordinarily convincing in their story and their effects. That ghastly trick phantom? Urgh! Such horrid ingenuity! You have nothing to reproach yourself for, Miss Wexley."

"It is Eleanor, please," she reminded me. "You are very kind, Dr. Watson."

"If I am to call you Eleanor, you must call me John. I insist on it."

"If the pleasantries are quite over, *John*, and if Miss Wexley is adquately recovered, I should like to ask her a few questions."

"As long as you don't over-excite her, Holmes," I warned.

"I will try to answer any question you may have, sir, even though you appear to know and understand much better than I what has taken place here."

"There is one thing I do not know. The woman who calls herself the Contessa Nascosta has gone to enormous trouble to gain a certain piece of information which only you possess, and it is this which contains the key to this entire grotesque affair. Tell me, Miss Wexley, what were your father's dying words?"

"How the devil can anything that old fool had to say inspire anyone to go to these lengths?" snapped Nicholas Wexley. "He spoke little sense during his worthless life, and at the end he was a raving wreck!"

"Nevertheless, it is of great importance. Well, Miss Wexley?"

"I don't know," she groaned, and her brow creased in deep concentration. "I did know it, but I can't remember. It's as if the smoke and the darkness have crept into my mind to fog the memory, and the harder I try to reach for it, the deeper the fog becomes. I try, but I just cannot remember!"

"It's the shock," said I. "If those fiends put pressure on her mind to recall that one particular thing, the horror of their other actions could easily have caused her to repress the memory."

"I am so sorry," said she, so forlornly my heart would have been stone not to go out to her in her misery.

"Don't worry, and do not push yourself to remember. Those fogs will lift, and the memory will return in time."

"Until Miss Wexley can recall what those words were, the solution to this particular mystery remains out of our grasp. Watson, I think we should get the young lady out of this foul place and ensure that there are no lingering after-effects of the drug." So saying, Holmes picked up and stoppered the decanter. "I suggest we return to Baker Street, where you can examine the patient more thoroughly, and I can examine the ingredients in this singular concoction."

"Certainly. Are you well enough to walk, my dear? We can summon a cab just outside."

"Mr. Wexley will be quite able to assist his sister," insisted Holmes, to my unexpectedly deep chagrin.

"Of course, Mr. Holmes. Come along, Eleanor." And taking her hand in his, our client escorted his sister toward the door.

"Once you have placed the young lady in the cab, I recommend you hail another one to take you home."

"What a ridiculous suggestion! I must stay with Eleanor!"

"And leave your home unguarded? You've told us already that many of your father's papers, books, and unique artefacts are there, and it would be foolish indeed to allow our enemies such easy access to them. You have a weapon to defend yourself, I trust?"

"There's a native club the old man brought back from his travels. That should prove the match of any intruder, have no fear. Thank you, gentlemen. Thank you, both."

I found myself sharing a last lingering smile with the gracious Miss Wexley, as she stepped back to return my overcoat which had engulfed her like a shawl. I watched she and her brother step outside, and that smile may have lingered longer on my own face had I not turned to catch sight of Sherlock Holmes raising a curious eyebrow. "Well," said I, brazening it out. "She is a very beautiful young lady."

"I know," Holmes replied. "You said so earlier."

"And awfully brave with it."

"No doubt. What she has faced down tonight might easily have broken the strongest mind. We have a cunning foe to face here, old fellow."

"Then why aren't we at Wexley's house, laying a trap for them?"

"Oh, Watson, if they believed that the information they sought could be obtained by mere burglary, do you think any of this would have been necessary? And if any one of those books in Professor Wexley's collection had real bearing on whatever final treasure he'd sought, he would surely have taken it with him. I merely wished to have his sister to myself." I fear I must have reacted in some consternation to this statement, as Holmes tut-tutted, adding, "To question her, my boy, without her brother's influence to interfere with my enquiries. His concern for her, and his overwhelming contempt for his father, could easily become disruptive, and I must have her frank answers with no outside pressures."

"In which case, I advise that you leave your questioning till the morning. Yes, I fully understand that she's the only one who can cast a light on these dark proceedings. Which she will be completely incapable of doing if she is in Bedlam suffering from nervous exhaustion. I insist you allow Eleanor—that is to say Miss Wexley—to rest and recover."

113

"Very well," said he as he gathered up the final vestiges of Jasper Montague. "You are the doctor. She may sleep in my room." Catching my unvoiced question in my startled eyes, Holmes carelessly dumped the bag that bulged with his disguise into my arms, announcing, "I will not require my room because I will not require sleep. I shall spend the hours of darkness attempting to identify the substance in this bottle."

"Gads!" I recoiled from the reeking clothes bundled in my arms. "It smells as if you may have already identified the contents of a bottle of gin."

"No need to look so alarmed, Doctor, I have not added to my list of vices. A drunkard who doesn't smell of alcohol is a most curious fellow. I merely poured the stuff onto my collar, and not down my throat."

"Very clever, I must say."

"I can ill afford to be otherwise. Those we face are no commonplace criminals. They are cunning manipulators and expert planners. And, if we are to follow that same trail they pursue, we must prove ourselves at least as clever as them."

"Well, old fellow, you have successfully outfoxed them so far."

"So far all they have done is played a game with Miss Wexley. Now they have seen that they cannot trick the information out of her, they must surely consider more drastic measures."

"Whatever they seek must be hugely valuable. But what?"

"Something old, Watson," said Holmes, gravely. "'*The blood ...*'"

"Blood?" I shuddered.

"'*The blood of four hundred years!*' And, if we slip in our quest," said he, gravely, "our own blood may well join it!"

Chapter 8: A Most Unhappy Reunion

Despite her protests—and much to my fellow-lodger's annoyance—upon our return to Baker Street I remained adamant that Miss Wexley should have a proper night's sleep before facing any of those myriad questions already circling in Holmes's head like famished vultures ready to swoop on any scrap of clue they may draw out. Though perplexed and filled with her own curiosity, the gruelling visitation in that dingy hall had evidently exhausted our guest, and her insistence that she was perfectly capable of withstanding any interrogation was voiced amidst much yawning and rubbing of weary eyes. Fortunately, I had an able reinforcement in my campaign to see her rested, as Mrs. Hudson brought her fresh linen, night-clothing, and cocoa, while I insisted on pouring a mild sleeping draught.

Sherlock Holmes, meanwhile, had loaded himself up with volumes on toxicology and botany, and, as I too retired for the evening, he sat hunched over his microscope, attempting through a process of elimination to find a match for the substance that had caused our guest's awful visions—visions she had described to me in such vivid detail that I can still picture them all too horribly clearly, these long decades later.

Some of these impressions I jotted down in my notebook, between unsuccessful approaches at slumber, and I had filled several pages with the day's events before weariness overtook me, and though I was vaguely aware of the pencil slipping from my fingers, I was asleep before it struck the rug. I slept fitfully, my mind filled with vile images of veiled witches and screaming skeletons that crept and skulked behind tombstones as they circled around the grave of my own sadly long-departed father. I stood guard, my army uniform pressed and brightly buttoned, my revolver raised and ready, as they stealthily advanced. It was only as I avidly scanned the mist-wreathed cemetery that I realised the footsteps pattering around me were in actuality the tapping and rapping of knuckles upon wood. With a settling dread, I knew then that the knocking was coming from inside my father's coffin, just as his muffled voice cried my name. Yet even as I scrabbled in the dirt to free him from his living grave, explosions to the left and the right of me became flashes of the dreadful war in Afghanistan, and as I dug with clutching fingers through the blood-caked sand, I uncovered the silently screaming faces of men I recognised—men who had died around me in battle. Men who had died on my table in the hospital tent, as I had fought to drag them back from abyss. Men whose blood was still slick on my hands.

You might well imagine my vast relief, therefore, when the sound of Holmes's violin woke me, and I realised that the morning sun that found me through the half-closed curtains shone down on old, familiar London, and not upon that field of blood on the other side of the globe.

Although still early, I found both Sherlock Holmes and Eleanor Wexley awake and dressed. Our fetching new companion looked much refreshed, even if I was less relieved to discover her intently reading my manuscript, which I must have left carelessly lying on my desktop the previous morning. As I would not permit Holmes to talk of our case until we had all enjoyed a good, sustaining breakfast, she insisted on finishing it, and I confess to fighting back a grin of supreme satisfaction when she informed Holmes that she not only found the tale utterly absorbing, but also that she thought it well-told and thrillingly written.

"I fear," muttered Holmes darkly, "that our young guest has not yet fully recovered her wits, and may yet be under the drug's mind-addling influence."

"While your own wit is as rapier-sharp as ever, my dear Holmes. I only hope I have it in me to dress my wounds before they prove mortal, for I am cut to the very quick."

"It's bewildering at first, I admit, but don't let it worry you," Mrs. Hudson confided to our guest, as she briskly laid the breakfast table. "And don't try taking sides. They're both as bad as each other."

"I find both my hosts very amusing."

"Amusing?" The landlady's eye roved round the three of us, before settling back on Miss Wexley. "It's a kinder word that I would use, miss. I shall be up to clear away in half an hour, and do try to make sure that one eats something." The thumb that was jerked in Holmes's direction was accompanied by a disapproving cluck of the tongue as Mrs. Hudson left us to our meal.

Over that hearty and excellent breakfast, Holmes revealed that his studies had taken him through beyond the small hours, but had finally borne fruit. "The substance," said he, "derives from a cactus that is indigenous to Central and South America, and grows particularly rife along the desert outskirts of San Pedro, where it is said to be watered in the blood of the enemies of that troubled nation's presiding tyrant. It can be administered by eating the flesh of the cactus, or dried and reduced practically to powder, which is then smoked like many other opiates. Had I experienced any of the same overwhelming feelings that oppressed Miss

Wexley last night, I might have suspected an attempt to combine it with the incense. But, of course, that would have led to the risk of the unwary actors running wild with their own delusions. It is an ingredient the natives have for centuries used in their religious ceremonies in order to bring about trancelike states and induce what they believe to be holy visions. In the most extreme of these rituals, the pulped flesh was rubbed into wooden barbs or long thorns, which were used to subcutaneously skewer the skin of their limbs and faces—Oh, Watson, I do hope I'm not putting you off your breakfast, my dear fellow!—allowing the toxins to work their way through the supplicant's system at a slower rate, leading to prolonged days of alternate euphoria and terror as the universe reveals its secrets to them. Ha! In reality, small doses actually cause docility and hallucinations, while greater amounts are known to provoke insanity and, in some cases, may even cause the heart to stop beating entirely."

Almost unknowingly, my hand found Eleanor Wexley's, squeezing it as I strove to mask a momentary stab of alarm behind a reassuring smile. "My heart," said she, gently returning my squeeze just as I moved to withdraw my grip, "beats quite as strongly as it ever has."

"As I would expect," agreed Holmes. "In solution, and as diluted as the dosage was in the alcohol, the effects are most likely to be passing, thus indicating that our unknown opponents must have recognised exactly how much of the devilish potion to administer to produce the desired effect."

Our fast broken, we could proceed from what had been discovered to what yet remained undefined. I cautioned Holmes about his choice of questions, but Miss Wexley appeared as keen as he to penetrate to the heart of the mystery, and declared that she would gladly answer any query she could.

Holmes had seemingly gleaned every last piece of information he currently needed about the Church of the Golden Star, as he instead chose to enquire about the death of Professor Oscar Wexley and the circumstances surrounding it. Obviously still feeling the sadness of her loss, our brave young companion gave a single sigh, before beginning her tale—which shall follow in as precise a recounting of her own words as my notes and my memory can provide—of how a telegram had taken her and her brother to a strange house in the north, for what was to be the last time they were to see their father alive.

The old priory to which Nicholas and I had been summoned (*began Eleanor Wexley*) was reached by a coach from the railway station at Harewynd, which carried us from the village through miles of winding country lanes. I couldn't even describe the village itself, nor any of the sights seen from the window of our train as it had sped northwards from London, and I only dimly recall the endless fields and grey stone walls that passed by agonisingly slowly as the coach rattled and shook over uneven roads and tracks. My mind was fixed solely on the contents of that telegram whose unforeseen arrival had seen me beseech my brother to put aside all other plans and hasten with me to the country.

That ominous message read, '*Oscar Wexley in bad way. May not last another night. Please come with all speed to Oldmire Priory, near Harewynd Village, if you would see your father alive. H. Rollistone.*' The sender's name was obscurely familiar to me, but I gave it little thought, as my poor father's dire condition was the only thing I could possibly consider.

Under skies as stark and dour as my frame of mind, we arrived at Oldmire Priory, a house that would have appeared gloomy and doom-laden even under considerably less trying circumstances. Behind its crumbling, moss-coated walls, it nestled within an overgrown park of thorny tangles and stunted, mouldering trees; as bleak, grey and damp as any ruined temple or toppled battlement. I thought for a moment we must surely have been delivered to the wrong place. No light shone in the grimy windows to the front of the house, and it was only the sound of raised voices, so jarring in the stillness of that forgotten spot, that led us around to the back of the building, where a set of French doors lying open onto the patio allowed us to clearly hear the heated conversation taking place in the room beyond.

"Wexley, Wexley, old chap," a rich voice purred, coaxingly. "Calm yourself, man."

This was answered by a hoarse roar. "Out, the pair of you! Get your filthy claws away from me!" I felt Nicholas clutch at my arm. We both recognised our father's voice, although never had I heard it so filled with fury. Fury and, I now perceive, fear. I wished only to go to him and calm him, but Nicholas gripped tighter at my sleeve and raised a finger to his lips, signalling for me to listen.

"Get your filthy claws away," echoed that first voice. "Out with you," it cried, still mimicking Father's tone, only to be answered with a ferociously vented oath.

"We only want to help you," countered another voice in a wheedling, appeasing manner.

"Jackanapes and jackals! Hovering over me like a couple of overstuffed buzzards. You might pick my carcass clean when I'm gone, but you can't touch what's in here, even if you dig my brains out with my own trowel. Oh, no, my good sirs, what's in this head of mine is not for the likes of thee or thou!"

That first voice came again, blithely jovial yet, I thought, subtly menacing. "You cannot honestly believe you've found it, old boy?"

"I've found it, and you know that I have. Otherwise you'd have left me to die back there!"

And again that pitiable pleading, "Oscar, you are gravely, gravely ill."

"Ha! I know I'm ill, you carrion crows. You think I can't see when you've got the scent of death in your nostrils? I've known you both far too long to miss the signals." Then gloating, despite his laboured breaths and painful sighs, he cried, "And I know something else. But it's not for you, grave-robbers! Scavengers!"

Despite my brother's desire to hear more, I could hold myself at bay no longer, and I stepped across to the open windows. Thus I entered a most peculiar room in that very peculiar house. Despite seeming very dusty and seedy, it was still rather a grand library, with towering bookshelves laden with ancient volumes dominating every wall. What little wall space was not devoted to shelves of books was taken up with primitive drawings and engravings, woodcuts, parchments, and maps of all continents, from contemporary charts of the latest shipping routes and lines of transport—as I had seen often when Father was planning his adventures—to crumbling fragments that must have weathered rough journeys in centuries long past.

There was a small landing atop a short flight of stairs from which a door lead off to the rest of the house, and below this a great table lay cluttered with yet more volumes—so many they spilled onto the floor around it. By what little light the clustered candles brought to that murky room, I saw that each surface not overwhelmed with books was decorated with exotic items from all around the world. Had some exotic Eastern bazaar overrun a corner of the British Museum's Reading Rooms, it might have matched the scene I now looked upon. There were hookah pipes, tribal masks, scimitars and spears, jade statuettes, tomahawks, Chinese lanterns, a cluster of grisly statuettes whose origins I would hardly wish to guess at, and enough items of exotic bric-a-brac to give any passing antique dealer or junk-shop proprietor grounds for battle.

These details I took in gradually, as my attention lay with the out-of-place bed set up in the centre of the room. Even this was covered with and hemmed in by books. Although its occupant was paler and seemingly more shrunken and lined than I could have imagined, his hair and beard now shot through with unfamiliar streaks of white, I had little difficulty in recognising my own father.

"Come now, Oscar," rumbled one of the two men who stood over my stricken father's prone form. He was a plump, elderly, man possessed of luxuriant side whiskers and brows, beneath the latter of which gleamed narrowed eyes, and a ruddy face. He was dressed in a velvet smoking jacket and upon his head he sported a fez, and despite the illness of my father and the grave expression etched deep on their other companion's face, he seemed excessively jolly. "If you don't tell us, then what use...?"

"Won't tell! Not you! Never! I'm keeping that for ..." And then my father saw me, waiting meekly in the window. And then he smiled. He smiled so broadly that for an instant his younger, more vital self shone through all the signs of his premature fading, and he sighed, "I'm keeping it for an angel."

The third man appeared a few years my father's junior. He was extremely tall and very powerfully built, dressed in sturdy country tweeds, with stout walking boots on his feet, yet with skin so pale it gave no indication that this was a man who spent any great time out of doors—at least not in any daylight pursuit. In contrast to his bulk, which he seemed keen to diminish by his hunching posture and small, precise gestures, he was nervy and softly spoken, and started in alarm as he followed my father's gaze. "Who's that? Hubert, who is she?"

"Why, surely," his companion remarked with a wide smile, "it is little Eleanor."

"Let her in, damn you," howled Father. "Let her in, or I'll go right now and take the secret to the grave, just to spite the pair of you!"

The jovial man hurried across to me, waving me over the threshold with a fat hand on which I now observed many rings, all the time beaming, "Miss Wexley, my dear girl. You received my telegraphic message, I see. My dear, dear child, I do hate to be the bearer of bad tidings."

"Mister Rollistone?"

"Yes, my dear. Hubert Rollistone, at your every service. You don't remember?" A slight frown flickered behind the grin. "Professor Rollistone? Of course, you don't. It's been many years since I last visited your delightful home and family. Come in, my dear girl. Come along in with you."

"Forgive me, Professor, but we saw no lights in the front windows and then, when we heard voices raised from this room ... Father? Oh, God, Father!" Ignoring the professor, I threw myself down by the side of the bed.

Father struggled to sit up, coughing and gasping with each movement. As I aided him, lifting him as gently as I could, he spluttered, "We? Did you say 'we', Daughter?"

"She did, Father. I am with her," replied Nicholas, stepping into the library and making no effort to mask his displeasure over where and with whom he had found himself.

"She's brought the whelp," groaned Father, and my heart, already heavily weighed down, sank yet further. "Come to see your worthless old man finally get his reward, have you, whelp?"

"I'm afraid," stammered the huge, nervous man who had stood silently watching, "your father has been like this for some time."

Professor Rollistone clapped this other man genially on the shoulder, causing him to flinch, as he explained, "This is our valued colleague and friend, Professor Ronald Flagstaff of Camford University."

Professor Flagstaff gingerly offered his hand to Nicholas, who shook it curtly before stepping past him, declaring, "Professor Flagstaff, my father has been like this for as long as he's been on this earth."

"Which won't be for too much longer," Father wheezed, "as you'll doubtless be glad to hear, boy!"

I fear my sorely tested patience entirely gave way then, for I cried, "Stop it, now! Both of you must stop this! Nicholas, you promised you would try."

My stubborn brother nodded grudgingly, before turning like a petulant, scolded child to stare out of the window, while I, seating myself by the bedside, tried so very hard to ease the fractious mood. "Father," said I,

"Nicholas didn't come all this way to fight with you. We received Professor Rollistone's telegram this afternoon and rushed straight here. He has been very worried."

"Worried he'd miss the chance to see me die in agony, like he thinks I deserve?" I opened my mouth to protest, but the spark was bright in Father's eyes. "He's hated me as long as he's known me."

Whirling round, aflame with his own fury, Nicholas cried, "When did I ever get the chance to know you? As far back as I can remember, you were always off with your," a disdaining gesture took in the two professors, "your learned friends!"

"Please, please," urged Professor Rollistone. "Nicholas, Oscar, now is not the time for such talk."

"When else is he going to get the chance to tell me how much he loathes me? Goading me in my death bed has to be more satisfying than spitting on my grave. You're right, boy. I was never there, but the reason I was gone was worth it."

"Was it worth it to abandon a devoted wife with two small children to raise?"

"Don't ever speak to me of your mother! She was an angel." His gnarled hand reached out to grasp mine. "An angel, just as you are, my daughter."

"An angel who took up with a devil," spat Nicholas. "It was a black day for her when she met you."

"And for all of us when she brought you into this world. You were a sour-faced whiner even then, and I see you are consistent with your temperament still."

"If it hadn't been for me, she would have died as destitute and penniless as you left her."

Unable to rise, Father shook a furious fist at Nicholas. "You speak to me of a few tin coins when there are all of the gems in the world to be had? If you but knew, boy! But you never have, and never will!"

Professor Rollistone helped me ease Father back into his pillows, where he lay coughing feebly, while the professor, smiling no more, insisted, "That is more than enough! Oscar, rest yourself. Nicholas, calm down. Think of the effect all this is having on your poor sister."

I quickly thanked him, grateful for his intervention, yet strangely angered that he was there at all in the midst of our family crisis. "Tell me, how did my father come to be in this condition? When we saw him last, he was healthier and in better spirits than I think I had ever known him."

"It's his lungs, my dear girl. Pneumonia, I believe, though I'm no doctor. It was a sudden attack. We brought him back here to rest, although he refused to be put in his room."

"He insisted on being close to the books," supplied Professor Flagstaff meekly. "He was most strict on that account. Most strict indeed."

"But to fall so ill so suddenly? How is this possible?"

"Having spent so many years in warmer lands, miss, your father is utterly unaccustomed to our colder climate," replied Ronald Flagstaff. "And our work has led to many nights spent out of doors."

It seems to me now that Professor Rollistone glared pointedly at his colleague, Flagstaff, but the meaning of this silent exchange escapes me—if meaning there ever was—for it was then that Nicholas, as has so often happened where our father is concerned, lost his composure. "'His work,' you say? 'Work'? I would laugh if I didn't see how seriously you believe that claim!"

.I heard the slap before I was even aware that I had raised my hand. "Nicholas! He's dying, and still you decry him!"

"I am so very sorry, Eleanor," he said quietly, his fingers straying to his reddening cheek as he strode away from me. "For your sake."

"What work was this?" I demanded of the two scholars, hoping at least to understand something of what had laid my father so low.

"Hubert, I think that, well," stammered Flagstaff, "I believe, that is, that we should tell them. They do have the right to know, don't you think?"

125

"My colleague is being over-dramatic, Eleanor, dear," beamed Rollistone. "It was just an investigation. A local piece of folklore. Our researches involved one of the nearby churches, but the only time our enquiries could be carried out without interruption was at night."

Scrambling upright again, Father snarled, "What are you telling her, Rollistone? Speak up, damn you! More of your miserable lies, eh? No, Eleanor, do not beg me to rest or to sleep, my girl. For I'd be dead as soon as I closed my ... I closed my ..." He sighed, slumping as if in defeat. "You realise that these are my final moments?"

"I do, Father. But only in this life. Your spirit will live on forever."

"Oh, God," I heard Nicholas groan. "Eleanor, please don't!"

"You still believe, girl. Not like this close-minded pup, never seeing more than the figures in his ledgers. But you've remembered what I taught you."

"I remember everything you've told me. And I know that even if we part this day, we shall see each other again."

"Good girl." Urgently, he beckoned me closer. "I have important things to tell you now, while I still have breath to utter them! You are listening? And not just you! No, I say nothing yet! Not with the sharks circling, scenting my blood. As if they can carry me back in bloodied chunks as another offering to the coiling darkness they hear crying to them from the deep."

"The sickness has left him delusional," murmured Professor Rollistone, looming once again at my side. "He's lapsed in and out of reason since he fell ill."

"I've enough reason left in me to spy a snake when it bares its filthy fangs! Get away, Rollistone, and take your whining lapdog with you."

"Oscar," yelped Flagstaff, plainly hurt. "After our years of friendship!"

Embarrassed, I urged, "These gentlemen have shown you great kindness, Father. They're your friends."

"Friends? Leeches!" With a sudden, unexpected show of strength, he seized one of the books from the mound upon the bed and hurled it at Professor Rollistone, who only managed to duck out of its path by a matter of inches. "Out! Out, you bloodsucking wretches! Slither away, leeches of the deep. You won't trap me! I'll say nothing till you go!"

"Sir, please," I beseeched the professor. "I am sorry to ask this of you in your own home, but could you leave us alone for a few moments?"

Hubert Rollistone hesitated for just a few seconds before answering. "As you wish, my dear girl. Pray, don't worry yourself on our account. We all know how stubborn Oscar can be."

"Yes," agreed Professor Flagstaff, moving cautiously up the short staircase and toward the door to the rest of the house. "We should go, Hubert. Should we not?"

"Of course, Ronald. Of course. We shall leave these young people alone with their dear father. If you should need anything, my dear ..."

That offer was drowned out with a roar of, "Get out, you grinning, poison-fanged cur!"

I turned imploring eyes toward the man on the landing. "Please, Professor Rollistone, I need only a few moments."

It was not until both scholars had exited and we heard the door firmly close that Father collapsed back into his pillows, coughing pitifully. I asked Nicholas to fetch water. This he poured from a jug on a table laden with dusty bottles, and as I held the glass to Father's dry, cracked lips, I urged, "You must drink, and lie easy."

"Uneasy lies the head, eh? No, stop fussing. I'm perfectly all right, don't drown me, Daughter! I just wanted those truffle hounds out of the way. They're fools, but not fool enough to allow me to take my secret to the grave. That is why you must make an oath, Eleanor. What I now tell you must never be revealed to them. You'll promise me?"

"These men are—or were—your good friends, your esteemed colleagues. Yet you talk now as if they were your tormentors."

127

"Give me your promise, and I will tell all. Swear to it, Eleanor!" He coughed drily, and I pressed the glass once more to him to drink.

"He seems so afraid," I whispered. "What could have happened to him, Nicholas?

Quietly, almost kindly, my brother said, "The illness is making him babble. Don't allow it to upset you. Promise what he asks, if that will stop his ranting."

Looking deep into those red and bleary eyes that had looked so often upon lands and skies that I have glimpsed only in dreams, I did as he entreated. "Father, I give you my word, I shall tell them nothing you do not wish them to know."

"Good girl. It's all been for you, Eleanor. For you and your darling mother." A palsied finger pointed briefly to my brother. "Even for him, should he accept it."

"I've never wanted anything you've had to offer." Nicholas grimaced in distaste as he lifted the carved ebony figurine of some ancient divinity whose many feelers or tentacles surrounded a face composed of darkly glittering eyes. "You can keep your myths and your monsters, for even had such abominations ever walked this earth, they're long dead now, and of use to no sane man!"

"You'd not turn your back so quickly if you knew just what it was I offered. What it is I have found!" He let loose a gurgling laugh that seemed to explode wetly from somewhere deep inside him. "Yes! It was I that found it! Not them! Never them! They have no claim here, only I! This is why they swoop around me, don't you see? They want that which shines inside my mind, yet they'll never see it. In order to see it they would need to look through different eyes, indeed!" And again he laughed until his face grew as purple as the dimming skies outside.

"If you have something to tell us, speak, man. Or is this another of your riddles and fairy tales?"

"Don't presume to question my word, boy!" A horrible look of realisation crept across my father's face, and he looked on my poor brother with suspicious eyes. "Or are you with them? Is that it? Are you their wooden horse, sent to trick me? All the king's horses and all the king's men couldn't put the clues I've followed together again! You and them, the laughing hyena and the hysterical dancing bear, plotting against me! Me? The one man left alive in this world with any idea of how the trick was done!"

"You don't know what you're saying," I cried.

"Obviously he doesn't," Nicholas laughed. "Me in alliance with those other fantasists? I've nearly as much contempt for them as ..."

"Lies! You're not clever enough to trick me, not one of you!"

"Eleanor," snapped Nicholas, seizing my wrists, as if prepared to drag me bodily from the house, just as he would go on to do from last week's ceremony. "I cannot and will not stand here and listen to this."

"Leave, then," I cried, snatching myself away from his grip. "I thought that now, finally, you two might make your peace. I can see that it will never happen! Well, you may deny him all you wish, but he's still my father. You go, if you truly can, but I must hear what he has to say."

"Very well, Sister," he muttered, coldly. "I shall not leave you here, but I'll listen to no more of his insults and accusations." And so saying, Nicholas stalked over to the windows, where he stood and stared out into the shadow-filled jungle outside, emphatically ignoring everything within the room.

Father tugged at my sleeve, pulling me close so he might whisper. "The crown! Over thirty years I sought its trail, and across so many lands ... So many false trails. Trails of blood! Oh, such blood ..."

I shuddered. "You mustn't talk of such horrible things."

"Not horrible," he murmured. "Beautiful! The most beautiful, deadly object. A beauty such as that often carries a darkness at its back. Golden and blue and scarlet ... A circle dipped in scarlet, scarlet blood. A glistening circle of blood. And one that sent those who sought it in circles of their own. How many circles of Hell did Dante describe? There are more than he dreamed of, for those who would seek them. More circles of blood, over centuries. Centuries lost! Until I ..." Tears flooded his eyes, though whether of joy or pain I doubt even he could have said. "I know now! After all these years. What were we searching for? Well, we thought we knew that, of course, but no. No, we were wrong. All wrong!" There was a chilling hysteria to his abrupt laughter, before he grew hoarse and his whispering resumed. "They still haven't realised. Only you! Tell no-one." Fearful, suspicion-filled eyes darted to every gloomy corner of the library. "Where are they? Creeping up on me, crawling on their bellies like snakes? Slithering like the coiling reaches of the deep ones? Or will it be their agents, lurking nameless and faceless in the dark shadows cast by the horrors they have committed? They must never know!"

"The professors aren't here," I assured him. "We're alone, just as you asked."

"And what of him?" He pointed a withered hand to Nicholas, shouting, "Are you listening, whelp? Are you spying?"

Without turning, Nicholas icily replied, "I've heard more than enough fantasy from you, sir. Your ravings don't remotely interest me."

But Father hadn't heard. His lips moved constantly, yet the words they strove to form were clear only if I strained to concentrate, and even then they made no sense. "Ha! Crown ... Crown ... Frown ... Flown ... Like a crow that has flown. A scrawny, greedy crow, black all over with claws to scratch, and a great black beak, sitting on a dead branch, pecking at the corpse's eyes. A murder of crows! Ha, ha! But why crow of murder? There has been enough of it done, damn their eyes! Thine eyes hath seen the glory of the coming of ... well, not the Lord ... the gory glory of the dawning of something that should have slumbered still 'neath ancient deeps... *'Far, far beneath in the abysmal sea, His ancient, dreamless, uninvaded sleep...'* But what if he no longer sleepeth, but

130

wakes and opens his mighty eyes? The eyes that shall see all that is to come, if they can but blind themselves to the warning of all that has gone before.... Had the captain truly seen through those long-sunken eyes, he would have scuttled the ship and drowned his deadly cargo once more, rather than bring it and the infection it bore ashore.... If he saw? The fool saw no further than the end of his own damned journey! Damn his eyes, and the Devil's eyes too!"

His own eyes glazed, and my heart lurched as I feared that he had gone. But even then a sudden clarity seemed to dawn in his gaze. As if waking suddenly he looked up at me in surprise, crying, "Eleanor, you're here, my child?"

"I am here, of course. Father, you're not making any sense. Try to concentrate. You have something you want to tell me."

"All this time ... All this long, long time, I was looking for it.... And it ..." These are the words I struggle now to recall, yet I know that they registered with me at the time, for I can still remember their utterly perplexing nature, and the helpless confusion I felt as I pondered on them. But I was given little time to question such things then, for my poor father's voice had grown ever more indistinct, and he slumped back into his pillow worn out by the effort of speech. I had to lean so close to hear them that his breath brushed my ear, and I could feel the clammy dampness from his skin upon my own, as he finally whispered, "Remember your sworn promise. Don't ever tell them ... don't deserve ... Never tell ..."

I wanted to protest that I didn't understand what any of it meant, but my father tore at his chest, heaving in a great sucking breath. His clawed hand pointed toward the windows, as a sudden peal of thunder crashed beyond them and lightning flared across the darkened sky.

"Please, Nicholas," I cried, as a strong wind gusted around the room, rustling the pages of so many fallen books that they fluttered like the enormous wings of strange white moths. "Close the windows."

131

But even as my brother did as I asked, straining against them to shut the gathering storm outside, Father gasped, "No! Not that! The ... the Devil ..." And then, as a final look of agony transfixed his ruined face, he fell still, and silent, and dead.

The approaching storm, the flapping of pages and wafting papers, and the last wheezing rattle from my father's chest, all faded to a silence alleviated only by the gentle ticking of an ancient clock, as the windows slammed shut and the swirling gusts abated. For an instant I considered that those winds had been the movements of some invisible force—an angel, although conceivably a dark one—and as they had blown through the sickroom, they had gathered Father's soul and carried it off as they departed. Then that thought itself fled, and a numbness froze me in that one instant of pure, inescapable loss, so that I didn't even hear Nicholas hurry to my side, or feel him lay his hand upon my shoulder. I was only dimly aware of his gentle words, before my own words, sounding distant and as if spoken by another mouth, reached my ear. "He's gone, Nicholas. Our father is dead."

"Yes. I'm sorry."

"Are you? Are you really?" The bitterness in the accusation was so startling that it shocked me back to my senses, and I flung my arms around my poor brother and sobbed. "Oh, I'm sorry, Nicholas. I'm so sorry! But the things he said! 'The circle of blood'? And such talk of murder! Could he really have been...?"

"Don't even think that. It was all just delusion. The illness robbed him of his reason. It was his own body that failed him, nothing more than that. His precious 'work' finally consumed him. Now we must forget about that and make his final arrangements."

"Must you always be so damn practical? Can I not have even one moment to mourn him?" Nicholas pulled back, stung by my anger, for which I could only apologise to him later. In that instant I merely wished to sit with Father, or what had once been my father, at any rate.

There came a gentle knock at the door, and Nicholas swiftly strode up the steps, opening it on Professor Rollistone, who enquired, with a smile in his voice, "Is there anything we can get him?"

"My father is dead, sir."

"Oh, my poor boy! Your sister! Dear Oscar," exclaimed Professor Rollistone, a babble of sympathy flowing as he moved down the stairs, bearing down upon me.

Professor Flagstaff, followed in his friend's wake, his head bowed, lamenting, "I am so, so sorry, my boy. So sorry. Such a dreadful thing."

Nicholas moved smoothly between these gentlemen and myself, before Professor Rollistone could sweep me up into some ghastly embrace.

"My poor girl. Such a waste. Such a catastrophic waste." Taking my hand instead, he declared, "If, somehow, there is any small way in which we can be of help at this terrible time...?"

Scurrying to stand by his friend's side, Flagstaff nodded vigorously. "Yes, indeed. Anything at all. You must not hesitate to ask."

Withdrawing my hand from Professor Rollistone's plump, rather damp grip, I replied, "You are both very generous."

"Nothing of the sort, Miss Wexley," Flagstaff protested. "This is a most tragic event. You shall want time to grieve, oh, yes, of course you shall. But there's always so much that needs done. Awful tragedy, dear, dear. Poor Oscar."

"Sirs," announced Nicholas briskly, "the arrangements will be made for the transfer of my father's remains to a chapel of rest. But first, I should take my sister home."

"I'm so very sorry your visit was concerned with such sad circumstances. I can only imagine how painful it was to see your dear father's sad condition. You mustn't dwell too much on all he may have said. But I know how much it must mean, to have been with him at the final moment. And I hope he had some final words of comfort for you."

There was in his gaze, now I think on it, something searching, and some sense of probing in his tone. "I'm sorry, Professor Rollistone. You have been most courteous, but I would like to get some air. Excuse me." I drew my coat tight, though I was too numb to feel either warmth or chill, and stood watching the threatening clouds from the garden doors.

"Oh, but there is such a storm building," Professor Rollistone protested. "Would you not prefer to remain here overnight? My home may not look much, but I've not quite forgotten how to provide guests with a degree of comfort."

"Our cab is waiting and we shall be dry enough on the train back to London. Failing that, there's a station hotel which will suit until morning. My sister would find it painful to remain here, I think."

"Indeed, Mr. Wexley," nodded Professor Flagstaff. "The poor young lady must have rest. Don't you think? Hubert?"

"Certainly. Dear Eleanor must be terribly upset. To see her father in such a way." Reaching to clutch Nicholas by the sleeve, again the professor allowed that questing tone to creep into his voice. "Did he regain his good senses? Was he able to give any helpful words, to you or your sister?"

Nicholas strode across to join me at the windows, turning back only to announce, "No, sir. He did not. My father remained, as he always has been, a man of little sense with nothing worthwhile to say. Good night, gentlemen."

And thus we departed, my last glance back before we turned the corner and returned to the coach being the figures of Professors Rollistone and Flagstaff standing framed in the window, grimly watching the lightning flash across the sky and heralding the oncoming storm.

"And that," said Eleanor Wexley, standing shivering before our sitting room window as if even now looking out upon that bleak and tempestuous vista rather than the altogether sunnier aspect of Baker Street, "is the sad story of my father's last moments, and of my one and only visit to the grim and unhealthy Oldmire Priory."

"Ah," replied Holmes, as he reached a long arm for his Bradshaw and deftly located the train times northwards to Harewynd, "your one and only visit thus far."

Chapter 9: An Official Caller

It was early evening before our train drew close to the small town of Harewynd—a settlement of whose very existence I had not, until that morning, even been aware—where we intended to interview the decidedly eccentric-sounding Professor Hubert Rollistone. Several hours later than we had anticipated that morning, it transpired, but in certain respects it seems a wonder we got there at all.

Even though Eleanor Wexley had finished recounting her sad tale in what Holmes was to describe as "admirably comprehensive and minute detail," there yet remained the frustrating gap in her memory concerning that last, urgent message entrusted to her. As there could be little doubt that these words related to some business in which the late Oscar Wexley had shared joint involvement with Professors Flagstaff and Rollistone, Holmes had decreed that it was with the latter, whose address we at least knew, that we were most likely to find the next scrap of information to build up his picture of the case. Yet even with this decision swiftly made and agreed to, if rather more readily by

Miss Wexley than myself, there had been much to do before we could make the journey.

While I would not willingly have lost her charming company, I had nevertheless been far from keen to bring Eleanor Wexley with us as we travelled into further potential danger. Sherlock Holmes, conversely, was of the opinion that the young lady's presence was imperative, declaring that Professor Rollistone would otherwise be entirely within his rights to refuse to entertain a pair of total strangers who turned up upon his secluded doorstep armed with a list of queries yet no official investigative credentials. He was also of the belief that her return to the scene of the tragedy might spark the concealed memory of her father's final, vital words.

I was unable to argue with my friend's logic, but there was another who could. How would Nicholas Wexley react to our proposal? Especially since Holmes made it abundantly clear that he did not desire Mr. Wexley's company on our journey, considering it likely that the young man's attitude toward his father's erstwhile colleagues might lead to significant difficulties. He also intimated that the knowledge we sought could put us at risk, therefore the fewer persons for whose safety he felt responsible, the better. It was this latter assertion that once again led me to question Miss Wexley's determination to accompany us.

It was not a question she was slow in answering. "John," said she, levelly, "Do I seem to you a witless, whimpering, helpless child?"

"Of course not. Far from it, indeed."

"Last night I believed myself to be wandering in infernal territory, beset by the spirits of the dead, in a realm where even my own father had turned upon me and threatened to drag me down into the abyss. If I can survive such an onslaught of terrors without finding myself permanently reduced to an hysterical wreck, I'm entirely confident that I can face an elderly scholar in his gloomy den. Just as I can face my dear brother and explain my choice to remain close by the man," she smiled, "rather, to remain close by the *men* who seem to offer my one clear chance of finding the truth about what has been set loose upon me. Yes, I am confident, and I would be even more so if I knew that you, too, had confidence in me."

"My dear Miss Wexley," I began, and I fixed her with an earnest gaze. "My dear Eleanor, I have every faith in you."

"Thank you, John." She squeezed my hand once more, and smiled with such radiance that I entirely forgot for one moment the dark forces that worked against us. Then she released my fingers, donned her hat, fastened her jacket, and declared, "Then I shall set off now to inform Nicholas of our intentions."

Despite our lovely guest's insistence that she was more than capable of returning home to face her brother unaccompanied, I was glad of Holmes's support in my decision to travel with her, lest she should encounter any unexpected delayed response to the drug that may yet have lurked dormant in her system. And so, with my medical bag in one hand and her delicate hand once more in the other, we stepped out to summon a cab to take us to Battersea. Though I was not then in practice, it was still my habit to keep a small medical supply to hand should an emergency present itself, and while this was an entirely different form of emergency to any I had envisioned, my revolver packed in amongst the bandages and powders might yet have proved an effective preventative. I was more than pleased to share the short trip with this lady, as the truth—which must be readily apparent by now to my unknown future reader—was that I found Miss Eleanor Wexley singularly entrancing.

I make no idle boast when I restate a previously published claim to an experience of women which extends over many nations and three—in actual fact, since that claim saw print, now four—separate continents. But in this young woman I found not only beauty, which can often prove so deceptively shallow, but also a certain nobility, and a bravery which I found quite extraordinary. Already the events that had so horribly upset her the previous night seemed to belong to a distant past. Seated opposite me now was a hearty, enquiring companion, with many questions about that adventure Sherlock Holmes and I had previously shared, and about the remarkable methods he had employed to reach a solution where normal police procedures had failed. Any slight twinges of jealousy I may fleetingly have felt toward my fellow-lodger as Miss Wexley exclaimed her admiration for his incredible expertise and fortitude was softened greatly by her repeated praise of my account of the case. "Perhaps," said she, blushing mildly, "one day soon you will find yourself writing of me and this astonishing adventure which has thrown us so dramatically together."

"Perhaps," said I, not daring to admit that on my bedside table lay the notebook in which I had already begun detailing the case, and where I had filled page after page with hopeless attempts to put into words the beauty and grace I saw in one of the interested parties. "Perhaps," I repeated, little knowing in my happy expectancy quite how many decades would pass before I would find myself fulfilling that notion.

All too soon, we had reached our destination. Having assured me that she proposed only to inform her brother of her intention to assist our quest over the next few days, and also to pack a few items of clothing, Miss Wexley skipped down from the cab, ran up the front steps and disappeared through her front door. I have no idea how long I stared at that doorway, as I drifted into a vivid daydream—one far removed from the grotesque and gore-drenched nightmare that had plagued me only hours before, the chief feature of this reverie being sunshine, warmth, laughter and, I admit, my recent companion and her soft, smiling lips—from whose embrace I awoke with an unpleasant start.

How long had it been since Eleanor Wexley had left my sight? Far longer than was necessary to throw some clothing into a case and bid her brother farewell, that was certain! Perhaps our client had objected to the proposed plan of action. I had seen and heard enough of Nicholas Wexley to recognise him as a most determined fellow, and one whose determination was backed up by a quick and fiery temper. Even now, I considered, he might be refusing to let his sister leave, or demanding that he too should accompany us, as surely he was as involved in this intrigue surrounding his family as any other! I strained, listening for raised voices in the full pitch of a bitter argument, for I had no doubt the brother's temperament and the sister's determination were an even match. I heard no voices. Nor any sounds at all save for the rattle of passing vehicles, a dull, persistent brushing of a street sweeper's broom, and the hooting of boats on the Thames, not so far away.

I fervently wished that I might consider this a good sign, but instead asked myself whether Holmes could have been mistaken in his assumption that the house was safe. Might not the woman I was supposed to be protecting have entered her home to find her brother a captive, the bait in some trap, or worse? Might she not, by entering that supposed safe haven, have fallen directly into the clutching grasp of those who pursued her with such ferocious cunning?

I was already out of the cab, fumbling within my medical bag as my hand sought my revolver, when the front door opened and, to my absolute relief and joy, sister and brother walked out, arm in arm, he carrying her small suitcase. I must have looked the perfect fool, standing gawping up at them from the pavement, my fists balled and ready to strike at imaginary abductors. I only concealed my embarrassment by kneeling to gather up the pills and draughts my fumbling with the bag had dislodged, snatching them from the path of the overzealous street sweeper, who regarded me as if I were a stumbling drunkard as I leapt in front of his brush. I may have groaned aloud as my leg bent stiffly beneath me, for Eleanor, rushing to help me gather my scattered supplies from the gutter, looked at me with some concern. "Just a minor twinge. It's only truly agony in the cold weather," said I, referring to my old wound through gritted teeth.

"But from what you wrote I gathered it was your shoulder that was injured?"

"Well, I was recounting an adventure yarn, not writing a medical journal," I shrugged. "And I chose to be selective. Boasting of two gunshot wounds may have shown me either as a braggart, claiming a more intrepid military career for myself than warranted, or as a clumsy, luckless oaf, which is closer to the truth of the matter."

"Hardly that," said she, handing me the last roll of bandages, and using that brief moment of contact to gently ease me to my feet. Upright again, I was greeted by Nicholas Wexley's warm, firm handshake, as he expressed understandable wonder at all that had occurred between his arrival on Baker Street the previous morning and now. He had already, with astute efficiency, sent word to both his and his sister's respective employers stating that there was illness in the house which kept both from their desks, and he was confident that he could prolong the pretence for the few days necessitated by Eleanor's absence.

As I took the suitcase and placed it within the cab, I gave brother and sister a moment while they hugged lovingly and she promised to take every care while away. I myself gave Mr. Wexley my oath that no harm would befall his younger sister, and with that promise hanging in the air, we shook hands yet again and parted company.

As we sped back to Baker Street, I imagined Holmes would be less than impressed by our tardiness, though I was in no genuine hurry to end the journey. Miss Wexley seemed in even better humour than before, and she smiled pleasurably when I finally commented on her change of attire—her fresh clothing, while not quite the latest fashion, being far more suited to country activities. "It is one of Mother's old outfits. Well, as a city dweller since childhood I haven't had much call for country dress."

I was beginning to find her strength of character a tonic following my weeks of worry, and also quite infectious. Let Holmes gripe over our prolonged absence, I thought. I will spurn his complaints as he was wont to do with mine. Let him see how he enjoys the boot being on the other foot. Thus emboldened I was, therefore, quite irrationally irked to find neither hide nor hair of him when we arrived back at our rooms.

As Mrs. Hudson informed us, "Mr. Holmes went marching out just shortly after your departure with the young lady. No, as usual, he gave no clue as to where he was going, nor when, indeed if, he would return." I could not even enjoy the further time this gave me with Miss Wexley, since my landlady took it into her head that the young lady would benefit greatly from a large lunch, numerous cups of tea, and generally being fussed over, while she herself set about making up a hamper for the rail journey that lay ahead of us.

I had almost given up on the afternoon as a total loss, when Holmes entered our rooms at a positive gallop, his eyes sparkling in a way that I had not witnessed since our last case, and with not a word about where he had spent his morning. Instead, he flung himself again upon his Bradshaw, declared that we had only a few moments to spare if we wanted to catch the northbound train to Harewynd and, bustling the startled woman abruptly from the room, ordered Mrs. Hudson to summon a cab.

But as she turned just as abruptly back, a strong word or two already on her pursed lips, our landlady's eyes swept past her impertinent lodger and she cried, "There'll be no cab going anywhere, unless it is to hospital. Dr. Watson, the poor girl!"

Before I could reach her, Miss Wexley, who had a mere moment before been smiling and chatting quite contentedly, dropped back in a swoon onto the couch, her hand to her forehead and her face ghostly pale. "Eleanor, what is it?"

With trembling hands she shooed me back. "I'll be all right. Please, I just need a moment or two. It's just a passing spell of dizziness."

"Watson, prescribe," Holmes instructed, with an impatient gesture toward my medical bag. "Otherwise we either must postpone our visit, which leaves our enemies a clear advantage, or else I leave you to minister to the patient, while I alone call on Professor Rollistone. Miss Wexley will surely pen a few words to vouch for me."

"That won't be necessary," said she, already up on her feet. "I told you it would pass. You may call that cab now, thank you, Mrs. Hudson."

"But what was it? Did you encounter any nausea, or blurring of vision?"

"It was just a moment of silliness," said she, and she granted me a terse and fleeting smile. "I thought, just fleetingly, that I saw a shadow in the doorway, behind Mr. Holmes. No, it was nothing threatening. More wishful thinking, and an over-tired imagination, for I thought ..." She breathed a sigh filled with feeling. "I thought I saw my father. Not like that dreadful phantom last night, but as if he were looking in on me, reassuring me that we are taking the right path. I'm so glad that we are taking it together."

I packed just as much as I had time for, my medical bag and its deadly contents squeezed into the corner of my suitcase, and was ready in the sitting room within minutes. But there was to be one more hindrance to our movements before we had even set foot outside our own rooms, and it came with a sharp knock upon our door and the arrival of a most unexpected visitor.

I have at times referred to Inspector Lestrade as rat-like in appearance, and this, I admit, is something of a harsh description. It is one to which the inspector himself has made frequent rueful allusions over the years in which our friendship has grown, usually when he wishes to make me squirm with embarrassment in good-natured revenge for the earlier slights of our sometimes volatile association. However, in this instance I can declare with all fairness that the twitching of his nose as he attempted to displace, or perhaps delay, a grin of triumph most certainly did lend him the appearance of an overgrown rodent. The grin, I would also discover, signified that the Scotland Yarder believed himself to be a step or two ahead of Mr. Sherlock Holmes, and that he knew something that the unofficial detective as yet did not.

"Mr. Holmes," said he as he stood in the sitting room doorway, surveying all present. "And, it is Dr.— ah, yes— Watson, if memory serves? Oh, forgive me, miss, I didn't notice you there. Inspector Lestrade of Scotland Yard. How do you do? Is this a bad time, Holmes? I hope I'm not interrupting you?"

"It is," confirmed Sherlock Holmes, "and you are."

"Well, I shall come straight to the heart of the matter."

Holmes's expression suggested that such would be a novelty, and that suggestion was borne out as the noticed our suitcases and attire, and smirked, "You're not fleeing the city, are you, Mr. Holmes?"

"Merely a business matter to attend to, Lestrade," Holmes replied, irked yet still mildly curious as to whatever it was that was not yet being said. "Business which is rather urgent, so unless you have any genuine point to make with this visit, we must bid a very good day to you."

"Only," continued the official, as if Holmes had not spoken, "there is something rather, well, rather strange that has come up that I felt certain must be of interest to you. I should rather say 'someone' than 'something', of course."

"Someone?" I prompted, eliciting a frown of disapproval from Holmes.

"At the Yard, it was. Was and still is. This someone, I mean, for he's still there. Most peculiar set of circumstances, too, for he burst in during the night banging on desks and kicking up a fuss, and demanding protection."

"Lestrade, I really don't have time to consider this," cried Holmes, "and for your future reference, I do not lightly offer my services as a bodyguard."

"He had run, he says, all the way from the East End, and was so out of breath from it that my sergeant was an hour or more fetching the story out of him. I reckon you'd be able to trace his steps in scorched shoe-leather from Scotland Yard back to Cyrus Road."

"Cyrus Road?" demanded Holmes, impatience switching seamlessly to anticipation.

"From the old derelict assembly rooms and hall. Quite a trot, wouldn't you say? Though hardly surprising when you hear that this terrified fellow had a pack of ghouls on his tail. Yes, gentlemen—and your pardon, please, miss—pursued by 'ravening, blood-sucking ghouls', to use his exact words. Well, he was a little heated in his excitement, and prone to fantasy and exaggeration, I should warrant. Very theatrical, you could say. But the thing that brought me along to Baker Street, certain of finding a fellow who could provide the key to this most curious business, is this. These ghouls that he sought bed and board in one of our most impenetrable cells to escape were, he swears, set upon him by an archfiend! And he ..."

"'He'? Surely you mean 'she', Lestrade?"

"No, most definitely it was a man—or a fiend in the shape of a man, if you want to take the fellow's view—that he spoke of."

I caught Holmes's keen glance and knew that he had already reached the same conclusion that I had now formed, and that the snivelling Vincent Fitzhugh had surely meant the Contessa's mysterious accomplice whom he had last night denied ever meeting. "Did he offer any description of the man he feared?"

"That's the mysterious part. He offered not one, but *two* very vivid descriptions, claiming this sorcerer had the power to switch appearances at will. Now what evil might a man commit who possesses sufficient diabolical skills to become first one man and then another, and who can tell how many more, and pass undetected among normal folk? But you will no doubt be wondering at this devilish adversary's name?"

"You have his name?" I cried. "But this is marvellous!"

"His *names*, as I believe the inspector is about to reveal," said Holmes with a dejected groan that baffled me almost as much as did Lestrade's absurd chortle of utter pleasure.

"You begin to catch on, Mr. Holmes," he grinned and clapped his hands gleefully. "Would you care to name your suspects?"

"The first name will have been Jasper Montague," began Holmes.

"A most insalubrious sort, I gather, of quite revolting habits. And the other," crowed Lestrade, "was Mr. Sherlock Holmes!"

"These ghouls," said Holmes confidentially to Miss Wexley and I, while the little inspector wriggled helplessly in his mirth, "are the overly dramatic Fitzhugh's former cohorts, seeking their lost wages. But coward though he may be, he is unlikely to have revealed the extent of his own activities, and nor should we if we wish to set foot aboard any train today."

Turning a beaming grin strategically on the official, Holmes told him, "Yes, you caught me out there. Very well done, Lestrade. You would have certainly proved them wrong at the Opera Comique recently, when they sang so vigorously of a policeman's lot not being a happy one. I did, in fact, run into your current guest, Mr. Vincent Fitzhugh, in the course of some minor misdemeanour or other, and I may have used a little method of my own to shock him off the dark path toward deeper perdition. But that case is closed without incident, and we have other matters that press, as you can see."

"Well," laughed the inspector as he showed himself out, "whatever chance it was that brought your path and that scoundrel's to a crossroads, I'm grateful for it. For he'll be sitting safe in that cell for some time to come, as there's a writ of breach of promise against him under that name of Fitzhugh you spoke of, plus half a dozen charges under as many other identities of conning besotted old landladies out of their savings and a few provincial theatre managers out of their takings. It seems that your Mr. Jasper Montague is not the only man who can change his name to suit his devious ends."

"And was there anything more, Lestrade? You didn't just pop in to amuse yourself at my expense."

"Just passing through. For some of us the solving of mysteries is a full time profession. Well, you enjoy your little jaunt, and don't worry, Mr, Holmes. While I know you think the whole of the Metropolitan Police Force will be lost without you to take our hands and lay them on clues and point our heads toward evidence you fear we might miss, I'm *tolerably* confident I can handle any simple little bits of business that come along. And speaking of which, I don't have time to stand around here now we've all had our laugh. Good day to you, gentlemen. Good day, miss."

And as the Scotland Yard man went off, finally, about his business, still chuckling at his own merciless wit, it was Eleanor who brightened our own moods by suggesting, "I think my most marvellous escape was not as you rescued me from those phantoms, Mr. Holmes, but that Nicholas could not persuade Scotland Yard to take my case." Sherlock Holmes and I exchanged a blank glance as her innocent expression broke into a sly smile before simultaneously exploding with laughter. And I was still laughing as I found myself in short succession in a cab, and then upon the northbound platform of King's Cross Station.

The great engine's rising roar and the guard's impatient whistle were second in urgency to Holmes's cry of, "Despite Lestrade's untimely jest, our schedule will stand, if we can just pick up our pace a little. Come along, Watson!"

I said nothing, conserving my energies for trying to lift my awkwardly limping gait to a run. I was both embarrassed and grateful when Miss Wexley hooked her arm into mine, her own pace brisk. I say 'embarrassed', as I was then still gauche enough to believe that a man ought to bear his injuries silently and without fuss wherever possible, but 'grateful' because this simple act of kindness seemed to reach beyond that embarrassment and tell me that this other belief was foolish and outmoded.

Then, very abruptly, we were no longer moving, and she stood rigid, her head craning back toward the mass of travellers flowing between platforms. "John," she cried. "Mr. Holmes! We're being followed! We're being watched! She's here! No, please don't look at me as if I'm imagining it. It's not like earlier, and I'm very much alert! And I saw her, the Contessa Nascosta, standing right there, where we have just passed. A tall figure, all in black from top to toe, with her face veiled. Although even with that dark lace masking her face, I could sense she was watching us!"

Holmes's suitcase landed at my feet as he sprinted back along the platform, his head snapping from side to side as he scanned the throng for that sinister, draped figure, before plunging headlong into the crowd. How long had she been our unseen shadow? Or had she not followed us, but instead anticipated our movements? Was she, too, journeying north to call upon the man we sought? And, if so, was she visiting as an ally, or as a deadly stranger?

I tried to keep my stick to the fore as I juggled with my additional baggage, lest it be needed as a weapon or form of defence, and searched for any sign of Holmes in that great, noisy chamber with its constantly shifting tide of bodies. At my back, carriage doors slammed with finality, and the whistle blew one last time. "Holmes," I yelled, my voice drowned by the movement of enormous pistons and the building clamour of steel wheels upon iron track. Had my friend emerged from the crowds at that instant, I felt that we might have just made it aboard, safe in the knowledge that the Contessa would be unable to follow on the same train.

When Holmes did return a bitterly disappointed expression clouded his face, and the distant, echoing vibration in the tracks and the smell of soot and steam were the only lingering traces of our intended transport.

"The Contessa?" began Eleanor Wexley, her reply coming back with a shake of Holmes's head. "I didn't imagine her. There was a veiled woman, I swear."

"I don't question what you saw, Miss Wexley, for I saw her too. A tall woman dressed as if in mourning. I followed her as best I could without attracting unwanted attention by barging my way through the swarm. I'm glad I opted to hold back and observe, rather than attempt to apprehend her, however, for when she re-joined her companions I saw from their own sombre attire and dismal expressions that the woman had good reason to be dressed in mourning. Yes, Watson, it's only by a narrow margin that I avoided launching an assault on a funeral party just returned by train from the Great Northern Cemetery at Barnet." Holmes snatched up his suitcase with all the good grace of a child wishing for Christmas who has just been reminded it is still October, and as we marched back to wait for the next north-easterly train, I distinctly heard him grumble, "I may have to alter my opinion on the effectiveness of curses, as this day's travel arrangements appear so far to have been decidedly ill-fated."

Chapter 10: Three on the Trail

The minutes and hours having flown past as steadily as the towns and cities, fields and pastures, and those occasionally glimpsed shimmering stretches of sea beyond our train compartment's windows, the dotted lights of surrounding farms and more concentrated cluster of illumination spilling into the darkening sky above the town itself could now be clearly seen as the train slowed into the rural station of Harewynd.

With Holmes having chosen his pipe over conversation, I was relieved to step out of the smoggy compartment and into the clean country air. Miss Wexley looked less eager than I, but she had no reason to think of the place fondly. She pointed out the building across from the station, The Harewynd Halt Hotel, and grimaced at the memory of its cold comforts as she had found herself an unwilling guest there on the night of her father's passing, and abandoned to its gloomy hospitality still throughout much of the following day while her brother had consulted the local doctor and made funeral arrangements. Thus, to Holmes's declaration that we should deposit our luggage at the nearest hotel then depart immediately for Oldmire Priory,

I had insisted instead upon a short walk to exercise my cramped limbs, during which I kept a keen eye peeled for any other comfortable looking inns with less unhappy associations.

Thankfully this took no real time at all, as a likely looking establishment stood just beyond a pleasant, tree-lined village green, and, our baggage checked and a cab summoned, within an hour of our arrival at Harewynd we found ourselves deposited on the doorstep of that unusual and uninviting house so recently described to us by our companion. In her wholly reasonable concern for her father, she had not taken in just how odd a dwelling it seemed from the outside. While the bricks above were the dark grey of wet granite or rain-slicked slates, the walls of the lower levels were so furred with moss that it seemed like a mass of damp, green caterpillars were swarming up the building. That sensation of moist unhealthiness was not lessened when I caught sight of an enormous snail, slowly oozing itself up the glass panes of one of the darkened windows.

While the coach horses stamped and whinnied, impatient to be out of the Priory's crooked shadow, Holmes knocked smartly at the weathered old door, the knocker's loud retort echoing away into the murky heart of the house. With Eleanor Wexley close by my side, I fought the urge to reach for her hand—in a gesture purely of comfort, naturally, for this was the house in which her father had died before her eyes. But my sidelong glances showed that she stood with her head upraised, her entire manner resolute, and she met my gaze with a quick, tight smile.

The pair of eyes that peered out at us when the door at last opened were blue and watery, and flickered rapidly between us from within deep creases above plump, rosy cheeks. This was a face accustomed to smiling, those creases declared, and the grin that broke out upon finally recognising our young companion confirmed that supposition. "Young Miss Wexley, my dear girl! Come in!

Come along in, do," cried Professor Hubert Rollistone, and we followed the bobbing motion of the oil lamp in his hand as he led us along twisting corridors made all the narrower for the overflowing shelves and bundles of books that lined the way. So many of these chaotic piles were there, and so deep the shadows all around, that I was never entirely confident that my stick would not disturb some dark-dwelling creature that had made its nest somewhere deep in the jumble.

The door our host flung open at the end of this slow procession led onto the small, railed balcony overlooking the library, just as cluttered and crowded with obscure and esoteric objects as we had heard, though with one notable exception. As she nodded to a space on the floor only marginally less overrun by books, Eleanor Wexley whispered, "That was where Father's death bed had lain."

The library was in almost total darkness, the sky outside the glazed double doors a deep, dark purplish hue above the twisted trees and overgrown bushes, whose restless rustling could be faintly heard through the slight opening there. The additional candles the professor set about lighting were clustered mainly around the book-bedecked table, next to which a large, shabbily luxurious chair sat vacant. With a close-at-hand side table on which glasses, bottles and a water jug sat, these furnishings formed a neat little study within the larger room's depths.

The candles now lit, I caught my first proper view of Hubert Rollistone. The almost permanently affixed smile I already knew to expect, but the long, quilted dressing gown and slippers speckled with a myriad stitches and repairs of countless different colours and patterns, the battered fez, the pince-nez with their elaborate silver frames that hung at his neck, and the large and heavy rings that gleamed dully on several of his fingers, all conspired to add to the overall aura of eccentricity that may only have been the natural state of mind for any inhabitant of such a disordered house.

As I followed Eleanor Wexley down the short flight of stairs, Sherlock Holmes, senses keen, lingered a moment longer upon that narrow landing to survey as much as could be perceived in the dim light. As he gripped the railing, his pale face impassive above his dark overcoat and tightly wound scarf, he looked for all the world like some stern cleric glaring down from his pulpit onto a congregation amongst whom he suspected sin and ungodliness to be rife.

Our host turned his broad smile upon our fair companion, announcing, "Ever such a nice surprise, Miss Wexley. And I do trust that your visit to this corner of the land will have a happier outcome than your last. So sad, it was. So very sad. I would have come to the funeral, of course, but I so very rarely venture as far as London these days, and, besides, I would have only intruded upon your family's private time for thought and contemplation. Thus I did my grieving here. Oh, but what gloomy talk is this? You brighten the place admirably, dearest girl."

"I apologise for calling so late and unannounced, Professor," said Eleanor, who attempted to match the scholar's broad smile, but only shivered in spite of herself.

"Not at all, my child," insisted Rollistone, who shuddered himself as if in answer to a sudden chill in the air, and shuffled across to close the windows. "Think nothing of it. I was still quite awake. My books take up most of the night, you know. But I must apologise for leaving you waiting so long on my doorstep. And also for the rather dusty nature of this room. I'm afraid I lost my housekeeper some years ago. Wretched woman! The money ran out and so did she. All gone on books and the oil to read them by."

"There was certainly money at one point," remarked Holmes as he plucked a crescent-bladed dagger of some age and beauty from a shelf and he descended to join us. "Items such as these do not come from church bazaars or junk shops. But no photographs, I notice."

"Do these graven images strike you as my family portraits, sir? Or might this woodcut of the damned entering Hell through the mouth of a serpent strike you as a formal study of my faculty colleagues and friends? Well, ha-ha, that latter might err on accuracy. It would certainly fulfil my last wish for them after I departed their cloisters. But, no, I have no need of photography, for I have a memory instead, and it is well-exercised." Hubert Rollistone rather fussily placed his lamp on an exposed corner of the desk near the overstuffed chair, then returned his damp gaze to Miss Wexley. "You've brought friends, my dear. And I so rarely see visitors."

"This is Mr. Sherlock Holmes, who has been kind enough to help me in certain matters."

Rollistone nodded in greeting to my friend, before turning his face to me. "And this, I presume, is your young gentleman?" I can only imagine my cheeks burned bright enough to be seen in even so tenebrous a light, but I chiefly recall looking to Miss Wexley to judge her reaction, though I looked away again before I could fully read her expression. "Alas, I've embarrassed you. I do apologise."

"Not in the least, sir. In fact, you flatter me."

"This is Doctor John Watson," Eleanor smiled, "who has also been of the greatest assistance."

"A doctor?" A frown fought its way through the grin, and heavy rings clicked and chimed as Rollistone rubbed his hands anxiously together. "Oh, dearest Eleanor. I do hope you're not ill?"

."No, it's nothing like that, Professor."

Hubert Rollistone loudly sighed his relief, settled into his comfortable throne, and threw his arms wide. "Ah, then that is all well. But what brings you to my humble home? You surely haven't made this long trip from London's civilised climes to this remote outpost merely to see me?"

It was Holmes who replied, greeting the enquiry with one of his own. "Professor Rollistone, you knew and worked with Miss Wexley's late father for many years, did you not?"

"Yes, sir. That I did, as dear Eleanor has surely told you."

"And what is your particular field of study?"

"Mythology and folklore. A most fascinating field! An obsession, you might call it, though not, I'd hope, a monomania. There are too many other pleasures in the world to get affixed to just the one. But it has been an abiding interest since I was quite a child, and will follow me until my end of days. As a matter of fact," he grunted, rooting around among the mound of books on the table before him, "I was just reading a very interesting account of a mediaeval Norwegian tradition common amongst carpenters...."

"And what of Professor Flagstaff?"

"Flagstaff?" mused Rollistone, as if trying to dredge up a sunken memory. "Oh, I only met Ronald a couple of years ago. Quite a brilliant mind, and a jolly nice fellow, all in all, though an absolute bundle of nerves, and, strictly between us, possessed of virtually no sense of humour."

"His area of expertise being...?"

Rollistone peered sharply at both Holmes and me. "Sir, I do believe you're trying to interrogate me. I hope I'm not being excessively rude in asking what the deuce is going on?"

"Please, Professor, Mr. Holmes is acting on my behalf."

Hubert Rollistone raised a quizzical brow. "Ah, my girl? This mysterious business in which he is kind enough to help. Very well, Ronald Flagstaff was a professor of chemistry."

"An interesting little cabal," noted Holmes. "An archaeologist, a folklorist, and a chemist."

"No less intriguing than a charming young lady, a gallant doctor, and a ..." Rollistone raised his pince-nez to his pale eyes and inspected my friend. "What are you, sir? I can tell you're no policeman."

"As Miss Wexley has told you, I am helping her to clear up a small matter. It would also be of help if you could clear up some points for me."

Said Eleanor Wexley, earnestly, "I should not wish to cause you such trouble in your own home, but the matter is of the utmost importance."

"Then I shall do all that I can to assist. Ask what you must, and I will answer to the best of my ability. But you must be tired after your travels. Sit. Sit. I'm afraid there are only the two chairs, but Mr. Holmes seems a fit enough fellow."

I moved to pull out an old, plain wooden chair for Eleanor, but Holmes unobtrusively placed an arm in my path. Understanding the gesture, though not the meaning behind it, I took a backward step and Holmes removed the teetering books from the other chair, before presenting it to Eleanor. How long those books had occupied that chair was anyone's guess, as I saw my friend blow quite a cloud of dust from the topmost volume, before adding them to the mass of tomes already occupying the desk.

"Not sitting, Doctor?" Rollistone nodded toward my stout stick. "I see that your leg troubles you."

"I should prefer to stand. It doesn't do to avoid exertion."

"As you will, so be it. Now, Mr. Holmes, you may interrogate away."

"Thank you. I understand that the bout of pneumonia which claimed Oscar Wexley was brought on suddenly in a church at night."

"That is a statement of fact, not a question."

"Then let me phrase it in this manner; what were three eminent men, specialising in three different disciplines, attempting to discover on this nocturnal visit?"

"We didn't discover anything. Poor Oscar's condition put paid to that."

"That is not what I asked. What was the object of your quest?"

"A myth. Naught more. A clue to something which, as all evidence conspires to indicate, doesn't actually exist."

That smiling face and these riddling answers irked me, and I snapped, "You are being very vague, sir."

"That's quite all right, Watson. The deep-rooted rivalries that exist in academic circles make loose tongues a rarity. And, if anyone else had been making enquiries into your work, I believe that would also add to your caution, Professor."

"It would," admitted Rollistone gravely, before grinning once more, "if anyone *had* been making enquiries. I've mentioned that I don't often entertain callers, I believe? My house is isolated, as I like it to be and, apart from the old gossip in the village store, her lackwit son who drives out with the deliveries, and the postman with the latest book consignment, or bill for books previously consigned, I've seen no-one in weeks."

"You speak of a myth," said Holmes, undeterred. "That is your field. A search falls into the domain of the archaeologist."

"But where does a chemist fall into the equation? There, I fear, you are concocting a mystery around nothing, gentlemen. Our researches involved endeavours to decipher the tiniest scraps of clues in ancient manuscripts. Educated men such as your good selves will be aware, however, that even a parchment which was written by one single scholar or scribe hundreds of years ago can, in the course of time, have become the work of many hands. Ancient texts have been altered, rewritten, censored, corrupted, until the original meaning is all but obliterated. A hugely frustrating factor, naturally, for anyone hoping to decode the true message. But, were it to become possible, with the aid of chemicals, to lift away the added layers, one by one, until the original article lay revealed once more, would that not be a remarkable aid to our quest?"

It was rare that Sherlock Holmes so readily displayed his amazement and admiration, but both were clear as he exclaimed, "Professor Flagstaff had achieved such a feat?"

"Partial success only. But nothing remotely as crude as those awful efforts with ammonias and sulphurs or tincture of gall that have destroyed so many a tantalising palimpsest or codex. No, these are far subtler methods, and promising enough to have made Ronald an invaluable ally."

"Indeed," mused Holmes, his mind still filled with possibilities. "Yet your investigations yielded no result."

"How could it? We were old men chasing a chimera, following trails in the dust, and going round and round in circles."

"'The circle of blood ...'" In unison, we turned our eyes toward Eleanor Wexley, who seemed as startled as were we by the words she had just uttered.

"What was that, my girl?" enquired Hubert Rollistone. "Blood, did you say?"

Eleanor Wexley shook her head. "It was something my father said to me, just before he died."

"Really? A strange thing to speak of. But dear Oscar was far from coherent in his final hours. I'm sure he said many things which sounded odd to you."

"But not odd to you, Professor?" said I, pointedly.

"I would have thought blood was more in your line of expertise, Doctor."

"You are certainly a well-travelled man," declared Holmes, "as any observer might tell from the eclectic ornaments in this room." A sweep of his long arm took in gargoyle-faced statuettes and carved reliefs depicting obscure ceremonies, candlesticks shaped like coiled serpents, and ancient mariners' charts depicting horn-headed dragons and colossal aquatic beasts breaching the waves, their tentacles wrapping themselves around ships and dragging them to watery perdition. "Eclectic and arcane."

"Souvenirs, sir. Relics of a peripatetic existence. My travelling days are long over but, as you so rightly deduce, I have roved and roamed both far and wide. If one hopes to untangle the truths and the lies that intertwine to make up a legend, there's really only so much that can be achieved with books." So saying, Professor Rollistone hefted a compendious volume from the pile. "No, even the most thorough tomes only provide so much. To separate the strands, one must have first-hand knowledge of the environment from whence the mystery originates."

"I couldn't agree more. You have been to the Far East, India and China, Africa too," observed Holmes, and he indicated in turn the silks and screens and masks that spoke of these destinations. "But what of other lands? South America, perhaps? Or Italy?"

"Damn you!" With this furious cry and a thunderous crash, Rollistone slammed the thick volume violently down on the desktop. Miss Wexley and I both flinched, and we exchanged startled glances. But with a sickly grin the scholar raised the book, displaying the object of his curious ire. "Ha! Got you!" Messily adorning the leather covers was an enormous spider, its skinny legs crooked and kinked at crazy angles, its fat body even fatter, and infinitely flatter, than when it had dared venture across the surface of the desk. Its many-limbed remains put me strangely in mind of the great Krakens on the maps, and the tentacle-jawed figurines and carvings that lurked on shelves like grotesque miniature sentinels.

"I cannot abide spiders," said he, that last word whispered in disgust. "Never could, but it's been all the worse since I was caught in a cave-in during a dig in some tropical spot. As the dust drifted and I tried to make out what was around me in the rubble, I reached for what I thought was my guide's hand pushing through to help dig me out. Instead my fingers brushed against spiny fur, just as I saw those horrid, tiny black eyes glinting back at me. My heart turned to ice, and it still does every time the corner of my eye catches the movement of long, spindly legs. Which is why I've long-since left the digging to the archaeologists, and devoted myself to more theoretical pursuits, for it's an unfortunate condition for one whose calling might have led to a life raking through darkened ruins, and who now finds himself entombed alive in just such a place. Urgh! Dreadful brutes! Nothing really needs that many legs, surely!"

Discarding the book and its besmirched cover, Rollistone reached across to the side table. As the professor unstopped the brandy decanter, Sherlock Holmes raised his hand in silent warning to Eleanor and I; a gesture that went unnoticed by our host. "Forgive me, sir, you were asking after my travels. Well, I've spent most of my life on the move. So many countries, over more years than I care to admit. One loses track after a while. Never South America, though. I do know that. Do you know they have"—his fingers made a spiderish scuttling motion in lieu of the word—"grown large enough to eat birds? No houseflies or beetles for them. Ugh! Birds! If that doesn't make it sound a place forsaken by God, I cannot think what does. But travel makes me thirsty, and talk of it more-so. Would anyone care for a drink?"

"Not for me," said I, "thank you."

"I think," Holmes added, "Miss Wexley would appreciate a cup of tea?"

"Yes, indeed," agreed our companion, picking up instantly on Holmes's signal. "If that wouldn't be too much trouble."

"Tea? With biscuits, I suppose?"

"Tea will be sufficient, thank you," said Holmes, smilingly grateful.

"Just as well," huffed the professor as he mounted the steps and lit a candle retrieved from a shelf by the door. "There haven't been any biscuits since the housekeeper left. Excuse me a moment."

With our host's departure, I protested, "What is all this nonsense about tea, Holmes? The man is being deliberately unhelpful, and you are letting him get away with it. Why don't you demand a straight answer, so we can get Miss Wexley out of this gloomy place?"

"You mustn't fret on my account, John," she assured me.

I pulled out the unoccupied chair and was just lowering myself to sit when Holmes raised an abrupt hand, crying out, "What are you doing, man?"

"My leg aches. I was just about to rest it."

As he pushed past me and stooped to examine the seat of the chair, Holmes admonished, "You were just about to destroy a valuable potential clue. Hah! As I thought." Then, leaping smartly to his feet, he demanded, "What is unusual about this chair?"

I peered at length at the shiny wooden surface, then finally admitted, "There's nothing remotely unusual, as far as I can see. What do you expect me to find?"

"Something which is all around us," replied Holmes as he ran his forefinger along the edge of the desktop and raised it in the air, "on every shelf and surface."

"Dust? But there is none."

"Precisely! Just as the posts on an unused boarding house bed will rapidly gather dust, so a used chair will not. Thus indicating that Professor Rollistone has not led as reclusive a life as he wishes us to believe. All right, Watson. You may sit, now."

"How very kind," I muttered, and I lowered myself onto the seat only once I was certain it was not to be snatched out from under me again.

"Here," Holmes called, and he threw a slim, compact, red-bound book to me. "Read this aloud."

"Which part?"

"That is unimportant."

Perplexed, I opened the book and squinted at the pages of neatly handwritten text. "Let's see ... '*The train grows ...*' No, no, '*The trail grows even ... grows ever colder with each damn ...*' Oh, I do beg your pardon, my dear! '*... with each dawn ...*' No, it's no use. Pass the lamp, would you?"

"Thank you, Watson. I've heard quite enough."

"Well, I haven't! Not nearly enough. You really have lost me this time, Holmes."

"And me," admitted Eleanor Wexley.

Holmes moved swiftly to the bookcases, examining spines, running slim fingers along the shelves to snatch up volumes apparently at random, sporadically darting up and down the rolling library ladders to reach higher placed volumes, and all the while he called back over his shoulder to us. "Hubert Rollistone is a creature of habit. As the upholstery of that rather ugly armchair shows, that is his preferred vantage point. His posture betrays the fact that he spends his waking hours hunched over his books, which also accounts for his poor eyesight, as shown by the spectacles he wears around his neck. Now, even if he were to abandon his favoured chair to peruse a volume, it seems unlikely that he would choose one in which reading is impossible, as your own keen eyesight's struggle with the text in that book just demonstrated. But could he not have moved the lamp, you will ask? No, he could not, as the layer of dust on that one exposed spot upon his desktop reveals that the lamp sits in its fixed position, thus bringing us neatly back to the fact that he is a man of regular habit. The deductions follow a circular pattern."

"Brilliant, Mr. Holmes," cried Eleanor Wexley through a broad smile. "Quite brilliant!"

"Not in the least. It was quite ... Watson, you fancy yourself as a man of words. How would you describe it?"

I considered carefully, before replying, "I would describe it as... yes, as 'elementary'...."

"My dear Watson! You have hit the nail squarely on the head once again. That is exactly the word. Elementary!"

"Thank you, Holmes," I grinned, though he was far too busily engaged in his inspection of the shelves to note my joy. I tossed the red book on top of the morass on the desk and said. "And, if it's not too elementary a point, might I ask what you're doing now?"

"Wait, Dr. Watson!" Miss Wexley darted to the desk to snatch up that same volume. Then, with a series of short gasps she flipped rapidly through its pages, and finally declared, "This is my father's journal!"

I struggled hastily to my feet, and joined Eleanor over the book. "Are you sure?"

"Of course I'm sure," she retorted sharply, before hastily adding, in a far gentler manner, "Forgive me,

John. But I can tell you that this is certainly my father's work. There are many further volumes like it in his study at home."

"I thought his study was locked. According to your brother, it remains closed up and unvisited."

"It's my brother who keeps it locked. You must know by now how he regarded our father's life's work. But I spent many an hour in there sharing his wonderment and enthusiasm for our vast world. He used to read extracts to me from his notebooks and diaries, and, when I was old enough, I'd read them for myself. I may not recognise this precise volume, but I know Father's writing, and I know this is certainly his."

"What have you there?" enquired Holmes, who placed down the disparate selection of books he had gathered and addressed his keen eyes to the single volume we held between us.

"Somehow Professor Wexley's journal has found its way here." I cursorily scanned the page it had fallen open to and read, "'*Romford or Venicciano? Which speaks the truth, if either?*'" I leafed smartly through the pages, then paused again at a heavily underlined entry. "'*Bosworthy, 347, dash, 695, lies, lies! Idiot!*' Look here, where the pen has torn the page. What does it mean?"

"'*347, dash, 695*'?" repeated Eleanor. "A code?"

"Perhaps we should ask Bosworthy?" Sherlock Holmes displayed the spine of one of the large volumes he had chosen. Sure enough, here the name 'Leopold Bosworthy' appeared in faded gilt lettering.

"Good grief," I cried. "At the risk of sounding like one of the Contessa Nascosta's dupes, anyone might think you had powers of precognition."

"Page 347," murmured Holmes, who then dropped the book casually onto the desk, where it fell open to a page in whose upper corner I read that very number. "Ah? Evidently this is a much revisited page, to present itself so conveniently to us," nodded Holmes, then he swiftly scanned the contents before locating page 695.

As he leafed through Leopold Bosworthy's gift to posterity, I picked up another of the volumes he had gathered, then another, their spines and title pages bearing recently heard names. "Venicciano? And Romford too? Now I'm sure there must be a perfectly logical explanation," I mused. And when my musings provoked no response, I added a more pointed, "And I'm sure Holmes is about to reveal it."

"Hmmm? Not precognition or foreknowledge, old boy, though you have yourself stumbled across something which may yet have relevance. No, it is dust again, Watson. A detective's greatest aid. Take a look at the shelves if you're in need of proof."

As Holmes perused the books and Eleanor read through her father's journal, reciting names of long-dead or forgotten scholars and then checking them off against the spines of the books before her—"'*Breaconridge has points of interest*'. And here we have Dr. Edgar Breaconridge and his *On the Origins of the Ancient Orders and their Gods*."—I hobbled over to the shelves, where I lavished particular attention on the empty spaces left behind by Holmes's inspection.

"What do you see, old fellow?"

"Where those books sat, there's no dust in front on the shelf."

"Meaning?"

"Meaning that these books were regularly removed from the shelves. Of course! That's where the information the three professors were following up is to be found."

"Why should anyone follow up something like this?" asked Eleanor Wexley. The reason for her distaste became apparent as I glanced quickly over the verses in the book she held out to me.

> *The ship ran hard aground, but no rock could be found,*
> *To answer why they'd stopped dead with a lurch.*
> *But they were snared in the power o' the Beast*

165

> *in the tower,*
> *Who'd cried them into his own deep, dark church.*
> *That answer as to why they sat stilled and becalmed,*
> *Was each man on the ship was now bloody well damned!*
> *Each one of them now answered to the Devil's command....*

"It is hardly 'Old Mother Hubbard'," said I, and my eye lingered warily over the primitive accompanying engraving of a ship besieged by revolting creatures that poured up from a submerged spire or turret. "Some foolish old sailors' song. Harmless, if a little vulgar."

"But what of this?" she insisted, reading aloud, "'*In their thirst, down they swallowed a ruby red flood, An' round each pale mouth glistened a circle o' blood....*' Those words again. The circle, and the blood!"

"The name 'Medaccini'," said Holmes, drawing us both back to the task at hand, "is the only one common to both of these pages. Do you think you could find that same name in these volumes?"

We sifted keenly through the accumulated tomes, which Eleanor and I split into roughly equal heaps between us. "Let's hope the authors were gracious enough to include indexes."

"If Mr. Holmes is right about much-revisited pages conveniently falling open to display themselves" said she, and she let a large book fall open onto the desk, "we won't need them. Here we have page 789. And, ah, here we have our Medaccini, whoever he, or she, may have been!"

Holmes took the open book she presented and cheerily remarked, "Splendid, Miss Wexley. If all our clients are to prove as resourceful as you ... Now, Signor Medaccini. Hmm.... This case grows in interest with every development."

I could only follow their lead, and in so doing had found a much-perused page in a small, brown edition with yellowed pages. "Holmes, here! Medaccini is prominently mentioned, and I think ... Good God!"

Sherlock Holmes pounced to snatch the book from my numb hands. Here he quickly located the words that had provoked my utter surprise. "'*The Crown*'! Well done, my boy! You've found it!"

My surprise was compounded, though delightfully so, as Eleanor Wexley threw her arms around my neck in a tight hug of victory, from which it took her several long seconds—though not nearly long enough, I considered—to disengage herself. "John! I can see that finding you gentlemen, both of you, has been my extreme good fortune."

Holmes, his eyes fixed on the page before him, countered grimly, "Perhaps what we are learning this evening will change your views on that matter. This is a sad and sorrowful tale."

The door thumped opened loudly and Professor Rollistone awkwardly returned to our midst, a tea tray balanced in his arms and the candle less steadily balanced upon the tray. As he slowly descended the stairs, he announced, "You will pardon the delay, I trust. The cups were in hiding."

"And here is the very man to tell that tale," continued Holmes, startling the scholar by dropping his book next to the tray just as the old man had cleared space enough to settle it upon the table.

"What the Devil?" came Rollistone's querulous cry. He furiously snatched up the book like a parent scooping up a fallen and injured child, though his action was not quick enough to prevent my catching sight of the monstrous figure depicted in a colour plate within. Even in my brief time in India I had seen the temples with their statues of the many-armed Vishnu and his more dreadful counterpart, Kali, whom I had heard described by the local believers as the 'black one' and as being from 'beyond time'. Yet even with such a profusion of arms, these deities shared certain features with the humans who worshipped or feared them. There was little humanity in the squirming, tentacle-draped effigy displayed here, beyond possibly the darkest, most base desires of our species at its worst.

"The Devil?" echoed Holmes. "Perhaps, if what I have seen is true...? We have been admiring your library, Professor."

"How dare you, sir? How dare any of you? These books are of enormous value! You have absolutely no right to come in here and toss them around like this. Miss Wexley, I thought better of you. What is this man's purpose? I feel it is my right to demand an explanation."

"No, sir," countered the young lady, standing fast in face of the old man's anger. "It is you who should try explaining to us how my father's journal comes to be here, and not in his study at home."

The professor blanched. "What's this? Now you interrogate me too?"

"The lady asked you a question," said I.

Hubert Rollistone dabbed his brow with a garish handkerchief and forced out a dismissive chortle. "Well, I see nothing to get hot about in this. Oscar was an old friend. An old, dear friend. He shared many of his findings and papers with me. I daresay you'll find more if you insist on tearing my library apart. He wanted me to have them."

Eleanor Wexley glared coldly at our host. "My father died desperate to keep what knowledge he had from you. Why should he wish you to have his journals?"

"If they are to cause so much bad feeling, take them. I wish you would. They are singularly uninformative."

"I should like to judge that for myself," replied Holmes.

"And you're an expert, now, based on a cursory pillaging of my bookshelves?"

"Riddles and crowns," said Holmes, with impatience. "I have experience enough of both."

"What can you know of the tracing and recovering of crowns?" snorted the professor.

"This is not the first I have tracked. Not so many months ago I returned a rather pleasant opal tiara to a distressed lady who had thought it irretrievably lost."

"A tiara? Petty baubles!"

Then, just as the sneer of derision widened on the old man's face, Holmes blandly added, "And I'm also the man who recovered the ancient crown of the royal Stuarts, former kings of England. There was death and perhaps madness associated with its discovery, too. My name was kept out of it, but if you were to mention it around Hurlstone, or enquire of my old colleague, Musgrave ... Yes, Watson, I'll find time to give you the story someday, I'm sure. Now, Professor Rollistone, instead of sitting with your mouth open, gawping at me like I'm in an exhibition," smiled Holmes, "why don't you tell us all about the Devil's Crown?"

Hubert Rollistone, already quite taken aback by my friend's extraordinary claim, now turned so rapidly pale, with his eyes flying wide, and his large frame overtaken by such overt tremors, that I believed my medical skills might imminently be called upon. He stumbled into his seat, which groaned almost as loudly in protest as he, and poured himself a large measure of brandy which his trembling fingers succeeded more in spilling down his shirt-front and dressing gown than they managed to direct toward his slackly writhing lips. Then finally, beaten, he croaked out, "I have grossly underestimated you, Mr. Sherlock Holmes. How much do you know?"

"Only that this fabled crown was the object you sought, and that its history, as its name suggests, is an unpleasant one."

A dry chuckle escaped from the scholar's whitened lips. "You have a considerable knack for understatement, sir."

"Now, we could, with time and patience, learn about this remarkable item from these precious books of yours. However, both commodities are in increasingly short supply, so it would save us a great deal of trouble if you would give us the facts, which you obviously know so well."

"Must I?" Rollistone groaned, dismally.

"I think you owe it to us," I insisted. "To Miss Wexley at least."

"As you say," admitted our host, the sheen of perspiration on his puffy, pallid face as it hovered in the lamp's light lending him the appearance of a talking corpse. "But, I warn you now, this is a history of horror and of violence following upon violence. As your father described it, Eleanor, *'a circle of blood'*, indeed. It is blood that has been spilled over this most beautiful and lethal object since it first made its presence known to man. The blood of four hundred years ..."

Chapter 11: The Circle of Blood

"**T**he dreadful story of the Devil's Crown, and of the hideous curse that is said to follow it, can be traced back to the year 1421," began Hubert Rollistone. "However the legend's roots run far deeper into history than we can even judge. But in that crucial year, in the mighty Ottoman Empire, a wealthy merchant and landowner, by name Halil Hodja, fell swiftly and far from favour with the Sultan Mehmet, due to certain ill-considered comments the merchant was reported to have made concerning Mehmet's governance. We need not go into court politics to detail the precise nature of the controversy, merely note that, in order to restore his slipping position, Hodja resolved that, to amply demonstrate that his allegiance to both emperor and empire was above question, he must make a significant gift to his ruler, before one of his many rivals might make a royal gift of his head.

"This gift, or bribe if you favour accuracy, would come from the pick of a cargo of silks and spices and jewels at that instant journeying under full sail across the Mediterranean in one of his merchant vessels. When, at last, that ship docked, Hodja elected that as fitting homage to his royal master he would have a crown fashioned, into which he might place his prized treasures: twin, perfectly formed diamonds, identical and of the most startling blue, and to balance them, two large, blood-red rubies. But the crown may as well have been forged in the furnaces of Hell itself, for madness, fear and death was to follow in its wake!"

In light of his recent curt dismissal of my own poor efforts at story-telling as sensationalised and garish, I felt somewhat irked by the absorbed attention Holmes paid this melodramatic fare. Had I thought this prelude outlandish, however, it little prepared me for the utter excess of macabre weirdness that was yet to come.

"Hodja, with a retinue of guards, set out at once for Constantinople, where he would present the crown to Mehmet as a symbol of his loyalty. They had gone no more than fifty miles when they were waylaid by fearsome bandits, whose chief was the notorious Hamid, known also as Şeytanın Kulu—literally 'the Servant of the Devil'. This was the time of such cults as The Order of the Dragon, and soon would come the great enemy of the empire who proclaimed himself Drakul—the Dragon—and his notorious Wallachian son, the bloodthirsty Impaler himself, whose name translated variously as *Son of the Dragon* or *Son of the Devil*, depending on the banner of which faith you fought under. Hamid, however, wasted no thought on faith or nation, and gave no quarter to Muslim, Christian, or any other, and Hodja's party fell under the bandit swords.

"Hamid's men returned to their hideout, the booty was shared or fought over, and they danced and drank and debauched themselves senseless in celebration of their victory. The pickings had been good, for the canny merchant, wishing to leave no breath of bad feeling or festering resentment, had also set out laden with gifts for the Sultan's many courtiers. But Hamid had eyes for only one trophy. Seizing the Sultan's gift, he placed it upon his head, declaring himself duly crowned as high king of all

172

murderers and thieves. Was he not, after all, the Devil's Emissary and special chosen one, for was his not the last face so many saw before being despatched straight to Hell? Who, more than he, deserved to be honoured as royalty amongst assassins?

"Had he ever ventured out of the wilds and into the cities and ports, Hamid might have known the dark reputation already earned by the glistening jewels he wore at his brow. Would any man who claimed the role of devil made flesh have paid heed to such ghostly stories? Or would he have seen it as bestowing yet more of the Archfiend's authority upon his own brutal actions? We cannot know, for the ignoble reign of King Hamid, murderer royal, wasn't to last the long desert night.

"As his pack of vile cutthroats caroused, he fell, poisoned by his favourite lover, who snatched the crown from his head and made off into the night. But with the last of his formidable strength, the Servant of the Devil clawed his way from his tent to fall before the campfire, his face a mask of agonised terror, his head bare, and the crown gone. Yet, before his bandit thugs could pursue the girl to avenge their chieftain, they were set upon by the Sultan's troops, brought to the den by a spy who had been working in their midst—a spy who had played his role with such dedication that his own blade had tasted many an innocent throat. The justice dealt these brigands was swift and savage, and all were put to the sword. But when he apprehended that the crown was not among the vast hoards recovered from the slaughtered thieves, the spy raced into the desert after the girl, and when he found her no great distance from the encampment, terrified and raving, he showed her no more mercy than was shown those they had both betrayed.

"Even with the bandits slaughtered, the expedition was ill-starred. A heated argument erupted between the head of the troops and the spy over whose honour it should be to present the regained crown to Mehmet. The quarrel was bitter and prolonged, and only brought to a close

173

when the spy drew his dagger, still crusted with Hamid's lover-turned-murderer's blood, and stabbed the captain furiously and repeatedly, before he himself was seized by the fallen soldier's men. And as the prisoner was dragged back to the city to face trial, so too was brought back word of all that had happened in the Devil's Servant's camp, and a fresh chapter was added to the growing legend of the bloodied crown."

"Professor Rollistone, you say the merchant had ordered the creation of this crown," remarked Sherlock Holmes. "How could an object so recently minted have already gained a lore of its own?"

"Ah, yes, well, you only asked about the crown," began our host, evasively. "The sinister reputation sprang from that quartet of great jewels, not from the crown itself, although you may say it inherited the infamy."

"Then you bring us in partway through the tale, instead of plunging in at the deep end and starting at the beginning."

"Those are very leading words, Mr. Holmes. Yes, then, it begins at sea, with the jewels, and with that vessel whose return the merchant had so impatiently awaited. But you surely cannot have ascertained so much from just a few moments amongst my books."

"It wasn't your books that gave the clue, but the other objects in your collection. It would seem unlikely that so predominant a gathering of specimens would not be associated with your quest. And as only those whose lives and livelihoods depended on the oceans and their great bounties and calamitous cruelties would invent gods or monsters that take such subaquatic forms, and as you spoke already of a merchant vessel ..." Holmes let us draw the connection for ourselves, returning his gaze to the ceiling and allowing the professor to resume.

"Alas, what should have been a routine journey under the guiding hand of an experienced captain—a born sailor named Murad—and his equally skilled crew had proved a nightmare passage, in whose course madness, pestilence, murder, and worse, rendered the craft that crawled into port a floating charnel house. A ship of the damned, the dead, and the dying, where even the flies and scavenger birds showed unwilling to settle on the remains of those crewmen that had perished just a few days from home.

"Of the half-dozen mariners still clinging to life, only three retained enough semblance of sanity to speak of what had befallen them. On some stretch of open water, though they could not, or would not, specify where, the vessel had come to a halt. Not becalmed, but snagged, as if run aground. Impossible! They were far from any beach or crag or known obstacle. Indeed, the ship had passed through the self-same spot a score of times and never yet run any risk. The sails billowed and flapped, yet something held them fast. Like a butterfly trying to take flight while pinned already in the case, you might say."

"You might say it, Professor," retorted Holmes. "I would attempt to stick to concise facts, not add grim atmospherics of my own."

"Don't forget it was you who demanded this account, sir. I would have happily left it buried in half-forgotten books. And it will need few of my personal flourishes, for it is grim enough, as you'll soon find," returned the professor coolly.

"What was to be done about releasing the vessel to resume its journey? Only one thing to do. Diving overboard, a reckless but dexterous crewman called, I believe, Orhan, surfaced again, gibbering of great sunken buildings. Mad babbling, indeed, until the others that dived down in answer to his cries saw for themselves the spire that had scraped along the ship's keel, like a giant finger tickling a trout's belly. How long it had lain submerged, or if it had been disgorged by some vast underwater earthquake, many have already speculated, but there it was! A great circular tower, its sunken base so concealed in the wriggling mass of seaweed that climbed the length of the structure's outer wall that it was impossible to judge the true depth at which the ancient edifice lay. As to its purpose? While those who first described it could scarcely have known, it, does that cylindrical turret surmounted by a clear chamber not sound remarkably like one of our modern lighthouses? Yet it was no lamp-room that sat atop this spire to light the deep for jellyfish and crabs to find their way. What it appeared to be was a shrine. And within, perched above its forgotten altar, sat some fearful, primordial idol whose golden scales shimmered amidst the green and squirming weeds, and from whose inhuman face many burning eyes balefully glared."

"'... the Beast in the tower,'" whispered Eleanor, as she recalled that dreadful verse. "'Who'd cried them in to his own deep, dark church.'"

"Some swam so far and so fast from the sight of this unknown 'Iblis'—that is to say, *devil*—that it was only sheer exhaustion and the prospect of the miles of sea surrounding them that brought them back aboard. There they shunned those who spoke of treasure, and set to praying as their fellows constructed a rope pulley in hopes of hauling the statue, all ten feet in height of it, up on deck. And with the ropes secured, the crew hefted and heaved, while the sculpture slowly ascended toward the surface. From the sounds that emanated from within, it appeared to be hollow, but concealing some secret consignment deep in its belly. Hidden riches was the cry, and they heaved all the faster.

"Our impetuous Orhan, his initial shock abating, dived yet deeper to establish just how far down the tower truly went, and to prise out any further treasures. Captain Murad and his men watched their crewmate's disappearance into the darkening deep, while the thing he had found emerged into the light after untold centuries. Had it ever truly belonged above the waves in the first place? Those survivors' accounts spoke of a thing that, while it may have possessed horns and hooves, and even wings, was most surely akin to some massively-tentacled and clawed ocean-haunting titan!"

The laugh I uttered brought all eyes so suddenly upon me that even the masks and mannikins seemed to regard me with watchful disdain. As I have gained more experience of the world and its many mysteries, I have seen things that the younger, brasher man who stood in that library that evening would have likewise mockingly dismissed. The contents of the great Red Barrow of the Addletons, the loathsome unknown worm, and the now infamous Sumatran Horror—an adventure which itself began with a stricken merchant ship, a crew driven to madness or beyond, and their unnatural, entirely unbelievable, yet very much living cargo—all lay in my future. And though he will argue the point, even the arch-rationalist Holmes is less inclined now to entirely reject the notion of phenomena as yet beyond the ken of man. But in the arrogance of my youth, such things sounded eminently laughable outside of the pages of one of Monsieur Verne's excellent scientific romances. "Cyclopean towers and shrines to water-dwelling demons that throw themselves up from the seabed? Surely this is all utterly preposterous?"

It took but a single curt nod from Holmes to silence my mirth. "That particular area of the world has long been prone to volcanic and seismic activity. You will know of the destruction of Pompeii, and may recall that both the Colossus of Rhodes and the Alexandrian lighthouse fell victim to earthquakes. Perhaps what the earth and sea may suddenly claim they may just as suddenly give up again?"

Suitably chastened, I acknowledged the possibility, allowing the folklorist to resume his narrative. And, as he did so, my conviction that this was mere phantasy dwindled steadily away.

"You talk of the Great Wonders, Mr. Holmes. If there were Seven Wonders, perhaps in balance there were Seven Terrors of the World? This might yet have been one such terror, for the sight of it sent more crewmen to their knees in prayer alongside their devout fellows. Those remaining

177

struggled to keep their haul from going under again, and the ropes were tied off as securely as could be managed. So it hung on high like some ... some snared beast that might, at any second, break free from its bonds and plunge down upon its captors." The heaving shudder as he sought to describe it suggested another image in my mind's eye—that of a great spider, hanging from a single webbed thread above its intended prey.

"Half his crew mad with fear, and the weight of the thing—seemingly carrying more mass now it had been raised from its watery resting place—threatening to topple the boat from beneath them, Captain Murad took his knife to cut the ropes. I wish I could claim that khanjar you were appraising earlier was that very one, Mr. Holmes, but it was not dissimilar. Let the iblis go back to the deep once more; it would not claim his vessel! But Timur, the brother of Orhan, just as nimble as his kin, snatched the knife and shinned up the ropes. His aim was to salvage the great jewels—those twin diamonds of the most startling blue, and the matching pair of perfectly formed rubies, as well as the shimmering green emeralds, and the agates, carbuncles, pearls, and more—that stared out from the coiled mass of a face.

"One by one, he plucked out the most dazzling of the devil's eyes, holding them triumphantly aloft. There he froze, a look of horror rendering his face that of a man who has seen the shadow of his own destruction. Casting the stones down onto the deck, he pointed to the waters below. The seas swirled with red, foaming traces before his brother, or what was left of him, broke the surface. Thickening strands of slick seaweed clung to his thrashing, jerking form, like the poisoned embrace of a gigantic jellyfish, before slipping from him to reveal livid, sucking pads like red-rimmed mouths—aye, more circles of blood, you could say—that left their ravages on the sailor's body, and on his face, the flesh eaten away and the skull showing beneath."

"Utterly monstrous!"

Hubert Rollistone nodded emphatically, mistaking my disgust at the ill-disguised relish with which he now addressed his discomfited audience for horrified awe at his tale.

"Monstrous, indeed. And the atrocity continued. For even as Timur raised his gaze from his brother's death agonies, he looked into the dark fissures left in the sockets of the creature's eyes. It was indeed hollow. And by removing those stones it was as if he had unstopped Hades. From out of the hollowed face rapidly oozed every mean and lowly beast that crawled or swam. Leeches, worms, slugs and eels and crabs, tentacled things and eyeless ones, and I daresay ... rather, I dare not say," and he made that scuttling, spidery finger motion again, "as if all of the things that make men shudder had been locked inside this devil's heart.

"The leeches that crawled out were thin and white, but they were fat and red by the time they fell sated from Timur's body. And as the horrified crew darted to and fro, crushing and stamping on any of the squirming horrors that fell onto the decks, the ropes finally snapped, and the blinded idol and the sailor whose blood it ran slick with plunged back into the waves.

"Well, those crewmen did not seek far for explanations of their ordeal, and not one of them was founded on this being a tragic accident. Orhan had disturbed an ancient, slumbering deity. His brother had inflicted wounds upon it. Both had paid the price. And whatever lurked once more in the darkened depths had received its sacrifice. Its revenge would be a far longer, further reaching process.

"It was the violent pitching as the idol broke loose that jolted the ship free of the very thing that had trapped it. As the winds drove them on from that evil spot, the only remaining evidence of this encounter was the cluster of jewels—twin diamonds, twin rubies—that Captain Murad snatched up, reckoning them a poor exchange for two good sailors and the nerve of his crew. But whether it was the crew's disordered state, the loss of the brothers, or some other factor that weighed upon him, from the moment those gems were in Murad's safe-keeping, his own behaviour became erratic and unpredictable. He developed a habit of staring at individuals among the crew with a look of haunted sadness. One by one the men upon whom he had set his gaze fell ill, and it was whispered that Murad had seen their fates, and that any he marked out was doomed.

"The men couldn't simply avoid their captain, though some conspired to close his eyes permanently to save him conferring that ominous glance upon them. Murad himself claimed that whatever enchantment he was under was not the fault of his own eyes, but of those other eyes he found himself looking through; eyes that showed not what was, but what would be! And all the while the men grew sicker, wasting away, their skin paling, their muscles shrivelling."

"Malnourishment," said I. "Most likely scurvy, too."

"On so short a voyage? Well, perhaps there is an answer in science. But there is no scientific definition for ghosts, is there? Yet the brothers were seen, Orhan and Timur, walking the decks of the ship, their forms like wraiths, wet and pale as the bellies of fish, but with ruby-red round wounds on their bleached skin, and one with only half a face upon his skull. They had followed the ship, perhaps, clinging to its bulk like ticks on the side of some vast, ripe animal. Night by night they clambered aboard the vessel, and night by night the crew weakened and died. There's a rough translation of a traditional song that recounts the voyage, which states;

> They swarmed 'neath the waves, not held fast in
>   their graves,
> Gripped wi' thirst that could never be slackened,
> With their flesh pasty white, they shone out in
>   the night,
> And with their touch, they left each man's soul
>   blackened...."

It was Eleanor Wexley who concluded the grisly recitation;

> *"In their thirst, down they swallowed a ruby-red*
> *   flood,*
> *An' round each pale mouth glistened a circle o'*
> *   blood...."*

The professor's eyes went to the book of verses by Eleanor's hand, and he nodded. "Whether the brothers truly did return by night, the captain grew ruddier and plumper, and was found in his cabin with blood on his lips, and meat upon his plate that did not come from the galley. *'They must be fed if they are to see, and what's meat and drink for them is you and me!'* That's from that same song; I don't suppose the real Murad had bothered to make his words rhyme."

"The things that must be fed? He meant the jewels?"

"Yes, my dear girl. Thus springs the first rumour, that the stones possessed some power of second sight."

"Well, if the monster had a second pair of eyes, why not second sight?" My attempt at leavening the atmosphere was received coolly.

"I've heard that song sung in a babel of tongues, by men who could never have heard faintest whisper of the legend it pertains to. I heard it last in shanty form in a tavern near Plymouth. A much more recent adaptation from the source, naturally, but in its basics it tells the same tragic old tale. I had a squeezebox long ago, but its workings were eaten by mice, alas, so there's a small mercy for you in that, if you still feel inclined to thank the Heavens for anything. It's called 'The Red Jerkin', in honour of the captain's bloodstained bib. His own end in the song goes:

> *Said the Captain to the mate, 'The Devil's eyes*
> *   saw my fate,*
> *I'll be damned 'fore this ship reaches shore,*
> *My feet ne'er more will touch land!' He took*
> *   dagger in hand,*

And to match his red jerkin, the Captain soon
wore,
A red neckerchief of his own bloody gore,
Aye, neckerchief soaked in his own rich, red
gore...

"With no command and a reduced crew, the vessel drifted finally into port. Here the statements of the crew, even tallying as they did in all important respects, were decreed the ravings of men with minds turned by the sun and salt water, and from witnessing the lingering deaths of their mates. What couldn't be denied was the existence of those glorious, flawless rubies and diamonds that were cut from the pouch worn around the neck of the dead captain, its cord embedded deeply into the flesh of his throat where his own blade had bitten into it."

Unable to bite back on my ire any further, I insisted, "You can't know this, surely! You said you would resist embellishment, and there is entirely no call to add such repulsive detail to an already grotesque story."

"It has been part of the legend these four centuries. While aspects of the merchant vessel's last voyage may, rather like that mysterious idol, have grown arms and legs, all I've related comes to us from the folk tales that spread throughout every dock and port from Rhodes to the Black Sea in the aftermath of the ship's return, and which remain the closest we have to a contemporary record of the events. I don't add to the retelling for mere effect, Doctor. But if I was to censor myself to avoid upsetting or alarming any of your party, there would be little of the story I could safely tell."

Eleanor Wexley squeezed my hand, stating, "When I was still a child, Father told me of so many antique legends, of gorgons and harpies, banshee and golems, that I can't be easily frightened by what is just another ancient story. Professor, please continue."

"Thank you, dear girl. Now you will remember the merchant, Hodja, who had waited in growing concern for the arrival of his ship and its cargo. Scornful of all talk that linked the tragedy of his crew with the treasure, but now in possession of unexpected riches, the merchant set out to make his crown. It is said by some that the intricate pattern into which the jewels were set took inspiration from the hydra-like coils credited to the underwater deity that had furnished the gems. From other sources come claims that, in mockery of the Redeemer prayed to by the empire's enemies, it was modelled upon a crown of thorns. A mare's nest, whatever the design, for it became a focus of ill-fortune and madness. It is also stated in some retellings that the artisan who fashioned the crown was so stricken by the perfection of his work that, fearing his hands would never again craft anything so beautiful, he plunged them deep into his own furnace.

"And now, the merchant slain, his murderer eradicated, and both the girl's and the guard captain's blood upon it, the crown was taken to the capitol, where the Sultan watched as the disgraced spy was executed. Already those legends of the jewels had escaped from the taverns and ports and reached nobler ears, chief amongst them the claim that foresight was among their gifts to bestow. In jest, the Sultan presented the crown to a courtesan, Sidika, famed as much for her wit as her great beauty. 'Tell me of my future triumphs,' he cried. 'Will my empire live on?' 'Yes,' she told him before the entire royal court. 'Yes, the empire will live, but without you to rule it, O great Mehmet, for you, before this year is out, shall be with your forebears!'

"Outraged at the dishonour shown his master, the Sultan's bodyguard wielded his scimitar, and Sidika's head was taken in one sweep. Mehmet demanded the disposal of the malevolent crown, no longer such a desirable trinket, and the executed harlot's remains. But while her delightful body was consumed by the pyre, the head, along with the crown it still wore, was snatched away by another who owed no allegiance to any of the great religions that clashed in those warring states. And

Mehmet himself? He was dead and lying in the mausoleum he'd had built for himself at Bursa within months of that fatal warning."

Rollistone paused here to run a finger delicately across the heads, if such they could be termed, of the misshapen statuettes and ghastly homunculi lurking on the shelves, and his watery eyes drifted with his memory, as he recalled, "I have stood in a house that still endures on the outskirts of Constantinople, that has lain tended but untenanted for many years owing to a certain reputation as a place where bad things have happened, and may yet happen again. From without it looks as any other in those cramped streets, but it is known that certain rites were performed there that have poisoned the spot for centuries yet to come, and there is such a blackly oppressive atmosphere within that you pray it will not cling to you as you leave.

"The walls, floors and ceilings are black, so that even lamplight is swallowed as soon as it falls, thus the rooms are forever dark. Those who made it their lair purportedly spent so long within those dark confines that they grew hateful of light and, in shunning it, became night creatures, emerging only after the shadows had lengthened to go about whatever furtive business drew them from their nest. It was in this dark residence that I, let us say, *acquired* several of these unusual specimens for my collection. Legally attained them, I should stress, or as legally as any business in such a place might be conducted. Many of them were left as offerings or tributes, and over centuries it has become night impossible to move for likenesses and graven images of elder gods whose favours were entreated in that black fastness."

"What kind of gods would you call these impossible accumulations of ill-fitting anatomical scraps?"

"That was never spoken of with the curator of those black rooms, Dr. Watson. But if you were to ask that question in certain benighted towns in New England, perhaps ..."

"But I'm not in New England, Professor! While practically everything I read tells me we might believe anything could be possible in America, I'm in *old* England. Plain old, feet-on-the-ground England, where the most our chosen God demands of us is to don our best suits and hats on a Sunday, and to offer up a few humble words and hymns of thanks. I still am in that England, or at least I think I am, unless we're further north than I'd supposed and we've slipped over the border? In which case, even the imaginative and romantic Scots won't give these Fiji Mermaids more than short shrift!"

"You say 'offerings', Professor," interjected Holmes, deftly applying a stopper to my outpouring of impatience. "Offerings to what?"

"Why, to the severed head of Sidika, of course! And to the prescience granted it by the Devil's Crown. Many sought guidance; farmers seeking news of the coming harvest, merchants, of new ventures, soldiers, of battles not yet fought. Did the disembodied head speak through her own dead lips? Or were her visions put directly into the minds of those who laid their tributes—and doubtless made further, more immediately transferable contributions to this church's idea of a collection box—and placed their hands upon the head that wore the crown? Both have been claimed. But what is common to all variations is that the courtesan's head neither withered nor aged, and her lustrous hair continued to grow until it overflowed the altar in great tumbling coils.

"And so it might have continued yet had the city guards not heard tell of these dark goings on, and in raiding the house found the solution to certain nocturnal vanishments and abductions. For while the preserved head of Sidika could neither eat nor drink, it had been feeding. The altar on which it sat was a shallow trough of sorts, you see. A trough which these stealthily creeping disciples replenished nightly with fresh blood from those unfortunates they found who could be quietly taken. And as their object of worship absorbed the blood offering, her

185

creatures also supped on gore for, as with the doomed crew in the tale of 'The Red Jerkin', those victims weren't just bled, but entirely devoured.

"Those priests and priestesses of Sidika that were captured were destroyed by a traditional method, with long iron nails hammered through their foreheads. The Devil's Crown was seized once more, and the head, denied sustenance, was left to shrivel and go to dust. On the single expedition I made to that obsidian museum, I was presented with what were claimed to be the surviving relics of Sidika. Had any residual gift of prophecy remained with it, when I held it in these hands I might have been warned that my own quest for the crown would be a lifetime squandered. Alas, I heard and saw nothing. But, then, what might I have expected from a hank of hair tied round a dusty old jawbone?"

Professor Rollistone reached for his glass and the decanter. "And speaking of jawbones, mine could do with some lubrication, as I feel like I've been talking nearly as long as the legend has endured. No-one else? No? Well, so much for the skull of our Cassandra. When next the crown was taken up it was by a general who proclaimed it would grant him the vision to foretell his enemies' every move, who then swiftly lost his position and his life leading a skirmish against Christian troops on Rhodes. Yes, it does rather undermine the supernatural claims for the jewels' powers. But one theory I rather favour states that this general knew his mission to be suicidal—had even been shown his own death—and the entire intent was to pass the crown and whatever darkness surrounded it into the hands of the enemies of the empire and the true faith, so that the evil infection might take hold in the opposing force's heart and eventually bring it down from within.

"For twenty years, though, the crown remained safely out of harm's way in a vault of treasures in the Christian camp, while the world moved on without it. In Rome, the Church had fallen into the hands of the Borgia Pope, Alexander, whose infamy and appetites are a legend in themselves. Alexander's greed stretched out like tendrils throughout the Church, and countless treasures were called on to fill the coffers. Amongst them was the cache containing the Devil's Crown, which must have thirsted ravenously for blood following its long confinement.

"It certainly did not have long to wait, as Alexander was soon to follow the diadem's previous bearers into the grave. The Borgia name is synonymous with poison, and it's ironic that this is likely to have been the cause of Alexander's demise, as the Catholic Church soon fell into the hands of his greatest rival, Giulliano della Rovere, and il Corona del Diavolo was placed in a supreme position in the increasingly overcrowded Vatican vaults, alongside the infamous black Borgia Pearl, and much else that glimmered and sparkled but had run red with the blood of those reluctant to donate towards the pontiff's might."

Professor Rollistone pointed a plump finger and said, "Miss Wexley, you see that calf-bound volume by your elbow? It is a translation of an edition by Aldo Venicciano; a name I see you are familiar with already, though these things no longer surprise me. If you would care to turn to page 206, and the last two paragraphs."

As she did so, Eleanor Wexley cleared her throat and read in a clear, precise voice, "*Under this new reign, the Church of Rome remained as corrupt as it had been for many long and sordid years. Criticism was scarce, as the dreaded Inquisition was still a valid cause of fear. However, there were those who could not bear to see their faith abused in this depraved manner. Chief among these was Gregorio Medaccini, a young cardinal of noble birth, whose forefathers were grand dukes and who had been raised in palazzos and on grand country estates, yet who had forsaken title and wealth in pursuit of salvation and spiritual illumination. Thus was Cardinal Medaccini appalled to find the love of gold considered more precious than that of souls, so he lashed out at the corrupt administration in the surest way he saw to hurt them.*

"'On a fatal night in Our Lord's Year of 1506, the young cardinal entered the Vatican, where he had free access thanks to his newly exalted position, and there, using purloined keys, broke into the deepest vault. From it, he removed a large quantity of gold and jewels, as well as the legendary cursed crown won in battle with the Turks. Had he been less dazzled by its charms, his escape might have been won. Yet his taking that of that object, so steeped in evil deeds, must explain what followed, as Medaccini found himself trapped by Vatican guards and faced little option but to subject himself to the Inquisitors' mercies—of which none were listed—or to fight his way to safety. Thus the noble crusader for purity and light escaped into the night's dark cover, fleeing Mother Rome and the Church with il Corona del Diavolo and the blood of two men on his hands.'"*

"What became of Medaccini has been a mystery for centuries," concluded Professor Rollistone. "Even whether he truly killed those guards is debated, as there are grounds to believe that His Excellency, furious and wrathful, had them summarily executed for their failure to protect his riches, then used their deaths as the crime by which he blackened the young cardinal's name. Whatever the matter, had he remained in his homeland, Medaccini would certainly have been killed and the crown would have returned to the Vatican treasury. As neither of these things ever came to pass, we must assume that he fled. But to where? Whatever may have happened, Cardinal Gregorio Medaccini seemed simply to vanish, and with him he took the Devil's Crown. But with it, did he also take the curse?"

Chapter 12: The Abbot's Cry

Professor Rollistone resumed his seat with a grimly satisfied smile and purred, "A gruesome tale, is it not?"

"Indeed! And I still think you might have spared us some of the more horrific details."

"Come, Watson," chided Sherlock Holmes. "I would have thought so gaudy a tale would be exactly to your tastes."

I felt no need to reiterate that any concerns I expressed were for Miss Wexley's sake, but with that thought in mind I turned to see her youthful face creased in worried concentration as she gazed out into the night. Did she, too, imagine unseen eyes watching from beyond the glass, and envision the wind-blown stirring amongst the overgrown trees and brambles as the thrashing of countless tentacles whose origins lay incalculably deep beneath the dank soil? Her eyes darted fearfully from the windows as I quietly spoke her name, and she cried in sudden surprise, "The curse? That was what she said. A curse—a malediction—would be upon us!"

"She?" murmured our host, arching a curious brow. "I wonder who you can mean."

Holmes gave no answer, merely insisted, "The curse is a mere legend. Such things have no place in a rational world."

"But the world from which this legend sprang was not a rational one. Far from it! The superstitions of the middle ages contain many tales whose basis in reality is tenuous, at best. But here, that cannot be said to be true. You must admit, gentlemen, that the unnatural and violent deaths of all who have dared claim the treasure do seem to suggest some malign force at work."

"Since you feel this way, Professor, I'm astonished that you would wish to expose the world once more to this malignancy."

"Well, I don't think we need fear on that point, Dr. Watson," he smiled, ruefully. "I have no hope of ever discovering the crown's resting place. The damned thing— and before you protest, I use the word in its most literal form—disappeared with Medaccini."

"Nevertheless, you must have spent that night in a cold church for a reason. How did you conclude that Medaccini had fled to Britain?"

Professor Rollistone's jaw dropped, even as he raised himself up to his full height with a cry of, "This is becoming damned tiresome, Holmes!"

"Kindly lower your voice and watch your language, sir," I cautioned.

The folklorist sighed and nodded his assent. "Forgive me, but the unexpected nature of your visit, and your friend's quite formidable powers have rather jarred my nerves, I fear, for I feel perfectly skittish. Foolish fancies, I'm quite sure. My dearest Eleanor, I suppose it only right that you should be told the reason behind your father's demise."

"I would be very grateful, Professor."

"It was I, then, who originally told Oscar Wexley and, much later, Ronald Flagstaff the legend of the Devil's Crown. Should I feel guilty for that? No, there is no need to answer, for I already do endure those deep feelings of

190

remorse. Had I not dragged my friends along this path with me ... well, they might just have been able to drag me back off it, given half the chance.

"For myself, I first encountered the tale on my travels, some thirty-five years ago. I must admit it obsessed me. Well, look about you; how can I deny that obsession? I was determined to succeed where so many before me had failed, and find whatever trail Medaccini may have left. Wexley was to be my ally there. His archaeological training led us to many scattered fragments of the story in as many lands. Medaccini had moved far and wide after fleeing Rome, yet each site we visited seemed to be but a short stop on his travels, while so many others proved to be false trails and blind alleys. The more we looked, the more tangled the trail became.

"Finally, indeed a mere few months ago, I realised—a little later than I should have, no doubt—that I had grown just too wretchedly old for the chase. Wexley would hear nothing of quitting, however. I believe that he wished to prove himself, Eleanor, to you and your brother. Believe it or not, he was devoted to you both."

"So devoted that he abandoned us to search for this horrid thing? Yes, I know I sound more like my brother when I ask it, but Nicholas is right, isn't he? Our father left us adrift, and all in pursuit of such a poisonous prize! I do not mean to shout, nor to decry his name, but simply wish to understand such an action."

"He was as obsessed as I ever was, and as poor Flagstaff would become. But, as fixated as he was, he talked constantly still of his family, and of how this would be the find of all time; the find to prove he was not the fool he feared you considered him."

"I never thought of him so," Eleanor Wexley protested. "Not ever! But he knew those legends, just as you do. Was he not afraid of the curse?"

"Oscar was afraid of nothing," laughed Hubert Rollistone, his long watch-chain jingling over his vibrating stomach. "He'd survived enough scrapes and earned himself enough scars to harden his nerve against anything. It's only a pity that it also left his body weakened, and his mind ... Well, any matter, he was not a man to be afraid of centuries-old folk stories. Where others saw monsters and misfortune, he saw riches, prestige, and knowledge." Another chuckle escaped him. "Poor old Flagstaff used to have to face a lot of ribbing from him."

"Professor Flagstaff took the stories seriously?" asked Holmes.

"Ronald took everything seriously. Oh, those stories upset him half to death, but he'd go over them again and again, looking for the secret. He tried to mask his obsession as scientific enquiry, of course, but he would happily have combined the ancient sorceries with the newer sciences, like some alchemist in his lair, if he thought they'd produce results. If these crystals genuinely offered some glimmer of foreknowledge, he would have ground them and buffed them, and fitted them as lenses in some great brass telescope to extend and direct that future vision, bringing into focus the clear path of progress. Ronald Flagstaff was never one to walk willingly into the unknown without a steady torch-beam to guide the way. In truth, he was frightened by his own shadow. I've never seen such a burly man jump so, or be reduced to a quake over such little things as a cloud's passage across the moon, or a snapping twig in a dusk-filled forest."

"He did appear rather nervous when we met."

"Nervous? My sweet girl, your poor father's shouting nearly caused him to keel over more than once. But shout about it all he wanted—and Oscar most assuredly did—I had more or less given up my pursuit of the elusive Medaccini, had retired from university life, and had taken myself here to this remote spot, where I planned to spend my remaining years with my books in the study of some of our domestic folk stories. This area is rife with them. Were you to credit just a few of them you would find that within a twenty-mile radius we have had mermen washed ashore, a house so malign that even those spirits haunting it have gone mad with fear, a well that cures all ills as well as a neighbouring spring that causes them, and enough pixies and fairies, goblins and imps to enchant any child or terrify any adult who hears their singing in the woods at night. I had no fear of boredom, but I little realised that my escape from what I thought was a pointless search was to uncover possibly the very clue we had sought all along."

Sherlock Holmes leaned forward keenly, and in that moment I detected a certain sympathy between the two men, both seeking elusive clues to allow their progression along an obscure trail toward some goal invisible to others.

"I wasn't the first to posit these isles as a potential resting place for the crown, of course. When I was first beginning my own search, Haworth Romford, whose works you may already have found, got it in his head that Medaccini's crown may even have somehow been entangled within the legends of the three holy crowns of Anglia; you know the tale, I expect, of the crowns buried clandestinely around the coast to keep invaders at bay? 'The Devil's eyes, plucked from the sea,' he declared, 'would surely be appeased by lying in full view of the very waves under which they had once long bided?' He was wrong, of course. Quite the wrong period, as the Anglo-Saxons had been gone nearly four centuries before the Devil's Crown was even conceived of. But, as with any obsession, the heart leads the head, and old Romford imagined he had identified an undisturbed mound somewhere along that stretch of coastline that showed promise. Well, he disturbed something, sure enough, whether it was some crazed local who didn't want him digging on his land, or something else. But my old mentor was found floating not so far out to sea. Not drowned, but with his skull caved in, and with his jaw smashed all into bits, as if to stop him telling what he'd found even if he came back as a ghost. The search for Medaccini's legacy is littered with such curious exits, and even those not fated to find the crown itself seem fated to be found by ... something.

"Some manuscripts I was studying concerning the local history had proven very badly obscured by centuries of addition and corruption. I passed one of these—the most obscure and badly rewritten of the lot—to friend Ronald. It concerned the foundation of some of the many churches in the area, but much of it was clearly fictional, with dates transposed and the source of funds obscured or hidden behind false names. How curious! Nothing with which to alert the British Museum, but a rare excuse for Ronald to practice his alchemy. Beyond that, all I'd truly hoped to find was some minor local scandal to add to my collection."

"Instead you found Medaccini."

"That was something I utterly refused to accept at that stage, Mr. Holmes. It was too fantastic! Too ridiculous, that we had traversed the globe when, all the time, our goal was here! But the more Ronald revealed of the censored text, the more my conviction grew. The original contents of the manuscript, which later generations had tried to conceal, referred to a foreign monk who arrived unannounced in the district—descending upon it out of nowhere, it appeared—and who set about moving from parish to parish, restoring churches which had fallen into disrepair, or building new ones where none had previously stood."

"How could a single monk achieve all this? How could he possibly afford it?"

"Ah! There you hit the mystery full square on, Doctor! That, according to our long dead informant, was a great talking point. The monk himself lived a simple life and would speak nothing of his past, beyond that he was 'an abbot of an order of one'. There were rumours that he had once been a harsh landowner who grew rich on the backs of his peasants, until he renounced his ways and devoted his life to making up for his past misdeeds. Or that he was a murderer who had seized a miser's hoard and was now haunted by every coin of it not yet spent in repaying his debt. Or a former bandit who had set out to use his stolen wealth in God's name, in hope of buying forgiveness on his deathbed."

"I fail to see anything censorable in this."

"It was what happened to the monk, Mr. Holmes, that caused the story's suppression. As the account goes, the nameless abbot's actions incited the curiosity of the local bishop, who demanded an audience with this mysterious pilgrim. This bishop was not renowned for his own devotions, unless those included a devout worship of various very earthly pleasures, and his abiding failings were luxury and vanity. When this invitation was refused, the bishop grew deeply suspicious, making enquiries whose trail of whispers may even have reached back as far as the Vatican. What is certain is that, not long after the abbot's rebuff of the bishop's hospitality, several more foreign monks arrived."

"Vatican agents," I ventured, my knowledge of the history of the Spanish Inquisition limited to the more gruesome and bloodcurdling activities for which this ancient purge was still ill-famed.

Hubert Rollistone looked thoughtful for a moment, replying, "It's a safe assumption, for their sudden departure coincided with the monk's violent death. I shall spare you the details, as enough horror has been described in this room tonight. But the man died slowly, under such tortures as can be found in descriptions of the Inquisition's worst atrocities. In the account, it was stated that '*The poor abbot's final cry was so sustained and so piercing in its agonies that it was heard echoing into the stillness of the night throughout all the neighbouring lands, where folk woke affrighted and prayed for their own souls, even as far off as the bishop's palace, where the Lord Bishop, being so mortally terrified by the ferocious sound, suffered a fit of the brain and a babbling in tongues that left him crippled in both mind and body until his own eventual, painful demise.*'

"That eerie cry, you will hardly be surprised to learn, has proved an enduring ghost story in these parts, although whose voice it's still thought echoes horribly between the pillars and porticos of every church in the area at times of crisis has long been forgotten. Until Flagstaff's processes peeled away the layers of lies that had helped mask the truth of it. That these agents had a definite object to their mission, beyond the murder of the monk, becomes apparent when you learn that all of the restored and newly consecrated churches in the area were searched, their interiors torn apart with vicious force. They were looking for something."

"The Devil's Crown," said Eleanor and I in unison.

"That had to be it! The dates, the Papal agents, the mysterious wealth, all tally with Medaccini's legend. Even the monk's motives are at one with Medaccini's. If his ransacking of the Vatican vaults was prompted by his disgust over the corrupt use of the wealth contained within, surely using that same wealth to provide churches for the faithful and needy would be his ultimate aim?"

"It is a convincing argument, Professor," admitted Holmes. "Though not the only one. The Inquisitors may be a safe assumption, perhaps, but your manner suggests they are not a foregone conclusion. Who else sought the crown in those far gone days?"

A flabby hand drummed unhappily on the table, and the professor's eyes darted from the darkened windows to the library door and to seemingly every shadow in between. At last assured no lurking presence listened nearby, he whispered, "That sect who had made such an icon from poor Sidika's felled head have been immortalised in certain legends of the crown under the fanciful term 'The Alliance of the Faceless', as they shunned the daylight so completely they elected to wear the night close to them, contained in cowls and hoods so deep their faces were never seen."

"But were they not supposed to have been put to death with the fall of their temple?" I asked, grimacing at the thought of a cold iron spike pressing against my skull, awaiting the hammer's fall.

"Some were believed to have escaped, even to have crawled into the very blackness of the walls themselves. An effort was once made to locate any concealed panels, or even bones within the walls. All that were found were more offerings, some older even than the house. Had any survivor or their descendant located their lost crown, you might be certain they would have returned it to that house of dark worship. But does it matter if those hooded clerics were the agents of one church or another? They came seeking their relic and the foreign abbot perished. Can any say that one order did God's work, and the other the Devil's, when the result was surely the same?"

"So you contacted Professor Wexley, and all three of you resumed your search here."

"Oscar returned from the continent, where his researches had led him aimlessly in circles these last few years, and he, Ronald, and I made a detailed study of all the churches in the area. Ronald overcame many of his worst fears at the prospect of the wealth and fame he imagined might be his should our search bear fruit."

"You spoke of having retired from your quest," prompted Holmes, "but not entirely, I imagine."

"Can you imagine any man would be able to completely ignore the apparent close proximity of something he has spent so many decades seeking? I do find myself often going through my books long into the night, hoping to find some clue that has thus far eluded me, even though I drew as much information as it's surely possible to glean from them many years ago. I suppose there lies a natural streak of stubbornness in most men which will not let them yield to defeat."

"Does Professor Flagstaff possess this same stubborn streak, or did he also give up in his pursuit of the crown?"

"Ronald? No, he certainly was not ready to quit. I never had, in the long years we had toiled together, seen him so determined before. I suppose greed can have that effect on a normally placid man. We argued long and loudly about it. The transformation from a nervy, edgy, gentle soul to a cursing, quick-tempered brute was quite the most shocking thing. Any thought of riches lying just beyond his grasp inflamed his fury, and I took my life in my hands ejecting him from these very premises when his insults and tantrums proved unendurable. It was at this point that our paths separated."

I reflected on this description of an irrational, obsessed and desperate man. "Could he be the one, Holmes?"

His attention solely on Rollistone, Holmes asked, "Is Flagstaff still seeking the crown?"

"I find that unlikely. No, I haven't spoken with him about it. I haven't communicated with Ronald in three weeks. I have not been able to. You see, he has disappeared."

"Disappeared?" echoed Eleanor, horror plain in both her face and voice.

"Yes, my girl. I have no wish to alarm you further, but he has vanished! And I think it unlikely that any trace of Ronald Flagstaff will ever be found. Not on this earth, at any rate."

"You appear certain of this, Professor."

"I am, Mr. Holmes. I had no hand in whatever fate has ultimately befallen him, I assure you, but I am certain he is lost to us all. That is all I can say on the matter."

"In which case we shall trouble you no further," said Holmes, and he stepped smartly toward the stairs. "Come along, Miss Wexley, Watson."

"Mr. Holmes, a moment further?" called the old scholar. "Sir, your questions have shown an uncanny—I'm almost tempted to say 'supernatural'—insight, and this has created questions in my own mind, which I would very much like to hear answered. If you would not mind humouring me?"

"Briefly, then. It is getting very late."

"Ha! You have nerve, Holmes, I'll give you that. But why should you, your friend, Watson, and young Eleanor travel all this way to ask this old man questions about an even older legend? Especially since you could have saved yourself the trip and simply consulted Oscar's journals?"

"Those that were still in the family's possession,"

muttered our companion, gripping the small volume she had earlier discovered.

"I was interested," replied Holmes, "in seeing the type of man who might covet such an object."

"Then," said Rollistone, with an elaborate bow, "I hope you enjoyed the view. No response, sir? Ah, a diplomatic reply, if ever I've failed to hear one. Yes, it must be disappointing to have come looking for a treasure-seeker only to find a man who is tired of the chase."

"Surprising, perhaps. Considering that the information which could conclude the trail exists. One person knows where the crown is."

"Then I would very much like to meet him," chuckled the folklorist. "Or do I mean her?"

"Miss Wexley," cried Holmes, as if in sudden recognition that he had been neglectful of his manners. "I'm afraid you must be exhausted following our long journey. Watson, the cab driver shall no doubt be growing impatient, even with the extra sovereign I gave him for his time. Kindly escort our young friend out."

"Of course. Come along, my dear," I replied absent-mindedly as I proffered my arm.

"Thank you," she smiled, "my dear."

"My apologies," I stammered, "I only meant, rather, I should have said, if you are quite ready, Miss Wexley ..."

Then, leaning close so that I was the only one to hear, she laughed, "You are going to be so easy to tease, aren't you?"

Seeking escape before either Holmes or Rollistone might spy the blushing grin I strained to conceal when she, with her father's old journal tucked under one arm, accepted my own arm with the other, I led Eleanor Wexley toward the staircase, but took a backwards step as our host rushed up behind us, declaring, "You shall need the candle. There are enough twists and turns in that hallway to lose a native guide. And, in the dark, it's ..." His next sound was a strangulated croak, as the struck match hovered near the candle on its shelf by the door.

It was no easy task to take the flame from his trembling fingers without being burned, but with the candle finally lit, I sought the source of his fright. "There's nothing there, sir."

"Did you look closely? No, of course. I just thought I saw ... within the shadows, just the movement ... The small ones I don't mind so badly. With dimming sight such as mine, I can't usually see them. So when I do spot one, it means it's either not small at all, or far too bloody close!" With a shudder, he concluded, "My apologies. I fear I am getting as nervy as dear, lost Ronald. Good night, dearest girl, Doctor."

We nodded our goodbyes, and as I turned my glance back, Holmes simply waved us on, while he stood casting a last, long look around the room. I wondered then, as I would wonder since on many occasions and in many locations, just what his senses might perceive in our surroundings that my own had failed to grasp.

"Your friend is very mysterious," whispered Eleanor Wexley, close by my side in the doorway.

"Sometimes," said I, "I think he does it just to annoy me."

"One last question, Mr. Holmes," said Rollistone, breaking in finally on my friend's meditations. "If you did not consult Oscar's notes, how did you know exactly where to find what you were looking for in all these books?"

"Our professions are not too dissimilar, Professor," said he, as he stepped up swiftly to join us in the doorway. "Like you, I too follow trails in the dust."

And on those words, we departed, leaving Hubert Rollistone to pour himself a large measure of brandy with a far from steady hand, and to gaze curiously and nervously about himself as he stood alone in his gloom-filled study while, from shelves and charts and cases, the faces of myriad inhuman beings glaring impassively back at him.

Chapter 13: An Ethical Dilemma

Night had fully fallen when we left the questionable comforts of Oldmire Priory, and as the surly cabbie drove us back to the Drovers' Pass, our hotel in Harewynd village, the combination of the darkness, our lack of conversation, and the motion of the coach wove their soporific spell on our travelling companion, for I can remember vividly the moment her head rested against my shoulder and her fingers gently curled around my wrist. My heart was beating so strongly within my chest that I felt sure the vibrations would waken her, which was the last thing in the world that I could have wished. She needed rest, to gain some respite from this strange adventure into which she had been thrust. I was concerned for her wellbeing, of course, yet it also pleased me greatly that even after so short a time in one another's presence, she seemed so at ease with, and so trustful of me. I had already sworn to offer what protection I could to this brave and beautiful lady. Now I knew without doubt that I would gladly die to keep her safe.

Sherlock Holmes said nothing throughout the coach ride and, even though I was bursting with questions, I was grateful for his silence. As the village lights filtered through the cab's windows, I observed that my friend's grey eyes were closed and his expression was as peaceful as Miss Wexley's. I knew he was not sleeping, however, and that beyond that serene mask lay a furiously racing engine, rapidly driving fragments of data through all conceivable permutations, and adding fresh knowledge to that ever-shifting process as his mind turned over every detail of our encounter with Professor Hubert Rollistone. My assumption was borne out when the cab drew to a halt outside our hotel. Before the horses had come to a complete standstill, Holmes flew from his seat, flung the door open and tossed a handful of coins to the driver.

I woke Eleanor as gently as I could and, as we climbed down from the cab, we could see only the tails of Holmes's coat as he disappeared into the hotel. I would not easily be able to catch up with my friend. The cold night air still caused my wounded leg to ache dully, but with an encouraging smile the gracious lady offered me her arm for support, and we followed in his wake. Inside the warmly comfortable hotel, we found Holmes waiting none too patiently outside Miss Wexley's room. Absent was the placid expression, replaced with one of intense urgency. I realised then that it was likely to be some little time before we would get any sleep that night.

What little light there was within Eleanor Wexley's room came from the corridor, throwing our three long shadows across the rug, and from the large window, where the moonlight cast a silvery patch of light upon the bed. "What is it that's so urgent, Holmes?" I hissed, and as he pressed a thin finger to his lips, I tensed, anticipating perhaps some sudden ambush from unseen lurkers in the dark corners of the unfamiliar room.

Holmes hurried across, drawing the blind swiftly down as he passed, and lit the lamp atop a chest of drawers, revealing nothing other than a sparsely but comfortably furnished, room, uninhabited by any skulking foe. Framed rustic scenes, rolling hills, seascapes, and sketches of churches hung around the walls, colluding with the florid wallpaper to render the décor both bland and busy. There was a single bed, upon which Miss Wexley's suitcase sat, a chair nearby, with its twin facing a compact dressing table. In the corner stood a set of screens, behind which I discreetly cast a glance, just to allay any lingering suspicions of intruders and spies. Eleanor, caringly mindful of my old injury, insisted on escorting me to the chair by the dressing table, placing Oscar Wexley's rediscovered journal on the table top in front of me. As our companion closed the door, Holmes, his sharp vigilance dropping away, sprawled back atop the bed, his long body an ungainly slump of angled limbs, but his mind still deep in thought.

Eleanor Wexley, unfazed by this liberty, discarded her hat and coat across the foot of the bed. But even one as unworldly in so many respects as Sherlock Holmes must have known that certain proprieties existed, so I hissed again, "You're sitting on Eleanor's ... I mean to say, on Miss Wexley's ... Dash it all, Holmes, you're on the lady's bed!"

"I'm sure she will find it very comfortable," said he, blandly, as he rose.

Eleanor failed to hide her amusement as she explained, "The good doctor is being very gallant."

My embarrassment burned in my cheeks like a furnace. "You must find me terribly old-fashioned."

"Not at all," said she, sincerely. "But now I am very keen to learn what Mr. Holmes is thinking."

"Well?" I prompted, turning to Holmes, who now occupied the other chair, his chin resting on his pale knuckles, his hands in turn clasped on the head of his cane.

"Hmmm? Do you think I might prevail upon you for a cigarette, Watson? My own are in my room, and I'm sure Miss Wexley would find the smoke less disagreeable than my pipe tobacco. Thank you. 'Well', you ask. You were there. What did you think?"

"I can hardly see of what value the trip has been," was my morose response. "I found the house depressing, our host irritating and, apart from that ridiculous and repellent story, which, I must add, I found incredibly far-fetched, he said nothing which can help us."

"This may be true, but it is what he failed to say that I find very leading."

"How so, Mr. Holmes?"

"Yes. Speak sense, man! You're nearly as bad as Rollistone, with your half statements."

"Then I shall make a full statement," said he, exhaling a plume of smoke that briefly hung like a question mark in the air before him. "The professor has lived his long life following trails which have been laid by his insatiable curiosity. He has traversed the globe, fuelled only by the need to know where those glimmering trails converge. Now, two strangers and the daughter of his late colleague and fellow trail-follower arrive speaking of a problem for which they require a solution. How strange is it, then, that he shows little interest in the nature of this mysterious problem?"

"Most strange," mused Miss Wexley, "unless he, somehow, is involved with the problem!"

"Oh, he is involved, though whether willingly or not...?" Holmes frowned, the frown resolving into alert determination. "I will have to see Professor Ronald Flagstaff next."

"Then you don't believe that he has disappeared?"

"That is a question which will be easily answered, old fellow. Such an eminent man's vanishing could scarcely go unnoticed."

"Of course, there would have been an investigation! But will the police give out such information."

"If they do not, someone at the university will know something of the matter. I shall have to make enquiries. Without the data I need, I am not prepared to theorise."

Even so I persisted. "But could Flagstaff have been Rollistone's visitor?"

"Possibly I will have the answer to that very soon."

"You think so? How?"

A slight smile flickered at the corners of his mouth. "I have my ways, you know that."

I was on the verge of further protest at this deliberate, goading vagueness, when Holmes leapt to his feet and drew Eleanor across the room to settle her in his just vacated chair. From here she looked up, wide-eyed in bafflement and some alarm. Holmes calmly returned her gaze. "It has been a tiring day for you, and I promise you shall rest soon."

"I am perfectly alert, sir," said she, the determination I so admired quickly returning.

I stood and drew closer, my protective instincts flaring, as Holmes crouched down and stared directly into her large green eyes, transfixing her just as a serpent might paralyse its prey. "Good. You shall need to be fully alert and on your guard, as there may still be some degree of danger. But for now I need your mind focussed on one particular thing. I need you to think. To think hard! Was there anything, absolutely anything at all in that house which may have helped dislodge whatever is blocking your memory?"

"I cannot recall."

"Think!"

"I'm trying!"

"Your father's last words? Come along, now! Think!"

"Holmes," I protested, "This is atrocious behaviour!"

"Come now, girl! The Crown! What did he say to you! Damn it all, will you think?"

In utter horror at his hectoring manner, I reached out a furious hand to grab Holmes by the shoulder. Having since observed how capably and formidably he can handle such assaults upon his person, I may be grateful that I was merely brushed away by an abrupt raising of a pale hand, and silenced by a slim finger which pointed to Eleanor's lips, as they moved, slowly and quietly, in an attempt at forming the words that had been trapped inside for so long. With difficulty I made out the carefully, almost painstakingly enunciated words. "All … All this time, I … I was looking for it and it … It was … It was …"

"Go on, Eleanor," I urged, my whisper of encouragement almost as quiet as her own.

"And all this time it was …" Her eyes squeezed tightly shut and her brows knitted as the frown deepened, until a pained groan issued forth. Jumping out of the chair and turning savagely on us, she cried, "I don't know, damn it! I can't remember! Why must everyone try forcing me to remember?"

There fell a long silence, during which Holmes stepped clear. Yet just as swiftly as the anger had risen in Eleanor Wexley it dissipated, leaving her abjectly repeating, "I'm so sorry."

I lightly took hold of her hands and sought earnestly to assure her, "There's nothing you need apologise for."

"Dr. Watson is correct," confirmed Holmes quietly, drawing once more on his cigarette. "It is I who must apologise. Since it was shock that caused the memory to be lost, I had hoped its recovery also lay in shock."

"It was damn reckless of you, Holmes! She has endured enough ill treatment. Another trick like that could cause severe nervous collapse."

"You're right, old fellow. Miss Wexley needs her rest. I will bid you both a good-night."

"Goodnight, Mr. Holmes," said Eleanor, but the door had already closed at my associate's back.

I remained deeply troubled by all that had just occurred. Yet it surprised me still to hear my thoughts voiced, as I admitted, "Sometimes I find him the most inhuman creature."

I realised then that my hands were still clasped with Eleanor's. Just as I realised too that she was in no hurry to let go, and I grew even more deeply aware of how comfortable I felt in her presence. "You mustn't think that, John. Mr. Holmes is only trying to help me."

"I know," I sighed, and I repeated it, as if hoping to reassure myself that she had judged my friend correctly.

"I know. Now, you're sure you are all right?"

"Do you fuss over all your patients so?"

"That's the second time I've been called a fuss in as many days," I groaned.

Delicate fingers lightly touched my cheek. "With you around, I feel as safe as if I had no cares in the world. I am very grateful."

With no earthly desire to move away, yet aware of the feelings that already compelled me, and which would undoubtedly overwhelm my good senses should I not, I stepped away and paced the room, unwilling to let Miss Wexley observe the flush on my skin that I felt would surely singe her fingertips were I to allow them still to caress my face. "Well," I announced, staunchly, "neither Sherlock Holmes nor I will rest until your case is solved and those who have wronged you are dealt with. I can promise you that."

It was Eleanor Wexley's moment to turn her back on me, as she opened her suitcase and busied herself in unpacking. Even so, I heard her quiet words. "That is not what I meant, John."

I had hoped this was the case, even if I could hardly dare admit it to myself, let alone to her. "You must get some sleep, Eleanor. If you need it, I could make you up a sleeping draught."

"I think I'll sleep well enough without it. It has been a very long day," said she as she turned round, and I saw with a start that she held her nightdress. As she let down her dark hair, I averted my gaze, and backed clumsily toward the door.

"Yes. Well, yes," I stammered. "Of course, I won't detain you any longer." My hand found the door handle while my eyes desperately strove to look anywhere but in the direction I privately wished to gaze, and in so doing fell upon Oscar Wexley's battered old journal on the dressing table. "You might want to lock that away just in case." I cursed myself silently. In case of *what*, exactly? Did I wish to fill her dreams with shadowy intruders in the night?

"To be on the safe side, rather. Not that I think you're in danger, of course. Holmes is nearby, and my room is just along the ... Well..." I fumbled with the handle, then finally, after what seemed an excruciating age, edged myself out into the corridor. "Goodnight, Miss Wexley."

As I closed the door, my heart's pounding almost obscured her appealing, kindly laugh as she quietly replied, "Goodnight, my dear Watson."

I traversed the short corridor while consumed by a strange and disorienting mix of dreadful embarrassment and absolute, unadulterated joy. The red flush in my cheeks sprang from the knowledge that she had read my emotions so easily. How could she have failed to? Here was I, a veteran of battle, a medical man, no mere boy, yet I was stammering, blushing and fussing like a pale-faced youth anticipating his first kiss. It certainly would not have taken a consulting detective to read the signs. My feet should have been dragging, and my head would have hung heavy were it not for the fact that I believed—no, I knew deep in my loudly hammering heart—that I was not alone in my feelings of love. I was not so inexperienced to be unaware of a certain light in Eleanor's eyes, or a lilt in her voice that suggested my emotions were shared, and were reciprocated.

How I envied her poise and the effortless way she remained unflustered, while I desperately tried—and hopelessly failed—to conceal my growing passion.

I was grateful to find Holmes's door closed as I passed. Knowing well enough, even in those early days of our acquaintance, his antipathy toward any notions of romance, as well as his views on what should be considered a professional distance between us and our clients, I imagined one glance at me would have provoked a stern glare, a haughty silence, and, inevitably, a prolonged and merciless lecture on the importance of objectivity in an investigation. Nonetheless, I did knock upon his door and bade him goodnight, but was unsurprised to receive no reply. Knowing Holmes, he could have been fast asleep the moment he lay down, or pacing the floor, his pipe filling the atmosphere with the reeking fog that seemed to clear his vision even as it obscured his surroundings, his mind so full of theories that anything less than an axe-assault upon the door or a fusillade of cannon beneath his window might go unnoticed.

With no wish to tempt fate by lingering too long in the corridor, I retired to my room where I knew I would not sleep for many hours yet, as my own brain whirled with thoughts of the lovely young woman I had just left and the perils which lay ahead. Yet, even as I primed myself for a wakeful night, I was unprepared for the sudden cry of stark terror that rung out along the corridor and which I knew, with a jolt of horrified certainty, issued from Eleanor Wexley's room.

My faithful old revolver came swiftly to hand, and after throwing my dressing gown over my nightshirt and seizing hold of a lamp, within the briefest of seconds I had pounded back along the hall, unmindful of any ache in my leg as I ran to rattle the handle and pound upon the door, demanding to know that Eleanor was all right!

In return, a pitiable voice pleaded, "Leave me alone!"

I was less able to put the aching of my shoulder out of mind as I applied it several times to the locked door, before the key turned inside and I fell, gritting my teeth against the pain, into the darkened room. Panic-stricken, and shivering from more than the coldness that seemed to have settled there, I looked around wildly before seeing Eleanor Wexley, clutching at the throat of her nightdress as she sank back into the chair with a whispered groan of, "Please, just leave me alone."

"Eleanor," I cried, and I set the lamp down on the bedside table so that she could see clearly that it was I and that I meant her no harm. "What is it? What happened?"

Her troubled expression cleared for an instant, and I hoped I saw recognition in her eyes, before abject horror distorted her face once more. She raised a trembling arm, a pale finger pointing toward the shifting curtains, from behind which came a regular tap-tap-tapping, as of something insistently knocking to be let in.

"Someone ..." She shuddered. "Some *thing* at the window!"

I dashed forward and threw back the billowing draperies to find the blind swaying back and forth, its lower edge tapping against the window's frame. I drew it up to find the window open; merely a sliver between sash and frame, but ample to admit the draught of chilling air that swirled around me. "It's nothing," I soothed. "Only the wind in the curtains. Fool that I am, I should have checked the window was secure. Was it Holmes's cigarette smoke? Perhaps you opened it to air the room?" I was about to lower and lock it when I sighted the ghastly thing that crouched upon the window-sill.

My first idea was that it was some horridly pale slug or snail, like that I had seen slithering up the darkened priory window. I must have given voice to my disgust, for Miss Wexley gave a start behind me, fearfully asking what was wrong. It was only as I turned my head to attempt to reassure her that I perceived, on the far side of the hotel's enclosed grounds, a dark shape that stealthily crept between the trees. I swiftly rejected the notion of a nocturnally strolling guest, for we were practically the small establishment's sole inhabitants, and the few remaining members of staff had no reason to tiptoe and skulk in the gardens. A pale smudge shifted as the figure turned its face to look directly back at me. With no further thought I flung up the window and raised my revolver, calling out, "Stay exactly where you are, or I shall not hesitate to fire!"

I was aware of Eleanor rising behind me, as she gasped, "Who is it?"

"A figure! It's in the trees! It's going! You, there! Stop!"

"Who, John? Can you see? Who is it?"

"He—I think it is a man, I can't be certain—is moving too fast. I've only one chance to get a clear shot." The grounds seemed to swarm with shadows, and it was only

210

the crashing of footsteps and the occasional glimpses of a half-concealed face or a darting white hand that allowed me to keep trace of my quarry. Yet before I could squeeze the trigger, all concentration was shattered by Eleanor's piercing scream, and the slump of her suddenly limp form tumbling to the floor.

I dropped my gun, the shot still chambered, and flew to her, gently lifting her wilting frame onto the bed. Here she lay gasping, "Who was it? Dear God, John, who was it?"

"I don't know. He ... they got away."

She clung to me then, tightly holding herself close to me so that I felt her shuddering. "I was so frightened."

I lowered her back into the pillow and murmured some feeble words of assurance, then weighed my revolver in my hand and hastened to the door. "I have to go after them."

"Please, don't! Don't leave me here."

"I won't be long, and Holmes can look after ... Holmes? He must have heard, surely? Stay here. I'm only going along the hall to check on him."

But my knocking upon Holmes's door again elicited only silence, and as I opened it onto an untenanted room, I cursed in apprehension. Where could he have gone at such an hour? Absurdly, my immediate thought was of that fleeing figure, darkly clad and pale of face, that had so frightened our charge. My anger rose as I considered the possibility that this had been yet another attempt to shock Miss Wexley's secret from her. Absurd, as I say, and when I spied the pale sheet of notepaper folded upon his table and with my name written across it, I already regretted the unworthiness of the thought.

I lingered no longer than necessary in Holmes's abandoned room, but dashed through to the front of the hotel, where I but fleetingly glimpsed the astonished gawp of the night-porter who had surely never seen a madman in a dressing gown tearing half-dressed into the street after dark. Had he realised the pocket of that gown contained a loaded gun, his astonishment would have been complete. There was no-one in the street itself or, from what I could see of the unlit expanse, on the village green, and I skirted quickly round to the hotel gardens. It was too dark to see much of anything, even had I any of Holmes's skills in determining detail from boot-marks and stride-lengths. I moved as silently as possible, not wishing the unnerved Eleanor to mistake my movements for those of the intruder, thereby causing her more unwarranted terror, and crouched low beneath her window to retrieve the small, white object that had fallen there. Here was the object I had mistaken for a slug, yet whatever it was, it was not alive. I slipped it into my pocket for closer analysis in the light, and looked up to see the face of Eleanor Wexley beyond the glass, gazing out and not seeing me. And surrounding her frightened, watchful face, as if grasping for her throat, I saw the clear outlines of two handprints smudged onto the glass where those unknown hands must have pressed themselves as they had begun sliding the window open.

With a cursory goodnight nod to the porter in passing, I returned to find Eleanor still gazing out into all the corners of the night. She turned, startled, and I wasted no time in guiding her away from the window, closing and firmly fastening it, and drawing down the blind. To her questioning look, I said, "Holmes has gone."

"Then they have him?"

"No. His room was quite in order. This was on his table," said I, and I opened out the letter and quickly scanned its terse contents.

"What does it say?"

I shrugged, hoping to dismiss it, but Eleanor Wexley's defiant spirit had fully returned. "Please, if it involves me I would like to know. You can't protect me by keeping me ignorant."

With no possible argument to make, I handed her the letter to read for herself.

Watson,
I fully anticipate returning before noon. Should
I be delayed, however, I am quite sure you will
need no urging from me to persuade you to keep
a close watch on Miss Wexley. Vital you do not let
her out of your sight at any point!
S. H.

"Then," she said, after a moment's thought, "Mr. Holmes believes the danger I'm in is very great? No, you needn't answer; your expression tells me everything. It isn't only your friend who perceives such danger. Whatever it is, I shall face it. Despite what Mr. Sherlock Holmes may think, I don't need you to watch over me as if I were a child."

"Believe me, I already know you to be both brave and resourceful. But, here, you're shivering."

She permitted me to sit her on the edge of her bed, where I draped a blanket around her shoulders. "You would shiver too, I think, seeing that ghastly shadow."

She then told me of what had occurred after I had left her alone in her room scant moments before. "I'd dressed for bed, extinguished the lamp, and had just pulled back the bedsheets to climb in when I remembered that the journal we'd rescued from the priory's library was still sitting on my dressing table, and not hidden away or under lock and key.

"'Stupid girl,' I told myself, 'You're getting forgetful.' And, by the moonlight still visible through the thin blind, I crossed over to the dresser and lifted the journal. I stood for a moment, my fingers pressed to the binding, enjoying the knowledge that, in another time, my dear father had held the same book in his own hands. 'Well, Father,' I wondered aloud, 'what kind of trouble have you got your angel into?'

"I'd opened a drawer, ready to place the journal into it, when the room fell suddenly black, as the moonlight was blotted out for an instant. I froze still, not wanting to move, and then I heard the window creaking and the noise of the wind outside growing stronger. Finally, unable to bear the agonising tension any longer I whirled round in time to see a grotesque silhouette on the blind, its long arms raised, palms pressed against the glass, sliding the window open.

"I don't know how I found the breath or the nerve to speak, yet, 'Who's there?' I cried. The reply was harsh and whispered, and my mind was instantly back in that awful séance room, plagued by the echoes of my own name being called. It was then that I screamed for it to go away, and the next I knew there was a hammering on the door, so that I feared whatever it was had found its way inside. I know now that was you, my brave rescuer. But my mind was a maelstrom of terror, and rather than go mad under the weight of my own fright, I thought to let whatever it was in and be done with me."

"I understand. But it is gone."

"Thanks to you," she smiled, taking my hand.

"But why did you cry out, even after the intruder had fled? When I had him in my sights, why did you scream?"

"The face! That dreadful face came back to me in a rush. I fear it will haunt me every time I close my eyes. A face like a living corpse." She stared hard into my eyes, seeing only confusion there. "The thing that tried to get in here. It was a thing! No living person could look like that. Those awful, hateful eyes!"

"It couldn't have been the thing ... the person at the window," said I, gently. "It was a person, make no mistake about that. What I saw was no phantom. But the blind was drawn. You couldn't have seen any face."

Eleanor fell silent a moment, then in a very quiet voice said, "Then I am going mad!"

"You are not mad! Don't ever think that. You've gone through a number of shocks; that sham séance, Rollistone's monstrous story, this attempted break in! Your imagination is bound to be working overtime. And, since you are clearly exhausted, it's far from surprising that an imagined horror might seem real. It is the only rational answer."

"Then I am grateful to have a rational man to bring me to my senses."

It felt like the least rational thing in the world to then say, "You must get some sleep. Even though I hate to leave you alone after this...."

"Then stay. For a while, at least."

"If that is your wish."

"It is."

I paced restlessly. "I blame myself, of course! I should have ensured that the window was secure."

"You can't think of everything."

"Holmes does."

"Mr. Holmes isn't here."

"No. He isn't." I wondered once more about the mission that had summoned my friend away at such an hour and, from this thought, suddenly mindful of the time of night, insisted, "You should lie down and, at the very least, try to rest."

Eleanor climbed into bed and, reminding myself that she was no different from any of the patients—female or otherwise—I had attended during my time at St. Bart's, I efficiently, with barely a quiver of my hands, pulled the covers up around her. I cannot imagine I was anything but awkward, and as I tried to control my nerves I felt myself tense suddenly in pain, my hand flying to my shoulder.

"You're hurt," exclaimed Eleanor, her hand lightly resting on mine. "Your Afghan wound?"

"I must have aggravated it when I put it to the door. The stupid thing is I didn't even notice at the time," I lied.

Eleanor drew me down, so that I sat on the bed next to her. "I have put you to a great deal of trouble."

"You? No, never! I have been called on to do nothing that any decent person could refuse."

"I think that you are more decent than most. You don't agree? No, but that is part of your natural decency. And to have done so much for someone you hadn't met before yesterday, and whom you have really no reason to help ..."

"There are reasons, I assure you. Despite the ghastly circumstances, I must admit I'm grateful that your brother secured our services. Firstly, there is Holmes."

"He's a very brilliant man."

"Brilliant, yes ..."

"Yes, but?"

"He has," I began, unsure of how I might, or if I even should, continue. But that sense of complete ease which I felt with this thoughtful and compassionate companion spurred me on. "He has problems of his own. I should not like to say more, but if this case can spare him for some short time at least from his own demons, then that alone is worth it. And you could not ask for a better champion than Sherlock Holmes."

"Nor he for a better friend."

"Holmes has helped me get over the horrors that befell me in Afghanistan. Whether he knows that or not, I have no idea. Should I tell him? I foresee that if I tried he would either dismiss my thanks as a display of gross sentimentality, or show me by a careful dissection of my shaving habits that he had known so since approximately forty-three seconds after we first met. He can be *that* infuriating! Yet without him, and the trust he has shown in me, I imagine I would be stuck in dismal lodgings somewhere, squandering my pension, unfit for work, feeling useless and bitter."

"That would be a sad loss. For your friend. And for me. Does that sound selfish to you? I don't think that I would be coping quite so well without you. I confess that I find Mr. Holmes slightly intimidating."

I smiled. "I cannot believe that any man could intimidate you."

"Oh, I know that he's your good friend and that you admire him. It's for these reasons that I trust him. True, he has found clues and secrets in a way which I find entirely remarkable. But he strikes me as cold, not quite human in a way. 'The most inhuman creature,' you said, though I know you said it in anger. But the things he says to you, his friend, so cold-bloodedly ..."

"If it were any other man I would take great offence. But you're right. He's not as others. When he has some puzzle to tax that great brain of his, he is something more than any of us could hope to be. But, when he is without work," I sighed. "Dark times."

"I'm sure you will support him."

"I do. Or try to. I just wish he would let me in on his thoughts. While he's immersed in a case, I find his actions as baffling as the mystery which surrounds us. Then he'll turn around and present me with the facts as a *fait accompli*, making it all sound absurdly simple." Little did I then know that I was putting into words a sense of frustration that would go on to become an all-too familiar experience—just as my own habitual insistence on the absurd simplicity of things once clearly explained to me would prove just as irksome to Holmes. At that moment, however, only the resolution of the pressing case was of concern. "Until he chooses to reveal his deductions, we just have to wait and watch. If there was only some clue that we might apply our own minds to! If you could remember what your father said, there might be some way we could untangle this horror. What I wouldn't give for one tenth of Holmes's abilities. I must seem a dull fellow next to him."

This had not been intended as a leading statement, but even so I was surprised to receive no argument, nor any response at all, until I saw that my gentle companion was dozing, her eyes shut but her lips moving as she murmured inaudibly to herself. As lightly as I could, I eased myself into a more comfortable posture, only to feel a sudden shifting weight in the pocket of my gown. With some horror I remembered my revolver, and carefully decanted it to the bedside chair. In that same pocket I also found the object I had discovered during my reconnoitre of the grounds. As I held it up to the light I saw that it was certainly no mere snail. It was around the size of a chess king, white and intricately carved. The craftsmanship was beautiful, though the subject was far from that. Winged like a bat and horned like a goat, it possessed a body that seemed in part spider, in part crab, and in equal parts octopus, yet with each tentacle bearing a minute, yet jaggedly barbed mouth upon which I had to take care not to snag my skin, as it would surely have drawn blood. Had it been one of those souvenirs with which we had earlier been surrounded in Professor Rollistone's study? That clearly had not been the huffing, ungainly professor who had raced off through the trees. I dropped the revolting carving back into my pocket, briskly brushing the fingers that had held it against my sleeve, only because I could not scrub them in scalding water. Because, as ancient as it was, and as polished by time, I had naturally recognised from what it had been carved. Naturally, I say, for as a doctor I can recognise human bone when seen at close quarters.

What purpose did this bizarre token serve? It had lain in the grass where I had knocked it in my haste to fire off a shot at whoever had delivered it. Was it meant as a warning, or as a threat? Or was it meant, instead, to somehow convey the curse, sending it forward to seek out new quarry? As ridiculous a notion as it may sound, I have since treated a most level-headed and unfanciful patient—a scientist on the board of several societies who had recently come under my care, and whose household staff I had not long since treated for a quite perplexing case of shell-fish poisoning—who told me, with all the seriousness of one who has researched such matters deeply, that these things are possible and that even inanimate objects may be used for malice; as the rueful, no-longer-sceptical Mr. Dunning would confide, he himself had felt some frightful fiend set against him by the agency of nothing more sinister than a slip of paper. But that story is for another to relate, and I knew nothing of such ideas as I sat in that hotel room, but still I pictured the grotesque thing sitting upon the sill, a morbid white beacon in the night, drawing some dark, faceless thing toward this hotel, toward this very room, and towards the sleeping and defenceless woman in this very bed.

And you, thought I, guiltily, *have allowed the damned thing in!*

I shuddered with alarm as this nightmarish idea beset me, before turning to see if my sharp movement had disturbed Eleanor in her sleep. But she was already awake. It was only when she urgently whispered my name that I noted the look of surprise that dawned in her eyes. "John! I've remembered. I do not know how. It must have been the shock of seeing that shape at the window, but the memory has come back. I can remember it all."

Holmes had been right, then, even if his own approach was questionable. "Well? Will you tell me, please?"

"Father was very weak. I could hardly make out his words, but he was so insistent that I hear him. I do not begin to know what it actually means, but my father's last words were; 'All this time I was looking for it, and I was looking through it, and it ... It was looking right through me!'"

I gazed at her, thunderstruck, and turned this curious phrase over and over in my mind. "Looking *through* him?"

"Yes. Those were his precise words. I'm certain of it!"

Frustrated at my own lack of understanding, I cried, "Holmes, where the devil are you?"

"Perhaps the Contessa, whoever she is, is wrong. What if it doesn't mean anything? What if my unfortunate father's mind had really failed him, and it was simply the fever talking?"

"Whoever she is, and whoever she's working with, they are convinced that it means something very important indeed. But we cannot let it occupy our minds any more tonight or we'll be fit for nothing in the morning."

"Remembering is like having a huge weight lifted from my mind. I will rest easier now."

"Good," said I. "You do that." What I had not expected was that she would choose to rest her head against my chest. I offered no protest, of course, merely put my arm around her shoulder and stroked her hair in what I fancied was a soothing manner. "Soon enough this whole awful business will be over, and you can get back to your normal life."

"I don't know that I want to return to normal. Not ever."

I had hoped for just such an answer, but my own reply was a measured, "You surely cannot be enjoying this nightmarish adventure?"

"At least it is an adventure. My whole life has been one of dull routine and boring normalcy. My work is tedious, typing out longwinded legal letters and dreary memoranda; my social life is no better. Dear Brother Nicholas has coddled me and protected me, as he likes to think of it, and in so doing has successfully prevented me from living the life I would choose. He saw what became of our poor mother, and it has made him determined that I should be comfortable in life, even though it is stifling me."

"It can't be much of an existence for him."

"That is just as I tell him. He had planned to marry once. Charlotte Parnham was a good match for him; rather proper and not fearfully exciting, but a kind woman and really very pretty in her way. They seemed deeply in love, but she, as is natural and proper, wished to set up as man and wife with him in their own home. What she did not need was a spinster sister mooning about the house with her head in a book and a mind full of dreams. I quite agreed, and took Charlotte's part, but Nicholas threw her over. 'Do you think it a Wexley inheritance that we simply abandon family to seek our own selfish pleasures?' he raged. 'I am nothing like he whose name I carry, and if I were then Charlotte would do better to find another! That is an end to it!'

"Had I found my own match, it would have been different. Someone who met his approval, naturally. A masculine version of stuffy Charlotte, perhaps; reliable, amiable, predictable, and ready to settle into a routine never to be broken by any threat of excitement or adventure, and not the sort of chap to run off leaving a wife and family, no matter how much she might secretly end up wishing him to go. No, no, any adulteries would be conducted in a civilised manner, in private, and tolerated in silence so as not to scandalise the neighbours."

I laughed, shocked by this forthright view.

"You think it indecent? Well, so you should, as do I. That's just not the life I could ever see myself choosing."

"What would you do with your life, then?"

She shot up again, her face alive with excitement. "I would get away from all that I've had to put up with these many years and travel the world. There are so many lands I've heard of, and dreamed of, but never have seen, and so many cultures I long to experience outside of the pages of books." Quietly, she added, "Maybe I will not have to experience them alone."

I said nothing, for too many different responses and possibilities tumbled and danced in my addled brain. Eventually it was she who spoke. "John? What was the second reason you were grateful?"

"I believe you already know that."

"I hope so, but I would like to hear it."

And then I told her, unleashing everything that had been building up inside my heart from probably the very second I had gazed upon a photograph of a beautiful, sad-eyed but bravely smiling young woman. "It is because of you, then. My dear, kind, clever, sad, laughing, fearless Eleanor! I have met no woman quite like you in my life and, if I can—and if you wish it, of course—then I am going to make damn sure no-one takes you away from me."

She cupped my face in her hands. Her lips were but a few inches from my own. "Let them try."

"We shouldn't do this," I insisted, making absolutely no move to break away. "Not now."

"Whyever not?"

"It is ..." What on earth was I floundering to say? "It's unethical."

"But it is my brother who is your client," she protested, "not I."

"No, but you are my patient."

"Well, Doctor," she gently informed me, "I have never felt better in all my life."

And then we embraced, eagerly enjoying to the fullness of our hearts this passing moment of light and joy in which we could pretend to be oblivious to the dark shadows that lengthened and swarmed around us.

Chapter 14: Guests at the Hall

On waking early the next morning—in my own bed, I hope I need not stress, having left Miss Wexley's room at around midnight, after which followed several watchful hours straining my hearing for any further disturbance before sleep finally claimed me—I dressed hurriedly and made directly for Holmes's room, anxious both to tell him of the attempted intrusion and of Eleanor's miraculously restored memory and to show him the ominous carved memento of the night's events. But no reply greeted to my repeated knocking, and his room lay as deserted as on my last visit.

Growing yet more anxious at my associate's continued absence, I was compelled to check on the young lady in our care. Yet something steeled my hand even as it was poised to rap upon her door. Would she, perhaps, be embarrassed to face me in the cold light of morning? Could the extraordinary closeness which we both had felt have been merely a product of emotions charged up by the extreme events of the preceding days? With these thoughts in my mind, I stood in that hallway for several moments before, after mustering as much courage as I possessed, I knocked lightly upon the door.

A few endlessly long seconds later it opened, and Eleanor Wexley stood before me looking as fresh and as happy as I believed any woman could. My heart skipped a military tattoo's-worth of beats as she smiled at me, that smile straying toward a discreet kiss, and, with my hand in hers, we strolled through to the Drovers' Pass's small dining room for breakfast.

Throughout the meal, she told me more of her dreams of travel and adventure, and her laughter filled every corner of the room. To think this was the same woman who had stood shivering in fright in front of me a few short hours before! Determined not to shake her good humour, I said nothing of my concern for Holmes and, excusing myself, I slipped out to enquire at the reception desk if there had been any word from my friend.

The receptionist was a dislikeable fellow, who wore a knowing smirk, so that I wondered momentarily what the porter may have told him of my late night perambulations. "Your friend?" he beamed, displaying as many of his teeth as he could humanly manage short of taking them out and placing the set on the counter. "Your friend, Mr. Sherlock Holmes? You were expecting a message from him, perhaps?" As coincidence would have it, it was at this moment the postman, face damp and pink from travelling the country roads on his well-used bicycle, breath short owing to the eight miles between Harewynd and the nearest telegraph machine, arrived with the morning's missives. He handed them to the receptionist, who made great show of sifting through the small pile of letters as slowly and methodically as possible, before reading the first of the telegrams. Then, putting his dentures on show again, he presented a second cable to me, and announced, "This appears to be for you, Dr. Watson. From your friend, perhaps?" I noticed his shark's grin transform into a no-more-pleasant look of anticipation as I opened the message and read:

Missing chemist is at Wynngrave Hall, ten miles east. Take a cab as soon as can be arranged. Do not bring our young friend. Instruct her that under no circumstances should she stray from her rooms. This is vital! Also, be so good as to give the receptionist who is no doubt waiting at your heels two sovereigns.

S.H.

I did as Holmes had bid, and the odd little chap pocketed the coins with an all-too-knowing grin, and a no-less-disagreeable wink, before disappearing into his office, doubtless to inspect his profits. Not a little bemused by this, I was more certain of the reaction I would—and, indeed, did—receive from Miss Wexley when I gave her my instructions.

It took a fair degree of persuasion before she would agree to remain where she was and, even then, she did so grudgingly, before finally throwing her hands up in mock exasperation and smilingly admitting that, no, she did not entirely mind remaining back at the hotel. "After you left me in the night, I barely slept with the noise and rumpus of all the things that are charging around in my poor head. It's merely the strange thrill of it that keeps me on my feet this morning, and purely elation that keeps the smile on my face; neither of which are any substitute for actual sleep, as I am sure an astute doctor might lecture me. I cannot promise that sleep will come, but I will try. On condition, mind you, that you tell me all that our friend has discovered upon your return. And on your oath that this return will be soon. I would so miss my gallant doctor."

The kiss that followed would have been somewhat less discreet had we not distinctly heard the clattering approach of the trolley bearing coffee and tea long before it entered the dining room.

I paused only to pocket my revolver and the winged figurine, before hailing a cab to convey me to this mysterious Wynngrave Hall. I was glad of the firearm's comforting weight in my pocket as I noted the driver's expression of revulsion on hearing our destination. He would say no more to my questioning on the matter, and merely shook his head sadly and insisted that his job was, "to take people where they asked to be took, not to tell 'em why they ought not to be so eager in goin' there!" And no sooner was that philosophy shared than we were on our way.

When the Hall itself came into view, I understood at once the cabbie's grim distaste. Surrounded by drably desolate moorland, miles from even the smallest hamlet, and enclosed by a stone wall topped with brutal spikes, Wynngrave Hall was a formidable, grey, crook-backed monstrosity, brooding in its own dreary solitude, its many windows black as the deepest pits and barred to keep anything out, or—as seemed more likely, for I could scarcely imagine anyone genuinely wishing to enter there— to keep its inhabitants in. I could easily have imagined that, as with the submerged tower in Rollistone's legend, this structure had been disgorged from the deepest chasm of the earth, its appearance seemingly designed to appeal to no human eye, and its function to afford no human comfort or kindness.

The closer we drew to this desolate edifice, the colder I felt inside. A bored looking gate-keeper slouched into our path. A hostile look gleamed dully in an eye that appeared to squint out of a mass of scars and dents instead of a face, and a vicious club was slung from his belt. "Private property," he growled, as if the sheer wall and its deadly ornamentation were insufficient to render that obvious. "Who might you be?"

"Dr. John Watson," I replied, with as much haughty authority as I could muster, while simultaneously quelling the urge to have the driver turn the carriage and fly. "I have an urgent appointment."

This last may have been stretching the truth, but the gate-keeper, with absolute disinterest, grumbled,

"Doctor, is it? Aye, well, you'd better go on in with you."
He flexed broad muscles then pushed back the immense
gate and waved us impatiently on. I did not look back
as we passed, as I had no great desire to see those gates
swing shut at my back, sealing me in with the Hall and
whatever or whoever inhabited it. I was deposited some
distance from the building itself and, before I could even
ask the cabbie to wait, he had whipped his horses around
and was speeding back through those same gates.

My apprehension over this fearful place at which I had
been abandoned was alleviated only when I perceived the
figure of Sherlock Holmes standing by the heavy front
door. He smiled grimly, but offered no word of greeting or
explanation as he led me inside. Here we travelled twisting
corridors, past ominous doors behind which I could hear
the most terrible sounds. I had gathered by now the nature
of the place, but that knowledge brought no comfort at all.
To keep my mind from the alarming surroundings, I took
the opportunity to give Holmes details of everything—
rather, *nearly* everything—which had occurred during his
absence. My narrative was accompanied throughout by
the stomping footsteps of the surly orderly—surely the
brawnier, even less personable twin to the gate-keeper—
and the clanking of heavy keys that formed a discordant
chorus with the shrieks, squeals, mutters, groans, and
whispers from behind barred doorways.

"There was no further attempt to gain entrance," I
concluded, "but I really am most uneasy at leaving Miss
Wexley behind."

"Would you have brought her into this place, Watson?"
said Holmes, as we paused to peer through the bars set
into one of the locked doors. The room beyond was little
more than a filthy cellar, its steep walls comprised of vast
brick archways between which wooden benches doubled
as cots for the occupants of the ward. For, appal me as it
does to credit this ghastly institution with the designation
of hospital, this it was. Had it been established by those
Inquisitors that had reputedly terminated the charity of

the nameless abbot, it might have taken pride among their famed torture chambers. On the benches or on the floor around them I counted a dozen or more pathetic figures, dressed—though barely so in some cases—in drab rags. Grimy, their shaven heads grey with stubble, and either wild-eyed or docilely blank-faced, laughing toothlessly or weeping without sound, these forgotten souls, whatever their misfortunes in life, were yet more unfortunate in finding themselves inmates of the Wynngrave Hall Asylum.

Would I have gladly exposed Eleanor to this degradation and despair? "Good God, no," I replied, as I clamped my handkerchief to my face to ward off the mingled scents of squalor, filth, and human suffering that issued up out of that grim abyss. "Though I fail to see why we are here."

"You shall," said Holmes.

"At least you're speaking at last," said I, and I hastened my stride to keep pace with him. "Well? Have you any idea what Professor Wexley's words meant? Or just who it might have been that attempted to enter Miss Wexley's room?"

"Those are questions which will be dealt with in their own time."

"Damn it all, Holmes! How long do you plan to keep me ignorant? You disappear without a word, just at a time when we might have urgently required your presence. Where have you been all night?"

"I should have thought you might be glad of my absence."

"And exactly what do you mean by that?"

"My dear fellow, I would never dream of interfering in your private life...."

"I would appreciate that."

"... but I warn you to take care. We cannot be sure that even the most innocent thing is as it seems."

For long seconds we faced one another in that corridor of torment, and it was only as I stepped aside to let a tiny, elderly figure shuffle past—with the brutally shorn head and shapeless garment that hung off the emaciated frame, I could not tell if it was a man or woman—and heard once more the cries and witless laughter, and even the tuneless singing of some vaguely familiar song, from the cells all around, that I again grew aware of the nature of the place to which our quest had brought us. I moved closer to the barred window from behind which that low, atonal chanting emanated, only to hastily step back as I observed the pale, bloodied fingers that flexed around the window's edges, as if ready to grab at any unwary passing throat.

"Tread careful along here, sirs," called the orderly. "Watch your backs. An' yer fronts too. Some o' they is awful sly! The fellow you gentlemen wants is this way, so don't dawdle, now."

"As you rightly say," offered Holmes, as we resumed walking, "I do owe you an explanation as to how we come to be in this unfortunate institution."

"Your telegraph said you had found Ronald Flagstaff."

"Yes. After we said our goodnights at the hotel, I caught the late connecting train to Camford. It is from there I have only just returned. Honestly, Watson, I have spent so many hours rattling back and forth in trains and carriages this last day, I fear my bones will take a month to cease vibrating. Well, then! Once at the university town, I called in on the police station. If the professor had disappeared, as friend Rollistone would have us believe, that was the best starting point I had."

"And the police talked to you?"

"They were only too glad to. It seems the circumstances surrounding Ronald Flagstaff were a mystery to which they despaired of ever finding a solution. They were certainly desperate enough to give the facts of the case, what little they knew, to an unofficial detective—though I may have improved my standing by flaunting the names of Lestrade and Gregson, the heroes of the Lauriston Gardens business, as potential referees should my credentials be doubted—in return for what information I could provide about the professor's activities. It's only on the authority of the local inspector, one George Braddock, that I was allowed access here."

"So, Rollistone was telling the truth after all. Flagstaff did disappear," said I. "But, if that's the case, how do you come to believe we will find him in this place?"

"Our friend Rollistone was somewhat selective in the truths he told us. For instance, he informed us that Ronald Flagstaff was a professor of chemistry. That much is true, but what he failed to reveal was that he was also a botanist, specialising in the plant life of the Americas. If we were to check back on some of the scientific journals of the last few years, we might find some interesting excerpts from a paper on the ritual uses of extracts of the San Pedran desert cactus."

"That insidious, damnable drug!"

As the orderly turned a key in an ironclad door and passed a lantern to my friend, I stormed forward, furiously demanding, "Where is this man? If he is working here, I will have it out with him now!"

"He is here. But not, I fear, working."

Holmes read the ghastly realisation in my eyes and nodded. "Yes, you have it, Watson." He brought around his lantern so that it lit up a room, high-ceilinged yet not much wider than a cupboard, its walls painted a bilious green that did little to disguise a multitude of stains and scars where fingers had raked the brickwork, and with a cramped cot pressed back against the wall. On its meagre mattress slumped a bulky figure, loosely garbed in an unfastened straitjacket, who stared up with dreaming eyes at a patch of light in the cracked corner of a begrimed window high above in the opposite wall. As the lamp's light fell upon him, the figure turned, his eyes widening with longing as he gazed at the lantern's flame, and I saw that one entire side of his face was horrendously scarred and burned. "This is Professor Flagstaff."

"Good God," I cried, as I looked in shock at the livid swirls and whorls that branded him from jawline to high above the hairline—had any hair not been shorn roughly away—and which consumed most of his right ear and bit deep into his upper lip. "But what has happened to him?"

Holmes handed me the lantern and sat on the bed next to the pathetic figure, where he softly enquired, "Professor Flagstaff? Ronald Flagstaff?" The large man remained hopelessly oblivious to my friend's words or presence, and as the lantern's light shifted away from him, his longing gaze returned to the high window.

As Holmes softly repeated the professor's name, I became aware of another's scrutiny as a pleasant voice chimed in, sighing, "You'll not get much out of that poor fellow, I'm afraid. Nary a word has he spoken since he was brought in."

"You sound quite sure of that. What diagnosis have you made?" I turned in expectation of finding one of the medical staff looking in from the doorway. Instead, I faced a sharp-eyed inmate who sidled up beside me, looking me up and down with oddly inquisitive eyes.

"Am I sure? Blood would be sooner fetched out of a stone than words drawn past that fellow's lips. Not a cheep-cheep-cheep. It's not that his lungs wouldn't power them, if he actually wanted to speak up for himself, for he can scream. You just come here when it's an overcast day, or there's no moon at night, and you'll hear that with your own ears, although you'd as soon wish you hadn't. My diagnosis, as you asked, is cats. That is to say, a cat's got his tongue, it has." His grubby fingers stroked the material of my coat sleeve. "Great big cat, it was. Big fat tom-cat. A black cat slinking in from a blacker night. It lies purring on his chest, I reckon, waiting for his mouth to open, then— gulp—down goes another tasty morsel until there's not even a sliver or a stub of his tongue left. No need for you to fret, though, good sir. I can see you're certainly no canary bird." The fellow laughed at his own jest, provoking muffled squeals of harsh delight from the cells close by. But such merriment was cut dramatically short as the orderly struck his truncheon against the metal door, the clanging retorts silencing the laughter and prompting groans of misery.

"Get back from the gentleman, you halfwit," he roared, and rough hands dragged the little inmate back into the corridor, from where he scurried away, mewling piteously.

"There was no need for that, man. He was doing no harm!"

"That one plays with them he can get his claws into, like a cat wi' a mouse, sir, an' I never once seen the mouse come out the better o' that game!" Then, slouching out to wait by the cell door, he muttered insolently, "But you please thyself, if you want to have your throat or your eyes torn out!"

I bit back on my anger with this ignorant oaf and returned my attention to my friend's attempts to communicate with Ronald Flagstaff. "A severe state of catatonia," he sighed, producing his pipe from his pocket to aid his contemplation. But as the match flared, Flagstaff turned, the tiny points of flame reflected in his eyes. Holmes, instantly alert to this attention, slowly raised the match to the level of his face, and the professor's eyes followed until their gazes were level. "Professor Flagstaff? Can you hear me?"

Painfully slowly, Flagstaff repeated his own name.

"That's right, yes," urged Holmes. "You are Ronald Flagstaff."

The pitiable fellow ponderously nodded his head, but Holmes's triumphant expression darkened, quite literally, as the match burned out. Flagstaff, denied sight of the precious flame, raised his head automatically toward the window once more. Following his gaze, Holmes's darted a hand out to me, exclaiming, "Watson, the lantern! It's the light, man! He responds to the light."

Holmes held the lantern level with his face, illuminating his sharp profile and causing his eyes to blaze with more than his own fiery intellect. With the gentlest but steadiest of grips, he gradually turned the other man's face toward him, until Flagstaff's own eyes fell on the lantern's glow, and from then on he needed no additional coaxing to turn fully face on to the detective. There may even have been the beginnings of a smile, though the raw, red twisting of his skin made this difficult to judge. "Professor Flagstaff, can you hear me?"

"Flagstaff?" The man's voice was a distant rumble, as if buried so deep within him that it took every effort to draw it out. "Flagstaff is dead. Dead, dead, dead. Poor Flagstaff."

"Dead?" I asked. "Then who...?"

Holmes raised a hand to silence me, but never did he break his gaze. "How do you know that Flagstaff is dead?"

"He has to be." The man grimly nodded his firm assurance. "Has to be dead, for they buried him, don't you see? They put him in his grave, where he belongs. Under the earth. Into the deep. Poor Flagstaff, under a flagstone. Tut-tut, a tombstone, there was no flag, nor marker."

"Who did this to Flagstaff? Who buried him?"

"They did. The three of them!"

"The three?"

"All three of them. Medaccini ... and Wexley ... and ... and Rollis ... stone. Did Rollistone roll the stone, I wonder, as the stone was rolled at Golgotha? Roll the stone, to keep the dead in their tomb. Tombstone, not flagstone. Tut-tut! They put him in the ground. The cold, dead, dark ground."

"Why did they do this to him?"

"Because he went to that place and died there. Poor Flagstaff went to Golgotha and died from the horror of it. Died with the frightful fiends. Their bony, skeleton hands reached out...." As he said so, his own hands stirred. His fingers softly twitched, their motions growing ever more agitated, before reaching out toward Holmes. "The faceless shadows with their cold, dead hands reached out and clutched his heart, and then they squeezed it and squeezed it till it burst, and he was dead! 'Frightened to death of his own shadow,' Oscar bloody Wexley used to say, with his big, cruel laugh. He never would listen when Flagstaff told him the shadow he was afraid of wasn't his own! Though Wexley was right that Ronald would be frightened to death! How did he see? Wexley was dead long before it happened. So, to see what would be, did he glimpse Ronald's dying through the Devil's eyes? If anything could see through the deep dark down in Golgotha, it would surely be they."

As Holmes slowly transferred the lantern from hand to hand, the light's motion caught and held Flagstaff's full attention, and his grasping hands dropped slowly into his lap. "Why did Flagstaff go to Golgotha? Was it because of the crown? The crown that the merchant made and lost, and that Medaccini stole?"

"No. No crown." Flagstaff shook his head from side to side, yet still his eyes remained fixed on the light. "Only bones. Bones and dust and skulls, and things as cold and dead as skulls but with no faces, only darkness within their robes, and they reach out blindly, scrabbling in the dust and bones, but there's no crown there. None at all." And as Holmes stood, his hand shading the lantern, Flagstaff's voice grew distant again, and his eyes drifted upwards. "No crown at all … Would you be so kind as to tell the shadows that, so they may retreat and not press in on me so? There is no crown that I can find, so let them leave me the light...."

"How did you know he was here, Holmes?"

"As I said, Flagstaff did disappear. For four days, just a week before Miss Wexley became involved with the Church of the Golden Star."

"Four days isn't that long a time."

"Ronald Flagstaff was a compulsively ordered man, according to what his university colleagues told the Camford police. Any excursion, no matter how brief, was planned and detailed meticulously beforehand. His superiors were notified and, upon his return, he would laboriously note all of his findings. It struck them as very suspicious, then, that he should abruptly break this habit and simply fail to appear for his lectures one morning. On the second day his rooms were checked, just in case he had fallen ill. There was no sign of him. They did find numerous plants and samples from his various outings, but nothing to indicate anything amiss. They also found a very well equipped photographic dark room, in which there were copious photographs of field expeditions and finds. Without seeing these photographs I cannot say for certain that Professor Oscar Wexley featured among their subjects, but I am inclined to believe that here was the source of those lantern slides that conjured Wexley's spectre for his daughter's benefit. The police were notified but they, as you, did not see any cause for alarm over such a short period of absence.

"And, on the fourth day, he returned," and my friend indicated the pathetic figure, "but like this. How did it happen? None could say. He was found in his rooms late at night, when one of the dozens of candles he had lit to ward off the darkness fell onto some papers and nearly destroyed the whole building. It was only the remarkable clear-headedness and decisive action of some late returning students—remarkable because they had been vigorously celebrating a triumph on the rugby field that day until the sight of the flames quickly sobered them— that saved both residence and its occupant."

"That was a stroke of good fortune, and there has been a dearth of that lately."

"Not so fortunate for the scrum-half who carried Flagstaff from the flames, I'm afraid. No, he wasn't injured by the fire, but Inspector Braddock gave me this cutting from the Camford newspaper printed a few days after the catastrophe. Read it silently to yourself, old boy, as I would not wish our unfortunate friend to be affected by its contents."

'*Did Demons Raise Fire at Local College?*' was the astonishing heading, under which the following, no less astonishing account appeared;

The source of the dreadful blaze which raged through the college rooms of widely-respected scholar and eminent chemist, Professor Ronald Flagstaff, in which no lives were lost, thanks to the timely intervention of the heroes of our university's sporting fraternity, has yet to find suitable explanation due to the severity of the condition in which the professor still remains. But according to the professor's rescuer, Gerald Ferndean, whose efforts on the rugby pitch on the afternoon before the late-evening tragedy were vital to the triumphs of that day, and who is himself undergoing treatment for the effects of the blaze, 'The very Devil himself had risen within the professor's chambers, and had ignited the premises in his evil fury.'

Speaking from his bed in the Camford Infirmary, before he became too incoherent to be quoted, Mr. Ferndean stated; 'I found Professor Flagstaff just kneeling among the flames, as if he had not even noticed them. The smoke was thick, and choking, and some of my fellows had to smash the windows to let it out and let the clean air in, so I nearly did not see him, so quiet was he. When I tried to call him to his senses, he mumbled disjointedly about devils and imps and creatures in the smoke and shadows. As I have hopes of obtaining a doctor's degree, and also have seen the results of many a mistimed tackle upon the rugby field, I know something of shock, and put it down to that. Until I saw for myself, as clear as I see the pencil working in your hand, sir, the great looming shadow of some hideous visitant. No, I saw no face, only a writhing darkness, and though the flames around us were scorching, I felt in my very soul that if the apparition was to touch me it would freeze my heart. My friends

236

saw it too, for I heard one of them, who is not a church-goer by nature, cry out all he could recall of Psalm 23, and it was in those words I found the strength to lift the professor and carry him to what safety I could find. Though where any of us can be safe from such emissaries of evil, I can only pray to be told.'

While it seems absurd to think that the Great Enemy might make his presence felt in our town and in this day and age in such a manner, and that Mr. Ferndean's sincerely delivered words are naught but the delayed results of an ordeal that threatened both life and limb and which we may hope never to face, several of his teammates who likewise took part in the valiant rescue, but who wish not to be named herein, have guardedly corroborated Mr. Ferndean's account of something blasphemous and abhorrent lurking within the smoke. Could this be, your correspondent wonders, a case of a delusion shared amongst several under identical, life-challenging conditions? Or might we consider it a form of hysteria; one which brings to mind the events of February 1855, when the residents of Devon spoke of 'Devil's hoofmarks' appearing in the snow, and cantering over rooftop and field for a distance of up to 100 miles(...)?'

"This is absurd," said I as I returned the newsprint to him.

"So said the sensible Inspector Braddock, and so agrees the equally sensible priest to whom our rugby hero now clings, still protesting that Hell rose up in the professor's study. But, Watson, before you dismiss the report entirely, are we not now travelling in company with one who has seen a similar apparition summoned up?"

"But Eleanor was drugged. Wait! Wait, you said Flagstaff kept plants and samples in his rooms. You also mentioned this vile cactus could be dried and burnt and its fumes inhaled. So with a room filled with an intoxicating smoke, and Flagstaff babbling of devils and putting ideas into overexcited minds ..."

"Exactly, my dear fellow! Just as I told Braddock, though I left the more recent uses of the drug from my elucidation. If he can convince Ferndean, just as I convinced him, the young man may abandon his ideas of throwing in rugby and his studies to seek sanctuary in the nearest monastery. Alas, for Ronald Flagstaff, whatever terrors he had endured before the accident were simply made real before his eyes in those noxious vapours. It has closed him down. And, even though he was badly burned, as this knotted, seared flesh so clearly attests, he has given no indication that he has felt the slightest pain, or any other sensation, since."

"It's often the case when a person's mind has snapped," I agreed. "A total closure from the outside world. He had no family? Then I take it the university had him confined. But why here? There are many other institutes much closer to Camford, and much better suited to offering assistance and not simple confinement, locked away in the dark like shameful secrets."

"It wasn't the university who had him committed," said Holmes. "It was his old friend and trusted colleague."

"Rollistone? But how could he afford it?"

"I do not think the professor had much option but to find the means."

"Then, through Flagstaff, Rollistone would have access to both the apparatus to create the ghost of Miss Wexley's father and the drug to further the illusion! It has to be Hubert Rollistone who is behind all of this!"

"Rollis ... stone?" With an anguished howl, Flagstaff threw himself off his bench, his sudden dexterity truly startling as he lunged at my companion. "Rollistone," he howled. "No! Rollistone!"

Holmes, his wiry limbs tensed like cords, lost his cane in the surprise of the attack, and was barely able to hold Flagstaff's huge, clutching hands from his throat. Already I heard the jabber and shriek of the neighbouring inmates, as the violence of Flagstaff's actions sent ripples of shock and fear and excitement through the denizens of those filthy cells.

My own attempts to drag the berserk former-chemist away from my friend saw me thrown stumbling back as Flagstaff lashed out. As I strove to right myself, I was jostled aside by the orderly as he shoved his way into the narrow chamber, his bellow of, "Move out of the bleedin' way," ringing painfully in my ears.

But even as this uniformed thug closed on Flagstaff, Holmes cried, "Watson! The light!" I grasped at once what was required of me, and I pushed past the orderly and thrust the lantern into Flagstaff's gaze.

"Flagstaff, the light is here," murmured Holmes, his voice as gentle as a nursemaid calming a distressed infant newly woken from a bad dream. "You have nothing to be frightened of. You see the light? Look at the light."

Gradually loosening his grip on Holmes's collar, Flagstaff moaned, "Rollistone ..."

, "Rollistone cannot harm you. You have the light."

The very instant he released my friend, the orderly savagely forced Flagstaff to his knees, and set to fastening the leather restraints on his straitjacket. Heartily sickened by all that I had seen, I rounded on the loutish official to demand, "Why is this man kept here, in this accursed, dingy closet? Surely you can see that he's terrified of the dark?"

"Don't tell me, mister," he spat. "I only have to keep they lot quiet. I'm not one o' you head-shrinkers! Besides, this ain't his cell. He goes back down wi' the others once you're through with him. He's only above ground because visitors don't like goin' down below an' seein' where they've put them they haven't time for theirselves."

"I shall demand to speak to whoever runs this disgraceful institute. This is no hospital, man! It isn't even fit to be a bloody zoo!"

The orderly dumped Flagstaff roughly back on his bed, from where he meekly stared at the window, his violent outburst forgotten. "Hospital? What good would that do these loonies? They're kept off the bloody streets, an' out of decent folks' sight this way."

"Why, you insufferable—" I shall not record the full range of epithets I let fly here, merely remark that it was only the hooking of Holmes's swiftly deployed cane handle into the crook of my raised arm that prevented me from committing physical assault on the wretched official.

"Steady, Watson," he murmured. "There are other ways to deal with this without incurring a criminal charge."

"Quite so. But, I shall insist on speaking to the ... the impostor masquerading as a doctor in charge of this appalling place! I will also write to the medical board, demanding an immediate enquiry as to why such an outmoded, inefficient, and downright bloody cruel house of horrors survived the Lunatic Reform Laws and is still operating!"

If these remarks even registered with the orderly, he did not show it as he stumped off back to his post. But Holmes clapped my shoulder, declaring, "I shall back you up every step of the way, old fellow." He then glanced back at the huddled form of the once-brilliant Professor Ronald Flagstaff and sighed, "He was the last of the trinity whose actions brought us into this affair. Oscar Wexley is beyond our reach, and for his testimony we must rely on what his children have told us. Last night we heard Professor Rollistone's account. And I fear we will gain no more insight from this third member of that party. I was mistaken when I said that Ronald Flagstaff had disappeared for only four days. The part of his mind that made him the man he was has gone forever. There's nothing more here. Let us get out of this depressing place."

"Gladly. If this is the fate that awaits those who go looking for this evil crown, then I shall be relieved to have Eleanor under my watch again."

"As shall I," he agreed, and quietly closed the cell's door behind him, so as not to disturb the thoughts of the man within. I confess I thought it a kind but unnecessary gesture.

"Done wi' him?" leered the orderly. "Only I best get someone to take him back down wi' his chums. What, leave him restin'? An' have him takin' up one o' our luxury suites, when any other visitor might come a-calling an' wish to use it? Well, there'll be no more guests for this un, I know that, so he goes back down, an' you gentlemen will have to wait 'ere. An' keep clear o' the doors, if you remember as I said."

"I still can't understand why you give me instructions not to let Miss Wexley out of my sight, Holmes," said I, impatient to make my way back as swiftly as possible through that warren of tunnels, "and then turn round and tell me to leave her unguarded."

"It is because I have had certain suspicions confirmed since I wrote those first instructions. But before I burden you with them, show me this alarming object which your prompt actions retained. My, my," he murmured, examining the ugly figurine in the light like a jeweller might a dazzling a gem. "It certainly looks like it would be at home in Hubert Rollistone's menagerie. And you say it was left outside Miss Wexley's window like some weird offering? I might wonder ..."

I was not then to hear the remainder of Holmes's musings, for my hand shot up to quieten him as I again heard the tortured strains of an almost familiar song.

"Said one fool to his friends, 'The Devil's Crown
sealed our ends,
We were damned 'fore our search e'en started...."

Tiptoed and hushed, Holmes and I approached the cell door, not wishing to interrupt the occupant in his strange chorus. But the singer's senses must have been extraordinarily keen, as, swift as a striking cobra, from between the bars of the tiny window plunged out an arm, grabbing tight to Holmes's sleeve, as a voice whispered urgently. "Wexley's girl must be kept safe! You must get her away from here! You must all of you get away!"

"Who on earth?" I cried out in shock. Shock that was by no means lessened as Sherlock Holmes flashed his lantern's beam full through the bars to reveal a fearful, grimacing parody of a so-recently-familiar face; the face of Professor Hubert Rollistone, now struck stark mad with fear.

Chapter 15: The Last of the Trinity

The clutching hand withdrew as the man in the cell fell back from the bars, blinking in the lantern's glare. The rough grey uniform was cleaner and less worn, and his hair had not yet been shorn from his head, but Hubert Rollistone was as much a patient of this unwholesome establishment as those other sad wretches who shambled aimlessly past in the corridors or languished in cells all around us. Had there been any lingering suspicion that this was not so, it would have dissipated entirely when the lantern light gleamed on the short length of sturdy chain that tethered one ankle to an iron ring in the floor. Had it truly been only the previous evening when this man had greeted us in his home with a strained form of graciousness and faded gentility? Yet now he scuttled in circles on his hands and knees, like some vast, well-fed insect, before springing forward to thrust his hands out again, scrabbling at my coat front.

But the instant I reached up to prise his grasp away, Rollistone snatched his hands back as if my very touch would scald him. "No, sir! Not one finger shall you lay upon me, or it will be the worse for you. The blood is on me! You must keep your dear Miss Wexley from the same fate. If you love her—and you must love her, for there is not another who can save her—you must protect her. Take her away. Save her!"

"Save her from what?"

His roaming, wet eyes fixed themselves on the fragment of sculpted bone still in Holmes's gloved hand, and widened in outright terror. "From the curse! Save her from the crown, and from the curse that is upon it, and from the monster that enacts the curse."

Holmes swiftly pocketed the effigy as he cried over to the orderly, who had just then returned with two others of similar build and surly bearing to the tiny chamber where we had left Flagstaff. With an anger rarely allowed to run unchecked, my friend demanded, "How long has this man been here?" When a grudging shrug was the sole response, Holmes's voice was like a pistol shot. "How long?"

"Since gone two or three this mornin'," retorted the guard, adding a grudging, "sir."

"Then this—whatever it is—happened sometime shortly after we left him," said I.

"It was the curse," Rollistone groaned. "Oscar was wrong to doubt, poor man, for all the legends are true. Now it's got me, like it got him. Like it got dearest Ronald. And before that, Romford, and Aldo Venicciano, who strode into a forest in Transylvania with a shovel and a peasant's map in hand, and never emerged on the other side. So much for the land beyond the forest, then! Did he find something in its darkest passes? Well, if he did, he isn't telling. Nor is Edgar Breaconridge, who never spoke again, so could never tell of what he found beneath the monastery outside Kursk, or poor Augustus, who caught a serpent by the tail and was so intent on keeping hold that he didn't notice the creature had circled round, till both he and the serpent were eaten up and vanished. Or Gatford, or Michel Delamaine, Madame Dragosian and her travelling witchcraft show, Frederick Uschard, who killed three men to obtain a single page from a forbidden book then watched helplessly as it was used as a taper to light the pyre for his own execution ... or all those many others who didn't have the decency to take up the trails they'd left behind and carry them away with them when they died, leaving them glimmering for other poor fools to follow, until they too are claimed. Just like it claimed Medaccini, and the Sultan's headless harlot, and as it must have taken those architects who built the dread tower from whence those jewelled orbs first surfaced! Like it got every man, woman or child who ever touched or sought that beautiful, evil thing!"

"What happened, Rollistone?" I pleaded. "How did you end up like this? How did both you and Ronald Flagstaff wind up in this dire place?"

"Ronald's gone. Maybe it was not the curse, but maybe *they* got him too. Maybe they got Oscar. They are everywhere, creeping and crawling. They creep inside you and eat you from the inside out. Creep and crawl!" Making movements like fat, pale spiders with his hands, his fingers still livid and marked from where they had once shone with rings, and scratched bloody from where these had been prised off, he whispered, "Scuttle, scuttle, scuttle, they go, and in and out, leaving webs like woven ectoplasm, the ghostly threads of their terrible passing."

"More damned spiders!" I shuddered, as if his fear had transferred onto me and was crawling across my skin. Rollistone shrank at just the utterance word and skulked back to his narrow corner.

"Why is he chained in this foul hole if he has only just arrived?" Holmes snarled.

"Had to, didn't we?" snapped back the orderly as he left his comrades to attend to their other charge. "He attacked one o' the doctors when he tried to examine him. Soon as he even tried to lay a finger on him, this one starts yellin', an' punchin', an' with a hand full o' heavy ol' rings on him, he knocked the teeth clean from the doctor's jaw. So, they slung him in here on a tight leash, where he can't do no harm to anyone. Well, least not anyone who'd notice."

"Who brought him in? Man or woman? Think, man, if you're capable of such an action!"

With ponderous deliberation, the orderly replied, "A woman. His housekeeper, I think she was."

"He doesn't have a housekeeper," I protested, for I recalled the scholar's pleas of poverty, as well as the unruly state of his home.

"That's what she told me she was. For all I know, she's just as barmy as him, bargin' in here, demandin' a doctor's help to get this one in an' safely locked away. Middle o' a dark night, an' her still with a veil on an' everything, like she was in society, or at a funeral. Probably some 'eathen foreign custom. Did I not say? Mus' be trouble with my thinkin' capabilities, sir. She was foreign, I know that much. I seen 'er before, when him there'd come to visit that other one in our best parlour, tryin' to get him to talk some sense, same as you gents. But she'd just wait outside in the carriage, like some black-widder in its web. Never even heard 'er speak till last night, but she's some Spaniard or Eye-talian or the like."

"The Contessa," I exclaimed.

Hubert Rollistone lurched suddenly forward so he crashed with his full weight against the unyielding door. His hands reached to me before he again snatched them smartly back, and he sobbed, "You must find her! You must find her and keep her from me. Do not, on your very lives, let her near me! The curse is loosed, and she must not touch me."

"Open this door," Holmes demanded. "Look, the fellow is chained like a dog. He's hardly going to escape and run amuck. But I cannot discover what I need to know through several inches of metal, so open the door and let me speak to him in a civilised fashion!" As the orderly still showed himself reluctant, Holmes cried, "Lock me in with him if you must, and as my friend will witness, I take full responsibility for my own safety."

The brute's face wore such a defiant look as he turned the key and pushed the door ajar, that I would not have been surprised if he then locked us in as just another pair of madmen. "I am a qualified doctor, with full military training and experience," I informed him, "and I will keep close observation from the doorway. If anything arises that I can't handle, or any assistance is required, I will call you."

He grudgingly left me to mind the open door, where I held the lantern steady while Holmes stepped inside, his open hands out to clasp the older man's and still their frenzied clenching. But Rollistone shied away, scuttling further back into the corner of the room, kicking away thin blankets and the rough mattress as he scrabbled across the cot. Holmes drew back and asked, "Who is she? Professor, who is the Contessa Nascosta?"

Hubert Rollistone's pale eyes stared past my friend, not seeing him, but focussed instead on the shadows in the opposite corner, as if even in such a confined space they might find a figure neither Holmes nor I could perceive; a figure, perhaps, shrouded all over in darkness. "No! Not you? You must keep back! Keep away from me, I beg you!"

With that shriek, he fell back, as if to evade the grasp of an invisible presence that loomed over him. His own hands appeared to turn upon him, as if they were the clutching grip of some dreadful *other* that he could not escape. "You cannot touch me. You will not pass the curse on. Keep away, I tell you. Do not touch me!" His palsied fingers grasped at the air, as if plucking a floating cobweb from before his face. As he drew this unseen wisp down with a gasp of horror, he threw his arm up to cover his face, and sobbed fearfully, "The curse! It has claimed me! *Attenta!* Too late. No salvation now." And as he collapsed back this final time, his arm was flung wide to reveal a livid face, teeth bared in a rictus snarl, dark-rimmed eyes wide and glaring as he hissed in a voice utterly unlike his own, *"La maledizione della Corona del Diavolo sopravvive nel cerchio di sangue!"*

"What is this?" I gasped, as Rollistone thrashed around, his face and voice entirely alien to those we knew. And as he whispered and shrieked, the occupants of cells the length of that dank corridor took up the cry, hissing and howling as they thrashed against their immovable prison doors. With stamping feet and an oath at their lips, the orderlies marched to and fro, screaming for quiet and hammering on bars as if to drown out the din with a clamour of their own.

"What indeed?" ventured Holmes. "Ghosts? A ghost of the mind, perhaps. A last moment of sanity relived to haunt a mind from which all sanity has fled."

"You must keep them both safe," called Rollistone, his voice feeble, but his own once more. "Don't let those creeping horrors claim those we love. The curse is here! It is upon me, and it was placed on me by a devil! Do not trust the crawling, lying devil!"

"Who? Rollistone, who are you talking about?"

"One who keeps their true face hidden. You may catch glimpses, but nothing more. What lies inside is ugly, and wasted, and withered."

Again I uttered the name of that veiled woman, whose shadow extended to darken even this grim place. "Did the Contessa also cause Flagstaff's fate?"

"No, no," he snapped petulantly, something of our former host's manner returning. Though he rambled in his thoughts, and let his words trail after them wherever they wandered, some clear threads emerged that wove together into a narrative of sorts. "I've told you already—or someone rather like you, at any rate—that Ronald Flagstaff is missing. Oh, so you think you've found him? So did we ... at first. But not all of him, it transpired. The darkness had started eating away at him a long, long time ago. No, not the darkness of his moods, nor of his all-eclipsing ambition. It *was* you I spoke to of the Black Church in that Constantinople slum? Yes, you, Mr. Holmes, I *do* remember, with your own powers of seeing. I told you of my visit there, and you saw the ghastly trinkets I bribed the caretakers to let me take with me. But I don't recall that I told you of my companions on that excursion. No? Our dear old Oscar, of course, who had it in his mind to carve into the night-painted walls and claw out any secrets within, and had to be firmly dissuaded from attacking them with his own bare hands or shouting them down as if he were an Israelite at the Walls of Jericho. And cowering Ronald, who wished to add certain Turkish minerals and flora to his laboratory supplies, or so he said, though Oscar reckoned he wanted to keep us close in case we bethought it fine fun to cut him out of the prize.

"Never have I seen a grown man turn sick with dread so quickly as dear Ronald did in that house without light. Even while I paid the curators a little extra for a crude sort of exorcism of the offerings I purchased, he remained convinced they carried still some taint of that place and the deeds committed there. Would you think him foolish? You have one of those trinkets with you, I perceive. It burns in your breast pocket, chilling your heart with a bone-white glare. Does it feel heavy to you? As if it carries something else with it, or reaches out beckoning to some dark follower?"

"No," said Holmes, frankly. "It does not."

"No," agreed Rollistone, shaking his head. "No, whatever dark thing Ronald carried out of the Church of the Faceless, it was within his mind. A dread that those cowled killers with their blood-ringed lips on faceless skulls awaited him in each dark turn, lingering behind each nightfall. It was fear that was slowly eating him, though when greed conquered fear, it was that which finally gobbled him down in one gulp, as if the world had swallowed him whole. He faced the dark in hopes of seizing a sparkling thing that might shine fierce enough to burn the shade away. Had he learned nothing? The siren's song is a cautionary tale that we might all have been wise to heed. So heed this, sirs. Not all monsters look monstrous, and not everything that looks monstrous is a monster!"

"So it was in facing his fears that Flagstaff went missing," prompted Holmes. "How was it that he returned home, on the night of the blaze?"

"It was the Abbot's Cry that led us to him. Howling out its desolation where only angels and devils and the souls of the long-dead might hear it. And now, where he is, his audience is probably the same. And, on such a topic, I have something for you, my good sirs," said he, casting about with quick, irritable snaps of his head. "I was certain I had a squeezebox once. I might like some accompaniment, for my neighbours, vocal though they most certainly are, could not be classed as melodic. But the song goes on, gentlemen. The old sailor song of woe and warning. I think it was my singing that drew you to me, although I am plainly not that deadly enchantress of the sea. I have been using my solitude to revise the song that it might reflect the saga's latest turns, and I have composed a new verse. You will honour me by being its first and only audience;

> *The professor's brave daughter, sought where*
>   *she ought not ter,*
> *With champions who weren't up to the task.*
> *Like offerings for the slaughter, they got dragged*
>   *down in deep water,*
> *For they ne'er saw the face, just the mask.*
> *Now the eyes 'neath the mask are brimming o'er*
>   *wi' greed.*
> *And the eyes of the Devil are preparing to feed.*

"Yes, I agree, the first line needs more thought, but I believe it has a rough charm to it," sighed the professor. "And I fear there is no time for fussing, if I am to versify more than four centuries of horror. Not much time for anything ..."

"Then use the time you have, Rollistone, to tell us who and what brought you to this."

The old man's strength seemed spent in his raucous singing, so his mumbled words as he sank down upon the cot were lost amidst the slamming of heavy doors, and screech of keys in locks as those three brawny officials half-carried, half-dragged the trussed and senseless Flagstaff into the corridor, each man cursing his dead weight with every plodding step.

"The curse claimed me because, after so long mistrusting even my closest friends, I put my faith in a devil," insisted Rollistone. "Not all fiends lie drowned in the deep, and even if they do, their coils stretch wide, turning others into puppets and instruments of the dark. Do not trust this devil's puppet whose face is masked, or the curse will lay claim on you!" Then he heaved himself upright once more to cry, "As it has claimed us, is that not so, my dearest friend?"

I followed Rollistone's sudden sharp gaze to see Ronald Flagstaff's head jerkily rise, as his glazed eyes attempted to focus on the source of the cry.

"I think old Oscar, whatever he caught sight of that we never did, was right, and we were close to the crown by the end. Close enough to touch it, but not quite enough to see it. Or to be touched by it, at least, and its strange energies. For I believe I have been gifted a pointer to my own furthest future, not that there's any great distance to look." He called again to the man who now struggled and dragged his feet as the orderlies tried to usher him along, to ask, "Did you see it also, before the darkness descended, old friend? Did you see the moment of death? I told you, gentlemen, I would not have time to complete the song, but while I have breath in my lungs, let's hear it:

> "Said one fool to his friends, 'The Devil's Crown
>   sealed our ends,
> We were damned 'fore our search e'en started.
> The treasure's beyond our grasp!' Then he gave
>   his last gasp.
> And instead o' a red jerkin, the friend's hands
>   then parted,

> *To show red gloves of the blood of the dearly*
>   *departed.*
> *Aye, hands slick wi' the blood o' all those now*
>   *departed....*

"And now, Mr. Holmes, Doctor, my last verse is over, and my killer approaches."

Amidst loudly yelled oaths there came a harsh tearing of fabric and a rending of metal. Ronald Flagstaff, having torn his bound arms free, had gathered himself up to his full height, the shocking speed of this motion serving as much to throw off the orderlies as his undoubted strength. While the fallen men clambered to their feet, the huge figure hurled himself toward me and the doorway I stood in. And as he bore down, he proclaimed, "It was you who killed Flagstaff! You killed him!"

I got only as far as crying his name before a muscular arm crashed into my chest, and it was only the straitjacket's heavy padding that ensured I would be nursing bruised rather than fractured ribs, as I was thrown aside. Winded though I was, I had to act. But even as I hauled myself forward, the heavy door slammed before me, closing Holmes in the confined space with the two lunatics.

From within I heard my friend's command, "Behind me, Rollistone. Stay close, and stay down!"

"No," cried the folklorist. "You cannot help old Hubert now; '*Come not between the dragon and ...*'" The old man's words came to an abrupt close with a strangled choke.

"It was you," Flagstaff screeched again. "You killed me! You killed Flagstaff!"

The orderly was at my side, and through the bars we saw Holmes struggle to prevent the scarred chemist from twisting his straitjacket's torn straps around Rollistone's throat and viciously heaving on them. Rollistone, his face already purple and his eyes bulging horribly, offered no fight; while Flagstaff moaned his accusations he simply gasped, "Not I. It was the curse that killed us both."

Were we to barge the door open we risked crushing

Holmes to the wall, so I pushed gingerly, my grip tight on the handle. But before I had gained even an inch, Hubert Rollistone's heavy form was lifted in Flagstaff's powerful embrace and slammed mercilessly against the door, sending us reeling as it crashed back into its frame. Again and again he was thrust back, and as we pressed our shoulders and heaved, we saw at close quarters the snowy hair on the back of Rollistone's skull redden as it struck repeatedly against the bars in that narrow window, each impact a sickening crack.

Those wandering inmates not still cowering in corners pushed and jostled as they converged around the scene of this frenzied assault, the rough and tumble growing yet more violent as the orderlies strove to keep them at bay. The surly creature that had shown us in took violent charge, his truncheon raining down blows, until he too was seized and dragged to the ground by those he struck out against.

"You killed Flagstaff," echoed the dull groans from the cell. "You killed me!"

"Watson," rang the cry of Sherlock Holmes. "Have you the lantern, man?"

I grabbed the lamp from the filthy corridor floor and held it to the bars, calling, "Here is the light! Ronald Flagstaff, the light is here."

In the mass of shifting shadows I could see that Holmes had managed to drag the straitjacket from Flagstaff's back and loosen its straps from Rollistone's throat. As he tried to prise the massive scholar's fingers away from the older man's shoulders, he grunted, "He has the strength of the devil. The lamplight isn't enough."

I snatched an unlit lantern from where it hung on corridor wall, and as I fumbled with matches, I yelled to an inmate—that purring fellow who had earlier spoken of cats and canary-birds, and who now slunk edgily around the scrabbling mob—to fetch another. He moved nimbly and soon, feeling not unlike a lighthouse keeper amidst a stormy sea of violently tussling bodies, I held three brightly burning lights to the window, flooding the cell with their radiance.

"You are Professor Ronald Flagstaff," urged Holmes, his breathing ragged but his voice held calm and low. "You are a rational, peaceful, gentle man, and we have brought you the light. You have nothing to be frightened of while you have the light, Ronald."

"They killed Ronald. They killed him," the large man mumbled, the anger leaving his voice as his grip slackened and Hubert Rollistone's slack frame dropped into his arms. "They killed ... me."

It was an obscene oath from somewhere behind me that alerted me to the chief orderly charging the length of the corridor, his club striking every bar and door he passed, the reports and their echoes deafening. The inmates swiftly abandoned their brawling to bolt out of range of that club's indiscriminate swing.

I slid the cell door open and joined Holmes in his attempt to ease the sagging Flagstaff onto the crude bed, but he was not to be budged from where he squatted on the floor, a single great hand large enough to cradle his one-time friend's battered head, while the other vainly dabbed at the blood soaking into the old man's torn tunic, spreading out like a dark bib below his several chins.

"Filthy, stinking animal," came the sudden bark of the orderly as he filled the doorway. His uniform torn, his knuckles and brow bleeding, he brought his club swinging down and coshed Flagstaff at just the instant he released his hold on the lolling Hubert Rollistone. A second blow fell, and a third, but any further attempt to bring the truncheon down came to naught, as I, without pause to consider the consequences, grabbed his muscled arm to prevent the club's descent, and then punched him square in his hateful face, knocking him sprawling to the grubby corridor floor.

"You're the animal! He was half dead already!" Then, sparing the floored bully no further thought, I supported as best I could the dazed Flagstaff. Slowly I helped him from the cell and out into the corridor. Here he slumped against the wall surrounded by the glowing lanterns, staring dumbly at the blood and clotted strands of white hair that stuck to his palms, unmindful of his own blood as it dripped steadily onto the floor. I turned away, trying not to think of those 'red gloves' mentioned in Rollistone's grim final verse.

Inside the narrow chamber, Holmes dropped into a crouch to cradle Rollistone's head. "Can you hear me, Professor? Who is this devil's puppet you warn us to guard against?"

"The one who brought the curse upon me ... The curse will claim ... The curse ..." His breath rattled and his head drooped, his eyes and mouth still open wide, yet seeing and speaking no more.

It was strictly a formality to take hold of his wrist and confirm, "He's gone, Holmes."

After the briefest of reflective pauses, Holmes icily addressed the orderly. "Fetch help for the man you have just assaulted, then summon your superiors. Go now!" Without argument, the thug scrambled to his feet and raced away, red-stained fingers still clamped to his flattened nose.

"Sometimes," said Sherlock Holmes, quietly, "I fear my work causes more harm than it does good."

"Oh, come now! There was nothing you could have done here."

"Would this tragedy even have occurred if I had not interfered?"

"Perhaps not. But if you hadn't become involved, that evil woman would have continued using her hideous potion and those horrid illusions until she had tricked Eleanor out of her secret."

"And the Contessa would have gained the crown, if she could decipher that cryptic message."

"Exactly!"

"And what great harm would that have done?

"What harm? Holmes, you surely cannot be serious?"

"Can I not? After all that has happened to those whose lives it has entered, would you really wish that dreadful treasure upon Miss Wexley?"

"Maybe not," I replied. "However, I do not and will not believe in curses and legends. This is the work of evil people, not supernatural forces. Evil thoughts in evil minds, leading to evil deeds. Our task now must be to bring these vile scoundrels into the light, and make them accountable for the horrors they have caused!"

"What would I do without you, old fellow? You're right, of course. The guilty party must be made to pay." Holmes looked once more at the fallen Rollistone then rose, as I took the old man's head and, wadding a blanket into a makeshift pillow, lowered it to the floor. It was only in doing so that I perceived the curious discolouration around and inside the former scholar's mouth, which in turn sparked a memory I had carelessly allowed to lapse.

"Look here! His tongue, his gums, and the roof of his mouth all have a greenish-white tinge to them."

"You have observed something like this before?"

"With Eleanor, yes," I nodded. "It went quite out of my mind amongst everything else. When I examined Miss Wexley in that East End hovel after she had been surreptitiously fed the drug. There was a slight discoloration, but nothing near as dramatic as this."

"Our companion was given only the tiniest dosage, and significantly diluted. The desired effects of pliancy and suggestibility could be achieved with just that. But this? This reeks of far more dangerous goals."

I leapt to my feet, a thrill of horror coursing through me. "Then our opponents have become more desperate? And Eleanor is alone and unguarded! We must prove Rollistone's song wrong when it sings of her champions not being up to the task. And the only way to do so is to finally bring an end to this grim affair with all haste!"

"Agreed," said Holmes, and he closed the door on what remained of Hubert Rollistone. From nearby echoed the percussion of racing footsteps and a babble of aggravated voices, as the orderly headed up a procession of white-coated doctors, nurses, and stretcher-bearers who tore round the corner. Behind them, striding briskly, faces thunderous, came the neatly attired administrators, showing all signs of distress at being dragged from the comforts of their offices to find themselves amongst those to whose needs they were supposed to administer. "There shall no doubt be questions to answer before we are permitted to leave. Let me do the talking and I shall have us away within a few moments. We shall then return to our hotel, where I would advise you to say little of this morning's events to Miss Wexley."

"Indeed, no. She has been exposed to more than enough nightmarish events recently."

"The nightmare may be reaching a conclusion." Holmes glanced down at Flagstaff, who stared without seeing into the circle of light, unaware of the attentions of those who stooped to examine his injuries. "There are only a few minor details to be attended to. Foremost amongst these is locating a bookshop."

"More dusty old books?"

"Not a book; a guide map of the local area, pinpointing churches, hospitals, and other points of interest. Once we have that, I can plot our next steps. And then we may assemble the cast of characters for what can only be the concluding chapters in the long and sordid saga of the accursed Devil's Crown!"

Chapter 16: A Dark Assembly

C onsidering the cabbie's indecent haste to abandon me in such ghastly surroundings, I was relieved, if somewhat surprised, when Holmes and I found ourselves being rapidly conveyed back to Harewynd in the luxury of the institute Director's personal carriage.

My companion's supposition that we would face interrogation by those who ran the asylum at Wynngrave Hall had proven correct, as had his estimate of how swiftly the meeting would be terminated. Under Sherlock Holmes's baleful gaze, the trio of pompous officials who faced us across the expanse of the Director's desk stuttered and shuffled like schoolboys as they listened to his tirade against the deplorable treatment of their unfortunate patients. I allowed myself to puff up with self-importance as my threat of action was repeated. Though he did not say as much, Holmes's tone of voice was sufficient to make my humble position sound as though I had the ear of the entire General Medical Council, and to convince them beyond question that, should our many complaints be ignored, the consequences would be dire indeed.

To judge from the slack faces about that oversized desk, I felt certain that my exaggerated authority would not be questioned. And within the space of twenty minutes we were ushered into the carriage by its owner, a solemn promise on his lips that sweeping changes would be made, and within five minutes more we were out of those awful grounds and on our way back to our hotel, and to the lady I had left there.

I hardly need state my growing anxiety, and I several times thrust my head from the window and urged the coachman to spur his horses on. In marked contrast to my nervous state, Holmes sat quietly, his eyelids drooping, his face once more an inscrutable mask, behind which he concealed that mind ever-racing with ideas and theories. I was in no mood to interfere with his train of thoughts, however, as my mind was consumed with its own very particular fears.

If the devilish woman we knew only as the Contessa Nascosta had resorted to such fateful actions with Rollistone, how long could it be before her evil gaze was once more focussed on the young lady we were hurrying to meet? That is—Heaven forbid!—if it had not already occurred! Could it have been the Contessa, or some unknown acolyte, who had tried to gain access to Eleanor's hotel room the night before? Had she some perverse reason for delivering that revolting talisman? And all this for what? I could discern no possible clue in Wexley's words, *'All this time I was looking for it, and I was looking through it, and it was looking right through me!'* I imagined them most likely the semi-conscious ravings of a weak and dying man. But our foe could not be aware of this and, having seen with my own eyes the look of stark terror on the wretched Rollistone's face, and having heard his terrible cries at the mere mention of that veiled enigma, I knew that I could never allow my sweet Eleanor to fall into her hands.

It was with great urgency, then, that I leapt from the carriage as it drew up before the Drover's Pass. I was halfway to the door when I turned back, a question on my lips, and to my surprise found that Holmes was not at my shoulder, but was instead moving away along what passed for a high street, swinging his cane in what I considered to be an inappropriately jaunty fashion. Exasperated, but already fully aware of his bizarre mood swings, I turned back and threw myself through the hotel doors. I nearly shouted with joy when Eleanor Wexley opened her door upon my second knock, though I fancied she might already have heard the hammering of my heart as I had approached her room. All my deepest fears must have been clearly etched upon my face, for she gave a little amused laugh, and took my hands in her own in a comforting gesture, before lightly kissing my cheek. "You kept your promise, then, for you were not long from my side."

My further promise, to tell all that had been discovered, was less easily kept, however. I told her little of the morning's events, save that Holmes had uncovered certain clues and that all would soon become clear. My bluff manner must have been just a little forced, for I saw the questioning look in her bright eyes, though she had the good grace not to press me on the subject.

As I had not been allowed to finish my breakfast, Eleanor agreed to join me for an early lunch, and we left her room to discover Sherlock Holmes in a whispered conversation with that disagreeable receptionist. Waving us on, he joined us momentarily in the dining room, where he wafted a large and detailed tourist map in one hand and blithely informed us that the case would be wrapped up before the day was out.

"Then why not now, Mr. Holmes?" asked an eager Eleanor Wexley.

"That would hardly be appropriate without our client present to witness the outcome of the case he was good enough to present us with," insisted Holmes. "But we shall all bear witness to the truth of this most convoluted affair just as soon as Mr. Wexley arrives, which should be on the next-but-one train from London, in response to the telegram I shall send him within the hour."

Pleased at my friend's confidence, I enjoyed a hearty lunch. Even Holmes's erratic appetite seemed keen, and we must have appeared exceedingly voracious in front of Miss Wexley, whose meal sat barely touched.

With a long afternoon ahead of us, I was eager to see some of the district without the case overshadowing our every move. I had visited areas close by on both sides of the Scottish Border at various times, but this stretch of the borderlands was unknown territory to me, and I had hopes that it would offer some more pleasant vistas and places of interest than the two establishments I had thus far been given reason to visit. I was greatly surprised when Holmes greeted this as a capitol notion and insisted that I take our companion with me, and then equally infuriated when, just as we were on the verge of leaving, he called me back, as if with vital information to impart, greeting my protests with much dismissive gesticulation and very little interest.

The 'vital information' he so discreetly disclosed was that there were thirteen churches in the immediate area and that his map had proved a very good investment, were I to care to examine it closely to see just how thorough it was.

"Indeed, remarkably thorough, yes! And does it have a designation for 'resting places of diabolically cursed crowns' marked on it? No? Such an oversight; I should write to the publisher if I were you," and I was in a foul humour as I took my leave of him. But this mood lightened instantly on finding Eleanor standing in the shade of a tree in the small park opposite the hotel, sweetly smiling as my icy expression melted into a grin of relief.

For a few pleasant hours we walked and talked and laughed together, and I was to be immeasurably grateful for this short period of normalcy for, upon returning to the hotel, we discovered Holmes waiting impatiently, having returned himself some time ago from the distant post-office whose elderly telegraph machine had conveyed his summons to Nicholas Wexley. "If he is sharp, as I have every reason to believe him, he will have made the express in good time and even now be well under way." Holmes then instructed us to prepare, after dinner, for another journey of our own. In making his own preparations for his excursion to the post-office, he had learned from the receptionist that carts and coaches could be hired for the day from a Mr. Carnham. So we were spared the lugubrious pleasures of the local coachman as Holmes, suitably caped and capped for country activities, took the reins and we left Harewynd behind at a brisk but not breakneck pace.

The verdant scenery we traversed, the passing trees in full leaf displaying colour enough to put a muster of peacocks to shame, the brooks we passed over flowing with crystal water a far cry from the foetid sludge that so often threatened to spoil the mighty Thames, and the clear vistas, free of any townhouse or chimney stack, palace or slum, all conspired to help me forget that our destination was to be the last resting place of the source of all our recent troubles, and the troubles of so many others over the last four centuries. For who could believe that here, amidst all that seemed pure and healthy and natural, we were going to find the Devil's Crown?

We must have travelled more than an hour; out further even than Oldmire Priory, which we passed, brooding dark and untenanted—for, as Holmes had assured me when I had earlier suggested we storm the priory in search of the Contessa, it was certain that the spider would have deserted that nest. With the sunset threatening at our backs, the sky before us was already darkening with the fingers of evening when the silvery blue of the sea added itself to our view. As our cart veered from the far-from-even country road and through a gap in a low, tumbled wall marked with the crooked remains of gateposts, we found ourselves jarred and jolted over a track that made those twisting lanes appear as smooth in comparison as Mrs. Hudson's kitchen linoleum.

Was it the prospect of coming into close proximity with that object whose dread reputation we had so swiftly learned that made me conscious of the rich and vibrant colours giving way to sickly yellows and whites among the scrubby grass, and the grey and blotchy leaves on the branches of those trees that grew meagrely in the approach to the skulking ruin ahead? Did I only imagine that those trees had grown stunted and warped, with many distended cankers in their stooping trunks, and that pale and unhealthy funguses seemed to eat them from the roots up? It felt to me that nature itself was sickening, as if tainted by some nearby poisonous influence.

The blighted land ahead appeared to drop away directly into the sea, with no feature atop the stark cliffs save the hulking remains of what I guessed to be one of those thirteen churches which the locale boasted. The roof and turrets had long since toppled, as had half of the transept, but the remaining walls were surmounted by tall, arched windows, all, or nearly all of them, devoid of glass; these broken frames formed ragged teeth in the gaping stone mouths of some fossilised, many-headed primordial beast that might once have clawed its way from the ocean's floor to die beached on the clifftop when the tides had fallen. Through these and many other gaping wounds in the thick hide of the building, the open sky and its rolling darkness were framed.

Holmes tethered our horse, then led us to an arched doorway in a corner of the building, the door long since rotted from its hinges. Perhaps it was the coolness of the sea breeze, blowing directly in across mounds of gargantuan rubble and over the ledges of those empty windows beneath which a stark cliff dropped down to the chill, relentlessly churning waves below, but a shudder passed through my every muscle as we stepped across that threshold. I started as the violent rustling of the beating of great wings filled my hearing. For an instant the air seemed filled with darting, wheeling shadows. It was only as they climbed into the sky, and my heart had regained its normal rhythm, that I saw we had merely disturbed a flock of screeching seabirds with our arrival.

"Are you certain this is the place, Holmes?" said I.

"This is the place," he firmly replied, glancing keenly around, his eyes stopping on nothing but taking in everything. "Bleakcliff. How appropriate a name."

Holmes strode ahead, and I was on the verge of following when, with the sudden falling away of my lantern's beam, I discerned a sheer drop just inches from where I stood. Throwing up a protective arm to keep Miss Wexley from straying closer to the edge, I cried, "And are you sure it's quite safe?"

The upper level upon which we balanced was little more than a narrow, stone-slabbed balcony, chiefly supported by the broad pillars of the archways below. The edges were irregular, crooked, jagged hunks of stone that jutted out above a yawning maw where the floor of the nave had, over the long centuries, caved and fallen into the crypt. Against the inner wall, and thankfully intact, a flight of steep stone stairs led down into the exposed vault. As I sidled around, giving those frayed stone verges as wide a berth as possible in so constricted an area, I saw that this manufactured cavern was peopled all around with broken statues. These carvings, many with heads or arms missing, their angelic wings chipped and snapped, seemed either to spring half-formed out of the pillars, or perhaps to have been absorbed by the very substance of the building as they struggled vainly to take flight like those now distant gulls. In their midst, beyond even the grasp of the few intact limbs, lay a huge sarcophagus, some twelve feet along each side and rising to chest height. Atop it lay a crumbling stone lid, its surface pitted, dented and cracked clean across by the stones and ancient pews that must have gradually fallen from above. Most of this debris lay heaped around the tomb, the wood splintered and mouldering, amidst towering piles of heavy masonry and broken slabs. It may have been the spongy moss that furred the walls, or an effect of the sea air, but an unwholesome greenish mist seemed to hang in the air of the vault, drifting listlessly in the shaded recesses between the arcade of pillars and those wounded statues.

"Safe?" repeated Holmes, as he stepped lightly down the stairway to find a better vantage point from which to view one of the shadowy alcoves above. "That depends, old fellow. We are, after all, seeking an item which is said to carry a deadly curse."

Following his line of view, I perceived that not all of the window arches were as empty as I had first thought. Set in a curiously angled wall that sheltered it from the worst excesses of the wind, this remaining window housed a practically intact image in murky stained glass. While a family tapestry spun by several hundred generations of spiders had done much to conceal it—that thick curtain of dust-blackened webs seeming to breathe in and out in what scant breeze crawled through those gaps where the glass had cracked or fallen free—from what little I could discern, it crudely depicted a warlike and not notably benign or saintly angel caught fast in the manifold grip of a dragon-like serpent. Even what little daylight remained seemed reluctant to squander its illumination upon the scene, and I could not condemn its refusal. Between this artless apocalyptic scene and the leering and scowling gargoyles that loomed out of the corners of each shaded arch, and craned at every height from footing to apex to glower in obvious disapproval at our intrusion, I had sufficient cause to shudder yet again. "Well, if cursed, it certainly is in the right place. But, as I recall, you said there are thirteen churches in the area."

Holmes rapidly descended the stairs, calling, "Unlucky for some. Not, I hope, for us. Fortunately, we do possess a certain amount of additional data which our predecessors did not. We also have the path they laid for us to follow."

Following more cautiously in his footsteps, and taking Eleanor's hand to guide her, I replied, "I don't see how. It all seems to have been nothing but dead-ends."

"That really is an unfortunate choice of words," remarked Eleanor with a grim smile.

"Unfortunate and inaccurate. Now, Miss Wexley, I have no wish to remind you further of the tragic circumstances of your father's demise, but ..."

"I know, Mr. Holmes. But you must. And it's not something you need concern yourself with. I'm entirely resigned to the fact that he has gone. Please, do go on."

"Thank you. Now, as strange and obscure as your father's final words may sound to you, his vehemence in passing them on, coupled with the determination of this other party to learn the message, makes it unlikely that these words do not convey some allusion to the treasure's hiding place. Your father knew. Of that, I'm certain. And what we know is that he was stricken down in a church at night, and it was in this place that the secret of the Devil's Crown's eventual fate was revealed to him." He moved to the sarcophagus, idly shining his lantern through a large gap where a corner of the lid had broken away, and peered into the gloom within. "As you so rightly recalled, Watson, there are thirteen churches in which we might have continued our search. However, thanks to that excellently detailed map, I know that four of these were constructed long after the monk, Medaccini, met his doom. A further five are still in active use, making them unlikely candidates for nocturnal visits, especially by a trinity of eminently respectable professors who wished to keep their researches secret; a desire that would be very much compromised by an investigation of burglary."

"That still leaves four," observed Eleanor Wexley, who stepped gingerly over rubble and rocks as she negotiated the vault's irregular pathways.

"Not when you consider their positions in relation to the local hospitals and surgeries."

"Well, then, of course not," said I, sardonically. "And why not?"

"To protect their secret, the professors could not leave Miss Wexley's father here to die. They had to take him somewhere else. To reach Oldmire Priory from any of those other churches, one must pass closely by either the local cottage hospital or one or other of the two surgeries nearby. Yet Professor Wexley was taken to the priory."

"Perhaps they feared he would reveal their purpose to the doctors."

"His words could easily be dismissed, as even his own family have been tempted to believe, as the senseless outpourings of a dying man. No. This is the place," he said firmly, and he nudged a discarded crowbar with his foot, "as I find it hard to believe that fallen flagstones can stack themselves neatly without outside aid." His lantern flashed around expansively as Holmes enthused, "Yes! Look! Can you not see it in the very stones that surround you? No, you may not exactly be an expert on church architecture, my boy, but you will concede that it is rare to find a church with so many of the gargoyles on the inside. A motley gathering of hobgoblins and malevolent sprites, indeed. I can imagine no uglier or more primitive a grouping outside the confines of Scotland Yard. Within the cells, of course, should you need clarification."

"Hideous, fearful things," said Eleanor, and her eyes darted to those malignant creature etched in the stonework, the erosion of their features rendering each yet more grotesque than the last. Winged and clawed, horned and fanged, they swarmed and crawled in the upper reaches, and huddled and skulked like troglodytes in dingy nooks lower down, each beady-eye and lascivious tongue proclaiming, 'Beware!'

"That is their purpose, to frighten away devils and other evil forces. And if, like the renegade Cardinal Medaccini, you believed that the Church itself—that corrupt mediaeval church of the Borgias and their ilk—contained more evil than it fought, and it was the world beyond its walls that needed protection, hmmm? A veritable Pandora's Box, to borrow from another myth, with the wickedness trapped within. The man had a fine sense of irony."

I shrugged, far less taken than he with this mediaeval joke. "It seems a little futile now the place is in ruins."

"Even a structure designed to withstand evil spiritual forces cannot stand immune from the forces of nature. Soon enough, erosion of the cliff will conclude what it has started and bring the whole lot down. But I don't think we need worry about it happening tonight."

I looked around myself, at the crawling tendrils of mould-speckled ivy, and the tangled plants and twisted trees that had taken root amidst the ruination as nature reclaimed its own. Letting dour fancy take me, I pictured those green-grey strands trailing away, merging and mingling to weave vast cords with the seaweed that clung to the cliffs. These great coils might form the tips of vast and monstrous tentacles, stretching out through limitless expanses of the deep, ready to flex and grip, and finally to heave together and bring the entire edifice crashing down into the waters below, where something incalculably patient and cunning had waited centuries to reclaim what had been stolen from it.

Shaking my head to clear it of the ludicrous phantasmagoria that legends, extremes of emotion, and recent tragedy had fostered there, I merely said, "All the same, I would prefer to be out of this place as soon as possible. If you know where the crown is, why don't you just fetch it, and we can be back in far more comfortable surroundings before it gets too dark to see?" So saying, I hung my lantern from the outstretched hand of a nearby statue; be it angel or demon I could not judge. "Or are you beginning to believe in the curse of the Devil's Crown, too?"

"Not at all. But it was Miss Wexley's brother who brought the case to our notice, and I feel it only fitting that he should be here at the conclusion." Pulling an oft-consulted book of railway times from the voluminous pocket of his travelling cape, and referring first to it and then his watch, Holmes announced, "We should have only a short wait ahead of us. According to my Bradshaw, the London express should have reached Harewynd some fifty-three minutes ago."

"I don't see why we couldn't have waited for Wexley, instead of hanging around in this accursed place. Out of common courtesy, at least."

"When he goes to the hotel, he will find the note and map I left with the receptionist."

I frowned, and I imagined the ragged pile of grey slabs nearby as the grin of the irksome hotel official. "That receptionist appears to know more about this affair than I do. And he's making a healthy profit from it also, I imagine," said I in remembrance of those sovereigns Holmes had volunteered from my wallet.

"Dear Nicholas," beamed Eleanor. "He will be astonished to hear of his baby sister's adventures."

"Then you may tell him now, if you wish," announced Holmes, and he swept his arm up toward the doorway just as Nicholas Wexley, stoutly booted and clad in country tweeds, raced into our view before pausing, noisily out of breath.

"Eleanor," he panted, as he mopped the sweat from his brow and he drew in gulping breaths.

"Nicholas! My dear brother!" Eleanor Wexley rushed carelessly up from the chamber and the two met in the middle of the staircase and threw their arms around one another, she embracing him so tightly that whatever breath he had regained was surely forced out of him again. They parted and smiled fondly at one another.

"My brave Eleanor! It's such a relief to see you safe and well."

"You may thank John ..." She paused, blushing, then continued, "Thank Dr. Watson and Mr. Holmes for that. They have both been very kind and very vigilant on my behalf."

Wexley sprinted down the remaining stairs and clasped my hand in his, shaking it vigorously, all the while favouring me with a delighted grin. "Then I am most grateful, gentlemen."

Sherlock Holmes appeared not to notice the hand our client presented to him, and showed far more interest in inspecting his surroundings, as his eyes flitted quickly between pillar and statue, gargoyle and slab. "Mr. Holmes," said Nicholas Wexley, rather plaintively. "May I thank you?"

"You have made a speedy journey, Mr. Wexley."

"Naturally. As soon as your telegram reached me, I caught the earliest train—the express, in fact—and when I was handed your note, telling me where you could be found, I hired a carriage and whipped up as much speed as the horses could bear. I ran the last few hundred yards; I was that keen to see my sister once more and to find out the whole story of these mysterious events. Tell me, Mr. Holmes, what is it all about?"

"That should not take too much explanation."

"That will make a refreshing change," I remarked, dryly.

"I'm afraid that I will not be the one doing the explaining." Then, with a grave nod in my direction, Holmes commanded, "Have your service revolver ready, Watson, but wait for my word."

Without pause, I produced my gun, even though I had not the slightest idea where I was being asked to point it. Holmes's own eyes were fixed on one of those shadow-haunted arches between the ancient pillars, and it was only then I realised that the central arch framed a doorway that lurked like a black chasm sunk deeper below the church.

"What on earth is going on, Mr. Holmes?" cried Nicholas and Eleanor Wexley in near unison. Then, as they followed the direction of my aim, they turned in time to see the black-clad form that emerged silently from the darkness and glided into the vault's murky light.

Sheer instinct saw me step sharply between this creature I had only briefly encountered as she had fled into the London night, and Miss Eleanor Wexley, whose presence felt to me as natural as it might had we known

271

one another our entire lives. I levelled my revolver at the very centre of that veil and whatever it concealed, and warned, "I have never shot a woman before, and as much as I should hope not to alter that claim, I must ask you not to put my resolve to the test."

Holmes brought up the tip of cane and gently pushed down my arm and the gun with it. "On my word," he reminded me. "If we can avoid bloodshed, we shall. I hope we have not kept you waiting long, il Contessa Nascosta— *'the hidden countess'*, if my Italian does not fail me."

"It does not fail you, Mr. Sherlock Holmes," said she in a coolly lilting tone. "As I am glad Dr. Watson's steady nerves did not fail him while his finger was upon the trigger."

"It remains upon the trigger, Madam, and I need merely raise my arm again." Then, boggling at the calm manner in which my friend addressed our adversary, I gasped, "You knew this ... this person would be here?"

"Where else? After all, it was her actions that led us into this train of events. I thought it unlikely she would wish to miss the closing stages. But the lady has the advantage of us. She knows our names but we, as yet, do not know hers."

"My name," she began, before resuming with a hint of a challenge, "that is to say, my family's name, is Medaccini!"

A gasp of confusion escaped from Eleanor Wexley's lips, and I could simply stand and stare, entirely startled by this claim. Only Holmes seemed to accept it as the only possible answer, murmuring, "Ah, yes, of course."

I heard surprise in the woman's voice as she asked, "You did not know this?"

"No. But I should have."

"Why is she here?" asked Eleanor, voicing the one question that seemed to my jumbled thoughts to make sense. "Does she intend to do us harm?"

"Yes. I imagine Signora Medaccini intends to do a great deal of harm," replied Holmes, "to someone."

"You are quite wrong, Mr. Holmes," insisted the veiled woman, before clarifying, "It *is* Contessa; the Contessa Adelina Mariana Medaccini. You said before that you had knowledge of the noble names of Europe, but ours is one that has long fallen into disuse. You have been told of the Faceless? We are ... we *were* the Nameless."

Sherlock Holmes offered a slight bow in apology, and this gesture of deference to one who had caused so much fear and suffering left me incensed. "Why in blazes are you even talking to this devil, Holmes, after all that she has done?"

"Because she is the one person who can fill in the missing pieces of this puzzling affair. If you would be so kind, Contessa?"

The Contessa slithered forth from the shade as if she were one with it. While I ushered Eleanor Wexley and her brother back, keeping myself as a shield between them and the Contessa, Holmes lingered, perfectly still, his grey eyes fixed like knives upon the veiled woman.

"Then your powers are not absolute, Mr. Holmes?"

"I'm afraid I cannot claim omniscience among my attributes. There are certain events even I cannot perceive, either because they took place too long ago or too far distant."

"I think you do know, but I shall confirm your suspicions." The Contessa's voice rose, and as it echoed in that ancient burial place, I could imagine just how commanding it must have seemed in the darkened meeting hall, amid smouldering incense and dancing shadows, during the course of her staged séance.

"My ancestor, Contessa Nicoletta Medaccini, was the sister of that Cardinal Gregorio Medaccini whose action, when he first seized upon the unholy Corona del Diavolo, has brought only horror and almost four centuries of torment upon us. We Medaccinis had palaces once! For centuries, land, wealth and power belonged to those who proudly bore the name Medaccini. Our people were privileged. Possibly we were over-privileged for, when that fool's deed forced us to flee, leaving our homes, our servants, and all we possessed behind us, the skills we needed to survive in our new poverty were not to be found within us. Many of our line died of starvation, of illness, of broken hearts or broken spirits, and of unrelenting terror in those early days of oppression and fear. Those who survived, they lived as nomads. Our name, once so proud, once respected, was changed from village to village to hide our shame, and from city to countryside, to forest and mountaintop, valley and cave, on our passage through lands far from our own. For we could not stand still, and had to remain ever on guard from the assassin's dagger and the inquisitors' talons. But, no matter where we ran, how far or how fast we flew, the curse that had befallen us could not be escaped."

"You talk as though you were there," whispered Eleanor, pity in her voice.

Her reply was a furious, hissing snarl. "I *am* there! Even now, I am there with my family who died hungry, cold, and alone! The knowledge of what our ancestor has made us burns in the hearts of every Medaccini! We are still in the clutches of that dark past. For the malediction is still with us!" So saying, her hand drifted to the edge of her veil, involuntarily plucking at the lace before dropping swiftly back to her side. "All these many years, we have dreamt of the time when the object of our destruction, *il Corona del Diavolo*, could be discovered by another. For, on their touching it, the curse would pass onto them and away from our line."

"Which is why Hubert Rollistone was brought into the story," prompted Holmes, "though not by you."

"It was my mother who first divulged the legend to him. This curious, ridiculous man with the ever-smiling face and fingers that sparkled with gold, who had come to our new land far beyond the great, dark forest, to seek tales of times past; he would be the one to lift the curse from us."

"And onto himself," I scowled. "A cruel exchange!"

274

"Cruel?" she echoed, before nodding, the sneer leaving her voice. "Yes, cruel. But she had known much cruelty all her life, from those who shunned her as *mostro*, as *strigoi*, as *wurdulak!* She had learned life's cruel lessons well, and she had the right to be less than compassionate to others. She worked—like a slave works—in a museum, in the cellars deep below, tending the exhibits no-one wished to see. Sometimes, if a visitor with money called by, the curator would bid her come up from the dark where she preferred to remain, and she, like his old bones and stuffed, glass-eyed dead things, was made a display, while the visitors laughed and jeered or screamed in her face. Why should she care if this stranger who had come in search of old books and charts lived or died? He was the right kind of sacrifice. He had the curiosity to seek, the taste for jewels and treasures, and may even have had the wit to find what needed to be found. That was all that she cared about. She did not know him. Not then ...

"It was he who changed her mind, and changed her life. It was he who was the first to show her that kindness existed outside of fables and nursery tales. He took her out from where she skulked among the shadows and dust and dead things, and it was he who was the first to show her love."

"And she grew to love him in return?" asked Holmes.

"I am living proof of that," she replied, "should you call this existence living. Ah, I see even Mr. Sherlock Holmes had not surmised that. Yes, the man you call Professor Rollistone is the man I have always known as Father. He saw past the cruel effects our family curse had wrought on her flesh, to the fine woman within. He was a man who saw much below what lay on the surface. Despite the fact that they never were married—my mother would never allow it, for to become one family with us under God would have been to curse him also—each remained devoted to the other, and to the child their love created. A child who was tainted! This is why he swore to find the Devil's Crown. It was why he recruited his friends as my saviours, though they never knew that this was their quest. To find the source of the great pestilence of horror, and to destroy it!"

"*'The professor's brave daughter'*," murmured Holmes, "*'With champions who weren't up to the task ...'* Oh, I should have seen other possibilities there! I apologise, Contessa. Please continue."

"*Grazie.* My mother and I remained in that land, while he crossed both the lands and the seas in search of the cursed thing. When she died, not so very long ago—as peaceful a death as any of our line had known in so many generations, thanks to his gentleness and love— the strength to continue his quest died in him, and he returned to this place a broken man. In his mind, he had failed those whom he loved most, and he could not face the daughter he had left behind."

"Until he found the document containing the hidden clue which led him to this place?"

"Yes, Mr. Holmes. He needed me then. My presence helped restore his strength, which he poured solely into his pursuit of the goal he believed would deliver me from my suffering. This desire became his whole life."

"Your own father?" I spat. "You are indeed a most wretched creature!"

Her response was a perplexed, "I, wretched...?"

"That abominable potion!"

"Yes, Mr. Holmes!" Nicholas Wexley jabbed an accusatory finger toward the dark-clad woman. "This miserable horror is the one you've been pursuing. It was she who nearly drove my sister to madness. Why do you force us to endure this nonsense about curses and not have her arrested?"

"I could have the Contessa arrested, true," said Holmes, mildly. "She will admit to her part in the crime."

"Yes. I do confess it, along with my deepest regret at what my actions have led to."

"Then what more is there to be said or done?" I cried. "Our case is closed."

"Are you sure, old fellow? There are factors which remain unaccounted for."

"The treasure?" prompted Wexley. "This crown of which you all speak!"

"Ah, yes. We cannot forget the foundation upon which so many of our recent endeavours have been built, can we?"

Eleanor Wexley looked at Sherlock Homes with wide, amazed eyes. "Then you do know where it is?"

"For Heaven's sake, Holmes, don't keep us in suspense any longer," I urged. "Where the deuce is it?"

"We have all seen it. And it has seen us."

Nicholas Wexley, all patience lost, exclaimed, "What in all blazes do you even suppose that to mean?"

His sister took his hand, urging, "'All this time I was looking for it, and I was looking through it, and it was looking right through me.' Our father's final words, Nicholas. Yet I still fail to see what they are supposed to tell us."

"That is because you have been looking for a conundrum where there is none," Holmes informed us, producing his magnifying lens from a deep pocket. "It is a plain statement. For something to look at, or, in this case, through you, it must have...?" As he spoke he brought the lens up in order to peer expectantly down upon us.

"It must have eyes?" ventured Eleanor Wexley, while her expression flitted between confusion and exultation. "It is something with eyes!"

"With eyes?" cried Nicholas as he bolted to the weathered figure from whose stone grip my lantern still hung. "A statue, maybe?"

"More likely one of those repulsive gargoyles," said I, as I tried in vain to count the swarming demons that leered down from on high. "But which one?"

"None of them," announced Holmes, his stride swift upon the staircase. "Those fiends are, like the building itself, carved out of cold, solid stone; not the easiest substance in which to conceal something, and certainly not one that you can look through. But there is one other architectural point of interest."

With a harsh scrape, Holmes struck a match against the window's frame and held the flame before the glass. Here it reflected redly in the scales that clad the coiling tentacles of the thrashing demon, while his lantern shone upon the barbed feathers that tipped the wings of the warrior angel. If you have seen Gustave Dore's depiction of 'The Destruction of Leviathan' in an illustrated Bible, you may have some idea of the scene; while the stained glass possessed none of that craftsman's delicate artistry, the dark, dramatic power and the subject itself—the brightly burning Heavenly forces in conflict with the great, dank devil of the deep—shared some vague kinship. Though a further variance might have lain in the impression that this ocean behemoth resisted its destruction with more formidable savagery than Dore's despairing sea serpent, and thus the triumph of the forces of light seemed infinitely less assured. Yet even as Holmes swept away the loops and strands of black web, I saw only the poor proportions and negligible craftsmanship that stripped the scene of its true drama and power. "The purpose of stained glass is to catch the sun's rays and illuminate a glorious scene. Why, then, place one at a point which is almost totally shielded from the sun? You will have observed the deep archway which surrounds it as we made our approach." Hanging his lantern on the wall next to the window, and stepping nimbly onto the window's ledge where he pressed against the glass like a huge grey moth, Holmes applied his lens to closely examining the remaining panes and their framework, here and there scraping lightly at the lead with the blade of his pocket knife.

"An oddity," I suggested, "like the indoor gargoyles?"

"Odd?" he said, enquiringly, not turning from his task. "Not if you also find that the archway protects it from the other elements, which is why it has survived nearly intact in so seemingly miraculous a fashion. But what is it that needs such protection? Certainly not the design."

"Then what?" demanded Wexley, turning his impatience on me. "Can you explain this, Doctor, without feeling obliged to lecture us on ancient architecture?"

My eye caught Holmes's as he mouthed two words to me whose relevance I had to cast my mind back two nights to recall. The words were 'chewing tobacco', and I said, in paraphrase of Holmes's own words, "Nothing so garish and obtrusive as that horrid design could possibly be seen as an attempt to go unnoticed or to conceal secrets. Therefore its purpose is never questioned. But had the artist given it the truly grotesque power the scene deserves, that would attract interest."

"Well said, Watson! It is primitive enough and ugly enough," proclaimed Holmes, "though as my friend astutely perceives, I fancy this too was deliberate, to dissuade curious eyes from looking too closely or lingering too long upon it. There is also Professor Wexley's last conscious action to consider. As I remember it, he raised himself from the bed, and with his declining strength he pointed? But where did he point?"

"He pointed at the window," answered Eleanor.

"But there was no-one there," insisted her brother.

"Why should there be? It was the window itself he wished you to note. He was far more aware than you give him credit for. His breath had failed, and he couldn't find the strength to form the words, but his resolve was still strong. This was him communicating in the only way he could."

"Ah! '... and I was looking through it....' Through it! He was looking through the glass. Through the glass in this window," exclaimed Eleanor Wexley, wonderingly, her face upturned in awe, as if gazing upon the elaborate and majestic windows of some vast cathedral lit up by the sun at its full, unclouded power, and not this crudely unedifying scene of violence and dread. "Then there is some clue in the image there? One of the arms of that monster is reaching for something! Is it pointing to some hidden nook?"

"Or the tip of the angel's sword," I ventured. "It looks to point, yes, you see? It looks to point down into that sarcophagus."

"You are all looking on it as some pictorial cryptogram, when it is the glass itself that you should focus on."

"But, Mr. Holmes," sighed Eleanor, "how can a window contain the Devil's Crown?"

"Quite obviously it does not," replied Sherlock Holmes, blandly. "For the so-styled Devil's Crown, which so many have sought in vain all these long and tragic years, does not exist."

Chapter 17: The Fall of the Curse

This shock of this pronouncement rendered our gathering dumbfounded for what seemed immeasurably long moments. In the end, it was Nicholas Wexley who was first in finding his voice, and he prefaced his words with a somewhat shrill and uncertain laugh. "You surely are not serious, sir?"

His sister wore a look of surprise equal to his own, but when she spoke there was none of the same upset in her intonation. "There is no Devil's Crown?"

I cannot say that my own question was quite so calmly spoken. "You mean to say that all this appalling tragedy has been for nothing?"

"Would you call this nothing?" asked Holmes, and he dropped back to the ground from the task that had seen him worrying away at the window with his knife. A strangulated gasp from beneath the Contessa's veil saw me whirl abruptly to find her as frozen as one of the derelict statues. And when I turned sharply back to the cause of that choking cry, I saw with horror Sherlock Holmes looking down upon me with eyes of blood, while an immense and glistening black spider crouched upon his face.

I blinked rapidly to free myself of this horrid image, and only then did I see that what I had pictured as a spider was only Holmes's darkly gloved hand, and that between his slightly splayed fingers he gripped two of the largest, reddest rubies I had ever seen. With the passing and exchanging of hands, like a stage magician before a rapt crowd in the theatre stalls, he exchanged his bloody-eyed glare within an instant for the brightest, bluest gaze imaginable.

As a final flourish, he drew both hands away and revealed his own grey eyes glittering with quiet satisfaction. Between thumb and forefinger of one hand were gripped two large and sparkling blue gemstones, while between the fingers of the other he held two crimson stones of similar size and lustrousness. And when I saw the hollows in the faces of that grim glass scene, I understood that what he now displayed were the plucked-out eyes of the saint and the demon.

'All this time ... it was looking right through me.'

Perhaps there was some force within these jewels, like lodestones compelling iron, which drew us toward them. While I saw a trembling Nicholas Wexley fight an inner struggle to hold from charging up the staircase, I felt his sister instinctively grip my hand, and as she stepped forward I followed. Out of all of us who had witnessed Sherlock Holmes's discovery, only the Contessa appeared immune to that power. It seemed, instead, to repulse her, for she backed away in alarm, repeating, "No! *La maledizione!* The blood curse."

Holmes folded his knife into his pocket along with his magnifying glass and, swinging his cane jauntily over a shoulder, he tossed the gems casually in his gloved palm, before stepping down to join us, his attentive audience, in the lower reaches of the ruin.

"But what of this Devil's Crown?" urged Wexley. "Where is that?"

"*It* has gone. Melted down, I would imagine, with the gold put to another use; perhaps even funding the building of this church and its neighbours. That is what your father meant when he said they had been seeking the wrong thing all along. This is what has allowed the real treasure to remain concealed all this time, from the professors, from their many predecessors in the hunt, even from the Vatican spies. They were all looking for something which could never be found, for how can you find something when it no longer exists?"

"Until my father realised the truth," murmured Eleanor Wexley, notes of sadness and admiration both in her tone.

"With every possible nook and cranny investigated without result, the only remaining answer was that the treasure had been hidden—if you will pardon any unintentional wordplay—in plain sight."

Eleanor Wexley, despite herself, reached out a trembling hand to touch the gems. "Who would have thought it, after so much horror?" she sighed. "They're beautiful."

"No!" shrieked the Contessa, her hands extended like claws to snatch at the stones. "You must not touch them!"

My revolver still in hand, I halted the dark woman's rapid movements with a warning yell. "It is I who warns," she hissed in return. "These baubles shall bring nothing but destruction on any who would hold them."

"Yet you sought them to pass them on to some other soul to take the curse from you," said I, coldly.

"I sought them to ensure no other hand might touch them! I am the last Medaccini! The last spawn of that polluted bloodline. And as I may die, that line dies also, and with us must end the malediction! If you claim them then all that I and my father worked for is as nothing, for you shall claim the curse also!"

"More superstitious rubbish," sneered Nicholas Wexley.

"Let us hope so," remarked Holmes. "In any case, I would not wish to tempt fate by keeping them in my possession for too long. Beautiful they may be, Miss Wexley, but as we are all aware, beauty is no guarantee of virtue." Waving me to lower my gun—which I did with some marked reluctance—Holmes took a small drawstring pouch from his pocket and, one by one, dropped the fabulous jewels into it, then drew the string tight. Weighing the bag in his hand, he continued, "But, since their true ownership is obscured by so many bloody deeds and the thickening mists of time, the question remains of what must be done with them."

"There surely is no question," I insisted. "They must go to Miss Wexley and her brother. Who else can possibly make any greater claim? I cannot comprehend why the decision troubles you."

"It no longer does. I merely had to see the claimants here in front of me, before choosing the path I must now follow. Miss Wexley's presence was always assured, and I felt it certain that *il Contessa* would certainly not be absent. That only left Mr. Nicholas Wexley unaccounted for."

"But I'm here now."

"Yes, you are," smiled Holmes, grimly. "Perhaps you would care to explain how."

As she turned from one to the other, her green eyes filled with confusion, Eleanor Wexley asked, "Nicholas? Mr. Holmes, what is this you ask?"

"Well," said her brother, with an uneasy laugh, "I'm here because you sent for me, of course."

Sherlock Holmes safely pocketed that tiny pouch whose contents were worth so many thousands, and only then responded, "I did?"

"What are you talking about?" I demanded, feeling as bewildered and lost as ever I had. "I saw you leave the message for Mr. Wexley at the hotel."

"Certainly you did. But Mr. Wexley is here because he followed us, very closely."

"I saw no-one following."

"Nor did I," agreed Eleanor.

Jovially, Nicholas Wexley enquired, "Come now. Is this another of your little tricks, sir?"

Holmes rounded on him with a fury so sudden and blistering that I felt myself recoil as if caught in its blast. "Mr. Wexley, you have used me as your bloodhound and abused my abilities to lead you to this place. Do not insult me further by trying to lie to me. You followed us here!"

When he had recovered from the shock of this volley, Nicholas Wexley smirked, "And you deduced this how, Mr. Holmes? From a speck of dust on the sole of my left boot, no doubt. Or perhaps it was my frayed shirt cuffs that led you to this conclusion?"

In charge of his temper once more, Holmes replied, "My deduction stems from the simple fact that the church named in the message I left with the receptionist lies fifteen miles to the other side of the village, as you might have realised had you bothered to check it. So, unless your map-reading skills are as woeful as your ability to spin a convincing lie, your presence here means you can only have followed us."

"But he has only just arrived from London," Eleanor Wexley protested.

"At your summons, if you remember."

"I did not summon you, Mr. Wexley."

"Then what was all that business about taking a cart to send a telegram?" said I.

"A ruse. I merely wished to be sure that he was in league with someone. And he was, was he not, Miss Wexley?"

My heart lurched horribly in my chest.

"Well, Mr. Holmes?" said she, a curious tilt to her head.

"Despite my explicit instructions not to stray, you were observed leaving the hotel this morning. I assume this was to meet your brother."

"Observed? Observed by whom?" Then, casting my mind back, I saw my answer grinning unpleasantly at me. "That receptionist!"

"Watson, an excellent guide to the quality of any hotel can be found in the level of bribe the staff will demand to betray their guests' trust. At only a pair of sovereigns, our lodgings barely pass muster. The station hotel, however, which we chose to forego in sympathy with Miss Wexley's recent unhappy experience there, deserves some credit, as the staff would not be coaxed into providing descriptions of any recently arrived guests. I could only assume, then, toward the true identity of 'Mr. Nicholls', who my briefly stolen glance at the register tells me had taken a room there some few hours before our arrival in Harewynd."

"You base this theory on one assumption?" said Nicholas Wexley, smugly. "Not very logical, is it, Holmes?"

"Watson has told me of the horrific face Miss Wexley so conveniently imagined at her window. Rather a macabre touch for a case already rife with them, miss. But you had to think quickly, if you wanted to distract Watson from shooting the intruder who, once your initial shock had worn off, you realised may have been your brother attempting to communicate with you unseen. I chose to test my hypothesis by telling you that a wire would be sent. It was then a small matter of distracting Watson— hence that necessarily long-winded lesson in cartography which you endured, my boy—allowing you the chance to slip away and inform your brother."

"You really are very crafty, Mr. Holmes," announced Miss Wexley with a small, gracious nod. "Yes, all you have said is true. Nicholas was here all along."

"With an eye to protecting my sister from this creature," snapped Nicholas Wexley, glaring at the veiled woman. "I can see no harm in that, yet you regard us as though we have committed some despicable crime."

"Yes," said I, somewhat downcast. "I admit to some disappointment that you didn't feel you could let me into your confidence, Eleanor. But there is no reason for you to treat this matter so gravely, Holmes."

"And none for our client to keep it so secretive," he countered. "Unless you remember our last meeting with

Hubert Rollistone."

"The professor?" asked Eleanor. "What has he to do with our actions?"

"Yes," demanded Nicholas Wexley. "I am rather confused as to what I stand accused of, sir."

"Then I shall tell you—*sir!* I accuse you of being the individual who visited Oldmire Priory before we arrived. I know that you had the opportunity because, yesterday in London, you were watched, firstly by myself and then by the Irregulars. That grubby messenger lad whose ears you boxed is their commander. You would not have seen the rest of them. Children make the most effective spies because no-one ever suspects them. My visit to the telegraph office today was not merely a ruse. I had arranged for any messages addressed in my name to be held there for collection." So saying, he pulled out a folded telegram. "From young Wiggins, sent yesterday afternoon. *'Mr. W left home shortly after Miss W and Doctor. My lads lost his cab, but not been home since.'*"

"Why in God's good name would you have wanted me followed?"

"To give you the absolute truth, it was your sister and my good friend Watson I was following, and even then, it was merely to ascertain that no-one else was doing the same. Watson, I shall have to teach you the signs for when you are being shadowed; such as a street-sweeper whose broom is lavished in front of only one row of houses when there is an entire road left untended. Not the most taxing of disguises, but enough to ensure that I was there when you, Mr. Wexley, a man who, only a day before, had been so consumed with fears for your sister's safety, were suddenly so uncharacteristically pleased to allow her to leave on an adventure with two men you had only just met. This alone made your motives suspicious enough to warrant closer attention. Perhaps the supporting characters in cheap melodrama will merrily leave the stage to the principals when their contribution to the plot has played out, but real life is rarely so convenient.

Unless, that is, one has taken inspiration from the play-acting of other parties, and has developed an inkling to direct the action from off-stage. You had, it seems, realised that your late father was not an incompetent dreamer, and that whatever it was the Contessa had gone to such lengths to discover was worth finding for yourself."

"Well done, Holmes," said he, sardonically. "While I was immediately impressed by your skills, it was from the vivid details Eleanor keenly told me of your previous adventures that I recognised how brightly chance had smiled upon me when I had been directed to the door of the one man who might actually be able to follow this trail to the end. But, still, I would have to have been very foolish to leave the investigation to chance." My heart, already weighed down, sank even further as I pictured Eleanor so avidly reading through my manuscript, and how my intentions for that narrative had been so twisted by the first person she had shared it with. And any hope that she may have been a reluctant participant in this subterfuge was not to be fulfilled.

"So, after persuading your sister to say nothing of your intentions, you boarded a train to Harewynd, hoping to arrive ahead of us with enough time to speak with Professor Rollistone. Fortunately, for you at least, you had a most capable ally to ensure that interview would not be quickly interrupted. I said that our travels had seemed ill-fated, and if the curse was at play in those delays and frustrations, then its human agency was with us all the way. When your sudden bout of fainting spells had to be abandoned in case they saw you left behind, you were very quick-witted in reacting to the sight of the woman in mourning on the platform."

"I was genuinely startled," asserted Eleanor Wexley. "I truly believed that the Contessa had found us."

"For a second or two, perhaps. Just as you must have realised in the instant of your cry in the hotel room that the loyal doctor would have heard and come running, and you were forced to play the helpless, hysterical victim."

"And very convincingly," said I, quietly.

"It was never that calculated. You wear elaborate costumes and become other people, Mr. Holmes. Not just play-acting, you inhabit them, and every thought and reaction they have is so intricately plotted in that extraordinary mind of yours. Who would need foresight when they could plot and predict so many potential outcomes by weighing up so many variables? I don't have that faculty! I am out of my depth in such an adventure, and my reactions were instinctive, with my first instinct being to guard my brother, as he had asked me to do."

"Your brother may have conceived his scheme in response to his own instincts, too, but planning swiftly followed. The separate hotels, of course, so we did not meet awkwardly in a corridor or lobby. And the transport you hired to take you to Oldmire Priory, was left...?"

"In a field, a half mile along the road," admitted Wexley. "It would have been rather unfortunate to have you trot up the drive and find it already occupied and the professor entertaining a familiar visitor."

"You took a souvenir from that encounter, too. My diligent friend found the fearsome carving you left behind as you fled your thwarted family reunion. Since you would hardly leave it outside the hotel merely to frighten your sister, I must assume that, having ascertained which room she occupied, you left it as a marker should you need to locate her window again in the dark."

My thoughts as I had regarded that eerie curio returned '... *a morbid white beacon in the night, drawing some dark, faceless thing ... toward this very room....*'

"But," said I, grasping for some dangling thread to unravel the case Holmes was building, "if Rollistone was in on the scheme against Eleanor, why should he tell her brother anything?"

"There is one sure way to get information, and that is to have information of your own to bargain with."

Eleanor's hand flew to her handbag, and emerged holding a small, red book. "Father's journal? You went down

289

into the cellar, into that room you have so long shunned, and stole one of his books to trade with his enemy?"

"That's right, sister. I told Rollistone that the old man's final instructions were to find the journal, and that it would lead us to a great treasure. A lie, of course, but I needed something to bargain with. So, I tricked him, Holmes, rather as he had tricked my sister. It was no more than he deserved."

"I will not argue the point. But, you took things too far, didn't you?"

Eleanor Wexley gasped, imploring, "What does he mean? John, what is he saying?"

I was still vainly seeking the words to explain the horrors of earlier that day when Holmes cut in. "Our trip this morning led us to an encounter with Hubert Rollistone, or what was left of him, chained and bound in a grim cell in an insane asylum."

As the full horror of it hit home, she howled, "Good God! No!"

"Yes," flew back the Contessa's accusing hiss. "My father too has been taken from me!"

"It's true," said I, gently, as Eleanor turned pleading eyes upon me. "He had been poisoned by that same drug whose awful effects you've already suffered. Though the dosage this time was far higher. Too high!"

"But not by Nicholas! I will never believe that! Tell him he's wrong, Nicholas! Tell him!"

"I'm not wrong, am I, Mr. Wexley?" prompted Sherlock Holmes. "There is no other who could have done such a thing. To his daughter, Rollistone was the only man who could save her."

"Then it was Professor Flagstaff! He knew all about the crown! He had the motive. They'd argued, and he's a dangerous man when thwarted!"

"It could not have been he, Miss Wexley. He is also confined in that fearful asylum. There is only one man who could have done this and that, sir," the tip of Holmes's cane pointed directly at Nicholas Wexley's cold heart, "is you!"

With the startling suddenness of black ink spreading across a page from an upset bottle, I became aware of the Contessa racing rapidly from the edge of my vision toward Wexley only after she had pulled from the folds of her garment that cruelly curving ceremonial dagger I had watched Holmes toy with in the Oldmire library. "It was you! Pig! *Diavolo!* Devil!"

Nicholas Wexley, taken entirely by surprise, and not sharp enough in his reactions to defend himself from the force of the attack, was knocked to the ground, tripping backwards over the triangular slab that had fallen away from the great sarcophagus's covering. The Contessa, dagger raised, swooped down upon him like a carrion crow on the carcass of some beast that still vainly clung to life. The pallor of his wide-eyed expression was starkly sullied by the crooked red dash carved into it by the khanjar's tip as it missed his throat and found his cheek. Another inch or so higher and he would have sacrificed an eye to save his neck.

With a warning yell, his cape flapping like enormous grey wings, Holmes flew upon the Contessa like one of the gargoyles swooping down from its high perch. He dragged her arm from within inches of Wexley's throat, then knocked the dagger free to clatter across the slabs. "Watson," cried he, but I was on it before he could even complete his command, wincing as my scrabbling hand caught the razor-edged curve below the jewelled handle. Had it found Wexley's jugular, his life's remaining span would have been numbered in seconds, I saw, and I threw it far out of the dark woman's grasp.

"Enough," demanded Holmes, releasing his grip only now that the immediate threat to our former client's life had been thwarted, and allowing the Contessa to back slowly away, whereupon I held her in my revolver's sights.

"My thanks, Mr. Holmes," panted Wexley from his crumpled position on the ground.

"I cannot accept them, as I currently find myself waging an internal debate on whether I should allow the lady to take her revenge. To kill is crime enough, but to rob a man of his mind while he still lives is an altogether more abhorrent thing."

"No! Nicholas!"

It was Eleanor Wexley's scream that alerted us to her brother's stealthy movement towards the fallen dagger. Nimbly, Holmes kicked it from his reach, leaving the young man to snatch at the abandoned crowbar as he lunged to his feet. Twisting deftly, Holmes brought his cane up, gripping either end in his fists, the polished stick's steel core holding as the heavy bar swung down toward the detective's skull. Thus locked together, face to face, the two men were joined in a ramshackle, shuffling, circling dance as they backed toward the staircase.

For my own part, the best I could manage was to shepherd Eleanor away from the battle, all the while striving to keep my gun trained on the Contessa, lest she attempt another murderous attack.

As sweat beaded his brow and his muscles strained tautly, through gritted teeth Sherlock Holmes enquired, "Shall I take this as an admission?"

"You're too damned clever by far, Holmes," came the growled retort.

"If I was, I would have realised your intentions before they cost Hubert Rollistone his life."

Even Wexley appeared horrified by the news, a hand clasping to his sweat-streaked and bloodied face. "No," he said, feebly. "I don't believe you."

"His life?" croaked the Contessa. "Then my father is dead?"

"You still have her covered, Watson?" asked Holmes, as he finally broke away from Wexley's reach. "Yes, sir. Your actions placed him in even graver danger than you imagined, but they had the desired effect."

With an incoherent snort of fury, Nicholas Wexley lunged again and again, the crowbar shrilling through the air. Yet with each attempt to dash my friend's brains out blocked by the adroit application of his cane and by the dexterous shifting of his angular frame, the fight continued its ungainly progress up the stairs.

Eleanor wailed her brother's name and tried to run to his side, but I just managed to grip her flailing arm and drag her back to me, where I pleaded with her to think of her own safety.

Through blind chance rather than design, Nicholas Wexley had manoeuvred Sherlock Holmes until he was hard against the ledge of one of those vast, empty window arches, beyond which lay only the ocean air and spray for over a hundred feet, before either the crags or the icy sea itself intervened. His reinforced cane still between him and our murderous client, Holmes reached into his pocket with his free hand. At such close range, Nicholas Wexley would be dead in an instant if my friend managed to get off a shot. Yet it was not his gun that Holmes produced, but a small, string-tied pouch, which he held at the furthest extent of his long arm, out above the perilous ledge. With a shriek of horrified comprehension, Wexley grasped at the tiny bag, until Holmes brought the tip of his cane up to his opponent's chest, propelling him back a step, then another, with a sharp jab of the ferule against his ribs.

"Attempt to advance just one step and the jewels go into the sea, Mr. Wexley. Then you will have killed a man for nothing."

His hands grudgingly raised and his head hanging resignedly, Nicholas Wexley backed slowly down the topmost stairs.

"That is a much better distance at which to converse. Now, how did you get access to the hallucinatory drug?"

"Easily, that was how." Nicholas Wexley wiped a smear of blood away from his eye and chuckled humourlessly. "The vain old fool showed me where it was. An entire bottle full of the filthy stuff. Well, eventually he showed me. At first he denied everything, of course, but I told him I knew it was all down to him. I was even kind enough to congratulate him on his little plot. 'The drug was a nice touch,' I told him. 'So very, very ingenious.' He rather enjoyed the flattery and desperately wanted the information I promised, so he admitted it all. He told me the whole story, or almost all of it. He said nothing of any family, but much about the crown, and the quest, and that preposterous legend of underwater demons and severed heads with second sight. Ha! All of it utterly nonsensical! That was why I took that ungodly carving, to convince Eleanor, to force her if need be, to see just how insane it all was; that anyone could look at such a thing and believe it ever could have existed outside a drunken fishmonger's worst nightmare! I suppose that little ornament must now count as evidence? How careless of me to leave it behind, but when I realised my blunder there was a pistol pointed at me. I shall have to retrieve it, I suppose, and take it with me when I go.

"Yes, it's all just as our clever Mr. Holmes surmises. Having watched your return to the hotel, and even having listened outside the window, I left it there as my marker, in case I should lose my bearings after checking the coast was clear. How ridiculous, Eleanor, that my attempts to bring you to your senses over monsters and curses should cause you to scream your heart out, as if Satan himself had tried crawling in through your window! But you always had that weakness, my dear. Rollistone knew it. He told me of our fool father's boasts to them of his darling daughter's fascination with the different cultures and legends he had filled her head with, and her openness to diverse faiths and beliefs and superstitions. It was from this, and the old man's recent end, that they devised their spiritualism scheme.

"Flagstaff had conceived the ghost projection, using photographs he'd taken of their little pack of pirates on their jolly jaunts. You knew about his knack with developing photographic plates, Holmes? Of course you did. If he is locked away, as you now tell us, then it really is no more than justice, as he was an active part of the scheme against my sister! But he betrayed his partner, or went off on his own, and ended up mad; as if he wasn't mad already! But the plan was already set. Hubert Rollistone had spent more time with our father over the decades than we were ever granted. He knew his tempers and his momentary turns of charm alike. Did we not hear someone mimic the old man's prattling on that last day, Eleanor? You remember, as we stood with our ears to the glass? It was Rollistone, and it was he who spoke through the smoke to you, and he who tricked you with visions of our wretched father. I could easily have run him through with one of his own spears, and might have done if I hadn't needed the possessor of that great brain I had set upon the track to hear and analyse the old fool's account. You will surely accept a compliment there, Mr. Holmes?"

"An explanation of your actions is all I wish from you," replied Holmes, coldly.

"Very well. I could hardly bash his silly old brains in, but then you arrived and I saw another chance. While he was seeing you in, I poured the drug into his drink, before slipping out into that jungle of a garden. From there I watched you rather craftily rifle the old fellow's den for clues; really, such an effort when you might just have asked. Yes, I knew my sister would be in the house, but I thought it unlikely you would have lost your senses enough to accept a drink. So I ensured he'd never use his poison on another by emptying the last of it into the decanter."

"The entire bottle? Enough to drive him out of his mind with terror. You left him to die, maddened and alone. But he was found."

"Crying out in abject fear," nodded the Contessa. "Convinced that the curse was upon him! His encounter with his guests had shaken him, and he drank to steady himself. This was how I found him after I'd heard his visitors leave and could emerge from my room. Yes, even in my own father's home I remained hidden away in darkened chambers, away from windows, lest any caller might see me and think his house haunted.

"But last night, the more he drank, the more frightened he became. I tried to help him, to comfort him! He would not even let me touch him, in case his nightmare should contaminate me! He shrank from my touch, as if I were crawling all over with spiders; as if this veil was a black, filthy web filled with thousands of those creatures he dreaded. He tore the veil away, and for the only time those eyes that had always looked on me with such kindness were filled with terror! Not the terror of what I am, but of what might overtake me if his touch redoubled the curse's ravages. That is why I had to take him to that sad, grey place. It was the place where we had put his friend. It was my father—when his own horror had worn him out so that he no longer screamed—who insisted I put him there, amongst those on whom the curse could not fall, for they, in their damaged ways, already bore curses of their own."

"But why, Brother?" cried Eleanor Wexley. "If he had already told you everything he knew, why did you not stay when we arrived and tell us all? Why do this dreadful thing?"

Nicholas Wexley bristled with indignation as he retorted, "He did it to you, didn't he?"

"He might also lay claim to a share in the treasure," observed Holmes. "That was your real motive, was it not? The trail had been set by joint claimants, of whom one remained very much active. But a treasure can be of no use to a man whose mind or heart has failed him."

With an anguished shout, Eleanor Wexley raced to her brother, urging, "Nicholas, tell him it isn't true! Tell him!"

"It is true! Damn you, you stupid girl! Can you not see what we could have? The very thing that led to Mother's abandonment can be taken in her name! Would you have the sacrifices she made for us, and the suffering and deprivations she endured all stand for nothing? We have the precious bloody thing that stole our father from us! These tiny pieces of sparkling stone took from us a father we could never have for our own, and we now have the one thing he craved above all others but never got to hold for himself! If you don't see that as justice, then you're as blindly foolish as he was!"

"Then the curse is real," she moaned. "It has touched you, and it has turned you into a monster. A dreadful monster!"

As she raised a fist to strike at him, Nicholas Wexley, his countenance purple with furious rage, slapped his sister hard across the face. "Enough of this! Enough talk of the curse! Will you shut up with that dead fool's rubbish?"

I ignored whatever warning Holmes was trying to issue, and I flew at Nicholas Wexley, enraged, vengeful, and entirely unmindful of my own physical aches and weaknesses. The jarring reminder came with the crowbar Wexley brought down on my shoulder; a glancing blow, thankfully, but forceful enough to blast every nerve in my body. My revolver fell from clumsy fingers as I clutched at myself and sank to my knees on the hard, mossy ground, dazed with the agony of it all.

Behind my eyelids, between canon-fire bursts of bright, fresh pain, those crouching gargoyles appeared to crawl, gathering in tightly, scrabbling and squabbling in their attempts to get a closer view of the kill. I was too blinded to see what happened next, and when my eyes focussed, through brimming tears, it was the eyeless gaze of the great glass serpent that met them. How had I ever thought it bland and lacking in ferocity? Its jaws widened in blind, silent fury that matched my own as I saw that, beneath its sightless gaze, Nicholas Wexley had retrieved my gun. This the craven creature now held to his sister's temple, while the rusted edge of the crowbar was squeezed tightly against her throat.

Holmes had drawn his own revolver and levelled it at Nicholas's head, while his left hand, the tiny, precious cargo dangling from his fingers, still obtruded over the window's ledge. Speaking so languidly one might almost have thought him bored of the whole situation, Holmes enquired, "Now, Mr. Wexley, what can you possibly intend to do?"

"I intend to take those jewels, Mr. Holmes. It seems I am already a murderer by default. I am quite prepared to commit the act in person if I must."

"Really?" said my friend, with a dangerously goading edge to his words. "Well, you cannot shoot me while I stand so precariously, as you would lose everything you've worked so very hard for. And I cannot believe you would kill your own sister."

Nicholas moved slowly up the steps, like a prowling beast pacing out its territory, keeping Eleanor at all times between himself and Holmes. "It would be a heavy task to undertake, but as she is so convinced of a reunion with Father, might it not be less harsh in her eyes? Yet so much of this was for you, Sister. So, perhaps," said he with a smirk, as I found my own weapon turned with cruel deliberation upon me, "I might kill the doctor instead."

"No! Don't!" Eleanor struggled against his grip, while her arms reached in vain across the distance between us. "John!"

As a glimmer of dawning realisation came into his eyes, Nicholas Wexley let fly with a term no man should ever use against any woman, much less his own sister. I believe I would have happily killed him with my own hands, such was the blaze this appalling slur stoked inside me. Yet the words with which he followed it turned my burning heart as cold as an iceberg. "You were only supposed to distract him, not fall in love with him!"

For the second time in so many days, brother and sister looked down upon me, a fool on his knees, struggling to find his words.

"He wasn't even the one you were supposed to keep close to, for God's sake! He's a lame, grovelling lackey; a jumped-up secretary, keeping watch for the clever one, and taking endless notes! And you've formed some ... attachment? It was never supposed to be him! Never anyone like him! Is this what you think I've put my own life into abeyance for, while I've tried to protect you and guide you? You were supposed to find a worthy match to provide all the things Mama never enjoyed. Someone ordered and reliable, with prospects! Not a half-crippled army reject, hobbling along in a lunatic's shadow!"

Eleanor sobbed, once, quietly. "I am so sorry, John."

That same irrational force that seconds ago compelled me to kill the man before me now twisted and reorganised itself within some deep recess of my soul, while from the shadowed alcoves where more hidden doorways noiselessly opened into the beyond, dimly glimpsed figures, faceless beneath cowls of night, urged me on with silently murmuring lips. I was only abstractedly aware of my actions as I heeded these insistent chants.

"John," repeated Eleanor, her face distorted in horror as these lurking presences emerged more fully, looming within the malformed shadows of the crippled statues as they impelled me onwards. "You mustn't listen! Don't, John, please!"

I rose slowly to my feet and took a determined step toward the gun. "Go ahead, Wexley," I seem to recall urging, though it may have been an other's command issuing from unseen red lips. "Kill me! Let your sister go, and kill me!"

Sherlock Holmes's clear and controlled voice broke through my self-destructive trance, and the shadows leapt back into hiding. "I think you have quite enough bullet holes already, old fellow. Besides, whoever you choose is not important, Mr. Wexley. For the very second you squeeze the trigger, you can be assured that I will squeeze mine."

"And you will have to live the rest of your days with the knowledge that you failed, and that your failure cost an innocent life. My sister told me you were a cold fish, but not, I think, that cold. I believe you shall do as I ask, Mr. Holmes." Placing the barrel once more to Eleanor's head, Nicholas Wexley drew closer to Holmes, whereupon he extended the hand which held the crowbar so that the palm lay open in front of my friend's face. "The jewels, if you please."

Eleanor gazed at my friend and implored, "Don't, Mr. Holmes, please...."

"I have no choice." Holmes dropped the pouch into Nicholas Wexley's palm, and in an instant had circled around him, away from the ledge.

"Thank you. I knew I'd made a wise decision hiring you," Wexley crowed, as he pivoted my gun away from his sister's head and directly toward Holmes's heart. "But does he even have one?" I heard him mutter, before raising the weapon so that Holmes's head was directly in line. Just as he seemed to weigh up his decision, and as I pondered the thought that my good friend—my only real friend—was about to fall victim to a bullet I had myself chambered, Nicholas Wexley gave Eleanor a violent shove, so that she stumbled directly into Holmes's arms. "Now, get back! All of you! Get down there!" He fired a single shot above our heads, then cried, "Down into the vault!"

With one hand Holmes helped Miss Wexley to her feet, while the other kept the gun firmly trained on her brother, and they descended together. Upon reaching the bottom, he passed her to my unsteady charge. Uncertain of what to do or to say, I finally, numbly, offered her my arm, and having ensured no hooded revenant prowled or waited within, I directed her toward a deeply shadowed alcove and out of Wexley's line of fire.

The brother, with half his face smeared red in his own blood, looked like the true face of a devil glimpsed through a torn mask of humanity, with all shred of civility, decency, and even sanity flown. He delved greedily into the little pouch, laughing, "I have what I came for, at last! I have it, Father! Where you failed miserably, the whelp has won! For I have what remains of the Devil's Crown!" His gloating cries poured from a demonic face that was crazed, exultant, and, finally, frozen.

"Father?" he repeated, his voice a moan of hopeless confusion, as his eyes flew from his task to the great crumbled stone casket below. And from out of the ragged edge of the tomb emerged the pale, dusty form of Oscar Wexley, his burial suit coated with grave dirt and worms, and his unkempt beard thick with cobwebs. His bushy eyebrows beetled, as stern eyes glared unhappily up at his wretch of a son.

A swarm of possibilities invaded my thoughts. It had all been a trick from the outset, with Professor Wexley's falsified death merely the opening of a scheme to dispatch his rivals before claiming his prize. No, it was another magic lantern show, put on by the Contessa for our benefit. "Don't look," I instructed Eleanor Wexley, as she craned to see what it was that had transfixed her brother. "It's another filthy trick, that's all." And then Hubert Rollistone, whose stilled pulse I had myself checked, heaved his bulky frame through the gap, his rings clanking like Marley's ghostly chains, his red fez matching the blood on his shirt collar, and I knew no human trickery had conjured this scene.

Fingers of mist crept over the window ledges, flexed and grasped hold of the brittle, stony frames. Nicholas Wexley shuddered as it curled and rolled at his back, but looked only toward his father as the old man dourly surmounted the lower stairs with his former friend at his back. "You can't have them, old man! They were never for you! The old dog is dead, and the whelp has grown fangs and can bark as well as the old one ever could! Shall we howl together, Father? You in defeat, and I in triumph?"

But as he slowly dropped the pouch's contents into his palm, any victory howl was reduced to a whimper. Nicholas Wexley's eyes shot directly to Holmes, his exultation shifting rapidly through bewilderment and horror before building into fury, so that he, as with the rest of us, did not see the Contessa until she was halfway up the stairs, hissing, "Then you, too, are cursed!"

He fired a shot, missing wildly in his surprise, and sent stone chips shearing from a carven devil's tail. The hazy, shifting forms of Oscar Wexley and Hubert

Rollistone parted, cordially allowing the Contessa to ascend unimpeded.

"You have become like me!"

Nicholas Wexley fired again, his aim truer. The Contessa's shoulder jerked back, and a gasp of pain issued from beneath the veil, but still she approached. "Stay back!" Another shot echoed deafeningly, and the dark woman flinched and clasped an arm to her stomach, her walk now a crook-backed prowl as on and yet onwards she came. And from alcoves and archways, forms as dark as her mourning attire, as hooded as she in her veil, swarmed behind her and into her, the folds of their robes becoming one with the shifting folds of her veil. As each cowled figure merged into her slender frame, her presence seemed to strengthen, her stride to grow in relentless determination.

"Contessa," cried Holmes. "Contessa Medaccini, you are better than this!" But to no advantage. The dark folds of her dress rustled insistently as still she stalked onward.

By my side, Eleanor Wexley whispered, "She's possessed!"

"You have become a monster," proclaimed the Contessa, venomously. "A devil! You now carry that curse! You now are as I!" Her hand rose in an ungainly jerking fashion from her stomach, the sleeve dripping and red from pressing on the wound that flowered across her abdomen. Clawing fingers found the edges of the veil, and as she wrenched it away savagely Nicholas Wexley screamed with an intensity of absolute terror.

My fleeting first impression was that a mass of roiling dark tentacles had been set tumbling loose to lash out at Wexley, thrashing and clamouring for his bloodied face. Then the waves of writhing hair parted, and I heard my own gasp, stemming from somewhere between horrified revulsion and sheer pity, as I saw revealed the face that this sorry woman had felt compelled to keep hidden from the world for so long. The skin, drawn tightly across what might otherwise have been noble cheekbones and a proud brow, was stretched and bleached as white as any skull I had inspected in an anatomical laboratory, or as the corpse pallor worn by so many on a dissecting table. Yet utterly unlike those specimens, the eyes that glared from this mask-like face were alive with hatred, and ringed as red as the grimacing lips that drew back in a rictus grin from snapping, snarling teeth, forming a hissing ring of red—a circle of blood! Those windswept tendrils of long, crow-black hair whipped around this shrieking skull, making the papery skin seem all the paler in comparison. As the woman staggered on toward the terrified Wexley, his shrieks were as nothing to the force of pain, tragedy, and loathing that powered her own cries.

"Monster! Like me, you are cursed! *Un mostro!*" The knife was in her hand once more, its crescent blade aglow in the reflected lamp light as it hung poised to fall on her quarry's heart. He fired once more as she closed the remaining few feet between them. Then, as the bullet found its target, she was upon him, the dagger finding its own mark as the vaporous hands of both her own father and the father of her killer closed upon her wrist to help the blade find his breast, before her lifeless weight drove it home to the hilt.

For a hideously long moment they stood in a fearful embrace. Nicholas Wexley's mouth hung open in a silent moan of disbelief, his eyes affixed to the rapidly dissolving form of his father, until the revolver dropped from his fingers, and the two figures, already past all mortal aid, teetered on the brink. Had some dark wave or colossal tentacle reached up from the sea to snatch them away, it could hardly have been as swift and final as the darkness that appeared to swallow them as they reeled back, locked together, and tumbled over the ledge and out of our sight.

The numbing silence, in which even the waves seemed to have fallen still, ended with an echoing scramble of feet, as Eleanor Wexley raced up the staircase. Fearing that she might, whether willingly or not, follow her brother over the precipice, I staggered after her and pulled her back

303

and into my arms. Fully expectant of a struggle, I was unprepared for her burying her head against my chest. But it took only a second or so of pained uncertainty before I did what I must, and put my arms around her and held her as she shuddered and wept.

Holmes gripped tight on the stonework and leaned his long frame out through the empty window, craning to look down. Softly, I called, "Nothing, Holmes?"

"Only the cliffs, and the swirling waters below. A fearful end."

With hindsight, were I to give credence to the phenomena of precognition, I might choose to ponder on the faraway look in Holmes's eyes as he said these words, and of the strange distance in his voice, and wonder if he had perhaps glimpsed some future shadow. Some inkling, maybe, of that fatal encounter in Switzerland which I would, for a long and painful time, believe to have ended my greatest friendship, and which did claim the most ferociously worthy adversary that Holmes had ever known. The legends had, after all, claimed that the quartet of stones had some power of foresight within them to bestow.

Yet the stones had been lost with the last of those who had claimed them. But if that was so, they had not quite finished with those who had survived their brief contact with the damnable things, for as I eased Miss Wexley in my arms, I saw the glistening crimson patch upon her shoulder, and the trickles of blood that smeared her coat sleeve.

"Dear God, you're hurt," I cried, my hand flying to my brow as I felt my years of training fly as if torn from my head. "When did it happen? I never saw. Was it him?"

Her eyes flew wide, as panicked as mine, as she pulled open her jacket, insisting, "I felt nothing. I don't think I'm hurt. There's no pain. No wound. No ... John. It's not my blood!"

"But if not yours, then whose...?"

A long arm slid around my shoulders. "Let's get you to a seat, Watson. You're bleeding."

304

"Nonsense," cried I, as I raised a hand to my brow again to wipe away whatever it was that seeped down into my eye and made it difficult to focus. It came back red, wet and dripping, and I felt a wave of nausea that doubled me over. The drip, drip, drip of my blood as it hit the dusty old flagstones became an oozing rush, and I cried out in utter revulsion as leeches, pale and slimy and gluttonous, alongside every other ghastly thing that had crawled from the eyes of the demon, swarmed from between every crack and cranny to feast on the meal I was leaving for them.

"John, please," gasped Eleanor, her face a pale halo around her wide-open mouth. She looked at me in horror, even as I saw those dark forms that slid again from the shadows now their living host was no more, hooded and silent and as ravenous and ravening as the parasites that flooded the vault. I flung out my gore-stained hand to her, but the glass-scaled tail of a great, blind serpent enfolded her, dragging her inexorably from my reach.

I ran across the green stones, furred with wriggling moss, slippery with my blood and with the slithering, verminous things that gorged in its pools. I had gone but a few steps when my foot slipped out from under me. I furiously cursed my clumsiness, and then I saw what had made me slip. The slabs themselves were tilting and rocking, and with absolute horror I observed the grey, reeking water that splashed and bubbled up between the shifting stones.

"Eleanor?" I yelled, as the slab beneath my feet pitched violently. "Holmes, where are you?" I leapt from where I swayed onto the next square of stone. The whole floor of the vault looked to be bobbing up and down on top of some vast, dark pool of unknown depths. I skipped and hopped between the shifting sections of floor, with even these irregular fragments cracking and splitting into smaller pieces, until I lost my footing entirely and the ground, and the whole world with it, slipped out from under me.

With a cry, I slithered into the icy water. My fingers scrabbled at the stone surface, but could get no grip on the damp moss. I held my breath—a futile effort—as I sank into the grey depths.

A frantic few moments of thrashing about in total darkness followed, as the dark sky retreated and even blacker voids claimed me. Tiny, rippling outlines of figures peered down from above a surface I had no hope of reaching and distantly called what I believed must be my name. I could not reply, of course, and my attempts to wave back were stilled as something moved by me in the water. Something darker than the murky liquid. Wider than my entire body. Powerful enough to send great eddies and currents through the surrounding pool. Something like an oily, black tentacle.

That gift—or curse—of foretelling must truly have worked on those whom the jewelled eyes had looked upon after all, I now saw. Had I not been right about some vast, inhuman thing dragging the remnants of Medaccini's forsaken church down into the depths with it? And as the old professor foresaw in his final madness, just like him and all the other offerings for the slaughter, I had got dragged down in deep water. What use was there in fighting such a fate?

My breath spilled out in frantic bubbles, and my mouth filled with freezing water. A few more seconds and consciousness would slip away entirely, and I would be left, floating eternally in icy darkness. But I would not be alone in my watery tomb. For there was a devil here with me to keep me company!

Chapter 18: Towards the Light

When I at last resurfaced, shivering, damp, and fighting my way free from the shroud that wound as tightly round me as the embrace of one of those infernal tentacles, a new day had dawned. From the drawn, grey-faced expression of Sherlock Holmes, it was evidently a dawn that followed a night without rest, and it was only my hoarse whisper of his name that creased his downturned mouth into a smile. "Back in the land of the living, then, Doctor? You're not going to go under again, I trust."

I was not, as I had feverishly dreamt, run aground upon hard stone slabs at the lip of some vast, obsidian pool, but in my disarrayed bed back in my blandly fussy hotel bedroom amidst its framed seascapes, not overhanging the icy ocean itself. The shroud whose folds I struggled loose from was a bedsheet, and I was slathered in sweat, while my throat ached as if I had been yelling for hours. "Just a nightmare?" I asked, and stretched thirstily for the glass of water my friend poured for me. My right hand, I then saw, was carefully wound in bandages, and at the sight of it I reached for my forehead, probing delicately for more bandaging, or any traces of a wound.

"More than that, old fellow, though from what you cried out and the way you thrashed and fought throughout, it certainly seemed particularly nightmarish. My, what an imagination to conjure such horrors! You may have the makings of a writer after all. You rallied once, when we got you back here and settled, but you sank rapidly again and for a few hard hours we thought you might have been lost to us entirely. And just when we could have used a doctor, too. Really, my boy, you must avoid getting yourself so knocked about and bloodied in future."

"I make no promises," I said, though my attempt at a smile I suspect was akin more to a grimace. "You spoke of 'we'? Then she is still here?"

"Miss Wexley dressed your wound, and made a neat job of it, as you will note. And, given your efforts to fight her off while I restrained you, it's astonishing that we didn't bind you from head to toe for your protection, as well as our own. I should inform her that you're now awake and coherent. If that is what you wish, naturally."

"If she's sleeping, let her rest. She needs it. As do you, by the look of things."

"That is clearly the Watson I know, but there will be a final task ahead of us this day before any of us may rest." He strode to the door. "And Miss Wexley isn't asleep. She only left a moment ago, when you began to stir. She was unsure that you would wish hers to be the first face you saw on reviving."

I was unsure of that myself. "She has been given enough worry without prolonging her concerns over my wellbeing," said I, after a moment's reflection. "Tell her I'll see her, would you, my dear chap?"

I took my brief moment alone to brush my sweat-slicked hair back and to bundle myself in my dressing gown. My head still swam as I attempted to sit, so I propped myself on pillows and tried not to look too closely at the wretched shambles of a man who stared back glumly from the mirror. So much for making myself presentable! Of whatever that haggard fellow had seen, or thought himself to have seen while in the realm of the unconscious, I am relieved to have only the vaguest, most fragmentary memories—memories of blood, and skulls with crimson lips, and hands that tried to prise treasures from a dead, fleshless, relentless grip that dragged both prize and seeker into the grave—and even as I sat, awaiting Holmes's return, the sunlight and the returning warmth in my bones helped me put the worst of those sensations aside.

The sound of a hesitant knock was followed by the sight of Eleanor Wexley's pale face as she peered around the door. As with my associate, there were signs of a night with little rest, and her eyes were puffily rimmed with red. "You look remarkably well," she said, her relieved smile clearly genuine.

"And you are a remarkably bad liar." I wished I could swallow the words immediately upon saying them. "Oh, my dear lady, I did not mean ..."

"No," she replied, and she took a seat by my bedside. "No, I know you would not try to make me feel guiltier than I already do. You are not so cruel, though you have every right to be. I had no wish to deceive you, or to use Mr. Holmes so. I barely knew either one of you, and so what he ..." I watched her struggle to force out the name. "What Nicholas suggested seemed like any other of his usual, thoroughly thought through, utterly practical notions. I didn't know you—not at first—but I thought I knew him. Till he became a beast! He became the very Devil! I knew he had occasion to grow angry, of course, at how unfairly he believed we had been treated in life. I thought perhaps finding our father's legacy, and seeing that he had not deserted us for a fool's errand, might finally have softened that anger. But I had no notion of how deep it ran, or how dark it had grown."

"At the cliffs," I asked, already aware of the answer, "there was no hope of rescue? For either of them?"

She shook her head, dislodging a tear. She wiped it brusquely away, then sighed, "We've informed the local police that there was an accident. They came to the hotel, the sergeant and a constable, and we each took turns to watch over you as the other gave a statement. On Mr. Holmes's suggestion, we said nothing of the legend, nor the quest, and certainly not of the jewels, for who would wish to spark a treasure mania in such a spot? He offered me a chance to save Nicholas's name, would you believe? With Professor Rollistone's daughter's profound grief at his sudden death, we might have offered the idea that my brother had sought to prevent her taking of her own life, and sacrificed his own in the attempt. But his was not a hero's end, nor should it be claimed for him. Instead, we offered no rationalisation. They were just two unfortunate souls swept away by tragedy. There may be an inquest, just to finalise the issue, but the police won't even go out and look. The sergeant was very sympathetic, but it's not such an uncommon thing around the cliffs, he said, and never once had they brought anyone back from those churning waters."

"What Nicholas said...?" My own words failed as she looked steadily at me. "What happened with you and me...? I don't mean here, in this hotel, but the growing fellow feeling I saw between us? Was it all just a distraction?"

"I kept something from you, but I did not lie. Not about that. What happened between us was real and true. If you can believe anything I say now, believe that. John, I truly am sorry that I hurt you so."

"I'll survive," I told her, and I forced another smile. "Not even bullets or iron bars can stop me. I'm beginning to believe I may be indestructible."

Her fingers found but did not touch my face. "I hope so. We worried ... that is, your friend and I did not know what to expect through the night. We didn't think we might lose you, at least not in body." She turned to the door, calling, "Mr. Holmes?"

Sherlock Holmes entered, and to his enquiry about 'the patient' I replied, "The patient would feel much better if he knew exactly what happened to him. My last memory, before I was assailed by abominable denizens of the deep, was of discovering a wound to my head. Now while a blow to the skull might explain my collapse, and a concussion might well have led to my nightmares, it doesn't explain why I can find no bump or scar, or even how or when it was inflicted."

"Your skull is as solid and undented as ever, Watson. The blood on your hands was the blood from your hand. There was a long, deep incision across your palm that you must have failed to note in the intensity of the moment."

A sharply returning memory brought with it a wince of jagged pain. "From when I threw aside the khanjar after the Contessa tried to slit Wexley's throat. Damnably clumsy!"

"Precisely. Both you and Wexley were cut by that knife's blade. And you both were affected by extremes of behaviour. Mr. Wexley's actions—I am sorry, Miss Wexley, but I must speak of them. Thank you for understanding— had been particularly cunning and cold-bloodedly committed. But his mania among the ruins at Bleakcliff was anything but refined and clear-thinking. We all heard him cry out, as if his late father was among us. You appeared to see some of what he saw, Watson, or rather to have had your imagination infected by his ravings, just as your blood had been infected."

"Infected? Then you can only mean by Flagstaff's drug?"

"You recall my mentioning of the various ways in which the cactus's potency might be administered? Inhaled in smoke, imbibed in solution, and injected into the skin? Here, I believe, we have seen the result of the substance directly entering the bloodstream. Alas, without the knife, which is far beyond our reach, I cannot be definite. But my supposition is that Rollistone's daughter liberally smeared that wicked blade with the noxious stuff, and that if we were to pay a visit to Oldmire Priory we would find the last remains of several eviscerated fruits of Ronald Flagstaff's researches. It is also my surmise that this was another weapon whose originally intended victim, before events overtook intent, was me. For, as far as Contessa Adelina Medaccini was aware, it was I who had been set against her family, I who had thwarted them in London, and I who had been the last to see her father while he still had his sanity. To repay the theft of that sanity, I believe she would have taken a long, patient time with that blade, ensuring its poisons did their work slowly."

"Then Nicholas's own end was mercifully swift," remarked the young lady with the slightest of nods, as she rose and strode to the door. "I shall be ready in a few moments, Mr. Holmes, but will wait in my room until Dr. Watson is sure he is recovered and that he is able to accompany us." Then she was gone.

I rose stiffly and tested my weary muscles. "A final task, you said, Holmes? Then I would guess that my poorly timed collapse last night left us with some unfinished business? And the only way to complete it is to go back to that ghastly place?"

"You are much the sharper for your long spell abed, though I shall refrain from parroting any warnings about dangerous stimulants. Strong coffee, cigarettes, and a hearty lunch will have to suffice, all of which I will order up as you get dressed. Then, fortified and fit once more, we shall return, briefly mind, to Bleakcliff, and also to Golgotha."

Within the hour we travelled along those same snaking roads, and through those same avenues of trees, passing fields and brooks that again spoke to me of life, health and tranquillity. There was little to forebode, though our horse seemed abnormally skittish and hesitant as it navigated the turns. "Poor old fellow," explained Holmes. "He pulled our shadowy follower's transport last night, and I think he was restrained and drawn to stop rather frequently to prevent the pursuer from becoming visible to the pursued along the straighter stretches. I tethered him with our horse last night as we sped you back to comfort, though our late client's cart will have to be retrieved separately.

Do you know, the cunning brute even had a rat-chewed old straw hat and the coat off a scarecrow stowed in the back of his cart so he might look the part of a farmer if we chanced to spot him from a distance? The nerve! You know, I had hoped my methods would catch on, but with the opponents of crime, not its practitioners."

The final approach to the ruined church appeared less blighted than in the dusk's gloom, and I saw fresh shoots of green and gold amidst the weeds and scrub. The church, too, looked altered in some way; less dourly imposing, as if the sea and the eroding cliff had claimed even more of its broken remains.

The glass serpent and angel were still trapped in their never-ending moment of frozen battle, each roaring soundlessly, and now sightlessly, at the other. As if only the accumulated cobwebs had been holding the coloured panes in place all this time, yet more seemed to have fallen away through the night to lie shattered on the stone, like brittle, discarded feathers from the angel's wings, or the old scales shed by the aging water devil. That ferocious power with which my delirium had invested these allegorical combatants was no longer present. "The place seems ... quieter, I suppose is the term."

"Why shouldn't it?" Miss Eleanor Wexley remarked as she peered out across the waves. "There's nothing here to haunt it now. The Devil's Crown has claimed its final victims. At least its last vestiges have gone with them."

"Not quite so, I'm afraid," confessed Sherlock Holmes. "I had certainly not intended to reveal this in so dramatic seeming a fashion, and would have done so last night if our friend's health had not taken sudden priority. You see, suspecting in advance that we pursued gemstones rather than a crown, and knowing that there may be some bitter dispute over who should take custody of them, I took the liberty of preparing another pouch, which I switched with that containing the jewels. The most apt substitute I could find was that effigy in bone. So the evidence of one of his crimes has gone with its perpetrator."

Holmes took from his pocket a pouch identical to that for which Nicholas Wexley had fought so savagely and held it out to Eleanor. "I know these can be of little consolation to you, Miss Wexley."

Slowly, and with all apparent reluctance, she accepted the pouch. As she cradled it in her hand, she sighed, "Such a heavy toll of horror in such light little things."

"You don't need to touch them. Not if you're afraid, or anxious."

"It can do no greater harm, John." Her gaze dropped from me. "I am sorry, Dr. Watson. If there is a curse, I fear it is already upon me."

"There is no curse," said I, with more assurance than I truly felt in my miserable soul. In the quest for these utterly inadequate prizes, so many lines had converged in this forsaken spot and had terminated here. Ronald Flagstaff was a bachelor with no living family, thus his line ended with him, lost in darkness and destined to gaze forever toward a light he would never reach. Oscar Wexley's final, rapid descent had begun here, and it was in his dying moments that the first steps along the path toward his only son's final end were laid. And within mere hours of one another, the father and daughter in whom the Rollistone and Medaccini lineages had become one were reunited again in a dominion wherein I could only fervently pray that no veils or secrecy were deemed necessary, and where they could walk with the light upon their faces. For them the curse that had consumed their lives was over, but what of the one that still remained?

Eleanor Wexley sat atop a fallen beam and stared at the still-sealed pouch in her hand. It seemed to me that she looked also into my thoughts when she mused, "Perhaps I will end up like that poor woman."

The sight of Contessa Adelina Medaccini's unveiled countenance returned to my mind, as it has done many times in the intervening years. "Her face, Holmes? Tell me, was that merely another gruesome part of my waking dream? No? Then what could have caused her face to look so stricken?"

"I spent part of the afternoon of our last day in London cloistered away in the library at St. Bart's trying to ascertain just that. You will remember I caught the briefest of glimpses of those concealed ravages during our confrontation in the Cyrus Road Public Hall. I could find no diagnosis in the medical texts, but I have my own thoughts. They're crudely drawn, and vague in their terms, and far further from defined science than I am remotely comfortable with, but you might lend me your medical opinion on their likelihood nonetheless."

"Anything to help this seem less horrific."

"As a matter of fact, it was in tales of horror that I found the basis for my theory, in particular the vampire myths of Central and Eastern Europe."

With memories returning of Sir Francis Varney's grave-shroud hood, exposed ribcage, and bloodied mouth, as depicted in a tatty contraband edition of *The Feast of Blood* that had passed through many hands at my school, or of Le Fanu's disturbing female ghost, Carmilla, and, finally, of that more recently recounted legend of the exsanguinated sailors, I protested, "Vampires, Holmes? Vampires are bats who lap blood from the necks of South American cattle, not diabolical leeches in human form. What are you saying?"

"Only that, as we have so recently seen, myths usually contain an element of truth. I suggest no supernatural solution but a disorder of the blood; one which causes a dispersal of the skin's pigmentation, perhaps an aversion to strong light. A tightening of the facial muscles."

"That awful grin!" I shivered. "A hereditary condition, you suppose?"

"This is my feeling. In less enlightened times, it has been claimed, certain isolated families stricken with mysterious diseases would drink uninfected blood in an attempt to lift the sickness, or alleviate its worst effects. The once-noble Medaccini family, under whichever name

315

they travelled throughout the most unwelcoming and insular realms of Europe, were certainly isolated. And, if you are also aware that the noble families of mediaeval Europe were rife with inbreeding …"

"Then," said I, with a thrill of disgust at what was suggested, "it is plausible."

"I am merely speculating, but perhaps this was a persistent strain of something we are nowhere near to defining. Might not the members of a haunted, fear-maddened clan, with no other to turn to, turn in on themselves for their needs? Or their desires. In a superstitious climate, perhaps a family curse was used to disguise a more dreadful secret. Sadly, the last of the line has gone where that knowledge can be of no help to her."

I shook my head, sickened and saddened. "Then, apart from the trickery of the séances, she was innocent of any crime?"

"Even then, there was no genuine harm meant, and every care was taken. What may have seemed a cruel deception was, after all, simply an act of desperation."

"And what of Flagstaff? What befell him to drive him mad?"

"He went to Golgotha." My lantern from the previous night still hung from the grip of a statue. Holmes lit it then lowered it through the wedge-shaped gap in the lid of the great sarcophagus. Beneath that crumbling slab lay an abyss of darkness that the lantern's beam singularly failed to lift. I dimly perceived, far down below in some vast, dripping chamber, a scattering of small grey-white domes whose nature I realised with a lurching sensation a mere instant before Holmes confirmed, "Golgotha, 'the Place of Skulls', as the Testament tells us. And the final confirmation I needed that this was the church I sought, as no other had such an extant subterranean charnel house. Perhaps it was the false clue of the angel's shining sword, pointing down from on high to reveal what is hidden, or so he may have thought? Perhaps it was a mistrust of his former friend, and a belief that something was being kept from him in a place they knew he would be hesitant to tread? Whatever it was that put the unshakeable notion in his head, in his monomaniacal fervour to find the treasure Flagstaff faced up to his worst fears, of the dark and what may dwell there, and descended into the catacomb."

He indicated the doorway from whose shadows the veiled woman had detached herself. "The entrance staircase to the crypt is blocked for most of its height, and even as burly a man as he could hardly shift the fallen rocks and beams, or risk the whole lot coming in on him in the attempt. So, he had but one other possible means of entry." From the ground close by the opening in the tomb, Holmes drew up a length of rope. One end was still tightly tied with multiple knots around an immovable pile of slabs. The other was frayed where it had snapped through. "It is quite a drop and utterly inescapable."

"He was trapped down there?"

"For four days, until Rollistone and his daughter found him, his pitiful pleas for help echoing out from every fissure and crack like the ghostly Abbot's Cry. Four days in the dark, among the dead? Enough to drive even the strongest man to breaking point, let alone one as highly-strung and nervous as Ronald Flagstaff. His friends may have rescued him physically, dragging him from the tomb's black reaches, but for his spirit, I fear there can be no escape from the terrors of the grave."

I had no wish to imagine the wretched scholar alone in the dark, counting the seconds, knowing that his lantern, if it had even survived the drop, would soon dim and sputter out. Rationing matches, unable to listen long to the dripping, rustling dark, yet dreading to see in the flickering glow the hollow eyes and lipless grins of his prison's other occupants. Nor did I wish to picture him deep amongst the fallen, with only a sliver of the sky to focus on. But no matter what I may have wished, these images came and I despaired for poor Flagstaff. I strode away from the tomb and moved by instinct toward Eleanor, who still regarded the pouch in her hand. "Thank Heaven it's all over," I sighed. "That people could be driven to such lengths over such trinkets."

"It is greed. Of all emotions whose consequences might entail such tragedy, it is second only to ..." As I heard Sherlock Holmes quietly voice this thought, I turned to see his guarded look pass from Eleanor to myself. He caught my questioning glance and murmured, "Well, there are more apt circumstances for idle philosophy, I would imagine." He then turned and mounted the stairs.

Eleanor Wexley looked up, prompted by my light touch upon her shoulder, and though her eyes were damp with tears, she no longer wept. "Shall we go?" We ascended the stairs, neither of us hurrying. "What will you do now?" I asked, simply hoping to quash the roaring silence between us, while also entirely unconvinced that any possible answer might be one I wished to hear.

"I really don't know. Things have changed so much, so very suddenly. The only thing I do know is that I can no longer stay in that house. It is full of ... full of him! I can't remain in London. Maybe I will finally get away. Far away from everything that might remind me of this."

"That may be the best thing."

"You could," she began, softly, and I nearly silenced her, as I knew that what was to follow was something I both wished and dreaded with each warring fibre of my soul. "You might come with me."

"I am tempted," I said at last. "But I fear that I would also remind you too much of this horror."

Her sweet face fell and my heart sank with it. I tried to smile, to lift her in some slight way, and nodded to the jewels in her hand. "Then there is nothing to their much vaunted powers, if you didn't know my answer before you even asked?"

"I did. I think I knew from the moment these were near, when I saw that you would have to learn the truth. But I hoped that perhaps they, and I, might be proved wrong."

"And you see nothing else?"

She trembled, the cool sea air catching her hair so that she had to brush it from her eyes as she stared out still across the waters. She pulled her coat tight. "Just an east wind," she said, finally, "but it's still a good way off yet."

"We'll be long gone before then," said I, lamely. "Are you coming?"

"In a moment. Our last trip together will seem a little anticlimactic. Instead of escaping the humdrum, we return hoping to find comfort in it. Such a waste. But it's probably just as well," she admitted. "This dreadful curse has destroyed everyone I ever loved. I would not ever see the same happen to you."

I nodded, no words I could then think to speak—nor any I can muster now—seeming adequate, and withdrew, mumbling something about waiting for her outside to give her a moment on her own.

"Thank you," said she with the saddest smile I hope ever to see. "For everything, John."

I found my friend quietly smoking in the doorway. I accepted a cigarette and grimly insisted, "Let us get far away from this place, this town, and this whole wretched affair, Holmes. There is nothing more to be done here."

"Certainly, old fellow. I have satisfied myself on those last lingering details. Our mighty London beckons. And you will have a gripping addition to your chronicles. Though I fail to see how even you could make it more lurid than it already is."

"I fear not," said I. The bitter knowledge of how my prior attempt to commemorate our adventures had only added fuel to the scheme that had brought us to this unhappy juncture saw me reconsider my literary ambitions, which, should they persist, would be tempered with a degree of self-censorship and restraint. "This tale will be a long time in the telling, if it should ever be told at all."

Holmes nodded and from a deep pocket in his cape presented me with my revolver. "This was the other reason we came back, as it was forgotten where it fell in our haste to be away. I should hardly want it falling into the wrong hands." In that moment I gave careful consideration to pitching it as far as my remaining strength could hurl it. Numerous are the occasions since that I have had cause to be thankful that I resisted the urge and pocketed it instead. My attention then turned to the lone figure framed by an empty window against the vast expanse of sea and sky. I cannot say how long I gazed on her before Holmes's words lightly drifted toward me. "She was entirely innocent of her brother's schemes, you can be sure of that."

"I am, Holmes," said I, and I truly was sure of the goodness and kindness of our recent companion and friend. "But she needs her freedom now. To travel, to see the world." I faced him with a wry grin. "I just don't think I could handle the excitement."

"Ha! Well, I hope you might be able to take one more piece of excitement. I have grown accustomed to your presence, and your assistance is invaluable. Your assistance, my dear Watson, and your friendship."

"Thank you, Holmes."

"Then it's decided," he cried, clapping his hands with barely suppressed exhilaration. "Splendid! You are familiar, no doubt, with Isadore Persano?"

"The sensationalising journalist? Well, who isn't? He's not planning another duel in Hyde Park, is he? No? Then he has been robbed? Blackmailed? Murdered?"

Holmes kept at bay the grin that threatened around the corners of his mouth for only as long as it took him to announce, "Mr. Persano has found a worm in a matchbox, and it has driven him quite mad."

I blinked several times, and wondered if I was truly free of the hallucinatory effects of my clumsily self-administered poisoning. "Did you say a worm?"

"A remarkable worm of a type unknown to science," he affirmed, the grin wider yet.

"Good Lord! Where on earth did you hear of this?"

"In several of our most trustworthy London newspapers on the morning before we left, not least the *Times*, where it dwarfed a fulsome piece praising my friend, Mr. Athelney Jones for his incredible theories concerning a knotty web of laundry lists and dusty bedposts that disentangled a crime of passion committed by a lethally jealous sailor."

"But that means it happened the previous night, if not earlier. Three days ago, at least. The matter may be resolved by now?"

"I think not. The article also mentioned which detective Scotland Yard had placed in charge of the investigation."

"Oh, surely you can't mean...?" I choked. "Not Lestrade? This is his 'simple little bit of business', then?"

"Indeed. That is why we should return as speedily as we can. Because if we are not back soon to rescue him, I believe our friend, the inspector, may also be driven mad."

I smiled in spite of myself. Perhaps, after all, a fresh adventure in more comfortingly familiar surroundings, with a newer, yet more abstruse set of puzzles to pit our intellects against, new trials to test our tenacity, and even unknown dangers to quicken our blood, was the surest way to put this all behind us, or to drive it from our minds, at least, until the great healer time might dull the sting of scars that would take longer to fade.

My smile died again as I looked out toward Miss Wexley, so worryingly close to the chasm's edge. Holmes's gloved hand clapped me gently on the arm. "She has an infinitely stronger spirit than her brother could ever have hoped for. She will join us shortly. Come along, old fellow!"

But this one time I did not blindly follow my comrade's orders. Stepping back into the shadows I watched Eleanor Wexley as she stared out, thoughtful and silent, over the sea, before lifting the pouch high and emptying its contents into her cupped hand. Even from my vantage point I saw the crystals gleam as they dropped.

"Well, you pretty little things," she said. "You have brought nothing but despair, horror and death to anyone who has ever felt your touch. You have destroyed my father, corrupted my brother, and lost me the only man who … Well, then. The only man! The blood of all who have claimed you is upon you. I will not keep you. You should never have been brought up out of the deep, and to the deep you should return."

Slowly, deliberately, she tipped the palm of her outstretched hand, letting the jewels slip away, sparkling and glistering as they fell—blue-white as ice and steel, red as blood and fire—into the waiting sea below.

"Have them, Nicholas. They're yours. Perhaps, in time, all the waters of the world can finally wash the blood away."

Epilogue: A Perennial Problem?

'**W**hat object is served by this circle of misery and violence and fear? It must tend to some end, or else our universe is ruled by chance, which is unthinkable. But what end?'* These words of Sherlock Holmes's which I appended to the opening of this account—sentiments first expressed in response to another tale of horror, though one in which no supernatural agency may be implicated, merely those all-too familiar human failings of betrayal, jealousy and vengeful rage—are ones that resonate whenever my mind should stray towards those few brief but intensely active days of 1881.

'What is the meaning of it, Watson?' How often have I voiced that self-same question? Had I hoped that by putting the whole thing down on the page I might find my answer, it was a vain hope. Even now, can I be sure that the circle of misery and violence and fear that drew us to Bleakcliff was truly just a catalogue of human failings; those evil thoughts leading to evil deeds that my younger self so assuredly proclaimed? Were we, and those that had gone before us, merely players in some enduring, ancient melodrama, playing out for no human audience

variation upon variation of the same scenario? That is the *'perennial problem to which human reason'*—this man's reason, at least—*'is as far from an answer as ever.'*

With the peculiar business that awaited us upon our return to London—an affair I have laid down elsewhere amidst my suppressed accounts under the designation, "The Adventure of the Unknown Worm"—bringing Sherlock Holmes and I so soon once more into a shadowed realm of legends, missing scholars, and entities whose touch appeared diabolical and whose origins seemed beyond man's ken, I feared that we were not yet free from the shadow of the Devil's Crown and its curse. However this latest bizarre episode, never rationally resolved though Holmes may long have considered it, was to give way to more mundanely earthbound adventures, yet each proving unusual and astonishing in their own right, which were to become the source of Sherlock Holmes's richly deserved fame.

Of our experiences in Harwynd, only a very few details remained to be resolved. At the hour—I will not go so far as to suggest it was at the very minute—when Eleanor Wexley finally jettisoned the stones to the waves, Ronald Flagstaff reportedly woke in the infirmary at Wynngrave Hall and announced, "The darkness has lifted. It is over." Sadly, this moment of unexpected lucidity was not to herald a recovery, as the injuries he had sustained and the ravages of long exposure to the hospitality of that institution were simply too much to bear, and though he prevailed through the night that followed, he did not see the new dawn.

True to his word, Holmes offered his every backing as I waged my campaign through the medical authorities against the deplorable conditions at Wynngrave Hall. I suspect now that my friend's chief contribution to my case was to prevail upon his, as yet unknown to me, older brother to deploy his considerable influence within official circles, for the swift and sudden reform that took place was likely not at the behest of a non-practicing army medic, no matter how impassioned and fiery my speech-making and letter writing proved. Whatever the catalyst, I gained hope that while Hubert Rollistone and Ronald Flagstaff may never have escaped their own private forms of the curse, the action taken in their memory may, in the years that the institute remained an active concern, have helped lift a curse for others in their place.

With the exception of the brief inquest promised by the local police, which took place some weeks afterwards, I saw Eleanor Wexley only once more after our return to London. Over a lunch that neither of us ate, in a restaurant I could not attempt to describe, she told me that she had put a match to her father's journals lest some future scholar find inspiration in them to seek something we could only hope was beyond all reach. The other books and artefacts were purchased by Oscar Wexley's former university, and with the money from these and the sale of her house, she intended to live out her dream. She left England that very day, moving on to America and, from there, to Africa, and in those years before I lost track of her she had gained a degree of fame for her numerous adventures, and her name appears on the spines of several guide books that adorn my shelves. This comes as no great surprise. She was one of the most remarkable women I ever knew. Indeed, at the heart of this whole business were two very remarkable women who, had motives and deeds not become so obscured by the swirling fog of darkness and secrecy surrounding their aims, might have made formidable allies.

I, of course, found happiness with another extra-ordinary woman under extraordinary circumstances a few years later. Again, there was treasure, again there was conspiracy, and again the lives that were touched by this wealth were made immeasurably sweeter by its loss. And again there was a brave, sweet, kind soul at the centre of it all. But in so many other respects Miss Mary Morstan, who honoured me by becoming Mrs. Mary Watson, was as different and individual a soul from Miss

Eleanor Wexley as one might find. Perhaps what seemed a tragic end to a friendship that glittered with such promise was not a curse, as it once so harshly seemed, but a blessing in waiting. For although our time together was all too cruelly cut short, I would not for any reward trade a single minute of any hour in the years Mary and I shared together.

But, as I have been as frank as possible in this account, it is only right that I should be just as frank as to what prompted me to make it. As I write, there is upon my desk an invitation bearing the stamp of Wynngrave Hall. I had maintained an obvious interest in the place, though it had not much troubled my thoughts in years. Having lain empty and neglected since before the Great War made an asylum of the world, the doors of the Hall are to open once more upon a fresh intake of inmates. Not as an asylum, but as a care home, hospital, and refuge for those for whom that war still rages in the scars on their faces, in the ghosts of limbs, and in their haunted thoughts. Where once I would have turned in horror from Wynngrave Hall, I eagerly accepted the invitation to view this noble enterprise, intrigued more than just a little by the Institute Secretary's insistence that the Director hoped very much to renew a valued former acquaintanceship.

Eleanor Wexley, in contrast to the once oppressive Wynngrave Hall, had changed remarkably little in the decades since last we spoke. Perhaps greyer of hair, and fuller of figure, with deeply tanned skin that was etched with a few well-earned laughter lines, but still with those lively, questioning green eyes, those same gentle tones, and that infectiously sunny grin, and still helping an old army medic shambling along behind a stick to stagger to a chair to recover from his astonishment.

Yes, my long-lost but never forgotten companion is now the Director and joint owner of the Wynngrave Private Home and Hospital. "It had felt the only decent thing to do, John. Well, you would know. You saw the state our boys were being shipped home in."

And so her story came out. She had travelled far and wide, and with no intention of ever stopping. Then that east wind came, cold and bitter....

"The war erupted, and it suddenly felt imperative to return home rather than staying away from it. I'd treated my own injuries and prescribed my own medicines in places where doctors' surgeries are hard to come by. So I volunteered as a nurse, an orderly, an ambulance driver, and anywhere else I might help. I would have carried stretchers in the trenches if they'd sent me. 'But some have to stay behind to hold the fort, they say. You're too important, we need your skills here, you're too necessary! Too necessary my eye! Too damn old, and too damn slow!' You may recognise the words, John. I heard you speak them one night at St. Bartholomew's in 1916 when you were doing your round of the wards. 'Better the old, and the slow, and the ones with bullets still in them than throwing away our young doctors, and their brothers and cousins too!' I would have gone to the Front without a qualm, but I still shook at the idea of letting you know the nurse changing dressings at the other end of the ward had once shared an incredible adventure with you.

"Too old? No, John, you were still handsome— yes, handsome still; the snowy beard suits you, like a rugged Father Christmas—and still full of passion and compassion. Still 'my gallant doctor'. Then the word came that the next consignment was coming in off the trains, so many that the platforms were choked with stretchers and crutches, and there simply wasn't the time.... No, I might have found you afterwards, but, then, I'd long known the route to Baker Street and never taken it. We'd last met in a time of madness and grief, and here we were in the midst of another; it hardly seemed fair. There were other hospitals, and too bloody many more nights like that."

She had administered to the war-wounded and, when the pandemic that descended upon an already injured and weary world was at its height, she had served on the

Influenza wards. And with both battles finally won, with a far higher cost than could be counted, she had resumed her travels, though now with the thought of return in mind. In her office she pointed me toward a shelf of recent travel books and gazetteers and journals—there to impress potential backers, she assured me—her chief purpose in writing them being to raise the funds to set up a clinic to ease just a portion of the suffering she still saw. Wynngrave, when she had discovered it was vacant and for sale, seemed a fated choice. I knew some of these titles, had seen them favourably reviewed, and had even browsed one or two in a bookshop, yet I had not equated the name on the covers with the lady I had briefly known.

"Ellie Wilton? A pen-name? No. Then you did marry?"

"Oh, yes. Not that very long before the war. A fine honeymoon that proved. He's my co-director in this colossal, insane scheme. You would like him, I think. In fact, I'm certain of it. He's a former army doctor. His name? His name is John. Dr. John H. Wilton."

I had no words to answer this. She looked at me earnestly, then a smile gleamed out. "I think I told you, a long, long time ago, that you would be easy to tease. He is a doctor, his name is Frank Wilton—no middle initial— and he spent his war serving at home, as did you and I. I don't know if Nicholas would have approved.

"Poor, deluded Nicholas ... Not even a marker of where he fell, for that grim ruin and the cliff it crouched on both followed him into the sea bit by bit, till the last went under a few years ago. It was never a memorial I would have wished for him, no matter what.

"Well, it took me a long time to find the man who might help me forget, and by the time he came trundling into my life, I no longer needed to forget. I still remembered that extraordinary adventure, but as a story, or a dream, or some fantastical legend from distant times."

I met Dr. Frank Wilton, and I liked him from the first. As we dined that night, I watched he and Eleanor together, ribbing one another one minute, the next earnestly discussing their newest fund-raising notion or the travel plans to some far-flung place to secure the best staff and equipment the medical world can offer, and I saw in them the devotion and excitement that lovers half their age might envy. I wish them every conceivable happiness. She remains one of the most remarkable women I know. She has not spent her years hiding away from the curse which so nearly destroyed her life, and if she was running it was toward something, not rushing, panicked, to get out from under the curse's shadow.

And if she is not hiding, then nor, I finally see, must I. The story is told.

As to my greatest friend, our many years of partnership are well known. Although my pledge to abandon all attempts to chronicle his achievements was one I maintained for several years, my overwhelming admiration as mystery upon enigma upon puzzle fell before his formidable gaze so impressed a colleague of mine with literary ambitions that my long neglected manuscript was brought into the light once more. That colleague—deftly editing my efforts to reduce rambling exposition to a few lines of dialogue, and expanding with imaginative passages those sections of the tale which had occurred outwith my presence—made my humble efforts an unforeseeable success. Indeed, the continued association with Doyle, my editor, agent, and very dear friend, has been nearly as consistent and long-established as that with Holmes, and it has ensured that, even a quarter century after his withdrawal from public life, the latter's many successes are legendary. And legends, as we know, have a tendency to linger.

The files and indexes, folders, scrapbooks, and shelf upon shelf of mementoes and memoranda left behind in Baker Street when Sherlock Holmes retired from practice to devote his life to quiet study in his Sussex hideaway have long since been packed away in boxes and crates in what once was his bedroom. After several years in which Mrs. Hudson and I preserved these rooms just as he left them—expectant of the day he would grow bored of the ordered lives of his bees and breathing the healthy country air and come stalking back to that disordered, chaotic London whose teeming lifeforms he had studied for so many years, and to the smog and smoke within which any manner of crime may be concealed—I finally resigned myself to solitary residence. I turned our old bachelor rooms into a home with all the comforts of our younger days but none of the untidiness and clutter—and absolutely no possibility of discovering a detached human thumb in the salt cellar, or stolen confidential treaties on the breakfast tray, nor a distressed parrot quarantined in the larder declaiming directions in Hungarian toward an unknown assassin's target!

Yet even so, it is still my habit when in reminiscent mode, to ransack those boxes and bedeck the floors with those scrapbooks and *aides-memoires* as if Holmes were still in tenancy, to relive for a few hours those halcyon days.

"Raising old ghosts, Watson?" I seem even now to hear my old friend enquire, as he steps deftly over the tumbled, jumbled papers to take up his familiar position in his well-worn chair.

"Laying a few to rest," I reply, setting down my pen.

"With ink, paper and nib, in place of bell, book and candle? No, this is a literary séance, resurrecting ghosts long-since exorcised through logic and diligent action. There are no mysteries here in these dusty archives. Not for us, at any rate. You are merely haunting yourself with puzzles already solved, crimes long since grown cold, words spoken that cannot be retracted, deeds that cannot be undone, and with no conclusions to seek now save foregone ones."

"Ah, my dear fellow, but even where the conclusion is already known, there is still the adventure of it to thrill to, the human drama to inflame the heart, the passions and eccentricities of our fellow men to be observed. And of course," I smile, "the calm, rational, and utterly unique methods of a brilliant specialist to be studied, emulated, and admired."

"Well, if you are going to start raising valid objections," the smile is briefly returned, veiled in a curl of pipe smoke, "I will concede you have a point. And we have a remarkable, evolving portrait of an enduring friendship through rapidly changing times, let us not forget. Where you may have erred in trivialising certain of the more technical aspects of our pursuits, as I may once or twice have mentioned, you may very well have left an important record of social relevance pertaining to the attitudes and behaviours of a certain class of English gentleman in this most fascinating period. Or just some luridly gripping tales of adventure, intrigue and horror, as you still clearly prefer. Ha!

"But surely we are not reduced to reflecting on a well-documented past? It is still crystal clear to us and immutable, while the present is around us to be seen, yet in places remains obscured. But the future, my boy, is undocumented. It is not set in stone, nor read in stones or in stars. It lies ahead of us, a vast, ever-shifting fog of possibilities. And in such a fog there must certainly be mysteries aplenty all round, the like of which even two old campaigners such as you and I have never yet encountered. That is, of course, if you'd care to breach the fogbanks now and again to investigate it alongside an old colleague?"

"Well, of course, Holmes. Need you even ask? I may be slower in step when it comes to giving chase, and I might need to find my spectacles before taking aim with my faithful old service revolver, but I would not leave you to face any further great adventures alone, old friend."

"Capital!" he cries, vigorously rubbing his hands. "I thought I knew my Watson!" And the laughter which follows still rings in my ears as I take up my pen once more to conclude this rather singular narrative.

Wishful imaginings? Not in the least. For, even though the Lestrades and Gregsons, the Athelney Joneses and

Alec Macs have had to make their own way, for better or for worse, without his assistance, my old friend's retirement has not been remotely as complete as he may have intended it, or as I had feared it. Nor is he as crippled by rheumatism and other complaints of advancing years as he once had me publicly claim in hope of discouraging persistent approaches from his still admiring followers with myriad mundane problems, commonplace puzzles, and trivial challenges.

Although it requires the most extreme circumstances, and the most fantastic, outlandish, and apparently impossible elements to interest him, it is still entirely possible to hear the impatient, spritely footsteps on the stairs of our once-shared lodgings in Baker Street, and to yet again hear the urgent, excited voice of the best and wisest man whom I have ever known, Mr. Sherlock Holmes, rousing me to action with that well-remembered cry of his.

"Come, Watson, come! The game is afoot."

Afterword;
or, The Case of the Dormant Document

It is common practice upon the discovery of a hitherto unpublished account from the pen of Dr. Watson to append some details as to its discovery. Those who have read the introduction to those rediscovered documents I transcribed some years ago under the heading of *Sherlock Holmes: The Impossible Cases* will know already of the cache of files, folders, journals and other sundry papers that were found concealed within a wall in a house on the Sussex Downs to which it is now well established that Mr. Holmes retired in the early years of the twentieth century in order to devoted his studies to the behaviour patterns of bee society rather than that of London's swarming criminal societies.

Among this great assortment was to be found a photograph of a singularly attractive young woman—to quote Watson's own description of the portrait's subject from the account this current piece accompanies: '*Her heart-shaped face is clear-complexioned and pale, though against the sombreness of her dress—still displaying unmistakeable traces of mourning—and the darkness of her lustrous chestnut hair and her large, inquisitive eyes, the pallor is all an illusion. She is evidently healthy and in full possession of herself....*'

But without the details to match this description from the good doctor's chronicle, there was to be found no other clue to the identity of the woman (leading to some short-lived speculation in certain quarters that queried could this woman be '*the* woman'?) it appeared that Watson had left us another mystery, yet without the benefit of his famous friend on hand to provide the solution, and the photograph was duly filed with the various other snapshots of a bygone world that he had thought fit to preserve. But in his own words the great detective did point his way toward that solution: *'You see, but you do not observe.'* For on returning to that raft of old pictures in an attempt to establish at least some chronological order I finally observed where I had at one time only seen.

This observation centred on a photograph of much later origin, in this case a group shot of three rather sprightly elderly people breaking off from a picnic lunch in the grounds of a large house to turn their smiles to the camera's lens. Of the two men shown, one is quite recognisably John H. Watson, whose apparent age— white of hair and of beard—would suggest the picture dated to a year in the late 1920s. The other gentleman is less easily recognised, and any hopes that this may prove to be a rare photograph of Mr. Holmes are dashed by the solid, stocky frame and head of curly hair that count against all known descriptions of the great detective. This laughing fellow is the subject not only of the camera's gaze, but of the gaze of the third member of the party, who looks at him with a fondness that is unmistakable. But what is also unmistakable, at least to an observant peruser of these old portraits, is that this older woman, with her hair now grey and face bearing traces of life, is that same much younger mystery woman almost five decades on.

Fortunately on this occasion there is an identifier inked on the back to point the way to the next stage of enquiry. *'Lunch on the lawn with the Wiltons, Wynngrave Hall'*. To locate Wynngrave Hall near the village of Harewynd is a matter of moments, even without Holmes's gazetteers to hand. The website of the care home that still operates at that site provides the necessary contact details for me to make enquiries concerning the Wiltons; a name that figures prominently in the institute's history, I quickly learn, and one which still has strong ties to the Hall and its work.

Although Eleanor and Frank Wilton—whose foundation of Wynngrave Hall as a convalescent home and clinic rapidly approaches its centenary—had no children themselves, Debbie Wilton-Lodge, a great-great-grandniece on Frank's side, still sits on the board and takes as active an interest in the Hall's hundred-year history as she does in its day-to-day running. She proved a highly knowledgeable guide when I accepted her offer to visit the facility—a world apart, I'm relieved to report, from the dire establishment visited by Holmes and Watson during that fateful excursion to Harewynd—and was delighted to be able to add framed copies of both photographs to the Hall's archives. And it was in this archive that a hidden treasure lurked, awaiting discovery.

When asked if she had been aware of Dr. Watson's visits to the Hall, Debbie Wilton-Lodge showed me some early documentation on which the name *J. H. Watson* appears among the list of Trustees. What had come as no small surprise to her and her fellows on the staff was that this same J. H. Watson was *the* Dr. Watson, friend and biographer of the world's most famous detective. Although a handsomely preserved run of bound *Strand Magazine* volumes occupies a bookshelf still in the Director's office, as with so many who chiefly know of the duo's exploits through film, television and radio dramatisations of variable authenticity, the presumption that Holmes and Watson were fictional characters had blinded them to any possible connection between the name in their hundred-year old ledgers and the one made famous the world over through Sir Arthur Conan Doyle's championing of his old medical colleague's very real reminiscences of a very extraordinary man.

With the dropping of this minor bombshell, the nearby presence of another, far yet combustible unexploded bomb was revealed to me in the form of an antique box-file with the seemingly insignificant words *'Collection of the Director, E. Wilton, re: J. H. Watson'* neat upon the label. The contents included a few brief pieces of correspondence, some affixed to cuttings from newspapers or medical journals that the sender felt might be of value or interest, plus several lengthier missives containing practical

335

advice on the care of the clinic's battle-weary patients and a list of potential benefactors *'whose gratitude to my associate for assistance rendered may yet warrant a spirit of generosity when presented with a truly worthy cause.'* (I have little doubt that, were one to check the Hall's early account books, the names of a gold-mining magnate, several racehorse owners, the wife of a former Home Secretary, a Duke, a General of some Indian renown and his daughter, the scion of a European royal house, and a popular Devonshire baronet will be found among the notables to grace the lists of benefactors.) Having spent no small time in transcribing the contents of that previous cache of cases, the not always entirely legible handwriting on display was as familiar—more-so, in fact, in these days of electronic communication—as my own.

But as fascinating and as welcome as these fresh Watsonian writings clearly were, it was the large buff envelope—addressed to *Eleanor Wilton c/o Director's Office, Wynngrave Hall* in that same unmistakable hand, and clearly unopened in the better part of a century— that quickened the pulse. Could this be what any Holmesian scholar dreams of discovering—an as-yet-unrecorded case to add to the collection? And if so, would this particular Holmesian enthusiast be permitted to inspect this document without undergoing the prolonged agonies of waiting for official verification and valuation by all manner of officials? To answer the second question first, it was a resounding 'yes', the original recipient's heir opining that had I not contacted them with my photographic find the contents of box-file *EW/JHW* might have gone undisturbed for a further century. (The answer to the first question should be obvious enough by now.)

The note, in that same handwriting that accompanied the manuscript I reproduce here in its entirety—

My dearest Eleanor,
It is written, as we spoke of on my last visit.
But rather than consign it, as I had originally

intended, to that battered old dispatch box in which reside so many accounts I choose not to share with the public, I commend the enclosed to your safekeeping, as it has attained the purpose of its writing, which was to make room inside my 'brain attic' (to borrow a metaphor from S.H.) without tripping over old and dusty ghosts. What you choose to do with it is entirely your own decision. Should you choose to read it and dispose of some of your own dusty ghosts, or to share it with that splendid husband of yours, then all is good. And if you choose to leave it unread, or—in light of how cold your stretch of country can get—to feed the fire with it, that is just as good—you of all people have no need to read it to read it to know what it contains.

Your ever affectionate and loving friend,
John

That enclosed manuscript comprised almost two hundred pages. To the relief of this putative editor, late on in life Dr. Watson had invested in both a typewriter and typing lessons, though any question of the document's authenticity was fully answered by the corrections and additional notes populating the margins of at least half the pages, all of them conforming to the recognised hand of Dr. Watson. This, naturally, rendered the account far easier and less headache prone—the occasional stubborn word or obstinate sentence among the marginalia aside—to prepare for publication than a lengthy process of transcription from written journals. It also made it possible for your present writer—no natural orator—to read aloud the entire affair to a small but generously attentive audience who gathered in the Hall's library for several hours that same evening. Thus *The Adventure of the Devil's Crown*, after decades in waiting, finally made its public debut.

Whether the recipient ever read the manuscript is, at this remove, impossible to ascertain. It is this writer's hope that the former Miss Eleanor Wexley was able to put aside any *'old and dusty ghosts'* of guilt and grief and to find some trace of wonder and happiness in the extraordinary memoir. As her great-great-grandniece remarked after the tale's first recitation in nearly a century, "It's an adventure yarn, and a mystery tale, and a horror story, yes, but above all that, *it's a love letter....*"

The above account is the true and accurate statement of how this book came about. Well, obviously it must be the truth, or else I would have had to make it all up....

But if we were to imagine—just briefly, and purely as an exercise in speculative fiction—that everything you have read so far in this volume had not been found in a document that had waited many decades to be let loose upon the world, how might they have come about instead?

In fact—or should I say 'in fiction'?—through a document that had waited several decades to be let loose on the world; this much I can attest is perfectly true. To discover its origins, we need not travel back to the 1920s, merely to the late 1990s.

As a writer—at the time fully employed in the field of humour comics—and lifelong fan of Holmes and Watson, I'd occasionally wondered if I might one day tackle a Holmes pastiche of my own, but these idle plans never got so far as pen touching paper. Until, during a lunch break, I found myself writing, not a story, but a short scene, no more than a page long, to set the stage for a mystery. One a darkened stage, a young woman sits in a circle of candlelight, with shadowy figures seated around her. Smoke or mist drifts, and in prowls a dark, veiled figure, who goads the entranced heroine to speak. Strange voices drift in the ether, and as she finally finds her voice the doors crash open, a figure races in with a furious cry, and the young woman stands and screams the words,

'*The Crown!*' Blackout. Curtain. New scene—

The curtains open to reveal a second curtain of white gauze, onto which projected images of Victorian London swim into view, as sepia-tinted photographs of the period or in shadow form, as silhouettes of rooftops and chimney stacks, Parliament and St Paul's.

There is a crackle, as of a needle being put onto an old record or, more precisely, onto a wax cylinder, and a voice speaks directly to us. It is Watson, but not the Watson who shall shortly appear. This is an ancient, rather crackly recording of 1920s vintage, of an OLD WATSON, in his mid-eighties, reading from his documentation of the case.

A violin solo creeps in, a slow, melancholic tune becoming steadily louder.

OLD WATSON (Voice):   Over the course of my long friend-ship with Sherlock Holmes, I have presented for publication nigh on sixty accounts detailing his remarkable achievements in criminal study and deductive reasoning. However, there are certain adventures which may never be brought to the notice of the public. In the case of "The Adventure of the Amateur Mendicant Society," or "The Sudden Death of Cardinal Tosca," it is since the details are of so scandalous a nature that, even after all these decades, the repercussions of such revelations would still be felt at the highest of levels.

In other instances, I am convinced that if certain stories were to emerge, I would be branded as delusional, an embellisher or a

339

downright liar, which would draw doubt on my other accounts and, thus, upon the accomplishments of Holmes. Into this latter category must fall the hideous truth of what was found upon opening "The Paradol Chamber" and the tale of that terrifying last voyage of the cargo ship, Matilda Briggs, itself only a prelude to the notorious "Adventure of the Giant Rat of Sumatra"... a story for which, I fear, the world may never be prepared!

It was among this collection of never-to-be-told-tales that I always swore the current narrative belonged. But, while I am still haunted by the cruel horror of the events, a horror stretching back over several blood-soaked centuries, the emotional strain under which I made my vow to withhold the details has long since passed. What is more, I am now an old, though I hope, not a foolish man, with few regrets. However, I could not happily live out what remaining years I have knowing that the full account of this most dreadful and terrifying adventure may one day die with me, denying the world the knowledge of how the singular skills of one man brought to a close the bloody tangle of events surrounding the cursed Murderer's Crown.

That man was, of course, Mr.

Sherlock Holmes.
Throughout the above, a backlight comes up slowly, casting
the silhouette of a legendary figure. At the last line, the
gauze lifts and the lights come up to show, in profile, Violin
in hand, the tall, slim figure of SHERLOCK HOLMES.

What was this '*Murderer's Crown*'? What was its
curse? Who was the young woman who screamed so
melodramatically? And what of the veiled medium and
the shadowy figure in the doorway? I was intrigued by all
these questions, but daunted by the realisation that if I
was going to have any of them answered I had no choice
but to keep writing till I found out. (And why a stage play
and not a short story? At that stage I hadn't actually seen
a Sherlock Holmes play performed. It simply felt the most
immediate way of working. And, to borrow a phrase from
the master, *'I can never resist a touch of the dramatic.'*)

Over the month that followed, that idle way of passing
a lunchtime lull led to the most intense writing period I
had up until then experienced. Without anything but the
vaguest of ideas as to where the plot was leading, I wrote.
While the plot—and I fervently hoped there would be
one—was still to reveal itself, what I most definitely had
fixed in my mind was the atmosphere I hoped to invoke.
Drawing on all the things I loved most about Conan
Doyle's creation, as well as the film and TV adaptations
I had grown up with (radio would come later for me), I
wanted mystery and adventure, an enigmatic foe, a brave
and resourceful heroine—one who screams and swoons
for the purposes of melodrama, I concede, though I was
pleased to discover she had a reason for this behaviour—
and a dash of romance for the intrepid Watson, and I
wanted to emphasise the gothic elements that seemed
to hang like a fog ever at the edges of Holmes's rational
world. Séance parlours, scholarly studies, grim asylums,
tombs and ruins all struck a suitable backdrops in
pursuing a cursed object. Treasure hunts and curses and
veiled presences and eccentric scholars and diabolical

toxins that led to nightmare visions: Doyle had already provided the ingredients, it was now a case of cooking up my own recipe, with additional serving suggestions courtesy of Universal Pictures and Hammer Films, the BBC and Granada Television, and too many others to list here. And the one thing in common to them all, the most important ingredient without which the whole confection collapses, is the enduring and exceptional friendship between Sherlock Holmes and his best friend, John H. Watson.

To keep my mind in the realm of Victorian London, while I typed in one corner of the room, in another corner my videotapes of favourite Sherlock Holmes films and shows played repeatedly. *Murder by Decree*, *A Study in Terror*, Hammer's rip-roaring *Hound of the Baskervilles*, *The Seven-Percent Solution*, *Without a Clue*, the entrancing *The Private Life of Sherlock Holmes*, and *The Crucifer of Blood*—a full-bloodedly gothic variant on *The Sign of Four* which does little to disguise its origins as a stage play, so was ideal for my mood—and the inevitable selection of Basil Rathbone and Nigel Bruce escapades, and episodes of the lavish series starring Jeremy Brett, David Burke and Edward Hardwicke were all to provide background accompaniment on regular rotation, while the Varese Sarabande album *Sherlock Holmes: Classic Themes from 221B Baker Street*, featuring re-recorded highlights from many a Sherlockian soundtrack became my own soundtrack of choice.

Over that month my nicotine and caffeine intake rose dramatically, while sleep became a thing of fond memory— on stumbling wearily to bed at some hour close to dawn early in the process, I had no sooner closed my eyes than I heard voices that gave no signs of quietening down. The characters were still talking. Not only that, but they were playing out a scene I had yet to write! I staggered from my bed, seized pen and paper, and wrote it down as quickly as I could, not trusting any of it to remain in my memory the few remaining hours till my alarm was due to go off.

From this point on it felt less like writing and far more like taking dictation, and that set the pattern over the weeks that followed. Go to the office, write at lunchtime and in coffee breaks, home by six, dinner eaten, work at the word processor until the typing errors get too numerous at which point switch to pen and paper (meaning the first stage of the next evening's session would entail typing up and redrafting these pages; an approach I've found very effective in beating the dreaded 'blank page' stage of writing and have used ever since), freshen up, go to the office, write at lunchtime, etc. Saturdays were surrendered to sleep, but most of that exhausting but utterly exhilarating month was spent trailing in the wake of the detective, the doctor, and the heroine as they closed in on their goal.

And then, a month after it began, it was done. *The Curse of the Murderer's Crown: A Sherlock Holmes Mystery* was now a play in three acts that filled 180 pages of script, broken down as so—

ACT 1
SCENE 1
"THE SINGULAR STATEMENT OF THE SCEPTICAL SIBLING"
221B Baker Street, *afternoon of the first day*
SCENE 2
"THE EPISODE OF THE SÉANCE IN THE SMOKE"
A Public Hall in London's East End, *the first evening*
ACT 2
SCENE 1
"THE TRAGIC ACCOUNT OF THE DYING ARCHAELOGIST"
The Library of Greymarsh Priory, *five weeks prior*
SCENE 2
"THE GHASTLY CHRONICLE OF THE BLOOD DRENCHED SAGA"
The Library of Greymarsh Priory, *evening of the second day*
SCENE 3

"THE DILEMMA OF THE VIGILANT DOCTOR"
An Hotel Room in the North of England, *the second night*
ACT 3
SCENE 1
"THE DREADFUL CASE OF THE CONFINED CHEMIST"
Wynngrave Hall, an Asylum, *morning of the third day*
SCENE 2
"THE CLIMACTIC ADVENTURE OF THE ASSEMBLED ANTAGONISTS"
The Ruined Church at Drearcliff, *the third evening*

It was with a mixed sense of elation and dismay that I typed *THE END* on that last page. Elation that, if nothing else, I had completed a new Sherlock Holmes adventure and could now answer all those questions prompted by my first random jottings. And dismay that I had to step fully back into the present day and out of the world of Victorian mystery and excitement—withdrawal symptoms from hansom cabs and gaslight and ticking mantel clocks over roaring coal fires quickly set in.

In the weeks to follow I was to hand across the printed out copy to a select few associates for feedback; I was still far too close to the whole idea to be in any way objective. First and foremost of these initial readers was my friend and colleague, Craig Ferguson, who returned it the next day, informing me he had sat up till the small hours reading it in a single sitting as he was so keen to discover the nature of the curse. High praise, and precisely the kind of thing I wanted to hear. He then followed up with, "You should turn it into a novel," which, having been set on writing a play for performance on the stage, was *almost* as frustrating as it was flattering. Though the reality that I was less than keen to admit, despite privately knowing it already, was that a three-act play that ran to at least three hours without intervals, had too much narration bridging the scenes, and carried a requirement for ambitious sets, costumes, props, and effects—and all from an untried playwright—was an impossible sell at worst, and only a promising first draft at best.

As tirelessly and wholeheartedly as I'd thrown myself into the writing, I felt entirely none of the same drive when it came to attempting to sell the thing—an obvious flaw when it comes to making a living as a writer, and one I still fight against. I submitted it for consideration to a local theatre, but even though the Creative Director wrote back to say that he had enjoyed reading it and spending time with Holmes and Watson, he saw no place for it among the theatre's plans. And on that anti-climactic note, that, for the time being at least, was the end of the adventure.

A lot of water has flowed over the Reichenbach Falls and under a great many bridges since that sleepless month. I would occasionally, over the following years, return to the script, sometimes just to read it to see if I was still a fan—I was, as it still felt like it had been written by hands other than my own—and sometimes to perform some surgery to scale it back to more manageable proportions, but never getting so far as sending it out again to any theatres.

Meanwhile, other Holmesian adventures awaited. In 2010 Joe Morey, then at Dark Regions Press, looking to follow up on my first ghost story collection, *They That Dwell in Dark Places*, asked if I would be interested in writing a book pitting Holmes and Watson against the supernatural. The result was *Sherlock Holmes: The Impossible Cases*, a collection of novellas in which several references are made to an adventure involving a cursed crown—one which had in the intervening years been promoted through the ranks of evil from *Murderer's Crown* to *Devil's Crown*. Among these accounts is "The Adventure of the Unknown Worm," which picks up with our heroes the very next day after *The Devil's Crown* case concludes.

At the same time as *The Impossible Cases* commission, I had also been asked by Larry Albert of *Imagination Theatre*, the syndicated radio mystery series which had produced several of my ghost stories, if I would put some thought to a supernatural-themed script for their long-running *Further Adventures of Sherlock Holmes* series. The resulting episode—which also appeared in prose form in *The Impossible Cases*—was *The Voice in the Smoke*, and it is a return to the world of séances and spirits that featured so prominently in my earlier stage script, though with a markedly different emphasis. A few more of my Sherlock Holmes radio scripts have made it to the air, my favourite—if writers are allowed to have their own preferences—being *The Case of the Confounded Chronicler*, a two-hander in which John Patrick Lowrie's Holmes and Larry Albert's Watson take on all the other roles, including each other's, to solve a minor mystery without ever leaving Baker Street. A few passages in this play were adapted from material first written for *The Murderer's Crown*, and with the radio episode recorded in front of a live audience at the Kirkland Performance Centre, this meant that finally a fragment of that earlier play has made it to the stage.

The script for *The Confounded Chronicler* was included in *Imagination Theatre's Sherlock Holmes*, a book celebrating the series and its creator, Jim French, edited by David Marcum, and containing scripts from every contributing writer to *The Further Adventures*. David is also editor of the ever-expanding *MX Book of New Sherlock Holmes Stories* series, to which I have contributed two novella-length adventures and a further radio script.

Which still leaves *The Devil's Crown*. By seeding references to the adventure throughout other stories, I may have been mentally preparing myself for the task of reworking the story to a different medium, though it would take some time before I actually plunged back into the world of 1881, and for a number of reasons nine years to the day have passed between completion of first draft

346

and the final version.

Naturally adapting a script into a novel isn't simply a matter of adding 'he said' and 'she said' to the dialogue and sprinkling in a few descriptions and a bit of verbiage. Which is a relief for this writer, as nothing could be more boring than simply reformatting a piece of old work. The action has opened out beyond the scenes and settings of the play. Events that originally took place offstage and were relayed either through reported speech or narration are now shown. And at least one character who was only mentioned and never seen in the script suddenly, while I was sitting on the bus home one night, popped into my head, demanded an actual appearance, explained how this would link certain events in a more satisfactory manner, would tie up a few loose ends, and also set up a moment toward the close of the book—thus allowing a certain Scotland Yard official to simply knock on the door at Baker Street and walk into the middle of the story.

The more serious changes between the play and the book are in being allowed to build up the histories of several of the characters, and in the level of horror the book allowed me to bring out, most specifically in the case of the legends concerning the blood-soaked history of the crown. While the play flirts with the supernatural before laying such ideas to rest, the legend becomes a far greater source of horror here, and draws on influences beyond Conan Doyle, with obvious elements of Lovecraft and a couple of brushes with the ghostly worlds of M. R. James in the mix, alongside some concoctions of my own.

One constant between writing the original version of this tale over a quarter of a century ago and finally completing it in a new and expanded form is that sleep has again become a rarity—though the nicotine and caffeine are both now things of the past—as the characters have yet again taken to telling me where I have misquoted them or in other ways urging me to set the record straight. I hope I have succeeded in telling their tale.

My thanks and endless admiration go to Sir Arthur

Conan Doyle for his immortal creations, and to all those writers, actors, directors and technicians who have kept them alive and present in the years since across every medium imaginable. To those who have commissioned or in other ways supported my own efforts to don Dr. Watson's mantle as chronicler of otherwise untold adventures for Sherlock Holmes. To my family, with all possible love, and—as befits a book centred on that most enduring friendship—also to my friends, with gratitude; not least among them the aforementioned Craig Ferguson. *You know, brother mine, there just might be something in that suggestion to turn it into a novel after all....*

Daniel McGachey
Dundee, September 2024

About the Author

DANIEL MCGACHEY is the author of the ghost story collection *They That Dwell in Dark Places* (2009), and *Sherlock Holmes: The Impossible Cases* (2010), both originally published by Dark Regions Press. His second collection of ghost stories, *By No Mortal Hand*, was published by Sarob Press in 2018.

His stories have appeared in the *Black Book of Horror, BHF Book of Horror Stories, MX Book of New Sherlock Holmes Stories, Best British Horror* and *Best New Horror* series, and as instalments of the long-running *Imagination Theatre* radio series.

As well as fiction and radio drama, he has written comics since 1989, audio comedy, animation, and for magazines and newspapers. He has designed and illustrated several book covers, and is a regular contributor to the small press M. R. James 'zine *Ghosts & Scholars*.

About the Artist

K. L. TURNER is a seasoned artist and illustrator with over thirty years of experience, known for creating captivating images across various media.

Influenced by the fantasy and science-fiction illustrations of the 1960s, '70s, and '80s, Turner infuses a touch of old-school painterly style into modern techniques. His work is distinguished by its expressionistic themes, drawing viewers in with compelling, evocative imagery. Turner's art has been featured in media and galleries worldwide and has become a celebrated part of pop culture.

In addition to his illustration work, Turner is accomplished in photography, sculpture, and the fine arts. After spending over fifty years in his home state of Colorado, he has relocated to Illinois, where he continues to find inspiration in nature and cultural influences, both locally and through his travels.

www.ingramcontent.com/pod-product-compliance
Lightning Source LLC
Chambersburg PA
CBHW022147010726
47493CB00002B/384